STIRRING GHOSTS

ALSO BY VICKI STEVENS

Abby Eaton Mystery Series

Shaking Trees

Saving Dragonflies

Other Fiction

Flames to a Moth

STIRRING GHOSTS

AN ABBY EATON MYSTERY

VICKI STEVENS

This is a work of fiction. Names, characters, places and incidents mentioned in this novel are products of the author's imagination or are used fictitiously.

Published by Bloodwood Press in 2025
Armstrong Creek, QLD, Australia

ISBN 978-0-6483831-7-8 (paperback)

ISBN 978-0-6483831-6-1 (ebook)

Cover design by Predrag Marković - Smashed Grid Studio

A catalogue record for this work is available from the National Library of Australia

For Sheron and Debra

There is no refuge from memory and remorse in this world. The spirits of our foolish deeds haunt us, with or without repentance.

— GILBERT PARKER

PROLOGUE

Grassington 1886

The empty manor house echoes with hurried footsteps. As Gerald Greenwood scurries through the unfurnished rooms, his nostrils sting from the pungent smells of sawdust and fresh paint, as sharp and unsettling as the fear that grips him. His blood pulses. Lungs burn. Where can he escape the malevolence?

A flight of wooden steps confronts him, urging his ascent to the first floor. Alas, neither of the bedrooms nor the wraparound verandah with fancy iron balustrade provides protection from his relentless pursuer. Winding his way up the spiral staircase—wheezing, knees creaking with the effort—he reaches the small landing. The door to the rooftop peels back of its own accord, and he steps into the tower lookout created to view Grassington Estate in all its intended glory. Arched windows reveal a vibrant blue sky that beckons him through a doorway onto the observation deck.

Eyes smarting from a strong breeze make it difficult to focus as he stumbles forward. Pressed against the stone parapet, he peers far below at the scraped earth, levelled to allow the recent construction of the grand home he designed. His castle. Measure of his hard work and standing in the community. Is he about to lose it all? Will guilt rob him of more than his mind?

A voice sputters in his ear: *Thief. You will pay.*

Gerald shudders and turns to challenge his phantom tormentor when an unholy force wrenches him off his feet in midair suspension. A scream lodges in his throat as the spectre materialises, the hideous sight turning the old man's heart to ice before he is hurled over the stonework.

For a moment, he takes flight, an awkward flapping fledgling, only to plummet, the impact with the ground shattering bones and smashing his skull, killing him instantly.

1

____

March 2019

I checked my escape in the rear-vision mirror and heaved a sigh of relief. The farther I distanced myself from Shadow Creek and the devastating last few days, the more the weight lifted from my shoulders. The dust would have settled by the time I returned home, my culpability in the failure of my new shop opening to the public diminished to only a twinge of regret.

I dodged another pothole and focussed my thoughts on Grassington. My sister's plea to help her and her husband launch the mansion on the historic estate as a luxury guesthouse was a godsend. Being involved in readying the venue for its first customers would be restorative—at least that was my hope.

No doubt Shane was already soaking up the peace and quiet afforded by the absence of a headstrong and impulsive wife. Though would he worry I'd go off the rails without him pulling me into line? *Stuff him.* If he couldn't trust me when we were apart, then it didn't give much weight to our twenty-five-year marriage. What woman in her mid-forties needed a minder, anyway?

My eyes stung, and my stomach growled. The three-hour country drive without a break, snacking only on peanut M&Ms, was taking its toll—not helped by sleepless nights incited by anxiety.

Directed by a metal road sign riddled with bullet holes, I slowed and drove through the aptly named village of Grimm —*Population 210*. My bright yellow VW Beetle travelling down the deserted main street stood out garishly amongst the smattering of dingy stores, lone-pump petrol station, and run-down pub, all closed. Shadow Creek was a bustling metropolis in comparison. Several side streets dotted with slouching timber cottages topped with rusted tin roofing showed where some residents lived, with the rest dwelling on outlying properties, unless the notation on the road sign needed updating.

The only thing to pique my interest was a wooden statue of a Yowie propped up outside a brick toilet block in the town park. Emblazoned with graffiti and missing an arm, this replica of a creature from Australian folklore looked more forlorn than ferocious, longing for the good ol' days when it had people shaking in their boots.

I emerged on the other side and drove roughly a kilometre through pastoral land until a reflective sign cut through the fading light, instructing me to turn right to *Grassington Historic Estate*. Veering the car onto a side road and climbing a forested hill, I noticed a sandstone turret with a flagpole poking above the tree line. Was the fluttering flag directing me up to the summit or signalling for help?

I saw no more of the mansion as I tackled the meandering incline. It was a tease, delaying gratification until fully visible. Confronted by a set of classic wrought iron gates bearing the estate's crest of two entwined G's—Grassington and Greenwood, the name of the original owners—I got out and entered the code Paisley had given me into the keypad. The gates opened with a mechanical whir, and I drove through.

Following the bitumen drive, I braked hard when something scruffy dashed from the roadside into the scrub. A wallaby? A wild deer? Or ... a Yowie on the loose? I chuckled and increased speed, soon arriving at a charming stone cottage on my left, surrounded by a white picket fence. Though the drive continued uphill and round a bend, I'd reached my destination.

With the car parked on the gravel verge, I removed my luggage from the boot and inhaled air redolent with promise before unlatching a creaky wooden gate. A cobbled path led me to a lit porch where a dog barked from inside. The door opened before I knocked and a large black German Shepherd burst out and crashed into me. My wheeled suitcase cannonballed into a potted topiary plant and ricocheted into a tight spin. Regaining my balance, I welcomed the slobbery canine kisses and sank my hands into his dense fur. 'Lovely to see you, too, Whitby.'

'You're late,' Paisley announced, wrenching her pet away. 'Did you get lost *again*?'

My sister's comment made me bristle. Would she ever let me forget that one occasion when I took a wrong turn and arrived fifteen minutes late for her wedding? My being the chief bridesmaid and causing the bride to wait in the decorated Land Cruiser until my arrival, I admit, was poor form. Yet, in my defence, she and Fletcher had blundered by choosing a secluded rainforest venue and not supplying me with easy-to-follow directions.

I forced a smile and retrieved my suitcase. 'Not lost this time. Google Maps helped. Though the razzamatazz of Grimm was a slight distraction.'

She cracked a smile and motioned me inside. 'You look exhausted. Remind me to slice up some cucumbers for those bags under your eyes. Oh, you've had a haircut. It's very bouncy looking. What's the deal with the shocking red tint?'

'No harm in a change.' Slipping out of my backpack, I stretched up and hugged my sister—a lanky fifteen centimetres above my diminutive height—being careful not to slice my cheek on hair straightened to the sharpness of an axe blade. 'Thanks for the invite.'

'More of an urgent cry for help. I bet you're relieved to have a break from everything for a while, what with—'

'Yep,' I interrupted, 'it'll be brilliant.' The last thing I needed was a postmortem on the catastrophe that had upended my life. 'Nice place you've got,' I said, peeking into the snug lounge area embellished with cosy furnishings and exposed rafters. A small wood heater adorned with a crystal decanter and two matching tumblers urged me to organise another visit in the cooler months.

'It's small but has loads of character.' Paisley pointed to a closed door to my right. 'Main bedroom behind there.'

Whitby and I paced after her when she took off in her usual haste down the narrow hallway. She gestured at the bathroom and study, allowing no time for inspection. At the end of the hall, she opened a glass door and led us into a rustic kitchen/diner with an island bench separating the two areas. Fixed spotlights lit the kitchen, while a dome pendant light in the dining section created flitting shapes on the distressed wood table.

I salivated in response to the rich aromas of spicy food bubbling in the pot on the AGA cooker. As well as efficient, my sister was an excellent chef.

Paisley opened one of two doors flanking a stone fireplace. 'This is your room. The other door leads to the laundry and backyard.'

She flipped a light switch, revealing a sweet little bedroom decorated in gentle shades of lilac and baby blue. White lace curtains tied back with satin ribbons bordered open casement windows that let in a jasmine-scented breeze. In a corner stood a wicker chair, home to a collection of soft toys I recognised from Paisley's childhood, including Cleo, a worn pussycat with buttons for eyes that had once been her closest companion. Nearby was a low bookcase stacked with books retained from different eras of her life.

I rolled my suitcase in and dumped my backpack on the bed. 'I need to use your toilet.'

'It's in the bathroom. Be quick, dinner's ready, and don't use too much loo paper.'

'Good grief, *Painsley*,' I said, using the despised nickname from our younger days. 'I'm only going for a pee.'

Sitting on the loo, I scanned the small room, admiring the claw-footed bath positioned beneath a stained-glass window designed with images of wildflowers. A decorative mirror cabinet mounted on the opposite wall reflected the wire rack above the toilet cistern, showing plenty of paper on standby. So, I rebelled, using eight squares from the roll hanging beside me to spite my sister.

Before leaving, I opened the cabinet for a snoop inside, discovering big-budget skincare products I'd only dreamed of buying. Dabbing on anti-wrinkle cream, I was about to close the mirrored door when a strange purple plastic dinosaur loomed over a tube of lip plumper. When lifted out, the long neck and head seemed to resemble a ...

I yelped and dropped the sex toy onto the floor, where it vibrated over the tiles in a robotic fit.

'What's going on in there?' Paisley asked from the other side of the door.

I stomped on Dirty Dino and flicked the tiny switch to the off position. 'Nothing. All good.'

'Make it snappy. I'm dishing up.'

On my return, I found the island bench set with only two placemats. 'Fletcher not joining us? Where is he, laid up in bed?' According to Paisley's phone call several days earlier, my accident-prone brother-in-law had suffered some kind of injury, limiting his workload—hence my invitation.

'Well ...' She poured kibble from a container into a steel bowl on the slate floor for Whitby, who waited for her hand signal before getting stuck into his dinner. 'Fletcher's not here.'

'Not in the cottage?'

'Not at Grassington.'

'No!' I plonked down on a bench stool. 'Don't tell me he's in hospital. How ill is he?'

Paisley's frown, as she served stewed meat and vegetables from the pot into two deep plates, worried me. She sat alongside. 'He isn't in hospital. He's taken time away to settle his nerves.'

'His nerves? So, he's not injured?'

'Not physically. Eat up, you must be famished. I want your opinion of this Beef Rendang. Did I overdo the lemongrass? Enough coconut milk?'

Confused by Paisley's apparent lack of concern, I tasted a mouthful of curry and told her it was delicious, perfect. 'C'mon, tell me what really happened to him. What's with all the secrecy?'

She sighed as she shifted food around her plate. 'Where do I begin?'

I ate while my sister explained Fletcher had experienced a mental breakdown due to exhaustion from organising renovations and setting up the guesthouse, even experiencing delirium.

'What do you mean by delirium?' I asked.

'Seeing and hearing things that weren't there.'

'How do you know they weren't there?'

Paisley's fork halted just shy of her mouth. By her irritation, you'd think I'd asked her to prove the validity of extraterrestrial life. 'Let's just say they were too ludicrous to be real.'

'Where is he now?'

'In Brisbane. I persuaded him to take a couple of days off.'

'I hope he's getting professional help while he's there.'

'He's staying with Joe. He'll talk Fletcher around.'

'Joe?' I shoved my empty plate aside in disgust. 'For crying out loud! Joseph Teo is no psychologist.'

'Fletch will listen to him, Abby. Joe will help him realise it was all in his mind. That it resulted from fatigue and stress.'

Fletcher's repulsive lifelong mate had a knack for hostility and coercion, and it wasn't because he had a background in law enforcement. A natural manipulator, he could persuade anyone to do anything. Regrettably, I could vouch for that. 'He needs a medical expert, Pais, not an egotistical blowhard with a taste for violence.'

'Don't be so critical, Abbs. You've not seen Joe for years, so you haven't witnessed his transformation.'

My goal was to maintain it that way—out of sight, out of mind. I changed tack. 'You've done an excellent job with Grassington's new website. Ultra-professional. Yet, I can't remember you mentioning there were three ghosts haunting the mansion.'

A glint in her eyes. 'It's just a gimmick we're using for marketing to help bring in the punters. The mention of ghosts inhabiting an old house sparks interest, especially if it involves gruesome deaths. Of course, the manor has a tragic history, and myths abound, but actual spirits of the dead occupying it? Nah. Fletcher's Aunt Bridget is the only one I've heard moaning around Grassington. There's no such thing as ghosts, Abby. It's all bunk.'

'That's not true. Don't you remember the seance we had when

we were kids? When we made our own Ouija board and Grandad Bill spoke to us from the afterlife? It scared us shitless. Mum was furious when she found out and burnt it. Made us cross our hearts and promise never to do it again.'

'I reckon Skye had her hand in that little stunt. Our big sis loved to get us youngsters riled up.'

I glared. Both my siblings riled me up in childhood, forcing me to gang up on the other sister or ordering me around to do their bidding. Even now, they could infuriate me. 'You think Skye set us up?'

'I wouldn't put it past her.'

Unconvinced, I went on to state, 'But Skye wasn't there when that poltergeist disrupted our stay in the old holiday house on Stradbroke Island. Who smashed the glassware and kept banging on the doors all night, then, huh?'

Paisley wiped a smear of curry from the edge of her plate and licked it from her finger. 'My recollection is that Mum and Dad were going through a rough patch. You must remember the huge fight they had there. Mum had a fiery temper back then.'

I had no memory of that at all. Only the crashing and thumping, then helping with the clean-up in the morning. 'I'm sure someone mentioned it was a ghost.'

'Or you imagined it was one. If someone told you that, it was likely because you were a child. We shielded you from stuff.'

'Shielded me from the truth, like Mum flipping out?' Annoyed, I snarled. 'What else occurred that I don't know about?'

My question went unanswered as Paisley stacked our plates. 'Want dessert? I've made a *tarte Tatin*.' My blank expression prompted her to add, 'That's a French apple tart. We can eat it in front of the TV while watching *Celebrity Bake Off*.'

Several episodes of *Succession* might have been more fitting.

'Sure.' Deflated, I topped up my wine. Maybe it was best to

believe my family was protecting me, rather than seeing me as insignificant.

Later in bed, mellowed by good food, alcohol, and a feather-soft mattress, I texted Shane of my safe arrival and gave a brief version of events, assuring him I was needed at Grassington. His quick comeback:

> That's great, goodnight

The terse response drove me to check the time and discover it was almost midnight. I sent the same message to my kids, both living away from home and possibly still awake, to keep them informed, not for a reply.

The phone set aside, I let my eyes adjust to the room, softly lit from outside by a hunchback moon. My thoughts dallied on Fletcher and the several incidences in the past when he'd had depression. As far as I knew, none of them included hearing voices, which led me to wonder if stress wasn't the only trigger in this instance.

A screech from outdoors: a nocturnal creature on the prowl or its unfortunate prey. Followed by a bloodcurdling squeal … closer … and a clatter overhead as something scampered across roof tiles. Why did Grimm have a more fearsome version of Bigfoot as their mascot? Was I about to discover the truth of the myth?

I shut the window and loosened the ribbon ties, the curtains meeting in a rush. Falling back on the mattress, I watched wispy shadows drift across the ceiling. What was the basis for the hauntings at Grassington? Paisley had mentioned tragedy. *Gruesome deaths.* A familiar thrill goaded me to discover more about the Greenwoods, yet it also set alarm bells ringing. Hadn't

I learnt anything from my recent perilous quest to dig up the past?

A soft thud on the floor. In the stippled moonlight, I saw Cleo the toy cat now sprawled on the rug and hissing at me through her stitched mouth. Tears filled my eyes in response to being spooked, and I hid under the bedsheet. Unlike my sister, I wasn't so dismissive of malicious spirits messing with the living. If something wicked were to come my way, would I have the courage to confront it, or would I, like Fletcher, topple over the edge of sanity?

2

Hot breath on my face.

I cracked open my eyes, expecting to find Shane snuggled up close to me, only to catch Whitby staring at me from the edge of the mattress and whining. Ah, yes. Grassington. Damn dog, why hadn't he woken Paisley to let him out for a wee?

Weary from another fitful sleep—this time compounded by a nightmare of being burnt alive—I got out of bed and narrowly missed stepping on a large rhinoceros beetle lying belly up on the floor. A prod with my toe proved it was dead. So, last night's hissing was a beetle in distress.

'It wasn't you, then,' I said, returning Cleo to the wicker chair.

Scooping up the beetle, I opened the bedroom window and tossed it into the garden. Answering Whitby's demand to be let outside, I found I was also desperate to relieve a full bladder. I tiptoed to the bathroom and eased the door shut so as not to bother Paisley. I shouldn't have worried. Her steady snoring cutting through the adjoining wall confirmed she was deep in sleep.

Keen to return to my comfy bed, I went to check if Whitby was ready to come back inside, only to discover him waiting at the rear gate, scratching on the wooden palings.

'Hey, are you allowed out there?'

He barked his answer, and I went over and flicked the latch. Whitby tore out and down a path, disappearing around a hedgerow.

I was about to head back indoors, when I saw him reappear a way off, yapping as if goading me to join him in his early morning adventure. Was this something Fletcher normally did? Birds chirped, and the section of sky I glimpsed through the trees was pinking up. A stroll before breakfast might be beneficial. I rushed inside, stepped into a pair of joggers, and yanked a hoody over my pyjamas.

Whitby ushered me along a bush-lined dirt track until we emerged onto the bitumen drive. Birdsong accompanied us as we traipsed uphill in the shade of sprawling acacias and eucalypts. Rounding a bend, an honour guard of pencil pines and Narnia-like lamp posts directed us to the top, where I pulled up with a start, my heart aflutter. Across a quadrangle of manicured lawn stood the Grassington mansion. Bathed in the peachy glow of sunrise, the two-storied, rendered-brick building took on an iridescence, its windows winking in response to my admiring gaze.

A porch surrounded the ground level while a verandah, supported by paired columns and protected by a decorative wrought iron balustrade, wrapped around the upper storey. The iron roof comprised an impressive tower with flagpole, and an observation deck—a lookout—no doubt to take in a 360-degree view. Unless I could master my intense fear of heights, I wouldn't be going up there anytime soon. Investigating the splendid interior would be thrilling enough.

I snapped a photo with my phone and sent it to Shane and the kids before twisting around to gawk at an unobstructed vista. Beneath a brilliant pink and gold mackerel sky lay a field lined with rows of woody vines. Beyond this ancient vineyard rose a sprawling hill bearing a colossal tree with wide-spreading branches. The website had suggested picnicking on Fig Tree Hill, and there it was—a delightful, secluded spot for reading, or dreaming, or ... *a moonlight tryst*. I took several pics of the landscape and sent them also to my family.

Coldness on the back of my leg—Whitby's moist nose urging me on. This time, he guided me across the lawn and down a steep path bordered by shady jacaranda trees and agapanthus. Passing through a timber arbour entwined with bougainvillea, we entered a clearing below a bushy terraced slope that offered snatches of the southern aspect of the mansion. I spied the words *Grassington Est.1886* carved into the masonry connected to the tower. Was this side the actual building frontage?

My attention returned to the colourful glade, where a kaleidoscope of butterflies now frolicked amongst stalks of blue delphiniums and candy-pink lilies multilayered with star-shaped petals. Tall spikes covered in purple bell-like flowers were also impressive. It was a perfect location to hold a garden party, or even a wedding.

A rock structure built into the earthen slope at the clearing's far end proved to be a garden grotto, with stone steps on both sides rising from ground level to openings halfway up. Rather than enhanced by a cascading fountain, a platform atop the boulder stack featured a life-size sculpture of a woman in a Roman toga.

Fascinated, I climbed the steps on the right and entered the cave, finding more roughly hewn stonework within, including a bench against the back wall. Crusty lichen engulfed every surface, and spider webs hung in profusion. One enormous wheel-shaped web sparkled with rainbow hues from sunlight seeping through the vent it spanned. My breath quivered the fine harp string strands as I leant close, careful not to disturb the plump orb spider at its centre. Peeking through the tapering gap to outside, I glimpsed a section of the garden below. Had someone inside the cave ever used this crevice as a spy hole to secretly watch the goings-on in the garden, or keep a lookout so as not to be detected within? One could almost get away with anything in here.

The lack of noise filtering in surprised me as I surrendered to the seclusion. Exiting through the second opening, I followed a path through scrubby bush to a set of stone stairs, which brought me up to the bitumen drive directly in front of the mansion. At close range, I admired the elaborate thistle-patterned lacework of the upper verandah's iron balustrade. So clever and creative, those Victorian era designers.

With Whitby nowhere in sight—off on his own escapade—I skipped up the four steps to the portico and stood before a pair of massive doors. Eager to use the large door knocker and rattle the brass knobs, I hesitated, not wanting to intrude. Instead, I walked to a bay window on the right side of the doors and looked through a curved glass pane.

The gold and crystal chandelier and a long cedar table showed the room was used for formal dining. Walls lined to ceiling height with red cedar panels were broken by two doorways—one accessing a central hallway, the other into the front foyer. A gilt-edged mirror mounted above an impressive dark grey marble fireplace gave an extra dimension to the room, reflecting the arched windows and scenery outside.

Through an identical window on the left side of the front doors, I saw a room of similar design, though furnished with a white marble fireplace, leather Chesterfield sofas, and a black grand piano—the drawing room. Startled by movement beyond one of the open doorways, I shrunk back. Had someone just walked down the hallway?

I raced to the other bay window to see if they were going to the dining room. My heart thumped as a blurry figure drifted in, floating across the floor in my direction. Before I could duck away, it flickered and disappeared.

Bewildered, I rubbed my eyes and glanced over my shoulder, catching leafy branches swaying in nearby trees. Could the image have been simply a reflection in glass?

A thud sounded to my right, followed by a cry.

Hurrying across the verandah, I nearly stepped on a green apple rolling past the corner of the building. I picked it up and manoeuvred around the edge of the house, discovering a woman crouched on the mosaic tiles, her bony fingers scrabbling to retrieve fruit spilled from an overturned basket. With a straw hat perched on a bird's nest of grey hair and dressed in an ankle-length dress with an embroidered shawl draping her shoulders, she resembled a time-travelling fruit seller from a previous century.

'Hello,' I said, hoping it wasn't my mind playing tricks.

The woman looked up sharply. 'Who the hell are you?' she growled, unfolding to stand. Even from a distance, I could tell she was taller than me—though, me being on the short side, most people were.

I inched near, discerning a crisscross of lines raking the woman's cheeks. Although past her prime, her cerulean eyes glimmered with the vibrancy of youth. She had to be Fletcher's aunt.

'I'm Fletcher's sister-in-law,' I said.

She cocked her head. 'Fletcher?'

'Your nephew. He and his wife, Paisley, live at the groundskeeper's cottage.'

'Zachariah's cottage?'

'Well, yes ... I guess so. And I gather you're his aunt?'

She swiped the apple from my hand and shoved it into the basket to mingle with pears, oranges, and an overripe banana. 'How old do you think I am, girl? Zachariah's dead. Long gone. How could I be his aunt?'

'No, not him. Fletcher, your nephew.'

'Fletcher?'

Oh, God, here we go again. 'You're Bridget?'

She nodded. 'Bridget Hawthorne.'

'Yes.' I clapped my hands together. 'That's correct.'

A scowl. 'I am not an imbecile. I know who I am. What's your name?'

'Abby Eaton. I'm staying with ...' I hesitated, reluctant to mention Fletcher again. 'Staying at the cottage. I'm here to help get the mansion ready for guests.'

'Guests? What guests?' She combed fingers through her hair and peered down at what was in fact a dimity nightgown. 'I'm in no fit state to greet visitors. Who arranged this? It certainly wasn't me.' She waved me away. 'Be gone with you girl, you are redundant here.' Then she swivelled on bare feet and scurried back inside the house through a side entrance.

Glued to the spot, I mulled over the awkward encounter. Paisley hadn't mentioned Fletcher's aunt was demented. My phone bleeped. A text message from my sister:

Where are you, Abbs? Breakfast is ready

Taking the steps down to the bitumen drive, I was dumbfounded by wet prints leading up to the portico. My joggers hadn't made them, nor Bridget's small bare feet. Large block-heeled boots had walked the dewy lawn before crossing the bitumen to reach the steps. Had the figure I saw gliding through the dining room been someone reflected in the window? Then where was this person now? Who had sneaked up behind me and disappeared in the blink of an eye?

I sat down in front of a plate of scrambled eggs, grilled tomatoes, and a glistening Bratwurst sausage. 'I think I just bumped into Fletcher's aunt.'

Paisley looked up from squeezing oranges for juice. 'Oh, so you've met her. How was she today?'

'Odd. Struggled to recall who you and Fletcher were.'

'Sounds about right. Bridget's more addled in the mornings. The cobwebs in her mind blow away as the day progresses, and by evening she'll remember the name of everyone she's ever met. A few shandies in, and she'll bore you to tears with her reminiscences.'

I chewed a mouthful of spicy pork. That last snippet of information could prove helpful. 'She called this cottage *Zachariah's*. Was he the groundskeeper?'

'Yeah. His missus, Maggie, was Grassington's housekeeper and cook. They were employed here until Zachariah's death.'

'Was the cottage left vacant until your arrival?'

'No way. You should've seen the place before our restorations. Someone modernised it in the 1940s or '50s and decorated it in shades of pinks and greens, including the bathroom. No-one saw fit to change it again until we moved in.'

'Hey, is there anyone else here? Someone who might wear oversized work boots?'

Paisley's hand stopped mid-squeeze. 'Why would you ask that?'

'There were wet boot prints on the bitumen out the front of the mansion.'

'You must be mistaken. There's no-one here who'd leave such prints. Not now.'

I regretted not taking a photo as proof. 'What's the plan for today?'

'We could start by making up the beds. Six guests are staying with us.'

'Three couples?'

'Nope, just two.' She reached for a notebook at the end of the island bench and flipped it open. 'Vince and Daphne O'Mara from Toowoomba, and Luke and Sandy Michaelson from Brisbane.'

Paisley passed me a glass of juice, and I took a long sip.

'Who else is booked in?'

'Let's see. Rowan Twomey from Byron Bay, and Hilary Bloodworth, who will arrive on Saturday.'

'Bloodworth? What a brilliantly creepy name.'

A grin. 'It is, isn't it. She's a paranormal investigator. Offered to use her skills while here.'

'A ghost hunter?' I gave her a nudge with my elbow. 'And you're fine with that, considering you're a disbeliever?'

Paisley's expression turned serious. 'It'll add to the experience. I'm sure the guests will get a thrill out of it. And you can always help out.'

'How do you mean? I'm not running around dressed in a white sheet.'

'I wouldn't ask you to. Historic houses make strange noises. You could draw attention to the odd creaks and rattles and inflame the guests' imagination. The power of suggestion might urge people to believe the noises are made by tormented spirits.'

My flesh squirmed. 'What if her investigations verify there

really are spirits haunting the mansion? Have you thought about that?'

'It'll never happen. She'll just psych people up and get them believing all sorts of spooky things. The more she makes them tremble with fear, the more enjoyment. As long as the guests leave positive reviews, I'm fine with it.'

'What if this Hilary opens a gateway to the spirit world? You'd better supply heaps of dried sage to burn afterwards to cleanse the place of evil.' I spoke in jest ... mostly.

'You and your wild imagination,' Paisley said, shaking her head. 'That and the inability to let go of things tend to cause you trouble.'

My muscles tensed at her caustic reference to my most recent brush with danger. What was wrong with being inquisitive? We'd still be primordial slime if it wasn't for curiosity.

Springing to my feet, I collected our empty plates and used cutlery and shoved them into the dishwasher. 'I'm gonna take a shower, and then I'll be ready to help out.'

Paisley pushed me aside and restacked the items. 'Well, get moving. I'll meet you up at the big house when you're done. Make sure you lock the cottage doors before you leave.'

'Why? I assumed you'd abandoned the idea of a trespasser.'

'There's no harm in being cautious.'

3

———————

The smell of the mansion's interior hit me first, a meld of odours from times past. Musty, like I'd opened a wardrobe and sunk my face into timeworn clothing.

Then came the sudden drop in temperature and the gloom—strikingly different to the dazzling exterior I'd observed earlier. Dark cedar panelling adorned with framed sepia photographs added to the suffocating atmosphere, restraining my movement. Anchored to the mosaic tiles in the foyer, I yearned to dispel the shadows by switching on the fancy chandelier suspended from the high ceiling; festooned with oodles of crystal beads and teardrops, it contained, at least, ten light bulbs. If only I could locate the wall switch.

Drawn by some mysterious force through open etched-glass doors, I found myself in a central hallway running the full width of the house. Walls closed in on me in waves, compressing and expanding as if the house was taking breaths—I could almost hear the sighs. Internal staircases stood at either end of the hall. The stairs on the right were plain timber, unlike the carpeted left stairs across from the drawing room, whose railing newel posts featured orblike caps.

Opposite me stood an intricately carved chiffonier built into a wall recess. Though impressive, a huge oil painting mounted above dwarfed its splendour, the stern features of a man with an impressive handlebar moustache leaping out of the portrait's dark background. A Greenwood ancestor, for sure. I squirmed under his frosty glare. Foreseeing a low rating in his appraisal of me, I moved close and gave him a dressing-down.

'Don't be such a snob. I bet you weren't perfect. I plan to explore your family's history and discover what actually happened here.'

The painting wobbled, and I reeled as a door nearby swung open and Paisley's head popped out.

'Abby, good, you've turned up. Come in here, I want to introduce you to my assistant cook.'

I blinked. Wasn't that my job?

I entered a vast kitchen, modernised with subway tiles and an abundance of stainless steel. At an island bench in the centre, a teenage boy—possibly fresh out of high school—massaged a mound of dough in a large ceramic mixing bowl. Sporting a green-dyed reverse mullet—shorn at the back, long fringe swept to one side at the front—and shimmering gold eyelids, he looked to be no shrinking violet.

Paisley draped an arm over the youth's narrow shoulders. 'This is Cole Sedgwick.'

I gave a limp wave. 'Oh, hi, I'm—'

'Abby, the younger sister,' Cole chimed in. Wiping a floury hand across a freckle-smattered cheek, he sniggered. 'Paisley's told me all about you.'

My glare shot skewers at my sister.

'Don't worry, sis,' she said. 'I kept it all legit.'

What did that mean? What story details did she omit?

'Cole's come up from the village to assist me in the kitchen. He's a star when it comes to cooking. His scones and shortbread are popular at the Grimm cafe. If he plays his cards right, I might wrangle a catering traineeship to help him get his foot in the door towards his chef career.'

Cole's face beamed back at Paisley. 'I'll do my best this weekend.'

She squeezed his arm and scowled. 'You'd better. Or else I'll have to rethink my commitment.' A chuckle softened the severity of her words.

More than a little concerned, I desperately needed to know more about this boy. Paisley and Fletcher chose childlessness years ago, believing it best for the planet, or some such notion. Watching my sister with Cole, I wondered if her motherly instinct had kicked in and she was funnelling it into something worthwhile: helping someone in need of ... what? ... motivation, affection ... *funds*? On impulse, I checked his footwear: red Converse sneakers, not work boots.

Paisley nodded in my direction. 'That leaves you to help me around the house.'

'So, I've been downgraded to a housemaid?'

'Stop fretting, there'll be plenty to keep you occupied. Come upstairs, I'll show you the proper way to make a bed.'

'Hey, I know how to make a bed, *hospital corners* and all.'

'Then it'll be a cinch.' She relieved me of my cross-body bag and hung it on a wall hook. 'It'll be safe here.'

Before following her into the hallway, I removed my phone from the bag's outer pocket. Cole may have been a shifty snoop for all I knew.

Paisley ascended the formal staircase, with me shuffling after her.

'Who's in that portrait above the chiffonier?' I asked.

'Gerald Greenwood. Fletcher's great-great-grandfather. He lost his mind in the end.'

I experienced an element of satisfaction until it was substituted by a solemn thought. Was this a family trait? Maybe Fletcher would be inheriting more than just Grassington.

Paisley reached the middle landing and turned. 'Better watch how you go. A maid fell to her death down this staircase. Some say it was an accident, others say she'd been *pushed*.'

A shove from her made me teeter and grip the railing for support. 'Hey! That's not funny. I might have lost my balance.'

'Lighten up, Abbs, it's a joke.' Laughing, she raced up to the floor above.

I seethed. Why were older siblings such frigging tormentors?

The initial room to prepare was a spacious corner bedroom with a prominent four-poster mahogany bed, featuring a canopy frame and lace tie-back curtains. Arched windows, like those in the two main rooms downstairs, let in light to counteract the darkness of the timber walls and maroon carpeting. Another fireplace, this one bearing a carved wooden mantle and above it, a gilt-edged mirror.

'This was Henry and Olivia's room—Gerald's son and daughter-in-law.' Paisley pointed to a framed photograph on the wall near a doorway to an ensuite bathroom, once a dressing room or nursery.

A strapping young man with a neat beard and sharp eyes seemed to be assessing me from the photo as I did him. Seated, and wearing a three-piece suit accessorised with a pocket watch and a buttonhole flower, he grasped the brim of a bowler hat resting in his lap. Standing alongside him, dressed in a high-necked lace gown and holding a trailing wedding bouquet, was a slender, doe-eyed woman with fair hair swept up from her face and piled atop her head. Henry and Olivia's blank expressions and stiff posture, typical of early photography, offered no sign of the state of their union.

A creaking hinge diverted my attention to Paisley, who had lifted the lid of a blanket box at the foot of the bed.

'Was it a happy marriage?' I asked.

She shrugged. 'No idea. Olivia's supposed to have kept journals, which might well have revealed how things were. But I haven't come across them. Maybe the journals were just hopeful gossip.' She extracted folded white linen from the box and held the pile out for me to take. 'The bed frame is antique, but the mattress and springs are new.'

Tempted to throw myself on the bed and check out its bounce, I removed the beige embroidered coverlet, and with Paisley's help, put on a fresh quilted mattress protector. Yet my sister stood back as I fitted the sheets, watching eagle-eyed as I crisply folded and tucked in the corners, replaced the coverlet, and slipped cases on four dense pillows. I expected her to give me a score out of ten for my efforts, but all I received was a grunt.

'Only five more beds to go,' she said with an irksome grin.

'Five? But there's only one other couple and two singles booked in.'

'The smaller rooms each have two single beds. May as well give the guests a choice.'

In the hall, we passed a cast iron spiral staircase leading to the rooftop when Paisley suddenly stopped and faced a wall. Had she gone catatonic? She pressed the heel of her hand against the timberwork, causing a panel to spring open and expose a narrow room lined with shelves of folded linen and cleaning supplies. How inventive. How many more secret doors were built into the wall panelling?

Paisley loaded my arms with bedding. 'These are for the pink, green, and yellow rooms,' she instructed. 'You'll be okay to do that on your own while I go double-check the food stock, won't you?'

If my arms weren't laden, I would have offered a salute and a 'Yes, ma'am'. 'Of course. No need to babysit me anymore.'

With a huff, she walked away.

A glimpse into the three other bedrooms revealed why Paisley described them by colour. Matching wallpaper and drapes in tones unique to each room added ample dimension, as if the curtains had grown right out of the walls rather than being tacked on to them. I would have inspected other rooms, to see if they were similarly decorated, had the doors not been locked.

The room decorated in yellow damask flourishes, though the brightest, turned out to be the coldest. It was like stepping into an air-conditioned space, only there was no air-con unit, just a motionless ceiling fan—perhaps due to the room's central location in the house. The pink room patterned with blushing peonies bore a heady floral scent, despite lacking freshly cut flowers, the result, no doubt, of absorbing residue from fragrant candles or oils. While the lush ivy design snaking around the green room gave the impression of the walls closing in, shrinking the space. It was easy to understand how these oddities might cause a person's imagination to run riot.

I lingered after making the bed in the pink bedroom to admire a lifelike painting hanging on the wall. With her hair fashioned into a low twisted bun, a jewelled headband, and a drop-waisted satin dress with tulle cape, the young woman looked the epitome of 1920s elegance. Was this delicate creature, her natural beauty enhanced by pale eyes and a heart-shaped face, another member of the Greenwood family? Fastening curtains back from the window, a set of letters scored in a corner of the glass near the frame caught my eye: *EG & WF 1921*. I slid a finger over the coarse markings and wondered who had made them.

While I stuffed a stubborn pillow into its case in the green ivy room, a flash of movement past the doorway and the pad of footsteps made me question Paisley's confidence in my efforts. Had she snuck up to check on me? A glance into the hallway found no-one there, only a lone milk-white glass marble with an orange swirl, lying on the carpet runner. I picked it up and rolled it in my palm, noting the chips and scuffing from use. If my sister wanted to play childish games, she was free to do it on her own. I placed the marble on a hall table between a pair of vintage Chinese foo dogs and completed my task.

With all beds made, I intended to return downstairs. However, when I approached the carpeted stairs, I swerved left, walking across the sitting area and through the doorway that brought me out onto the wraparound verandah.

Standing back from the railing and dizzying sight directly below, I made out distant tin roofs shimmering with sunlight, and a church spire rising above a band of trees to pierce the sky. With the hill cleared of vegetation to enable the build, residents of Grimm would have had a clear view of the mansion taking shape. *Behold my grandeur*, it would have declared from its lofty position. Was there resentment between social classes back then? Or were local folk grateful for jobs created by the Greenwood dream becoming a reality?

I went to take a photo when I received a text from my son:

> Good to see you're having fun Mum. Wish
> I was there and not getting ready for
> college

In response, I sent Elliott a pic of the view, along with a kissing emoji.

'Finished already?'

I turned and found Paisley standing close, eyeing her watch. I was unaware of being timed.

'Yep, all done. And what have you been up to?' I offered an opportunity for my sister to confess her spying and game-playing.

She squinted. 'Checking on food stock, like I said. Weren't you listening? I came to show you where the towels, soaps, and fragrant candles are kept so you can place them in the bedrooms. I also need gift bags made up.' She gestured for me to accompany her as she strutted away.

Was she telling the truth about being downstairs? I clutched my sister's arm, pulling her to a stop. 'What's in the other rooms, the locked ones?'

'Oh ... just like you to be a stickybeak. Rooms yet to be restored. Opposite the main bedroom is Bridget's domain, her living quarters. Out of bounds to *everyone* else.' I got it, that included me. 'The old girl may be muddle-headed, but she's highly independent. Does her own cooking and cleaning, as well as washing and ironing.'

'How old is she?'

'Eighty-four.'

'Never married?'

'Nope. A true spinster. Was a schoolteacher way back, somewhere up north. Returned when her mother became ill and needed full-time care. Looked after her until she died. Now she refuses to move, preferring to rattle around in this ancient house alone. Well, until we arrived.'

'What will become of this place once she's gone?'

'You mean who will inherit Grassington? Well, that's a bone of contention. As things stand, Fletcher will be the recipient, being the only other surviving family member since his mother's death. But if Bridget goes through with her recent line of thought, it will be gifted to the Heritage National Trust.'

'Are you serious? What prompted such a decision?'

'She says it's a money pit and doesn't want to burden Fletcher with the worry of it all.'

'Why doesn't she sell it, move to a smaller residence or a retirement community, and leave him any remaining funds when she kicks the bucket?'

'She refuses to shackle Fletcher to the past, whatever that means.'

I flung my arms wide. 'Look at this place. The possibilities are endless.'

'That's why we're trying to show her how it would pay for itself, generate a decent income, even. We talked her into parting with a little cash for basic renovations and giving us two years to prove how it can be run successfully as a guesthouse and function venue. Still, we're on edge, questioning whether she'll pull a swiftie and alter her will without consulting us.'

'I guess Fletcher doesn't have the enduring power of attorney over her affairs?'

'Correct.'

'Then she could legally do whatever she wants. I suppose it's up to you to change her mind. Two years isn't long. You'll really have to work some magic, Pais.'

A woeful sigh. 'Don't I know it. The hall's end bathroom cupboard holds soap, towels, et cetera. Once you've finished, I'll meet you in the rose garden for a cuppa and cinnamon teacake, if Cole has managed to bake it.'

The bathroom was a thing of beauty—dark timber, white porcelain fixtures, and black and white geometric wall and floor tiles. A leadlight window positioned in the wall above a deep, claw-footed tub enhanced with gilded tapware continued the opulent theme.

Collecting the items from the cupboard, and struggling to hold the bundle, a bar of lavender soap slipped from the top and slid across the floor. I squatted to retrieve it and spied a colourful object beneath the bath. When dragged out, it proved to be a small wood carving of a circus elephant standing on a wheeled platform. The crackled paintwork and iron ring screwed into the front edge of the platform showed it was a vintage pull-along toy. I recalled seeing a couple of these on a wall shelf in the yellow bedroom, amongst other children's playthings.

A brisk investigation in that room revealed there was now a lone elephant displayed on the shelf. Alike in design, yet larger, it bore an iron hook on the back of its platform. I positioned the smaller elephant behind it, connecting the calf's front ring to the rear hook of its mother.

How did the smaller carving end up in the bathroom and roll under the bath? I thought of the glass marble I'd found in the hallway. If it was Bridget I'd seen scurrying past the green bedroom, had her condition caused her to regress to childhood and play with old family toys?

4

OLIVIA

Grassington, May 1886

Olivia Greenwood is giddy with excitement as she races through the entirety of the manor house for the very first time, imagining how best to furnish each room. It is as if she's woken on her birthday to find the bed piled high with gaily wrapped parcels tied with satin ribbon.

After visiting the first-floor bedrooms, she descends the staircase with care, lest she slips on the newly varnished flooring. Stopping on the final step, she lets out a squeal. 'I can't believe this is all ours.'

Henry appears, stroking his dense beard as one would a cat. 'It is ours now, my love; every nook and cranny of Grassington Manor belongs to us.'

'It is a shame your father couldn't enjoy the house in its completed state. But, eight bedrooms. Such extravagance. What did he have in mind when designing it? What in the world are we going to do with all of them?'

Olivia's new husband draws her down to his level. 'Don't worry. We'll fill them with babes soon enough.'

She blushes as he presses his lips against hers and trails fingers down her throat to the buttons fastening the collar of her bodice. Fearing walls have eyes, she sidles away. 'We shall have plenty of visitors from the city. Imagine the functions we can host—the balls, the soirees, the banquets. Surely, we will be accepted into society as one of their own.'

Henry guides her through the doorway into what will be the grand dining room. Sliding his arm around her waist, he leads her in a silent waltz, twirling past red cedar panelled walls, and huge arched windows admitting pools of light. Their laughter echoes, their delight unfettered.

'We are going to be happy here. I just know it,' Olivia says.

'Happy and successful,' Henry adds.

'As long as you don't overwork and end up like your father.'

He comes to a sudden stop beneath the glorious crystal chandelier. 'You mean, leaping from the rooftop to my death?'

'I mean, turning as crazy as a loon.'

'I'll do my best.'

Olivia grips his shirt front and gazes into his nut-brown eyes. 'Promise me you won't ever change. I couldn't bear it if you did. I love you just as you are.'

Henry wrenches free and doffs his felt hat, bowing from the waist with an exuberant flourish. 'I promise I will always be charming and forever devoted to you, my sweet bride.'

'I'm holding you to that, Henry Arthur Thomas Greenwood.'

Still amazed he'd wed her, a plain-faced spinster with no obvious talents, Olivia wonders if it was the dowry that had piqued his interest, or her lack of objection to moving to an obscure rural setting. Whichever, she is grateful. Henry rescued her at the perfect time.

She tells him it is necessary to return to Brisbane as there is plenty of shopping to be done at the city stores. The selection of wallpaper, drapes, and furniture for each room will present quite a challenge. And she has ideas for the garden. Engaging a skilled groundskeeper with a full knowledge of roses will be a priority.

'A man named Zachariah Bright has come to my attention,' she says, 'a highly proficient gardener seeking employment. He has recent experience in groundskeeping at Brisbane's Government House, while his wife has worked in the kitchens. She may be suitable as our chief cook.'

Henry's face beams with pleasure. 'Well, it's up to you to organise, being the lady of the manor. What has been good for the Governor, will certainly be sufficient for us. But first I have a surprise.'

He ushers Olivia across the hall to the room due to become his office, and seats her on one of the many tea chests waiting to be unpacked. Plucking a brown paper package from a wall shelf, he places it in her hand. 'Open it,' he urges with a grin.

'What is it?'

'A housewarming present, from me to you.'

Intrigued, she unties the string binding it and peels away the stiff paper, surprised to find a leatherbound book, green cover with embossed gold lettering that catches the sunlight. Her fingertip traces the wording: *The Journal of Olivia W. Greenwood.* 'What shall I write in it?'

'Whatever you wish,' Henry replies. 'Our new life together will surely be filled with wonder.'

'*Or heartache,*' she hears whispered into her ear.

Her eyes sweep the room. Whence had the voice come? They were indeed alone.

With a sense of foreboding, Olivia springs from the tea chest and clings to her husband so tightly he winces.

5

———————

I located the walled rose garden out from the north side of the mansion. Passing through an ivy-covered archway, I was greeted by flourishing flower beds formed in concentric circles around a small pond featuring a stone statue of a man in dungarees, squatting, and spilling water from a shallow bowl. Untroubled by my presence, small birds chirruped and bathed, while a water dragon sunbaked on the paved edging.

In a corner of the garden, a metal gazebo entwined with purple foliage provided shade for an iron outdoor setting—a perfect location for morning tea. As Paisley had not yet arrived, I strolled the gravel pathways, taking photos and cupping blooms to smell their individual scents. Unable to identify roses by name, I appreciated their beauty and distinctive colours and features. The tranquillity of the surroundings was palpable, and I succumbed to the garden's enchantment.

The magic was broken when I caught a face peeking through branches of a rose bush, veined eyes swimming in a sea of wrinkles.

'What the hell! Who are you?'

Moments later, a short elderly man in bibbed overalls, black gumboots, and a broad-brimmed straw hat shuffled out from the greenery. Along with a bushy white beard and plump ruddy cheeks, he was a garden gnome come to life.

'Sorry, luv. I used to work here at Grassington. Mainly in this garden. Thought I'd drop in and check on the state of things.'

'Oh … how long ago were you employed?'

'Until fairly recently. Worked here for fifty years. I found nothing better than getting my hands dirty cultivating these roses. Most of them are over a hundred years old.'

'So, you knew Bridget's parents?'

'Mrs Hawthorne was the one who hired me. Desperate, she was. What other reason could there be for taking a chance on a young fella with more courage than expertise? It sure was back-breaking work, alright. The garden was a jungle. A right dog's breakfast.' He shook his head and tut-tutted. 'I've never weeded and trimmed so much in my life.'

'Did you live in the groundskeeper's cottage?'

'For a time. Until I bought my own place just outside of town. Nothing flash, a shack more like it, but comfortable.'

'You have family?'

He hesitated before answering. 'Yes and no.' Sadness lurked behind his eyes, and he changed the subject. 'Want to see my favourite rose?'

He led me to a rambling rose growing over a wooden trellis. 'The *Albertine*. Only blooms for a few weeks in the summer, so I'm surprised it's still flowering. Give it a decent whiff.'

I did. By my remark I could have been evaluating a pleasing fine wine. 'Gorgeous. It has a heady, fruity aroma.'

'Heirloom roses possess exceptional fragrance. New types boast beauty but lack scent.'

I fed the sprig behind my left ear; there was no escaping its pleasant smell.

He walked on, with me in pursuit. 'Another of my favourites is the *Lady Hillingdon*, that delightful apricot-yellow tea rose just to your right.'

I sidestepped over and leant my nose close, careful not to breathe in one of the many bees buzzing around the fully opened flowers. 'I guess the bees and flowers benefit greatly from each other here.'

'Yes, they have a wonderfully symbiotic relationship. What do you think of the *Roseraie De L'Hay*? It's a real stunner.'

I gazed around, clueless. 'Sorry, I'm not well-versed on roses. Which one is that?'

'The magenta-coloured shrub near the pond, on the right of Gerald.'

'Gerald? Is that another variety?'

His staccato chuckle reminded me of Woody Woodpecker. 'That's the statue in the pond. Gerald Greenwood was the original owner of the estate, and that's him panning for gold. Though Zachariah, the original gardener, had gotten it wrong when he commissioned a stone mason to produce the statue. I think Gerald was more into gold *digging* rather than someone who panned for it.'

'I thought it was a bloke quenching his thirst.'

The man grinned and removed his hat to wipe sweat from his age-spotted scalp. 'After making his fortune on the Gympie Goldfields in the early 1870s, Gerald moved to this area and bought two hundred wooded acres. Clearing the land, he became a saw miller and timber merchant before building the Grassington mansion.'

'Where did the name come from? The scrubby terrain?'

'Gerald named it after his birthplace, a village in Yorkshire,

England. Unfortunately, the poor sod didn't get to reside in the house. He died only weeks before moving in. His son, Henry, and new wife took up residence instead.'

'You could reinvent yourself as a tour guide for the estate. Just a suggestion,' I added, catching him grimace at the idea. 'How'd you get to know so much?'

'Like I said, I worked here for many years. Can't help but gather a lot of facts in that time.'

Facts or *secrets?* He was the perfect go-to person for further questions.

The man crouched to examine a cream-coloured rose with a bright yellow centre. Removing a tiny green bug and squishing it between his fingers, he wiped his hand on his overalls. 'Blasted aphids,' he growled. 'Someone needs to keep a watchful eye on things around here.' His geriatric knees creaked with the effort of straightening.

I followed his line of sight as he gazed up at the house, catching movement in a window on the upper level—curtains closing in Bridget's section.

'Yes, she also needs watching, that one,' I said. 'I heard she's showing signs of dementia?'

He looked shellshocked. 'Who told you that?'

'I witnessed it myself. Bridget was rather confused, the poor thing. Couldn't follow a simple conversation.'

'Maybe she's unsettled by all the changes. She should have sold up and started a new life after her mother's death, but she stubbornly stayed on, saying it was now her duty to hold the vengeful spirits at bay.'

I balked. 'Vengeful spirits?'

'Ghosts. The house is teeming with them.'

'Really?' Three wasn't exactly *teeming.* 'How do you keep ghosts at bay?'

His answer, if he had one, was prevented by the sound of clinking china.

'I'd best be off,' the man announced, shuffling over to the wall and disappearing through a gap in the decaying brickwork.

Paisley appeared near the trellis, struggling to balance a laden tray. 'Were you talking to yourself?'

'No, with the gardener ... or perhaps I should say, the *ex-*gardener.'

She pulled up with a start, her eyes roaming. 'What's he doing here?'

'He said he'd dropped in to check on things.'

'Well, he shouldn't be on the premises. Fletcher is capable of looking after a few plants on his own.'

Had they sacked him? Even I could tell the garden needed someone with more than a scant knowledge of roses to keep it under control. 'They're not just plants, Pais. They're heritage roses. And there's way more than only *a few*. You might want to revisit your decision. If Fletcher is struggling, having this guy tend to the gardens would help alleviate some of his stress.'

'Never going to happen.' She trudged over to the gazebo and banged the tray down on the garden table, knocking a teacup from its saucer. 'Now let's try this cake while we tackle the next job on the list.'

'Which is?' I said, forcing my hackles down.

'Running through the events of the weekend.'

We sat, and I was handed a plate. I took a bite of cake and fished a strand of green hair from my mouth. 'Ew. Better make Cole wear a hair net. Are the guests all arriving at the same time tomorrow?'

'They've been instructed to arrive by two pm for afternoon tea at three. That way, they can get settled into their rooms before eating. Oops, I almost forgot. I need to print out menus for each meal.' She tugged a small spiral notepad and pen from her shirt pocket and jotted something down. 'One guest is vegan. I can't remember who.'

'I bet it's that Rowan guy from Byron Bay.'

'Possibly. Now, a quick run-through of the meals. Tomorrow's dinner will be that Beef Rendang we had last night, plus a Lentil and Vegetable Korma. Then on Saturday we will provide a cooked breakfast with vegan options. For lunch I'm offering gourmet picnic hampers so guests can go eat wherever they wish, weather permitting. Darn, I have to print maps of the estate too.'

'I can do the printing for you. And Saturday's dinner?'

'A formal three-course affair. Sunday breakfast will be croissants, fresh fruit, and pancakes. I've a delicious honeycomb and blueberry topping I'm dying to try.' She made a show of licking her lips. 'Lunch will be an alfresco country-style barbecue.'

My mouth watered. With all this mention of food, the slice of teacake fell short of appeasing my appetite. A glance at my watch showed there was still another hour and thirty-five minutes till lunchtime.

'Seems you've got that all sorted,' I said. 'How about playing some games after the initial dinner to break the ice and help everyone bond? Like Charades, or Beer Pong, or ...' I grinned, 'Truth or Dare?'

Paisley screwed up her face. 'Let's get a feel for the audience vibe before we decide, okay? They might be a real chatty group and mingle by themselves.'

'Or retreat to their bedrooms for an early night.'

'Oh, no, we don't want them to do that. Grassington offers them more than good food and a comfy bed. It isn't just a hotel. Staying here should definitely be an experience worth sharing. Word of mouth is the best form of advertising, you know.'

I knew. That had been my wish for my own business venture

back in Shadow Creek. My gut spasmed at the memory of what I'd lost because of my impulsive actions. Robert Burns had it right: *The best laid plans of mice and men often go awry.* Mine surely had, and in spectacular fashion. To lift my mood, I jokingly suggested we get Hilary to look into her crystal ball for us while she was here. I certainly would be interested in hearing what good things were in store for me.

'That's a fortune teller, Abby,' Paisley said with an eyeroll. 'Hilary supposedly contacts the dead, not foresees the future.'

'Talking about making contact, have you heard from Fletcher?'

'Nope. I'll call him this afternoon, see how he's doing.'

6

OLIVIA'S JOURNAL

September 1886

This evening, Henry and I awaited the arrival of guests from the rooftop observation deck. The sun dipping behind the far hills, painting the sky in glowing shades of pink and purple, was a fitting prelude to our first spring ball. The dressmaker had worked a miracle in creating a wondrous evening gown out of peacock blue taffeta, giving a sheen to my pale skin and depth to my murky grey eyes. Maggie's niece, visiting from Brisbane, had taken on the role as lady's maid for the day and fashioned my hair into a work of art. I have never felt more alluring, so significant.

With new-found confidence, I grasped Henry's hand and told him there was something important I needed to share.

He said he hoped I hadn't changed my mind as Mrs.

Bright had prepared a feast, while the maids were at the ready on the lawn with silver platters of hors d'oeuvres and champagne.

'Listen,' he said, 'the string quartet on the patio have begun playing.'

My ears pricked to the sounds of Vivaldi's 'Spring' concerto. I affirmed with Henry that I wouldn't dream of cancelling the opportunity to show off our grand house in style.

He asked what concerned me and remarked on my flushed cheeks.

With excitement, I told Henry that I was expecting a child.

His mouth gaped, and he stepped back, studying my waist in disbelief. Of course it is too early for any visible evidence of my condition, especially when hidden beneath layers of fabric. So I assured Henry that Doctor Morphett has confirmed we will be parents by March of next year.

'Well, you're good at keeping secrets,' he said.

I told him I just wanted to be certain.

He kissed me and said I had made him the happiest man in the world. Said he felt like shouting our good news from this very rooftop.

I cautioned him to show some decorum. The guests were almost here. I pointed to the clouds of dust in the near distance, evidence carriages were making their way up the dirt drive to the estate.

Henry threw back his head and laughed. 'It didn't take us long, did it? What a splendid lot the Greenwoods are, they'll say. 'Young, successful, and fertile.' He pulled me into an embrace, careful to not crush the gown's finery, and promised to announce our good news tonight in the most proper of ways, with a speech and a toast to me, his sweet love.

I confess, my heart was filled with joy like never before, and the late-night celebrations that ensued were absolutely perfect.

7

———

The office was situated across the hall from the drawing room. Once again, dark timber dominated, with a ceiling height bookcase and massive mahogany desk giving the room a masculine vibe. As if to confirm this, a whiff of stale tobacco emanating from the woodwork tickled my nostrils.

I indicated a floor-length velvet curtain hanging from metal rings on a rod attached to the interior wall. 'What's behind that?' I asked Paisley.

'Just a strongroom.' She swept the curtain aside to reveal a grille door much like one found in a bank vault. 'Henry Greenwood built it to store important papers and valuables. We don't use it because we can't find the key to unlock the grille. Anyway, we have a filing cabinet for such things.'

I peeked through the bars into a shadowy space the size of a department store dressing room. All it contained were bare metal shelves bolted to the brick walls, and dust bunnies. A twist of the brass knob fixed to the large iron rim lock, along with a shoulder shove, proved the door wouldn't budge.

'Wonder if it was ever used to lock someone in as punishment … or fulfil a sadistic fantasy. Wouldn't be able to escape in a hurry, that's for sure.'

Paisley dropped the curtain. 'Your mind certainly goes to dark places.'

'It's not dark … it's creative. Critical thinking is my superpower, don't you know?'

'Critical thinking? I'd call it *feral* thinking.'

'Hey! Miss Marple would have just been an annoying busybody if she hadn't used her smarts to help solve crimes. When was the door last opened?'

Paisley gave a shrug and pushed me into the desk chair. When she brought the computer to life, the sight of the home screen crowded with a mess of folder and document icons set my teeth on edge. She clicked on a folder in the centre of the screen, and a list of documents popped up.

'They are the ones that need printing. Oh, and can you make up place cards for the Saturday dinner? I've saved a template along with guest names in another folder. Good luck with finding it.' She leant sideways and pressed the start button on the printer perched atop a filing cabinet. 'Should be enough paper. Otherwise, check the desk drawer. There's also some light card in there.'

Left alone, I eventually located the necessary template and produced the place cards. Resting back, I swivelled the chair and observed the room, while I waited for the printing to finish. It was easy to envisage Henry Greenwood sitting at this desk counting all his money. I could almost hear ice chinking in a glass of Scotch, papers rustling, and the hand crank grinding on an old adding machine. Pleased with his takings, Henry would light a cigar and …

A section of titles on a shelf in the bookcase caught my eye. In particular, an unfamiliar work written by Arthur Conan Doyle. I eased it out and studied the bold type on the front of the plain dust jacket.

<u>*What IS Spiritualism?*</u>
THE NEW REVELATION
by Arthur Conan Doyle
Can we, or can we not, speak with our beloved dead?
Sir Arthur Conan Doyle answers YES

I was aware the creator of Sherlock Holmes had a fascination with the supernatural and wholeheartedly believed in fairies. I even recalled reading that he and the prominent magician/escape artist Harry Houdini had famously argued about magic tricks. Houdini vehemently insisted they were illusions, while Sir Arthur was convinced sorcery was involved. Equally important to Doyle was his belief in life after death.

I opened the book to the inside title page and found it was printed in 1918. An inscription penned in ink at the top right showed this copy had belonged to Henry Greenwood.

The clanging of metal and a scraping sound drew me to snap my head around. The strongroom curtain, still gathered to one side, showed the grille door remained shut, the interior just as empty. Would my alarm have lessened if someone had suddenly appeared within to shake the bars?

Unconvinced my imaginings were due to sleep deprivation, I yanked the velvet drape to cover the grille, shoved the book back into its spot on the shelf, and raced out with the printed papers.

. . .

I delivered copies of the menu and the map to each bedroom. Finding the yellow room still chilly, I placed extra blankets from the secret linen cupboard on the ends of both beds.

Before heading down to the lower level, I stopped at the spiral staircase leading to the rooftop. A montage of scenes from horror movies involving such a relic flashed in my mind, along with a compulsion to test my fear level. With dread, I gripped the railing and placed my right foot on the first iron step, followed by my left foot on the second. I tackled the third and fourth steps, my ascent causing the structure to wobble slightly. Hesitating on climbing farther, I gazed up to the landing high above, finding it lit by a sliver of daylight seeping in from the door being ajar. Was someone up there on the roof?

'And where do you think you're going, young lady?'

I swung around. Bridget Hawthorne stood at the foot of the stairs, arms folded and one shoe tapping the floor. Being called a 'young lady' was as surprising as her sudden arrival.

'N-nowhere,' I muttered, stepping down to floor level, feeling like a naughty schoolgirl caught by the headmistress for wagging class.

'I wouldn't go up there unarmed, if I were you,' she said, holding out an empty glass pitcher. 'Take this.'

A fancy jug was not my weapon of choice for protection against whomever ... *or whatever* ... lurked on the rooftop. 'How am I supposed—'

'I've run out of milk,' she interjected. 'Ask Cook if she can fill this up, pronto.'

'Oh ... Cook?'

'You know, the woman in the kitchen.'

'You mean Paisley, my sister.'

'I mean Mrs What's-her-name, the bossy one with ants in her pants.'

'Mrs Croft. They are one and the same.'

She threw her head back and cackled. 'Don't be daft, girl. Mrs Croft is *my* sister. Wouldn't catch Kathryn cooking from scratch in that enormous kitchen.'

If Bridget was talking about Fletcher's mother, then she wouldn't be cooking anywhere—she'd been dead for five years. 'I'll get you the milk. Did you need anything else? Are you right for lunch? I think we're having ham and salad on bread rolls.'

'If there's plenty to share, please bring me a portion.'

I peered back up to the staircase landing. Was there more to fear up there than the height?

I returned a few minutes later with a tray loaded with a bread roll, milk, and a large lice of teacake. My first knock on Bridget's door went unanswered. So did the second. The door opened on the third attempt, and I handed the tray to the elderly lady who promptly said, 'Thank you,' before abruptly shutting the door on me. I gathered our getting more acquainted would not happen soon, if at all.

I ate my lunch downstairs while studying the framed photos on the foyer walls.

One picture showed a group of women seated at an outdoor table set with tea things. All frocked up in long, lacy dresses and outlandishly broad-brimmed hats, they posed demurely. However, the toddler, seated on the grass in front of them, dressed in a child's sailor suit, seemed too engrossed in playing with a toy horse to face the camera.

The next depicted the front view of the mansion, people grouped casually on the portico and leaning over the verandah railing on the floor above. Their clothing appeared to be the peak of fashion for the 1920s, with the women in low-waisted, knee-length dresses, and cloche hats, and men in pale-coloured suits or white shirts with baggy trousers. An event or celebration of some kind.

In another photo, two women of different ages stood outside the stone grotto. They were dressed in sensible skirts and blouses from, my guess, the 1940s.

Cole joined me with two glasses of iced tea and offered me one.

'I just love the 1920s style of clothing,' he said. 'Very Great Gatsby.'

I sipped from my glass. 'That reminds me. Whose portrait hangs in the pink room?' I pointed to the photo of the mansion. 'That might also be her in the group on the verandah.'

He leant in for a closer inspection. 'Yeah, you might be right. That's Elodie Greenwood ... well, Hawthorne after she married. She's Bridget's mother.'

That would explain the EG scratched on the bedroom window glass. 'Fletcher's grandmother?'

'Yep. A real hottie, hey? That's her again outside the grotto with her mother, Olivia. If you look closely, there's a smudge that resembles a man's face peeking out from one side of the cave. Some say it's the ghost of the guy who offed himself there.'

'Offed? He suicided?'

'Hanged himself from the grotto. You haven't heard that story?'

I shook my head and studied the ill-defined image that could have easily been discolouration on the rock surface, while Cole continued.

'Some homeless guy working at Grassington for a bit got drunk and depressed and tied his leather belt around his neck, fastened it to the grotto railing, and jumped.' He grabbed his throat and mimed being choked—eyes bulging, tongue lolling, gasping.

I shuddered at his depiction of a shocking death. 'Is he one of the three ghosts that supposedly spook the mansion?' Cole's grin urged me to add, 'You don't believe they're real?'

He dropped his voice to a whisper. 'Of course I do. But don't tell Paisley. She thinks I'm like her and reckon it's all crap. Heaps of people around here believe in the supernatural. The Grimm locals are convinced Grassington is cursed.'

A sudden clap of thunder would have been the perfect accompaniment to this ominous remark.

'So, let's see ...' I counted on my fingers, 'The ghosts are the maid, the homeless guy, and ...' I raised my eyebrows.

'Henry Greenwood.'

'Oh.' That was a revelation. 'What happened to him?'

'He drowned on the property. Then there's Mad Gerald's fatal leap from the rooftop, although Paisley thinks three ghosts are enough for guests to cope with.'

I risked a gamble. 'Are you sure there isn't a child ghost haunting the mansion? I've witnessed some odd occurrences that suggest a child's presence.'

Cole tapped his finger on the toddler in the photograph of the ladies at tea. 'Tommy Greenwood, Elodie's older brother, died when he was only four years old. But not everyone who dies becomes a ghost. An innocent without a grudge wouldn't bother returning to frighten anyone,' he said with maturity that belied his years.

I considered the pull-along elephants and the glass marble. 'Maybe frightening people isn't the intention. Perhaps he wants to play.'

Cole's frown mirrored the one pinching my forehead. 'Tommy has a lovely grave here in the cemetery. It has a weeping cherub on the headstone.'

'Grassington has a cemetery?'

'It's not a big one, but it's nice ... nice for a family graveyard, anyway. It's on the map you printed, just past the glade.'

Was it? I hadn't noticed it in my rush to exit the office after the grille door had rattled by itself.

'You should visit,' Cole suggested.

<h1 style="text-align:center">8</h1>

OLIVIA'S JOURNAL

June 1900

Grief splintered my heart this day. Even now I am awash with tears. Why has God taken my Tommy?

The silent house is unbearable. No more tinkling laughter and patter of feet. No butterfly kisses, nor tiny fingers wrapping around my own. No blond curls to brush from his sweet face. With his reaching four years of age after surviving bouts of ill health, I believed I had cast off the curse that has plagued our family for so long. Over a ten-year period, I have experienced two early losses not warranting proper burials—a much-celebrated first child being one of them—then a stillbirth, followed by another living for only a day. All extinguished with a click of omnipotent fingers.

Witnessing my precious boy being lowered into the

reopened earth this morning was almost too difficult to bear. As my nose dribbled, someone fed a fresh handkerchief into my clenched fist, causing me to lift my gaze. Beneath coils of jet-black hair, Tommy's nursemaid, Claudette, studied me. Her smouldering eyes and perfect Cupid's bow lips bringing a familiar pang of envy that cut through my misery. Yet again, I wondered why fate had blessed this young woman of humble origins and questionable beliefs with such beauty. Did it have anything to do with the beastly rabbit's foot pinned to her bodice, a good luck talisman she's been wearing since her arrival? In my anguish, I considered snatching it from her, keeping it as my own. Testing its power.

A sound seized my attention—Zachariah shovelling dirt onto the miniature coffin. With each thud of earth, I writhed as though whipped, imagining Tommy nestled on his bed of white satin, clasping his toy pony in his pudgy hands and opening his eyes to the darkness.

'I love you, my little angel,' I moaned, and crumpled to my knees, my woollen skirt soaking up the cold moisture of damp ground while the handkerchief soaked up hot tears.

A hand on my shoulder, trembling, squeezing—Henry suppressing his sorrow. His hope of an heir shattered again. Four times his icy glower has placed the blame on me—he planted the seed; my body failed to tend to its growth. But this time it was God who disappointed. God, who was deaf to prayers to protect our son. God, the life giver … the life taker. THIEF.

As I write, muscles cramp. Pain grips my innards. A vice crushes my skull.

Please, God, take me too!

9

____

On Cole's advice, I went in search of the graveyard. Whitby, my shadow, joined me.

Passing through the glade, I shunned the grotto, batting away visions of the hopeless vagrant hanging from the statue, kicking and choking. A path winding through a carpet of wildflowers brought me to an enclosure box-hedged by mock orange shrubs. I entered through an iron archway bearing three crucifixes on top and the words *Ego Sum Resurrectio*.

Within was a compact cemetery where gravestones jutted out of knee-high grass interspersed with dandelions and daisies. On a concrete plinth at one end stood a two-metre stone crucifix guarded by a pair of statues: robed women, one bowing her head, the other lifting her gaze to the empty cross. Were they the two Marys—Jesus' mother, and Mary Magdalene? I traipsed around the clutch of graves, stopping to read the inscriptions on headstones and two brass lawn plaques scarcely visible in the overgrowth.

The plaques belonged to Fletcher's parents, Kathryn and

Stanley Croft, who died respectively in 2014 and 2016. Older, decorative headstones grouped together showed the resting places of Gerald, Henry, and Olivia Greenwood. Alongside, was a smaller, simpler gravestone on which perched a weeping cherub. The inscription stated:

Thomas Gerald Greenwood
Our sweet son aged 4
Slipped from Earth to Heaven 1900

I laid a hand on the cherub and considered the cute toddler in the photo on the foyer wall. How heartbreaking to lose a child so young.

Age had affected another gravestone near Tommy's, cleaving it in two. By touch, I deciphered the weathered words carved in the pockmarked stone lying on the ground: *Female (stillborn) 1888,* along with *Reginald Henry Greenwood, born and died 1891.* Stone fragments of four smaller cherubs were scattered nearby. Had there been more unnamed losses? How could one survive losing so many little ones? Not unusual for the era, with many untreatable childhood illnesses decimating families, the parents' grief would have been almost insufferable. A new appreciation for the strides in modern medicine was gained in that moment.

I approached a black marble headstone.

Elodie (Greenwood) Hawthorne 1902-1991
Beloved mother of Bridget and Kathryn

Fletcher's grandmother. Beneath it, the name of her husband, *Samuel Hawthorne,* and the date of his death twenty years before hers. Was Elodie the only child of Henry and Olivia to make it to adulthood?

A separate grave with a simple tombstone was that of *Zachariah Bright 1859-1931*, the groundskeeper who had lived in the cottage. Paisley mentioned his wife left Grassington after his death. Loyal help, for sure.

An urgent scraping sound drew me to discover Whitby showering himself with dirt as he dug in a corner of the cemetery. I ran over and pulled him clear by the collar. 'Stop it. You don't know what you'll dig up in this place.'

Thankfully, all Whitby had unearthed was a dinted tobacco tin sealed shut by rust. I slipped it into my crossbody bag and noticed an impression in the ground, roughly the size of a grave. Why bury someone here, isolated from the others and without a marker other than a clump of candy-pink lilies?

A harsh *kaa-kaa* cut through the deathly quiet.

Whitby bounded over and barked until a black crow flew from its roost atop the tall crucifix on the plinth. Seconds later, the bird returned with its mate as backup. Four more appeared, until a whole murder of crows adorned the cross and the two Mary effigies to eyeball us with suspicion. I'm not sure which was more unsettling, their silent scrutiny as I deliberated on how to best exit, or the drawn-out growls they unleashed as we moved through the iron archway in our effort to flee a possible avian attack.

10

___

I joined my sister and her protégé for dinner in a small room between the office and scullery. Once a billiard room, and then a breakfast nook, it was now used as a more intimate dining area.

Paisley placed bowls of pasta steeped in a tomato-based sauce on the six-seater circular table, along with a basket of garlic bread and a dish of grated parmesan. 'Sorry, I didn't feel like cooking up a storm after all the baking we did today. Will puttanesca do?'

'No probs,' I said, twirling spaghetti around my fork and feeding it into my mouth before it unravelled and slithered onto my shirt. 'Yum. This is much better than store-bought pasta sauce.'

'Huh!' Paisley huffed. 'It had better be.'

Cole slurped up a wiggling strand until it disappeared. 'Puttanesca means whore.'

His random comment prompted me to seek confirmation from my sister.

'Actually,' she explained, 'the Italian translation is *in the style of a whore*. The story goes that the brothels in Naples invented the dish to attract clients with its aroma. Another claims it was a quick and simple dish ladies-of-the-night threw together in amongst their busy schedules. But some say people simply named the dish for its pungent aromas.'

I lifted the bowl and inhaled the spicy scent of an Italian prostitute. *Fascinating.*

'So, Abby, you've checked out the Greenwood cemetery.'

I glanced at Cole. 'How did you know? Did the crows blab?'

'Huh? I saw you from the turret when I was putting up the party lights.'

'Party lights ... on the rooftop?'

'Yep.' He pursed his lips. 'What's wrong with that? Paisley gave permission.'

She shot me an icy glare before patting Cole's arm. 'It should look quite festive when dark.'

Feeling the weight of their disapproval, I found solace in gnawing on garlic bread. If let loose, what else would Cole come up with? Fog machines, disco balls, strobe lighting ... a chrome rod for pole dancing? All *enhancements* to a 133-year-old mansion.

I reignited the subject of the cemetery. 'I discovered Tommy's grave. Olivia and Henry certainly experienced their fair share of sorrow. Was Elodie their only child to reach adulthood?'

Paisley answered, 'Yes,' at the same time Cole said, 'No.'

My sister and I met his gaze. 'Well,' Cole added, 'there's an old village rumour that a Greenwood child was born on the wrong side of the tracks. Chances are it grew to be an adult.'

'I think you mean the wrong side of the blanket,' I corrected.

'Whose blanket?' Paisley asked sternly. 'Henry's or Olivia's?'

'Who's to say it wasn't Elodie's?' I suggested.

Cole shrugged. 'The goss just states that someone here screwed around, resulting in a little bundle of trouble.'

'Was it adultery?' I asked, intrigued by Victorian-era infidelity.

'Though I suppose it may have happened before the person got hitched. If it was Henry's child, someone might have paid the poor mother to keep quiet. Or if Olivia's, or Elodie's, given away at birth. Was someone from Grimm possibly involved?'

'What if they were?' Cole grinned broadly. 'I might be related to the Greenwoods. Wouldn't that be a blast?' He spread his arms wide. 'This could be all mine.'

Paisley stabbed her fork at Cole. 'Best you shut that fucking mouth of yours or you'll be out on your ear.'

My shoulder blades smacked against the back of my chair as I recoiled at my sister's outburst. Paisley's bossiness often raised its ugly head when distressed, yet this was off the charts, even for her.

Cole's face turned a deep red. Pushing up from the table, he stomped from the room.

I locked eyes with my sister. 'Bloody hell, Pais, that was an overreaction. He was only repeating gossip ... ancient gossip, at that. So what if there was a secret illegitimate child. Every family has skeletons in their closet.'

The fork flew from Paisley's hand and embedded itself into the wall behind me. 'You know nothing. Something like that could ruin everything.'

In a clamour of noise, she too was gone.

Abandoned, I dwelt on my sister's atrocious behaviour. Was it a symptom of menopause, or had age just morphed Paisley into a spiteful bitch? Perhaps living with a shrew for a wife, not stress, had exacerbated Fletcher's anxiety.

Tugging the fork from the wall, I returned the bowls to the kitchen and stumbled upon Paisley begging Cole for forgiveness. Not wishing to witness my sister grovelling, I collected my bag from the wall hook and slipped out, intending to head back to the cottage. As I crossed the hall, a peculiar noise drew me to catch sight of something tiny bouncing down the steps of the timber staircase. Landing on the carpet runner, it rolled and came to a sudden stop at my feet.

I stared at the milky glass marble with an orange swirl, exactly like the one I'd found earlier upstairs. 'Bridget?' I called, peering up the flight of stairs. 'Are you there?'

No answer. No sound whatsoever. A thousand barbs pricked the back of my neck. I thrust the marble into my shorts pocket and ran outside.

The soft glow of the LED lighting in the ancient lamp posts assisted my walk down the driveway. They petered out after a hundred meters or so, forcing me to use the limited scope of my phone torch to light the rest of my way. Jittery, I ignored the shadows by concentrating on my shoes crunching over gravel.

Taking the bush path down to the cottage, a coughing sound above and swishing foliage drew me to spotlight a brush tail possum on the move in overhanging branches. The light also captured a barn owl perched in the fork of a tree, eating a mouse whole. Winding tracks in the dirt showed a sizeable carpet snake had recently passed this way, as had a wallaby, evidenced by two-pronged footprints and marble-shaped scat. It was sort of comforting to know I wasn't alone.

Yet, just as I neared the fenced yard, a rustling in the bushes to my left, accompanied by a menacing snarl, brought me to a stop. Two small fires pierced the dark. Of the three primary responses to fear, I always expected I'd choose *flight*. Despite dreading being mauled by a terrifying beast, I chose option three for this occasion. Frozen to the spot, I shielded my face with my bag—if I couldn't see it, it wasn't there.

A stench like rotting roadkill compelled me to sneak a look an instant before something black and furry pounced from the scrub. A scream tore from my throat, only to wither away when I saw it was Whitby with the remnants of a dead animal, possibly a gigantic rat, hanging from his mouth.

'Drop it,' I signalled in a shaky voice. 'Drop it, Whitby. Now!'

Surprisingly, he obeyed, allowing me to grip his collar and kick the carcass into the bushes, before steering him to the gate. Following Paisley's instructions, I extracted the key from beneath a ceramic frog near the back door.

'You pong!' I growled before turning the handle, my stomach churning. With difficulty, I dragged him to the bathroom.

He didn't seem to mind me unloading him into the bath or straddling him to wash the stink away with Paisley's sea sponge soaked in expensive shampoo, however, it was quite a battle towelling dry a large dog who kept shimmying and spattering the walls with canine-scented droplets.

I snatched musk body spray from the mirror cabinet to camouflage the lingering doggy smell, accidentally knocking Paisley's 'dickosaurus' onto the floor. Whitby seized it before I had a chance to retrieve it and took off down the hall. There was a chase, followed by a skirmish, yet I was unable to find the mischievous purple critter, only the battery. Whitby must have chewed it up. All for the best.

With him locked in the laundry, I stripped out of my damp clothes. *The glass marble.* I fed my hand into the pocket of my shorts, only to find it empty. No use searching for it. After my tussle with Whitby, it could be anywhere, outside even. I showered and changed into pyjamas. A scavenge in the kitchen for something sweet and calorie-loaded, turned up a stash of fudge squares in the pantry. With the whole container in tow, I retreated to the lounge room to watch mind-numbing TV until Paisley arrived.

I channel-surfed, striving to find anything interesting. Was this just my second night at Grassington? It had been a long day. A long and *rather strange* day. What would tomorrow hold? I envisioned a raucous group of strangers. Me needing to interact with the guests. Forced pleasantries, small talk, kowtowing. Was I up to the task? I should have recuperated on the coast in a flashy beachside hotel with a spa, a bar, and staff at my beck and call.

An episode of *Fawlty Towers* appeared on the screen, with Basil typically flustered as he fussed about. 'Please God,' I prayed, 'make the guests nice and friendly, and undemanding.'

I poured myself a measure of whatever was in the crystal decanter on the wood heater. Finding it was a tasty, fortified wine, I took several swings straight from the bottle and replaced the lid.

Half an hour later, with still no sign of my sister, I released Whitby from his incarceration, and he followed me to bed. Too hyped up to sleep, I opened my laptop and researched the Greenwood family. Exploring online records wasn't new to me, having helped my father construct our ancestral tree and, more recently, doing my own investigating to unearth family secrets.

I searched the Queensland Registry of Births, Deaths, and Marriages, and easily found the marriage between *Henry Arthur Greenwood* and *Olivia Winifred Innes* dated *6 April 1886*. In addition, I discovered children born to both Henry and Olivia, corresponding with the graves I'd seen in the cemetery. If there were others, as per the shattered stone cherubs, they were early losses not warranting a mention.

What if Henry fathered a child before he married Olivia? I typed in his name without filling in the mother's details. Nothing. I did the same for Olivia, without submitting a father. Zilch. Still, I wasn't confident I'd busted the myth about a mystery child.

Widening to a national search, I looked for children born to Gerald Greenwood, with only Henry's name coming up—born in Paddington, New South Wales, in 1860. Research revealed that his mother, listed as *Mary Anne Stromberg*, died the following year. I found Gerald's and Mary's wedding date in 1858, but no record of Gerald ever having been married before or after that time.

A search of immigrant passenger lists on a popular genealogical site brought up details of a *Gerald Greenwood, aged 34, born in Grassington, Yorkshire, England*, who had travelled by ship to Sydney, New South Wales, Australia in 1857, alone. That had to be him. He and Henry might have relocated to Queensland later to capitalise on the 1867 Gympie gold rush.

Nothing came up under Elodie's name.

All this information didn't rule out the existence of another child. For one thing, birth records online were only available to view once a hundred years had passed since the event. A margin of error also meant that record keepers didn't register everyone's major life event, or if they did, those records may not have survived to be digitised. Historically, people actively concealed moral failings like infidelity, crime, and especially illegitimate births. One also had to consider that the rumour Cole had relayed was simply a spiteful untruth.

Mentally taxed, I placed the laptop on the floor. Cleo's button eyes, watching me with evil intent, drove me to cover her with a cushion to hinder any more wicked night moves.

Sleep came as soon as my head hit the pillow.

11

OLIVIA'S JOURNAL

August 1900

I have snuck down to Henry's office in the dark so as not to disturb his sleep. How long has it been since I dipped the pen nib in ink and written in my journal? One month? Two?

Tommy's death has harmed my health. I have endured bouts of delirium, hearing my dead child giggling behind doors, scampering up and down the halls, and dragging his favourite pull-along toy across the floorboards. Once, I glimpsed him beside his bed—where I have been sleeping following his passing—and another time felt him stroke my brow. But that was weeks ago, before Dr Morphett reasoned they were products of grief and wishful thinking, and prescribed medication to ease my torment.

My gorge rises. How can I recount what happened

today? Poor Claudette.

If I do not commit the events to the page, it will be as if I have suffered another nightmare or derangement. If only that were the case.

The day began with such promise ...

Hours Earlier

Despite her frail appearance in the dressing-room mirror, Olivia's emotions seem more stable. Convinced a walk in the sunshine will do her wonders, she has dressed in a new mint green day dress made from a chintz fabric with a lovely pattern of daisies and gold lilies. Looping a silk scarf around her neck, she ties it in a bow and considers visiting Henry at the mill. He will be delighted she is up and about, feeling spirited.

Halfway down the stairs, on the landing, the nursemaid coming up startles her. Her attire of a fringed brocade shawl over a pale blue dress, in place of the distinctive uniform befitting her role, reminds Olivia the maid's position is now redundant. Her cheeks, having filled out since their last meeting, had a lustre about them as if she had raced here on an errand.

'What brings you here, Claudette?'

'It is necessary that I speak with you directly, ma'am.'

'Is that why you utilised the family stairs rather than the others?' Olivia nods to indicate the staircase at the far end of the hall, a more modest structure.

Claudette shakes her head. Her dark hair free of its usual cap and pins sways around her shoulders, giving her a more youthful appearance than her thirty years. 'I am no longer in service, ma'am. No longer a servant.'

Olivia's spine stiffens. 'Then why have you arrived unannounced? What gives you reason to gad about the house so freely?'

'Because I have every right.'

'Every right? You are not a Greenwood. You are just—' Claudette's grip on her arm shocks Olivia into silence.

'I am entitled,' Claudette says with an air of conviction, 'for I am carrying the master's child.'

What does she mean? Olivia's blood freezes. 'You lie. Such impertinence. Henry would never—'

Claudette clutches Olivia's hand and forces it beneath the shawl and between pleats of the blue dress. Presses it against a swollen belly. 'There, feel what your husband did to me. It's a lively one, alright. I'll not birth a weakling, as you have done. It will survive the defilement of its conception.'

Olivia wrenches her hand away as the protuberance bumps against her finger. She accuses Claudette of being a slattern. 'What makes you think I'd accept the notion Mr Greenwood is the father of … of this? You could have lain with any number of men on the estate: timber cutters, mill workers eager to taste your wares. Or even men from the village.'

'You want me to prove it, do you, ma'am?' Claudette steps close. 'Prove it was your husband who spurted his seed inside me?' Her belly juts into Olivia's sunken stomach, the rabbit's foot charm pinned to her bodice alive with the vibrations of excitement. 'Oh, I'll give you proof.'

Her breath smells of cloves as she recounts the event that resulted in her condition.

'Under threat of false accusations of stealing from the household,

Mr Greenwood forced me to undress in his office. He made me unbutton his trousers and undergarment before he violated me. That ugly jagged scar on his groin, the result of a boyhood injury, he explained, showed he'd been inches away from being gelded.

'He was quick to demonstrate that it had no effect on his performance, other than brutal dominance. I, like several other women here at Grassington, wished the barbed wire fence had successfully done its job and ripped his cock right off.'

A slap rings out, Olivia's hand burning with the effort.

Yet Claudette stands her ground. 'Did you learn that from him? He's not averse to violence in the heat of passion.'

A weight crushes Olivia's ribs, the surrounding air as cold as a tomb. Claudette's words bore truth. 'Does Henry know about the baby?' she asks feebly.

'He told me to put an end to it. When I objected to such wickedness, he demanded I leave before it became obvious. For him, young Tommy's death was convenient, making my duties obsolete. But I couldn't stay away. It's fitting the Greenwood heir is birthed at Grassington, whether Henry likes it or not.' A smirk. 'Maybe you could act as midwife when that time comes. That would be a change, getting your hands dirty.'

'Enough!' Olivia orders her to shut her mouth. 'Get downstairs where you belong.'

'Never. Though I didn't choose this predicament, I am the mother of Henry's only child. He will pay for his actions by giving me and this babe the favour we deserve.'

The rage bubbling within Olivia escapes its restraints to surge through every nerve in her body. In that instant, she transforms. As Claudette moves to ascend the second flight, Olivia blocks her way. 'Leave this house now, witch,' she commands in a strange voice.

It all happens so quickly. A tussle. Claudette stumbling backwards. Overbalancing. Tumbling down the stairs.

Olivia rushes down to the woman crumpled on the hallway floor. Falling to her knees, she rolls Claudette onto her back. Blood pools on the floorboards, fanning around her head in a crimson halo. Her eyes are slits. Breathing non-existent. The rabbit's foot is as still as death.

Maggie emerges from the kitchen and drops a glass bowl, spewing shelled peas every which way. Crouching beside Olivia, she lifts a limp arm and releases it. Together, they watch it fall with a thud on the floor.

Olivia cradles the oozing head in her lap, unconcerned her chintz dress is now ruined. What has she done!

'She's dead!' comes a shriek over her shoulder.

Jane, the young housemaid, her face as pale as her starched apron, stands in the hallway alongside the staircase, a polish cloth and tin of wax trembling in her hands.

Olivia cringes. How long has she been waiting there? What has she seen?

What has she heard?

12

———

Waking entangled in the sheets, I found Whitby snuggled into a cosy nest formed by the bed cover that had slipped off during the night. To clear away the cobwebs, I dressed in activewear and set off on a second early exploit—a route of my own choosing, this time.

Early morning fog, as warm and clammy as shower steam, shrouded the road uphill. No surprise, Whitby followed hot on my heels, accompanying me as I veered right and unlatched a timber gate leading into the vineyard. Undeterred by limited visibility, I jogged between rows of woody vines, their misshapen limbs stretching out in the swirling mist like crones casting spells. Other shapes lurked beyond the wispy curtain, along with muted sounds distinct from my own.

Happy to leave the creepiness behind, I scaled a steep grassy slope, my pace slowing with the effort, my breath laboured. The vapour thinned the higher I climbed until, reaching the top of Fig Tree Hill, I stared across a churning sea of fog to a clear view of the mansion sparkling like a fairytale castle. A heavy line of cloud suddenly hid the rising sun, the orange glow dulled to a sepia tint, exposing the mansion's age. As the mist melted away, revealing the entire vineyard, I was saddened that it no longer produced wine-suitable grapes.

Moving under the broad canopy of the fig tree, I spotted a swing. Despite being secured to a sturdy branch with chain stays, deep grooves in the bark revealed previous use of two ropes looped over it. Further evidence of damage to the tree included long-defaced initials carved into the trunk within a heart shape. The result of heartbreak? I plonked down on the new wooden swing seat and rocked back and forth while Whitby reclined nearby. Together, we soaked up the serenity.

I envisaged people from bygone eras, relaxing in the shade, reading literary masterpieces, while smoking pipes or roll-your-own cigarettes. Or picnicking on a tartan rug, delving into their wicker basket for scrumptious goodies and a flagon of local wine. Someone may have sat here to write a love note or pen an encouraging letter to a family member serving overseas in a war. My imagination was limitless.

Planting a foot, I spun, winding the chain stays together until they tightened. Lifting both feet, I let the swing untwist, whirling and juddering until it stopped at its original position. Dizzy from the gyrations, a childhood memory played out.

My much younger self squealing in protest at being pushed too high on a swing set, my fear escalating as the support poles lifted repeatedly from the earth and thudded back down. Somehow my tiny hands let go of the chains, and I hurtled through the air like an ungainly trapeze artist to land hard on the ground, my left forearm snapping, the agony rendering me mute.

I leapt from the swing and leant against the tree, rubbing a phantom pain in the arm I had broken over forty years earlier. A distant glint. I squinted to focus and made out a person in white clothing scampering from the mansion, carrying an object which reflected the sunlight. Cutting across the lawn, they disappeared down the avenue of trees. Was that Bridget? My watch showed it was barely six o'clock.

'C'mon, buddy,' I said to Whitby. 'Let's see what the old girl is up to.'

He sprang up and took off ahead of me. At least it was easier going downhill.

A trail of scattered fruit marked Bridget's journey—strawberries on the dirt track, a mango on the grotto altar, apples directing towards the cemetery, and passionfruit along the path on the western side of the mansion. What the hell had the mad woman been doing, delivering food to wildlife? Finding the door at this section of the building ajar, I entered.

The office was deserted. However, an undefined noise drew me to investigate the storage space beneath the carpeted stairs. Opening the door, I discovered a set of steps going down. *Aha! So, this was how one got to the cellar.* I ducked to avoid the angle of the overhead cladding and descended with stealth. Halfway down, a shuffling sound prompted me to crouch and peer through the railing, hoping not to be seen.

Long shadows cast by the narrow stair balusters stretched towards an archway, through which a figure hovered within the gloom. Bridget, in a white nightgown, stood alongside an oak barrel, engrossed in a duty I couldn't make out. Creeping down in the direction of the brick arch, I hugged the wall before extending out to spy on her.

I shivered in the chilly temperature, perfect for storing wine. Clouds must have parted outside, for sunlight filtered through the timber slats of a bulkhead door above a ramp leading to the open air. This enabled me to discern empty wooden wall racks, more dusty oak barrels, and several wine bottles strewn across the floor.

A thump pulled my gaze to Bridget just as she lopped the spiny crown off a pineapple with a carving knife. After skinning and slicing the fruit, she arranged the pieces on a silver tray and lifted it off the barrel. Thinking she would walk through the arch and return upstairs, I was surprised when she placed the tray on the paved floor. Waving her arms as if batting away mosquitoes, she mumbled a series of words. A blessing? An incantation?

Next, Bridget plunged her hand into the hip pocket of her nightie and tossed flower sprigs into the air, which floated down to scatter around the tray. Collecting the knife from the barrel, she focused on wiping the blade on her clothing. That's when I slipped away. Mystified by the event, I crept back up to the hallway and aimed for the foyer.

A pang of hunger urged me to swipe a banana from a glass bowl perched on the bottom step of the staircase. I peeled it and took a bite as I fled the house through the front doors, trying not to imagine what part the banana may have played in some weird voodoo ritual.

13

OLIVIA'S JOURNAL

August 1900

Though shocked by the news of Claudette's death in his house, Henry has shown little remorse, fuelling my suspicion that the woman had lied about his role in her pregnancy. Of course, I have not spoken of it with him. What good would it do? I am not so vindictive as to malign the dead. Yet, Claudette's distant burial offers solace, a respite from constant reminders.

February 1901

With Henry showing scant attention to anything other than the flourishing mill, I reacquainted myself with piano playing. Debussy's 'Clair de Lune' is a favourite of mine. I also began china painting and found I possess considerable skill in floral depictions. Maggie has encouraged me to progress from display plates to vases, which she says is more practical.

April 1901

It has not taken long for my joy to be crushed. Last week I spied Henry being too familiar with Jane Sedgwick in the hallway, stroking the girl's blushing cheek while complimenting her on her service. What is worse is that silly girl responded with a giggle. Claudette's assertion that my husband has a penchant for sexual indiscretions seems proven correct. How many has he charmed into sacrificing their innocence? To save our marriage and secure my future, I must take matters into my own hands.

April 1901

I surprised Henry in his office this afternoon.

He frowned as he glanced up from his desk to see me in the doorway. Asked, why the interruption? Complained that he was chin-deep in paperwork. Enquired if it was time for tea.

I told him, no, it was too early for tea. Said I came to offer something that may arouse his interest.

My hand perspired as I shut the door and turned the key in the lock. Inhaling deeply, I turned and undid the buttons of my skirt, letting it fall to my ankles.

Henry's eyes widened. His voice cracked as he stammered my name.

I unbuttoned my blouse and shrugged it free.

Unlacing my bodice, I removed all the petticoat skirts. Henry leaning forward in his chair and loosening the collar of his shirt showed I had garnered his attention. Still, I was unconvinced my risk would succeed. Was I brave enough to follow through?

I kicked shoes from my feet and peeled off both stockings. Slipping out of the chemise, I untied my pantaloons, which dropped with surprising ease to the floor. Standing as stiff as a statue, my flesh pinking with embarrassment, I allowed Henry to view me fully naked for the very first time. As his gaze raked my body, my heart leapt into my throat. I imagined Claudette being forced to do the same, giving him what he desired.

A scrape of chair legs and Henry stood. I couldn't bear to look him in the eye when he edged around the desk and halted in front of me. Reaching out, he touched me, his sweaty fingers enjoying my lack of modesty.

A moan escaped his mouth, a death rattle of sorts, when I unfastened his trousers and took hold of the rampant tool of his lust. Though I have endured intimacies in the past, I have never been the instigator. Therefore, when he quivered in my grip, I gave a smug smile. Today I was the victor.

June 1901

I am delighted that I'm pregnant again! No more encounters with Henry in his office are necessary. No more degrading myself to satisfy his lascivious desires. If he searches elsewhere to fulfil his needs, then so be it. My goal is achieved. Intuitively, I know I will give birth to a healthy living baby destined to outlive us both.

8th February 1902

Today our daughter eased into the world like a zephyr, with barely a whimper to announce her arrival. An easy birth, compared to the others, she was born with a membranous cowl covering her head, deemed to bring good luck to child and parents. We've named her Elodie, which means 'wealthy.'

1902/1903

A demure babe, Elodie hardly squalls or demands to be fed during the night, contentedly dropping off to sleep as full as tick until dawn.

~

With no urge to climb out of the cot as a toddler, Elodie is happy to watch morning light flitter around the room and refract off the crystal prisms of the table lamp, creating dancing rainbows on the walls. She gurgles in response, as if the sparkles speak to her.

~

Her father was smitten the instant Elodie uttered her first word, Dadda. He dotes on her, calling her his little gum nut baby. Meanwhile I am in the habit of cosseting my daughter, swaddling her tight against every chill, spoon-feeding her mush lest she choke, and walking her on a leather lead so she won't stray and fall in a ditch, or be stung by bees or bitten by snakes. Motherhood is a tiring responsibility.

14

———

I walked through the cottage front door just as Paisley staggered out of her bedroom, looking worse for wear.

'I see you're raring to go, sis.'

She grumbled and smoothed down her tangle of bed-hair. 'I'm gonna have a shower.' Then she made for the bathroom, the door banging shut behind her.

Invigorated from exercise—and inspired by Bridget's strange goings-on—I foraged in the kitchen for ingredients to make a healthy breakfast and found a large Mason jar of muesli. Taking two bowls from the cupboard, I shook a good serve into each and added fresh diced fruit, honey, and yogurt.

When Paisley appeared, looking less bedraggled, I handed her a bowl. 'Thought you could use a little fibre in your diet.'

She gave the muesli a sniff and wrinkled her nose. 'What gave you that idea?'

'Your reaction last night. I reckon you needed loosening up.' My smirk went unobserved as she cast her gaze over the slight mess spread out on the bench, her forehead puckering. 'Don't worry,' I assured, 'I'll clean it up.'

She popped two strawberry pieces into her mouth and set the bowl down. 'You're right, I was a bit tense.'

I pulled a face. 'A *bit* tense?'

'Okay, I was vile. No idea what got into me. Must be all the strain I'm under. Anyway, Cole forgave my outburst and everything's sweet again.'

'What's the go between you two? You seem pretty close.' *Is he the son you never had?* I was dying to ask.

'He hasn't had the easiest life, raised by a single mum struggling to make ends meet in a dead-end town with a declining population. Not the best environment for a lively teenager. I believed we could offer a helping hand in improving his situation. Broaden his horizons, so to speak. I'd hate for him to waste his cooking talent by only flipping burgers in Grimm.'

I ate heaped spoonfuls of muesli, an interesting grittiness to it with an earthy aftertaste. 'Heard from Fletcher?'

'I spoke to him before. He's doing okay.'

'What about you? Will you be up to the task after your late night? I assumed there wasn't much else to prepare.'

'Oh, you know me. Some necessary last-minute tidying up.'

That better not mean reorganising my creative hard work. The act of folding napkins into pinwheels had been a killer, let alone tackling towel origami—having ditched forming swans or monkeys for a simpler, yet classic, fan design.

'No need to be anxious,' she added. 'I'm fine. Soldiering on and all.' Her words didn't quite match the strain in her eyes.

'Hey, remember when I broke my arm when I was four?' I said, hoping to recollect more clearly what had happened.

'Sort of. You made a real mess of your arm. What brought that to mind?'

'I climbed the hill above the vineyard. There's a swing there. It sparked memories, but I can't recall how I fell.'

'You asked me to push you. You lost your grip and slipped off. It was all your stupid fault for not holding on tight enough.' She peered up at the wall clock. 'I'd better get a move on. Big day. I trust you won't be wearing that later.'

I stared down at my sweaty Lycra. 'Of course not. I have a maid's outfit I picked up from a costume shop in the city. You don't mind if the hem's a tad short, do you? Or that the apron barely covers the plunging neckline?' I tapped my chin. 'Still deliberating on the fishnet stockings, though.'

'You're joking, right?'

I squinted. 'Am I? You'll just have to wait and see, sister dear.' I pointed to her barely touched breakfast. 'Are you eating that?'

'Nah. Looks like puke.' Before I could stop her, she tipped it into the pedal bin.

While Paisley got ready, I tidied up the kitchen to avoid trouble. Returning the Mason jar to the pantry, I tripped over a basket of potatoes and smacked my head on the corner of a shelf. *Shit.* My vision fizzed with exploding stars. I collapsed onto a stool at the bench and rubbed my aching skull below the hairline. No blood on my fingers, therefore no gash. A cold shower might ease any swelling.

As I stood beneath the spray, dizziness kicked in, accompanied by a throbbing behind my eyes. Drying myself, I searched for painkillers in the bathroom cabinet and swallowed three pills with a handful of tap water. Despite sitting on the edge of the tub with my head in my hands for five minutes, the medication had little effect. I wished it away and faced the mirror to scrunch my hair with curling gel—anything more complicated in that moment was beyond my capabilities. Even applying makeup was challenging because I appeared to have four eyes and an extra mouth.

Was a migraine developing? I hadn't had one of those for years. I needed a dark room in which to recuperate. Instead, I pushed through my suffering and chose a chambray shirt dress from the few items hanging in the bedroom wardrobe and accessorised it with sneakers—*decent attire,* by anyone's standard. Half an hour later, I met Paisley on the front porch.

'Thank you,' she said, giving my outfit a once over. 'Though your sneakers don't match.'

I stared down at one grey sneaker with white laces, and a pink one with sparkly silver ties. 'Oh well, I'm sure no-one will notice.'

I accompanied her to the Hyundai hatchback parked in the driveway and gazed around in wonder, astounded by the myriad of verdant colours popping out of the bush foliage. How many shades of green existed? 'Wow, take a look at that,' I exclaimed.

Paisley followed my line of sight. 'Look at what?'

'Nature's miracles.' I felt light as air, ready to lift off and flit amongst leafy branches like a forest fairy. 'It seems I have fresh eyes.'

'Yeah, right.' Unimpressed, Paisley skirted the car and opened the driver's door. Had familiarity already numbed her to nature's beauty? 'Let's get this show on the road, hey?'

As we drove to the mansion, I dropped my window, and stuck my head out, breathing in air heavy with scents of eucalyptus, wattle, and rich earth. However, my bliss ended when the scenery turned ferocious. Creepy imps peeked out from the dense undergrowth, snarling at me through bared teeth. Trees stretched out knobby branches, striving to drag me from the car, while vintage lamp posts ran alongside like pursuing paparazzi, their lights flashing as if snapping photos of my turmoil.

Drawing back, I turned to warn Paisley and found her head had morphed into a crow's, with two beady eyes scrutinising me before its beak opened and released a harsh caw. I slapped my hands over my eyes to banish the bizarre spectacle. This was way worse than a migraine. Had the head knock caused a brain injury?

Once the car stopped, I tumbled out onto the gravel drive and wobbled past Bridget, who'd popped up meerkat-style from amidst a mock orange hedge. I tackled the porch stairs and entered the mansion foyer to the sound of Cole's off-key singing drifting from the kitchen. A splash of cold water might help.

I passed through the glass doors into the hallway and skidded on an overripe kiwifruit near the chiffonier—*blast you, Bridget.* Movement to my left. A woman in a vintage-style long dress stood in a pool of blood at the bottom of the staircase. The instant our eyes met, she evaporated.

In the kitchen, I headed straight for the sink.

'Are you okay?' Cole asked.

I twirled around to find him standing at the workbench and extracting squirming caterpillars from his ears. Blinking hard and taking a second glance, the caterpillars became wireless earbuds.

'You look as though you've seen a ghost,' he said. 'And there's a massive red lump on your forehead.'

A ghost? I touched the tender egg-size swelling on my scalp. 'I hit my head, that's all.'

Cole's face split into The Joker's overwide grin. 'On purpose?'

I ignored his distorted image and smartarse comment and fended off a wave of nausea.

'What happened to you?' Paisley walked in carrying a cane flower basket. 'My driving wasn't that bad.'

'It was the wicked forest and—' I stopped short of professing I'd seen someone that wasn't there.

'The wicked forest? We're not in Sleepy Hollow, Abby.'

I wasn't so sure about that.

'Do me a favour and cut some roses from the garden for the dining and drawing room vases.' She handed me the basket, along with a pair of secateurs and gardening gloves. 'Don't trim the stems too short,' she ordered, her face hideously melting like a waxwork in a bonfire.

I dry-heaved and rushed out the back door, disgorging my breakfast into a compost heap near a vegetable patch. In the rose garden, I slumped beside the pond and cringed when Gerald's statue lifted its head and winked at me. The flowers nearby also became animated, swirling and merging like 1960s artwork.

I willed my stomach and head to settle. Maybe the muesli was past its expiry date. Was seeing visions also a symptom of food poisoning? How would I manage the rest of the day in this condition?

I'm not sure how long I lay on the paving. However, a raspy cough forced me to open my eyes and catch the ex-gardener stepping from behind a trellis.

'Hello again, luv. Looking pretty rough this morning.'

'I'm not well,' I whined, sitting up. 'I suspect I'm going mad.'

'In what way?'

How many ways were there? 'I've been seeing and hearing things. I witnessed a strange woman near the main staircase disappear right in front of me.'

'Hmm,' he said, frowning. 'You're not bonkers. It's only them trying to get your attention.'

'Them?'

'You know ... the ones I mentioned yesterday.'

'The spirits?' I watched with dread as he nodded. 'You've seen them?'

'Seen them, heard them, had altercations with some. Hardly a Casper amongst that lot.'

I was oddly relieved. Though how could ghosts mess with one's mind to the point of lunacy? 'You said Bridget felt she had to *keep the ghosts at bay.* How does one even do that?' I imagined the old girl adopting a stance similar to Chris Pratt's *Jurassic World* character fending off raptors—knees bent, arms extended.

'Bridget devises effective techniques. Though I reckon it's taking a toll on her health.'

'You haven't spoken with her recently?'

He tugged his beard. 'It's been ... er ... rather difficult of late.'

'Want me to pass on a message?'

'Give her my regards ... and this.' He plucked a pink flower from the foliage rambling over the trellis and handed it over. An Albertine rose, if I remembered correctly.

I left in search of a remedy. A woozy head with guests soon arriving was highly inconvenient.

15

———

Caffeine helped somewhat, though I was still floaty and didn't trust my eyes.

I went upstairs and knocked on Bridget's door. Movement sounded from inside the room before the door opened a smidge.

'What do you want?' came a croak through the gap.

'I have an important message,' I murmured spy-like.

It worked. The gap widened enough for me to slip within. I'm not sure what I expected to find inside Bridget's domain, but it wasn't this. Jam-packed with ancient furniture and household paraphernalia, it resembled a storage hold for a museum.

I followed Bridget through a maze of aisles between oddities that would have brought shrieks of delight from my antique dealer friends in Shadow Creek. I did a double take when I glimpsed a freaky stuffed miniature dog, the size of a rat, encased in a glass dome. What was the story behind that? It snarled at me, and I quickly moved on to an area crowded with mismatched armchairs gathered in a semicircle around a fireplace, the polished timber mantle lined with an assortment of framed photographs.

'Have you found my turquoise necklace?' Bridget asked. 'Or the Rosenthal vase? Grandma Livvie loved that vase. A wedding gift.'

'Sorry. I know nothing about those items.'

'What about the black pearl earrings and bracelet, or the Margaret Olley painting?'

I shook my head. 'Are they missing?'

'Lots of things go missing around here. I'm keeping a list. People say I'm just forgetful or imagining it, but ...' She tapped her skull. 'I'm still as sharp as a tick.'

'As sharp as a *tack*,' I corrected.

'Thank you for agreeing. I wouldn't put it past the cook. The help are known for having sticky fingers.' She took a seat at a drop-sided table under a window, spotlit by a shaft of sunlight. 'You have a message for me?'

I sat across from her, the Bentwood chair creaking under my weight. For some odd reason I broke out in a sweat. 'The old gardener fellow sends his regards.'

She cocked her head in a baffled kind of way.

'The gardener,' I repeated, fanning my face with my hand. 'He worked here for many years until ...' I bit my tongue. *Until my sister and husband sacked him for no good reason.* 'I spoke to him in the rose garden. He asked me to give you this, a favourite of yours, I believe.' I plucked the Albertine rose from my breast pocket.

Bridget's face lit up with a smile as she gave it a sniff. 'Darius. I'd give anything to see him again.'

Darius, so that was his name. 'I'll try to put things right. I'll have words with Paisley. Tell her she can't stop friends from visiting one another.'

'Friends?' Her eyes fastened on mine. 'Yes. Just friends.'

Yet the way she stroked her cheek with the rose suggested something more intimate. *Lady Chatterley's Lover* crossed my mind. 'I'll arrange a meeting between the two of you. It can be a secret for now.'

'How will you do that? It's impossible.'

'You don't know me well enough, Bridget. I can occasionally be bull-headed, especially where ...' I stopped short of saying *romance*. 'Where affections are involved. Anyway, it's not like you're a prisoner here at Grassington.'

A tear slipped from one eye to weave amongst wrinkles. 'Oh, but I am.'

I shuddered. For the Greenwoods, was it a case of being able to check out anytime they liked but never leave?

A rap on the door. A muffled, 'Abby, are you in there?' Paisley on the warpath.

I made my way back through the miscellany of strange objects and opened the door. Bridget pushed me into the hall before slamming it shut. Face-to-face with my sister, I stared into eyes bulging with surprise.

'What were you doing in there?' Paisley asked.

'None of your business,' I growled, annoyed with her for separating friends of long standing. 'What do you want?'

'What's up with you? I was going to ask if you'd prefer to stay here tonight. You can have the old servants' quarters downstairs.'

I balked. 'The old servant?'

She spoke slowly, as if explaining to a child. 'An old room ... used in the past for the house help to sleep in. Although small, it has a functional bed.'

'What's wrong with my bedroom at the cottage?'

'Nothing. I just thought you'd enjoy experiencing the mansion in its entirety. Get a real feel for a *haunted* house.'

'But you claimed it wasn't haunted.'

'Yeah, well ... can't you at least pretend for a night or two?'

'Pretend? Who for, the guests? God, Paisley, don't tell me you want me to get them all spooked?'

She tugged me over to the sitting area leading to the verandah. 'If you stay here, you'll be on hand to … you know. I'm relying on you.' She stabbed a finger into my chest. 'If the guests aren't sufficiently frightened, you'll need to stir up activity.'

My hands curled in anger. 'If you're so concerned about the fear factor, why don't *you* stay over and make sure it's up to par?'

'Because it will look like a setup if the host generates excitement.'

'But it will be a setup.'

She stamped her foot. 'Stop being a pain, Abby!' Paisley's features transformed into a red devil with horns, her words accompanied with flames pouring from her mouth. 'Just do as I say, will you?'

Normally, I would've staved off her taunts, made excuses for her nasty behaviour—she'd had a bad day, her busy lifestyle, frustration … menopause. However, with hallucinations and nausea returning, my nerves were on the brink of snapping. Before I lost control and punched my sister in the face, I strode away.

16

ELODIE

1908-1912

An ethereal creature, with snow white hair and pearlescent skin—almost translucent—Elodie wafts through her early years with little disruption to her parent's life. Until she and Violet Bright become firm friends.

Zachariah and Maggie's only daughter, of similar age, is the total opposite. Dark haired and sun-freckled, she is rambunctious, exploring the property like a roaming goat, snacking on whatever nature offers up. Violet introduces Elodie to a world filled with adventure, and her clothes are no longer stainless, her face and feet no longer unsoiled. Under her friend's influence, Elodie comes out of her shell. Reborn and emboldened, she rebels—as much as a five-year-old can—questioning everything to the point of annoyance.

On turning six, Violet joins her two elder brothers at school in Grimm. Meanwhile Elodie remains at Grassington, suffering under the tutelage of a dour woman with chin whiskers, employed to teach the fundaments of her education until she is of age to board at a prestigious girls' grammar school close to Brisbane.

When not being schooled, Elodie enjoys moving about unobserved, sneaking from the house, and wandering the gardens —a tiny wraith, tempting fate, yet always keeping within safe reach of home. Her favourite spot is the fig tree on the hill, its sprawling branches offering a hideout where she can view the comings and goings at Grassington in the pretence as a princess or wood nymph.

One day, when she is ten, and contentedly reclining on a wide branch of the fig tree with her thoughts *away with fairies* as her father would say, a pretty-faced wallaby appears, its distinct white cheeks and ear-tips conspicuous amongst the dry grass. Curious, she follows as it grazes on new shoots, moving downhill and up again until arriving at the boundary of the forest. Elodie is on the verge of returning home when a ray of sunlight reveals an old stone well.

Her feet move of their own accord, and she inches over to the aged brickwork. With effort, she slides the rotting timber cover back so that it rests on the far edge. Gripping the rim, she leans over. Her eyes are drawn to the lime-green sludge coating the water's surface in a thick skin. She stretches and dips in a finger. Gives it a stir.

A bubbling sound.

Moss ripples, surges, and rips apart as the verdant seal ruptures. Elodie squeals when a hand thrusts out with wizened fingers splayed, followed by the dome of a head streaked with sodden strips of hair. When the two nostrils spurt muck, and icy fingers clutch her wrist, she tugs free and slips lightheaded to the ground.

Moments later, intrigue prises her up, only to discover a brown frog floating amongst the moss, yellow eyes blinking. Was her mind playing games? Or had the devil paid her a visit? She pulls the cover back over the well.

That night, Elodie takes the family Bible to her room for protection and sleeps with it under her pillow.

Several days pass and Violet is staying overnight at the mansion while the Greenwoods host a dinner party. When the guests arrive, the girls sneak up to the rooftop observation deck to view the finely dressed men and women and comment on their attire. They remain in lofty seclusion as the sky darkens, and the moon rises to hang like a phosphorescent globe.

Violet gives a wolf howl and dares Elodie to do the same. She goes one better. With hair shimmering, and face as pale as milk, Elodie climbs onto the parapet, her nightdress wafting in a strong breeze. Her sleeves take on the transparency of wings as she stretches her scrawny arms up towards the suspended orb and quotes a familiar nursery rhyme:

> *'I see the moon, the moon sees me,*
> *God bless the moon and God bless me.*
> *There's grace in the cottage and grace in the hall,*
> *And the grace of God is over us all.'*

Letting out a sharp wolf howl, she gives a bow and wobbles before righting.

'Get down,' Violet cries, clutching the hem of her friend's nightgown. 'I won't pick up the pieces if you fall.'

Elodie turns and shakes her head. 'I won't fall. I have perfect balance. Anyway, it's not my time to die.'

'How do you know?'

'Because God protects me.'

'But what does the Devil want? He has power too.'

As if announced, a form oozes out of the shadows and glides

into the moonlight. Thin-bodied and faceless, there is nothing to prove it is human.

Elodie gasps and jumps down, yet Violet—sighing with relief—doesn't seem to notice the grotesque bystander. Unable to form words, Elodie escapes inside, descends the spiral staircase, and bolts to her room.

For a whole week she sleeps with the Bible hidden under her pillow as protection against the No Face Man.

Over time, Elodie glimpses more spectres: a sobbing woman in a light blue dress, and a boy she recognises from photographs as being her brother. She mentions the appearance of poor dead Tommy to her mother, only to receive a slap across the face for 'lying'. Her mother's distress causes Elodie to cease sharing experiences brought about by the harrowing gift thrust upon her, and she keeps her visions secret even from Violet in case she blabs to Maggie.

17

The puttanesca room offered quiet concealment. Resting on a velvet chaise lounge, I covered my face with my arms, wishing I was anywhere but Grassington. I even longed to be holed up in my pole house at Rosella Ridge, on the mountain range overlooking the village of Shadow Creek. A rush of memories from the disaster I had fled suddenly brought a new wave of pain behind my eyes. If I'd kept to myself and not been hellbent on unravelling other people's secrets, I'd be the owner of a spanking new bookstore selling loads of stock to the masses. At least that's what I'd hoped before my 'meddling in other's affairs'—Shane's words—aborted that plan. Yet was running a bookshop my ultimate goal, or had I been influenced by circumstances and people thinking they knew best?

The seclusion shattered further as the door burst open and Paisley rushed in.

'Abby, there you are. The first guests have arrived. C'mon, it's showtime!'

I groaned and dragged myself into the foyer just as a mid-to-late-fifties couple walked through the entrance. Floral Hawaiian shirt, chinos, and straw hat for him. Capri pants, a bright silk kaftan top with matching headscarf for her. Anyone would have thought they'd just boarded a cruise ship. I slouched against the wall to view my sister in action.

'Welcome to Grassington,' she greeted, clasping the tall and hefty man's hand with both of hers and giving it a shake. 'You must be the O'Maras.'

'Vince and Daphne,' he responded.

His wife's grin exposed a canine tooth smeared with blood ... or maybe lipstick. 'We're thrilled to be here. It's a dream come true.'

My sister returned the smile. 'Glad to hear it. I'm Paisley Croft, your host.'

Vince peered over the top of his wire-framed glasses. 'And your other half?'

'What? Oh ... Fletcher, my husband, is indisposed at present. My sister will assist me for the time being.' She thumbed over her shoulder at me. 'Abby will show you to your room.'

I sighed and moved off, expecting to be followed, when Paisley sprang forward and hauled me back.

'Need help with the luggage?' she asked the O'Maras. 'Abby will oblige.'

'No, no,' Vince objected. 'I'll collect the bags while you ladies get acquainted.' He took off out the door and down the stairs to the drive.

Daphne clapped her hands, making me jump. Was I alone in hearing it as a clash of cymbals? 'This is palatial,' she gushed, eyeing the fancy pendant light hanging overhead. 'Do we get a tour?' She thrust her head into the dining room. 'Vincent has told me a lot about Grassington. I couldn't wait to see it for myself.'

Paisley's eyebrows arched in astonishment. 'He's been here before?'

'He's just done his research on the history and all. It's on the internet.' Daphne crossed the foyer to lean into the drawing room. 'Oh, my ... look at all the timber panelling. Cedar, I guess. And a grand piano. Just the ticket for a fun singalong. If you're looking for someone to tickle the ivories, I'm your woman. I know all the good show tunes.'

My sister nodded politely and shifted focus to Vince lumbering through the doorway, his face flushed from the exertion of retrieving two large suitcases, a cumbersome beauty case, and a laptop satchel. 'Would you prefer to pay the remaining amount now or later?' Paisley said, stepping behind a wooden lectern I hadn't noticed before.

'I'll pay now. Get it over and done with.' Vince dropped the luggage and paid via a handheld POS system Paisley produced.

I commandeered one of the suitcases and leant on its extended handle for support against my lingering lightheadedness, while Daphne perused the wall photos and walked by the glass doors to inspect the ornaments on the chiffonier. Upturning a painted china vase, she appeared to be reading the maker's mark or possibly checking for the price sticker.

Vince shoved his wallet into his trouser pocket. 'Righto, where's our room?'

'Upstairs,' Paisley said. 'You have the master suite.'

Daphne moaned with pleasure. 'Oh, how lov-er-ly.'

'Follow me, if you dare.' I sideswiped the grandfather clock with the heavy suitcase, causing a jingle of chimes, and wheeled it over to the main staircase. Gingerly scanning the area for any ghostly apparitions, I lugged the suitcase up both flights and led the couple into the main bedroom.

More 'oohs' and 'ahhs'.

'Who might this handsome couple be?' Daphne asked, standing in front of the framed wall photo.

'That's Henry and Olivia Greenwood,' I informed. 'This was their bedroom.'

She drew her husband over. 'Look, honey, the Greenwoods. You know, I can see a resemblance in Henry to—'

'... a young Russell Crowe,' Vince interjected.

Daphne stared at him. 'Yes, my exact thought.'

Frankly, I couldn't see it. I quickly pointed out the gift bags and the brochures and reminded them of the time for afternoon tea. 'Enjoy your stay,' I said, leaving them to unpack, or ogle, or do as they please.

Downstairs, Paisley was speaking with two men wearing matching khaki shirts printed on the back with an image of a Dalek and the word 'EXTERMINATE' in large lettering.

'Luke and *Sandy* Michaelson?' she queried, obviously baffled that one of them wasn't a female.

'Yep. I'm Sandy. Less of a mouthful than *Alexander*,' the stocky, light-haired one said. 'And he's Luke,' he added pointing over his shoulder to the tall, gangly, and much younger man behind him.

Paisley apologised. 'I'm sorry, I assumed ... no matter. And you are a couple?'

Sandy tucked in his multiple chins. 'A couple of what?'

'A couple.' Luke elbowed him. 'You know, a *gay* married couple.'

'Good God.' Sandy's eyes popped out from under their hoods of skin. 'You think I'd choose to spend a romantic weekend away with this string bean? We're father and son, for Pete's sake.'

'Oh, then I take it you won't be wanting to share a double bed?' Paisley queried.

'Not if we don't have to.'

'Let's see.' She studied the guest register splayed out on the lectern. 'I'll do a swap. The green room with two single beds is now yours.'

'Much better.'

Sandy handed over a wad of cash and Paisley ordered me to show the Michaelsons to the green ivy room.

Fortunately, they only had large backpacks, which they carried themselves. I guided them upstairs via the timber staircase—being closer to their room.

'You're Dr Who enthusiasts,' I remarked, opening their door.

'I am,' Luke said. 'Dad's more a Jack Reacher fan. If you're referring to our shirts, it's because we run a pest control business.'

'Oh ... I get it. *Exterminate!*' I stabbed the air with thrusts of an imaginary knife. 'Die, you pesky creepy crawlies.'

Their pained expressions did little to encourage my theatrics, so I repeated the instructions I gave to the O'Maras and left the men to argue over beds.

With Paisley absent at the front entrance, I ducked into the kitchen and poured another mug of coffee. Back in the foyer, I stood in for my sister guarding the door—if draped over the lectern, wishing I was curled up in bed with an icepack over my head, was considered as keeping watch.

Car tyres rolling on gravel urged me to straighten and attempt to appear normal. According to Paisley, Hilary Bloodworth wouldn't be arriving till tomorrow. Therefore, it had to be Rowan Twomey pulling into the driveway.

He never showed up. In walked a round-faced young woman with dark wavy hair, her pink-and-black polka dot rockabilly dress flaring out in a full skirt.

'Hello,' she said through fuchsia-coloured lips, viewing the surroundings from beneath huge false lashes. 'I feel like I've been sucked into a wormhole and spat out into the past.'

And into the wrong decade, it seemed to me, taking stock of her 1950s inspired outfit.

She held out a hand. 'I'm Rowan Twomey.'

'You're Rowan? From Byron Bay? But I thought you were—'

'A man? It happens all the time.'

'Welcome to Grassington then, Ms Twomey.' I echoed Paisley's mantra, 'Do you wish to pay now or later?'

'I've already paid, haven't I?' She produced a printed confirmation of her online booking from her patent leather handbag, showing she had indeed paid in full.

'Great. You are staying in the ... er ...' My attempt at checking the register was hindered by words crawling across the page like caterpillars. I rubbed my eyes and took a second look. The notations were now still. 'You're in the Yellow Room. Do you need help with your luggage?'

'I'll get my bags from the car later. I can't wait to see my room.'

As we started up the staircase, Rowan shivered and rubbed her arms. 'Ooh, did you feel that?'

'Feel what?'

'A heaviness in the air. As if a terrible incident occurred here. Someone may have suffered a massive injury.'

I gasped. *Massive alright, resulting in death.* Was Rowan familiar with the maid's unfortunate accident?

'I have a sensitivity to such things,' she said, and continued upstairs.

On the floor above, I spied an A4 paper sign now taped to the door leading into Bridget's rooms. *KEEP OUT! OFF LIMITS!* had been written with a black marking pen. I swiftly ushered Rowan to her room before she clapped eyes on it.

More shivering interrupted her delight in the decor. 'It's freezing in here. Do you feel it, or is it just me again?'

'I feel it too. That's why I've placed extra blankets on the beds.'

'Are all the bedrooms this cold?'

'Just yours, to be honest.'

'That's peculiar. Is this room haunted, do you think?'

'What?' I looked around and gulped. The two elephants on the shelf were now positioned back-to-back, not following, as I had placed them previously. 'I'll investigate. Let me know if you need more bedding. Or a heater.'

As I was about to leave, Rowan stepped in my way. 'Will I be sharing the room? I'm not the best sleeper. I occasionally suffer from night terrors. Sometimes I sleepwalk. I wouldn't want to annoy anyone.'

'You have the room to yourself. Though I suggest you lock your door at night. You don't want to trip down the stairs in the dark.' Instantly regretting my remark, I edged around her. 'I'll leave you to settle in.'

I snatched Bridget's sign from the door and went downstairs to the office to scribble a more favourable notice, choosing *Private Rooms* to replace Bridget's curt phrasing.

18

ELODIE

1920

Elodie follows the zigzag flight of a Blue Tiger butterfly with her eyes as she rests against the fig tree. With secondary schooling finished, and still at a loose end as to her future—other than marrying well—she considers how to convince her father to send her to university. She could study biology to become a botanist like Joseph Banks, who travelled to Australia with Captain James Cook on the HMS Endeavour. Her watercolour artwork of plants and animal life have won acclaim from the science master, so why couldn't she aim high—even if she is a girl.

Her mind drifts off at a tangent, fantasising on the possibilities, until Violet leaps from the tree swing and shoves a pair of brass and leather binoculars into her hands.

In contrast to Elodie, her best friend is not floundering but was assisting Maggie with cooking and cleaning for the Greenwoods. Her true talent, though, lies in dressmaking. Gifted and creative in this art, Violet has been employed by Elodie to create her a new outfit for an upcoming charity ball, the region's first since the horrid Spanish Flu of last year put a stop to social events. Maybe it had been worth it, living in the boring countryside, and taking inconvenient precautions. The number of deaths in Grimm and the surrounding areas was minimal compared to the thousands of poor souls who'd succumbed to the disease in the cities.

'Here, try these,' Violet says. 'They should help.'

Elodie peers through the lenses, searching in vain to locate the graceful insect.

Violet tugs her arm. 'What are you doing? He's not up in the tree, silly.'

'Who's not up in the tree?'

'The new labourer I just mentioned. The one my brother, Stan, says is a war hero. He's with the workers in the vineyard.'

Elodie redirects the binoculars to view the field below the hill. Because the sawmill slowed production, her father has diversified into planting and cultivating grapes for winemaking.

'Sherries and brandies will help fill our dwindling coffers,' he'd argued against her mother's comment that it was 'a foolhardy venture'.

She spots a light-haired stranger squatting amongst the workers as they prune stems on healthy vines. Stripped down to trousers and undershirt, his tanned, muscular arms shine with perspiration. It's pleasant having younger men working back on the estate now the Great War has ended.

'A hero, you say?'

'Yes. The way Stan tells it, this fellow was under heavy fire somewhere in France, dashed out in front of his company, shot two German gunners, and captured the machine gun, bringing it back for their own use.' Her voice drops to a whisper when she adds, 'We mightn't have lost our Roy if this chap had served with him.'

A pang of grief wrenches Elodie's heart strings at the memory of Violet's jaunty older brother who, at nineteen, eagerly signed up to do his bit for king and country, only to die three months into his service.

She again studies the man through the binoculars. 'Do you think my dad is aware of his bravery?'

'Hardly anything gets past your father. I hear this fellow learnt a few things about wine growing during his time abroad.'

'You make it sound like he was on a holiday, Vi, not trying to dodge the Huns' bullets.' Elodie returns the binoculars. 'It's hot out here. I suggest we scrounge a refreshing fruit cordial from your mother.'

She gets to her feet, and brushes leaves and twigs from her skirt before taking off down the grassy slope, only to skid on a patch of shale near the bottom and take a tumble.

'You silly duffer,' Violet says, catching up and crouching beside her.

'You're lucky you didn't break your flamin' neck,' comes a deep voice above them.

Elodie looks up to find the young man they were spying on flashing a smile, his bristled chin and cheeks bordering full lips. Appearing just slightly older than them, he must have lied about his age when enlisting for war duty.

'Do you need help to stand?' he asks, holding out a hand.

Elodie goes to take it and pulls away with a gasp. Violet hadn't mentioned this hero had suffered war wounds. Burn scars snake from his fingers to his elbow in shiny pink and purple ridges.

A vision takes shape, like those that have plagued her since witnessing the horror in the stone well. She sees a crowd of similarly young men gathered around him, their uniforms spattered with mud and blood. Some have horrific injuries—

missing limbs, disfigurements—yet all bear the hollow stare of the dead.

Elodie pays no heed to them and rises, wincing from a searing pain in her ankle. As she hobbles forward, the man kneels and inspects her foot through her stocking, his fingers pressing gently.

'Just a sprain, I reckon. But you'd best keep your weight off it.' He scoops her up in his arms and carries her towards the house.

Too shocked to speak, Elodie averts her gaze to the pale blue sky.

'I'm bettin' you're Miss Greenwood,' he says, breaking the silence between them.

'Elodie Greenwood.' Violet speaks for her as she keeps pace alongside. 'And I'm Violet Bright. What's your name?'

'Will ... Will Flanagan.'

'A pleasure to meet you, Will,' Violet says.

Elodie is more entranced by two shimmering cotton-ball clouds colliding midair and merging.

She is delivered to her mother who, tutting about unladylike manners, settles her on a sofa in the drawing room with a cushion upon which to rest her swelling ankle. Meanwhile, Violet takes Will around to the kitchen to ply him with cake and cordial in place of the *thank you* he failed to receive from Olivia.

While her mother leaves to rustle up tea, Elodie feels the tender touch of a small hand in hers. She turns to see her brother standing close, a sad look on his little face. 'I'll be as right as rain in no time,' she assures him.

Tommy holds out a toy tin soldier, and she smiles in gratitude for his childish act of consolation. Sometimes it is a ball, or a pull-along toy. Once he offered her a peppermint candy snaffled from the jar in her father's office. Her little protector. She wishes Tommy could speak, for there are many questions she'd love to ask him. As usual, he vanishes in a glimmering mist at the arrival of their mother.

'Tea and a sandwich,' Olivia says, placing the tray on a side table and eyeing the room, as if searching for the presence of another.

Had she heard her talking with Tommy? Though her mother never asks, Elodie is aware she remains watchful in the hope that she too might catch sight of her son in any form.

'I've telephoned Dr Morphett, Elodie. He will visit soon.'

'There's no need for that, Mum. It's just a sprain. Rest is the only remedy.'

'How do you know it's only a sprain? You could have fractured a bone or torn a ligament.'

'Will told her,' says Violet, entering from the kitchen. 'He had a good look at it.'

'Will?'

'The young man who carried her here.'

Olivia screws up her nose. 'A labourer is no physician.'

When Dr Morphett arrives, all flustered from being fetched by Zachariah in the Greenwood's new Studebaker, he examines her injury and agrees. 'Plenty of rest, young lady. I'll strap your ankle, but no walking on this foot for a while.'

'See, Mum,' Elodie says smugly, 'Will Flanagan was right.'

'Will Flanagan?' Dr Morphett's eyes widen.

'One of the vineyard workers,' Olivia explains. 'He helped Elodie when she fell. Have you met him?'

'He's a returned soldier,' Violet chimes in. 'A very brave and handsome one.'

Dr Morphett scowls as he says, 'I am acquainted with his parents.' He fumbles while extracting items from his medical bag, dropping a roll of gauze which unfurls on the floor.

Elodie reaches down and retrieves it, rewinding it for him before passing the roll back. What is the doctor hiding? Is Will not the war hero people believe him to be?

19

———

The dining room was abuzz with chatter as guests piled their plates from the buffet and milled around, getting acquainted. Paisley, as predicted, flitted from person to person like a pollinating bee.

Surprisingly, Daphne O'Mara was the vegan, caught stabbing her fork into arancini balls and spring rolls, checking for meat products. I repositioned an olive tapenade next to a bowl of crackers and informed her that all dishes at this end of the table were vegan friendly. She launched into espousing the importance of animal welfare, with which I thoroughly agreed.

'You wouldn't eat your pet dog or cat, would you?' she said, pointing a celery stick in my face. 'Sheep and cattle have feelings too. I've seen YouTube videos showing cows and horses playing with beach balls like puppies. They are affectionate and smart. Smarter than a few of my relatives. Yours too, I reckon.'

I glanced over at Paisley conversing with Vincent. My sister had her wits about her, that's for sure—unlike poor Fletcher. Her reluctance to comment this morning raised questions regarding her desire for his presence. Was life less complicated with him no longer in the picture?

I offered a serving tray of bruschetta to Daphne.

She shook her head. 'No thanks. I see it has chickpeas. I'm highly allergic to them. A spoonful of hummus almost killed me, once. Thank God for EpiPens.'

'Abby.'

Turning around, I noticed Rowan standing behind me, holding a cup of tea in one hand and a slice of carrot cake on a paper napkin in the other.

'Found out the history of my room yet?' she asked.

'No.' I beckoned Cole over, drawing him away from stacking cannoli pastries on a silver platter. 'Rowan's asking about the yellow room. Any idea whose it was back in the day?'

'It was the children's bedroom. During the room's makeover, they discovered nursery rhyme print under layers of old wallpaper. Bridget confirmed it. She and her sister shared that room as kids. I think it was also little Tommy's.'

I nodded. 'That would explain the toys on the shelves.'

'Yeah, Paisley's idea. She talked Bridget into handing some over from her *collection*.'

Rowan licked icing from her cake. 'Any reason why it would be so cold in there?'

'Have you shut the windows?' Cole said.

'They're closed. It's really freezing.'

'Must be a draught. You'll find more blankets in the linen cupboard.'

'I've already put extras in the room.' I turned to Rowan. 'I'll have another look later to see where the draught might be coming from.'

'There's a stepladder in the storage cupboard upstairs that you can use,' Cole offered, then he slipped from the room to return to the kitchen.

I had a sudden thought. Was it just coincidence, or was there a connection between the toys changing position, the marble's appearance, and the cold room that I now knew had once been Tommy's before his untimely death?

I busied myself, rearranging the remaining mini quiches and devilled eggs onto one serving plate when Luke Michaelson came alongside.

'Excuse me,' he said, botching my display by removing three eggs and a quiche and dropping them onto his already heaped plate. 'Can we wander around the whole property, or are some areas off-limits?'

'I think you're permitted anywhere on the grounds. The hill above the vineyard has an excellent view of the estate.'

'Great. Dad and I might go for a hike after lunch.' He stuffed two more quiches into a trouser pocket. 'Sustenance for the journey,' he added with a wink.

Oh, to be young and slender again, without the worry of overloading on carbs. I swiped a devilled egg from the platter and went in search of a cold beverage.

Vince poured me a glass from the punch bowl. 'The photographs in the foyer are fascinating. Do you have any information on them?'

I sucked passionfruit pulp from between my teeth. 'A little. Only the bare bones, really.'

'I'd be interested in viewing others, if they're available.'

'Me too. Bridget Hawthorne, the owner, probably has loads more, but I'm not sure if she'd be willing to show them to ... er ... strangers such as us.'

'A bit of a recluse, is she?'

'You could say that.'

'Not ill, I trust?'

'Not in the physical sense.' I tapped my skull.

'Ahh.' Vince nodded in understanding. 'Bats in the belfry. It happens to the best of us. No, not me. Not yet, anyway.' He laughed theatrically behind his hand.

'Are you a history buff? Or do you have a particular interest in the Greenwood family?'

'Well ... certain parts of history.' He eyed me over his glass as he finished his punch. Picking a seed out of his teeth with a fingernail, he asked. 'Any plans to revive the vineyard? A winery with a cellar door offering tastings would add to the estate's appeal.'

'Snap! I've thought the same thing. A rotunda on the lawn for weddings and outdoor entertainment could also be good.'

'And candlelight soirées in the glade. A swimming pool wouldn't go astray, either.'

I cocked my head. 'Have you managed similar venues before? Sounds like you're planning to add Grassington to your portfolio.'

'What? I wish. No, I'm just gifted with the ability to discern the economic potential of new ventures.'

'You should speak with Paisley. She'd be happy to discuss ideas.'

'Well, maybe I should.' Vince gave a sideways glance. 'Oh, Daphne needs me.' He sprinted over to his wife, who seemed too engrossed in examining her food to require her husband's attention.

Thinking about returning to the kitchen to see what other food needed bringing out, I froze when, through the large bay window, I spotted a vehicle pulling into the car park. Not just any vehicle, but Fletcher's blue hybrid, a Toyota RAV4.

Paisley was nowhere to be seen, so I bolted outside and down the stairs to greet my brother-in-law on her behalf, only to skid to a stop at the sight of a towering, broad-shouldered man standing beside the car. With ink-black hair gelled flat, black clothing and boots, Joe Teo looked like a hot Asian badass in a blockbuster action movie—too bad about his undesirable personality.

He, too, pulled up sharply. 'Holy shit,' he said, removing his aviator sunglasses. 'If it isn't Aberdeen Gordon. Haven't seen you for ... what ... ten years?'

I glared at Joe. 'More like fifteen. And Eaton is the name now, as you well know. What are you doing here? Did you tag along for the ride?'

'Tag along? I drove here.'

'Where's Fletcher?' I peered through the car's tinted windows. No-one inside—front or back. 'What have you done with him?'

'Huh? Oh ... he's in the boot, hogtied and sobbing for his mother.'

I groaned. 'Don't be stupid.'

'Truth is, Fletch didn't feel up to returning, so I've come in his place.'

'Well, you can simply turn around and head back.'

He took a defiant step forward, his lofty frame looming over me. 'Hey, that's not hospitable. I expected you'd be pleased to see an old flame.'

I craned my neck to give him a dirty look. 'You were never a flame of mine. Barely even a spark. How'd you know I'd be here?'

He gave that smarmy grin I despised. 'Paisley mentioned it. Anyway, more hands make light work, right?' He waved large jazz hands in the air.

'We're fine. Don't need you here. Go on, bugger off back to the city.'

'Still the same Abby, hey? Not physically of course. It has been a few years.'

What nerve! 'I could say the same about you. Some serious worry lines going on there, I see.'

'At least my shoes match,' he said, studying my feet. 'And my hair doesn't need touching up. What's with the tomato-ketchup tint? More efficient for covering the grey?'

'It's fire-engine red.' I tossed back my head in an attempted feisty hair-flip which, from Joe's confused expression, must have resembled a quirky spasm.

'Are you aware of a bruise on your forehead?' he said. 'Looks rather nasty.'

I touched the tender lump. 'Yeah, it's what you get when your head collides with kitchen cabinetry.'

He twisted his mouth and frowned, as if considering the worth of continuing that line of inquiry. He eyed the mansion. 'Where's Paisley?'

'Inside, entertaining the guests.'

'How is she?'

'Taking charge, as usual. Though more stressed than normal, what with Fletcher ...' No need to expound.

Joe sighed with understanding. 'I guess I'd better make my presence known.' Opening the car's rear door, he extracted an overnight bag and brushed past, aiming for the mansion entrance.

Was he planning to stay over? Unbelievable!

'Wanker,' I mumbled, and massaged my forehead to ease the ache of a fresh headache.

My mind rolled back to Paisley and Fletcher's wedding—*the one I was late for.*

Our older sister, Skye, was supposed to be the chief bridesmaid until she got pregnant and couldn't assure Paisley she'd last the distance of the wedding ceremony without puking her guts out. Hence, I was bumped up the ranks. Joe, being Fletcher's closest mate, was the best man, and therein, my downfall.

Filled to bursting with tasty tucker, expensive bubbly, and drawn in by Joe's good looks and animal magnetism—including his convincing argument that we only lived once so why fight a natural, positive, urge—we hooked up. A big mistake. Huge. Catastrophic, even. Not only had we made out under cover of darkness in the dense rainforest while everyone else linked arms and farewelled the happy couple. I had also cheated on my boyfriend.

Shane and I had just become an item, making our relationship official, and if it wasn't for his grandfather's funeral interstate he would have been there. Therefore, I could blame my shameful *faux pas* on Shane for being absent and not protecting me from myself, or his grandfather for choosing to die in the week leading up to the wedding. I never told Shane and never would, filing it away under Abby's Stupid Stuff-ups.

Joe, however, decided he wanted more of what I could barely recall, and pressured me for months to reconsider. It was only when Joe met his first wife, Barbara—a more shapely and amenable prey—that he lost interest in me. Still, that hadn't stopped him from reminding me of our misadventure whenever we ran into each other at events organised by my brother-in-law. Ultimately, I avoided functions Joe attended. Hence our not seeing each other for a decade and a half.

Armed with resolve, I moved inside.

20

ELODIE

1920

Violet soon becomes obsessed with Will Flanagan, making any excuse to hang around the vineyard. She offers him cold drinks and samples of her mother's baking or pretends to be fascinated with the process of growing grapes. Exasperated by her friend's infatuation, Elodie prefers to pore over books taken from her father's office. With Darwin's *The Origin of Species* tucked under her arm, and a cup of tea, she goes to the rose garden, taking up a position on a stone bench near the pond.

A sound interrupts her reading.

Will appears through the archway. He scans the surroundings and blinks when he notices her. 'Sorry Miss, I don't wish to disturb. I'm looking for a particular gardening hoe. Zachariah said there was one hereabout.'

Elodie points to what she thinks is the tool, leaning against a brick wall covered by a climbing rose. 'Might that be it?'

She watches him cross the lawn, flinching when she sees he is not alone. Shadowy figures follow close behind, as if tethered to him by ghostly threads. Is this how it is to be, the dead sporadically accompanying him?

Will flips the tool over by its hardwood handle and examines the flat sharp-edged blade. 'It'll do the trick well enough.' Lifting his gaze, his mouth opens as if to speak, only to clamp shut again. He turns and approaches the archway.

Elodie leaps up. 'What were you about to say?'

He spins around, the apparitions evaporating as he nears. 'I … I was about to ask if your ankle has mended.'

'It most certainly has. It's been weeks since I injured it.' She raises the hem of her sky-blue dress and wiggles her stockinged foot. 'See. As good as new. I danced without problems at the Grimm charity ball last Saturday. It was quite a popular event, yet you weren't in attendance.'

'No, I …' His face falls and he feeds his disfigured hand into a trouser pocket. 'I don't enjoy social events so much. Especially dances.'

'Please don't,' Elodie says, tugging his hand out. 'No need to cover your wound with me. It's not a scar; it's a badge of honour.'

Will frowns and pulls his hand away. 'I best be off. The foreman will have my guts for garters if I don't return with the hoe.'

As he leaves, Elodie surprises herself by calling out, 'I'll be here same time tomorrow if you need help fetching more gardening tools.' When there is no response, she doubts her words ever reached his ears.

Therefore, it is a delight when she comes to the garden the next morning and finds Will waiting. They share a more relaxed conversation, with Will's enthusiasm when talking about viticulture bringing a warm smile to his face that reaches his eyes. Elodie steers clear of broaching the subject of war, or the existence of his spectral companions, who at least have the decency to hide from view as their talk continues.

Over the following months, Elodie forms a friendship with this pleasant young man, gaining his trust enough that he begins to disclose his tragic war experiences. He even confesses to harbouring guilt for not protecting those who died alongside him. This grows into an attraction that scares Elodie as much as it thrills.

She keeps her emotions hidden, until Will startles her one day when he sneaks a kiss under the fig tree on the hill. Lovestruck, she responds eagerly, and he marks the occasion by carving their initials into the tree trunk, encasing them within an outline of a heart. Elodie, in turn, scores their initials into the glass of her bedroom window, using the diamond ring her father gifted her on her eighteenth birthday—another event Will failed to attend. However, the candlelight picnic he organises in the glade the next evening—amorous advances included—more than make up for his social reticence.

Keeping the news of the budding romance from Violet is the most arduous task Elodie has ever done. The girls' friendship ruptures when Elodie discovers the carved initials have been gouged from the heart in the tree. Only one person comes to mind who is capable of orchestrating such a jealous act.

21

I walked in on Paisley and Joe pulling out of a hug in the foyer.

'Isn't this a surprise?' my sister said, distancing herself from him. A pink tinge mottled her throat, a tell she was nervous or embarrassed. 'Joe has come to help out.'

What was going on? Had this been Paisley's plan all along, to replace Fletcher with Joe for the inaugural weekend? Or was she truly ruffled by his arrival, as was I?

She ignored my protest at being ordered to take his bag upstairs to a bedroom I hadn't yet seen, handing me her set of skeleton keys and separating one from the others. I watched, irritated, as she ushered Joe into the dining room.

Under sufferance, I carried his overnight bag up to the room next to the Michaelsons' which, when unlocked, turned out to be decorated in shades of blue. The peeling wallpaper, though damaged, still showed a design reminiscent of the Chinese Willow pattern. I cringed. Was Paisley's room choice for Joe a subconscious gaffe of racial stereotyping, or a flippant joke? Then again, did I even care how he would react?

I suddenly noticed an anomaly. The design in the oriental wallpaper gave an illusion of a 3D scene in which dragons writhed, and pagodas swayed. It resembled one of those Magic Eye books we enjoyed as kids, and I almost pitied Joe having to tackle the weird depth perception ... if that's all it was.

I dropped the bag on the bare floorboards and smirked at the difficulties he would face in sleeping with his limbs hanging over the mattress of the lone single bed. Forcing him to do his own bed-making, I dumped clean linen on a wobbly armchair cowering in a corner and walked out.

While upstairs, I chose to address the temperature fluctuation in Rowan's room.

She had already made her mark, arranging her belongings on one bed and hanging outfits on a clothes rack. Two blankets lay folded on the second bed, with a third draped over the armchair. A side table held her laptop and a pile of stationery.

The room really did feel like a walk-in freezer. I pressed my hands against the timber frames of the closed windows; minor rattling proved they fit snugly into the casements. No major gaps in the flooring, even under the beds. I dragged furniture out from the walls in case I'd missed a crevice through which a draught might enter. With no luck in finding any, I pushed them back into place, the movement causing a folder on top of the side table to slip to the floor. Picking it up, I read a label stuck to the front cover:

The Greenwood Curse
(The Renouf Question)

What was that all about? The urge to examine the folder's contents was strong, but respecting Rowan's privacy, I placed it down on the table.

Additional investigating revealed a break in the wallpaper near the ceiling, below the decorative cornice. What use was a metal grate comprising small curlicue holes? An air vent? Out of easy reach, I recalled Cole mentioning a ladder in the storage cupboard.

In the hallway, I pressed timber panels near the secret linen cupboard until another door popped open. Amongst cleaning implements, I found a tall stepladder, which I took into Rowan's bedroom and unfolded near the wall. Climbing halfway up, I extended an arm and felt a cool breeze wafting in. Was it enough to chill the room? I climbed farther, catching a scratching noise drift through the vent. Mice? The last step taken, I shouldered the wall and angled my ear to better listen. A mouse—not unless it was an anthropomorphic rodent—did not produce what came next.

Hissed through the vent was one word: *Abby.*

Jerking back, my feet slipped from the rung. I scrabbled for purchase and my legs got twisted up in the ladder. Both it and I toppled sideways and crashed to the floor. I may have screamed.

Struggling to extricate myself, sounds of running preceded the door bursting open and wide-eyed faces staring into the room.

Sandy rushed over and freed me from the step ladder. 'Are you okay, luv?'

'What are you doing in my room?' squealed Rowan, inspecting her personal items.

Joe, leaning against the door frame, shook his head and grinned at me in a condescending manner, no doubt thinking how pathetic I was. In that moment I had to agree.

Flustered, I allowed Sandy to pull me to my feet. 'I was checking on the coldness in here,' I said, examining my body for injuries. None, thank God.

'And?' Rowan asked, hands on hips, eyes gauging if I was telling the truth.

I pointed to the wall vent near the ceiling. 'A breeze seems to be coming through there, but—'

'It's not a haunted room?'

Her obvious disappointment could be relieved with one mention of the unnerving whisper I'd heard, yet I bit my tongue.

Sandy wrenched open the window. 'Let some warm air in. It's a beautiful day outside.'

'Duct tape should do the trick for the vent in the short term,' Joe offered.

And he'd have plenty on hand, I guessed. Along with handcuffs, mouth gags, hoods and whatever else a sadist would use for bondage play. I regretted not rifling through his overnight bag.

My shoulder gave his elbow a glancing blow in my hurry to leave. What was the real reason for him being here?

22

ELODIE

Business-wise, 1920 is a tough year, and by August, Elodie's father has closed the failing timber mill, selling the machinery to cover costs related to the vineyard and constructing the winery. Christmas is quite a sombre affair.

As the new year dawns, Henry's desperation leads to an obsession with finding an elusive gold nugget he believes his own father had not sold after discovering it. His manic searching within the house frustrates and annoys Elodie and her mother, and when his endeavours prove fruitless, they are relieved. Still, he comes up with an alternative plan.

'Let's visit the city,' Henry announces during dinner in the first week of January.

'Surely you don't mean tomorrow,' Olivia says sharply, her cutlery clanging down on the gold-rimmed Royal Doulton dinner plate.

'I was thinking early next week. We might stay a couple of nights and reserve rooms at the Bellevue Hotel, as before.'

'Am I included this time?' Elodie asks.

'Absolutely, my little gumnut. The more the merrier.'

Olivia's face lights up. 'Are you sure we can afford it? I could do with a new hat. That lovely milliner on Queen Street did a superb job on last season's order.'

Henry strokes his beard, clears his throat. 'Remember, we ought to watch our pennies. While there, we could attend a lecture at His Majesty's Theatre.'

'A lecture?' Elodie's joy turns to dismay. 'Don't you mean a play? A concert? It's been so long since we've attended one.'

'Not at all. Sir Arthur Conan Doyle is touring Australia and New Zealand, doing the rounds of the capital cities. His next stop is Brisbane.'

Elodie and her mother share a look of disappointment. That is until Henry reminds them of the celebrated author's passion in educating the masses on his beliefs in spiritualism.

'He'll be speaking on psychic phenomena, focusing on *death and the afterlife*. Newspapers are reporting that audiences have enthusiastically received his lectures, although the churches have offered some criticism.'

Eyes widen. The women sit forward, their interest piqued.

'My good friend, Albert Hawthorne, has acquired tickets and has asked if we'd like to join his party for the Tuesday evening session. We have also been invited to dine with them the evening before.'

'Well, we'll definitely need to explore the city stores beforehand,' Olivia says. 'Perhaps you deserve a new dress, Elodie. Something *à la mode*. I hear the Hawthorne's son is easy on the eye. If you play your cards right, you may turn his head in your direction.'

Elodie groans, regretting not enlightening her parents as to the situation between herself and Will. 'Maybe I'm not interested in turning anyone's head.'

'Of course you are. The Hawthorne fellow would be a most suitable match. Consider the security in snaffling a wealthy husband.'

'Are you implying her wealth isn't already secure?' her father asks, frowning. 'She'll inherit everything when we have passed.'

'Including the debts. Make your own future, that is my advice.' Olivia reaches for Elodie's hand. 'Romantic entanglements never endure, dear. Passion hardly ever does. You should prioritise security over affection.'

Elodie's mouth gapes. Was her relationship with Will no longer a secret?

A cough from her father. 'No need to be so blunt, Olivia. Now, just to confirm, what shall I communicate to Albert? All in favour of his invitation say, *aye*.'

'Aye,' his wife says, mirroring him by raising her arm high.

Elodie gives a shrug. 'I suppose so.'

Elodie slinks from the house after dinner to meet Will at the grotto as planned. The instant she reaches the glade, a shadow becomes a man, wrapping her in an embrace.

Guided up the stone steps, Elodie enters the candlelit grotto and sits on the rug spread out on the dirt. Will kneels beside her and kisses her with an ardour the leaves her breathless. Slipping down the straps of her silk dress, his mouth moves to her bare shoulders. Elodie responds by kicking off her shoes and unfastening the mother-of-pearl clips binding her hair. It is high time Will proved the depth of his fondness for her. Lying back, she slides the hem of her dress up to her thighs, revealing legs free of stockings. Will places a hand on her knee and drifts it higher. Excitement builds. Over the course of the next half hour, he introduces Elodie to the more intimate pleasures of touch.

She returns to the house and sneaks upstairs to her room. Lighting the oil lamp, she locks the door, changes into her nightwear, and crawls into bed. If only she and Violet were still close, exchanging secrets and thoughts, as she has much to share and inquire about.

The gauze curtains shielding the open window part in a breeze and she throws off the sheet to catch the coolness. Still clammy from the heat, she shamelessly sheds her nightgown. Lamplight illuminates her sweaty nakedness, while shadows define her curves. Was Will pleased by what he'd glimpsed, what he'd caressed?

Her hand traces the path his fingers had taken, causing flesh to goosebump. The floral wallpaper comes alive beside her, pink peonies nodding their heads in time with her thudding heart as she recalls Will's admission in the cave. Shocked by his honesty, she had remained silent, but now she replies in kind.

'I want you, too,' she sighs, becoming a blossoming flower, her petals unfurling.

Elodie snaps her head around as a moan enters the room— wind gusting down the chimney. It brings with it a cloud of ash that drifts into a corner to form a fuzzy shape. A shift in the atmosphere, air thick and oppressive, indicates an otherworldly presence.

Her breath catches and she averts her gaze to the ceiling, the paint peeling like sunburnt skin, only to have a sinister chuckle strike fear into her heart. A panicked cry lodges in her throat, her tongue a frozen block in her mouth. Deadweight limbs thwart attempts to move. Not even a finger can she twitch.

What spell is she under?

Unable to squeeze her eyes shut, a face smeared like a blurred photographic image appears in her line of sight. Hovers, releasing a stench that fills her nostrils before it vanishes. A frigid breath travels over her bare skin. Razor-sharp fingernails lacerate her stomach. Screams echo in her mind when her thighs are clawed in stinging slices.

Terrified by what may follow, she wills an extraordinary strength into being and with concerted effort breaks the invisible restraints. Bolting upright, she shouts rebukes, casting the phantasm back to hell.

A knock at the door.

Her mother's muffled voice. 'Elodie! Are you all right, dear?'

The mood in the room has returned to its natural state. No lurking shadows with evil intent. Had it just been her fanciful thoughts mutating into a horrid vision?

'I'm fine,' she rasps. 'A bad dream, that's all.'

'Well, leave the light on and try to get some sleep.'

Elodie reefs up the linen sheet to cover herself and balks at the sight of scored flesh, the scrawled words on her stomach—*blood for blood*—strangely fading the longer she stares. Wary of the menace reappearing, she lies awake till morning, proposing to revive the habit of sleeping with the family Bible under her pillow.

23

———————

Eager to distance myself from the house guests—and further embarrassment—I escaped to the verandah, my fear of heights momentarily assuaged as I gripped the railing and focused on a brown goshawk circling high above the treetops. Watching the bird of prey glide effortlessly on an updraft of air in search of food, I had an urge to drift away, too. This stay in the country was proving way less calming than expected.

A raised voice blaring through the main bedroom window prompted me to step back into the shadows and press flat against the outside wall.

'When are you going to say something, Vincent?' Daphne sounded irritated.

My nostrils itched at the detection of cigarette smoke, right before a freckled, hairy arm jutted out of the open window only centimetres away from me. The large hand gripped a cigarette between thumb and index finger, smoke spiralling before the arm disappeared inside.

'Are you listening? When are you—'

'I heard you, Daph. I'm not deaf.' The hand returned, fingers flicking ash from the ciggie onto the windowsill to lie in smudges amongst black-and-white gecko poo. 'Timing is important. At any rate, we need tangible proof.'

'How do you intend to get that?'

'For pity's sake, we've only just got here. Ow!'

His hand jerked, the cigarette dropping to the verandah flooring and rolling towards my shoe. I stamped on it before it set the century-old timber alight.

'No need to poke,' Vince growled. 'Trust me.'

Muffled voices revealed they'd moved deeper into the room, making it impossible for me to catch the rest of the conversation unless I thrust my head through the window to listen.

I turned quickly at a cough and saw Joe at the far end of the verandah, observing me.

'Who are you eavesdropping on?' he called in a loud whisper.

I hurried over and pushed him around the corner, out of earshot. 'I'm not eavesdropping. Not intentionally, anyway.'

'Was that the older couple's room you were sticking your nose in?'

'I wasn't sticking anything in anywhere. I was minding my own business when they ...' When they did what? Mention something I shouldn't have overheard? 'It was just small talk. Nothing of interest.'

'You looked pretty interested.'

Time to deflect. 'How's your room? Settled in?'

'The bed will be a tight fit, but it's not like I've moved in for good. Where are you staying?'

'At the cottage. At least I was. Now Paisley insists I sleep here, in the servants' quarters. She wants me to be on site to keep an eye on things.'

'Why? Scared the guests will run off with the silverware?'

'To make sure they have a productive time.'

'Good God.' He shook his head. 'Paisley wants you to spook them, doesn't she? Has she no confidence in the ghosts to do their job? If she wants moaning and groaning echoing around the halls, I could help you with that. Just tell me where your room is and I'll pop down at midnight to lend a hand.' A sly wink accompanied his vulgarity.

'You're revolting. Anyway, the house is creepy enough without human intervention.'

'You might be correct there. This old house used to freak me out a bit.'

'You've been here before?'

'In my youth. Came here a couple of times with Fletcher during school holidays. We experienced some crazy shit, alright.'

'Such as?'

He sighed at length while kneading the back of his neck. 'The usual things—strange shadows, eerie noises, objects going missing and turning up elsewhere. Imagination runs rampant in a place such as this.'

Busted pipes and air leaks wouldn't explain what I'd seen or heard. 'How much do you know about the tragic history of Grassington? Surely Fletcher told you stories.'

'Enough to give a kid nightmares. Exaggerations, of course.'

'How can you embellish stories about a maid falling to her death and a suicidal hanging?'

Joe eyeballed me like I was a dunce who'd accidentally cracked a complex code. 'Oh, so you're aware of those. Where's the evidence they actually occurred?'

'Apparently, everyone knows about the fatal tumble down the stairs. Regarding the hanging, Cole told me.'

'Gossip, created to cause a stir.'

I had to concede he may be right. I'd found no newspaper

accounts concerning the hanging at Grassington or the maid's demise. As far as I knew, the tale of the illegitimate child was purely based on word-of-mouth. 'But there must have been a basis for each story. One doesn't just make something up out of thin air.'

'Doesn't one?' he said in a pompous, mocking tone. 'Happens all the time. That's why you must look for a motive. What would goad someone to generate a fabrication? Jealousy is always a good start ... or retribution.'

'Retribution? For what?'

His shrug led me to wonder if the divide between social classes in this region was more a chasm than a crevice.

Rowan stepped through the verandah doorway closest to us. 'Hey, can either of you help me open the door at the top of the spiral staircase? It seems to be locked, or stuck, and I want to get access to the tower and observation deck.'

'Don't look at me,' I said. 'That staircase alone is too high for me.'

Joe got to his feet. 'Well, I'm no pussy. I'll give it a go.' Taking Rowan by the elbow, he steered her inside.

Although he may not be a scaredy-cat now, his childhood experiences here likely had a lasting impact, even if he dismissed them as mere fantasies.

Drawn by voices from below, I peered cautiously over the railing and spotted two men walking the gravel path. All geared up in hiking boots, backpacks, flat caps, and binoculars, the Michaelson duo could have been setting off on a reconnaissance mission. Were they twitchers, eager to spot local species of bird life? Glancing over their shoulders, Sandy and Luke also resembled looters on the run. They only had to raise their eyes to the verandah to catch me witnessing their getaway. I watched stock-still as they stopped to refer to a sheet of paper before veering west towards the lower paddock and the ruins of the sawmill.

Since everyone was busy with their own activities, I took a walk back to the cottage. As I'd been commanded to stay at the mansion for a night or two, I needed to gather some essential items.

I let myself in and flopped onto the bed in my room, while Whitby spread out likewise on the floor mat. A brief respite before tossing a few items into my backpack and returning couldn't hurt. My gaze drifted around the room and landed on the tobacco tin brought back from the cemetery, now sitting on the bookcase shelf next to Cleo-the-cat. To whom had it belonged?

A phone call from Gemma, wanting to know about the mansion and whether I'd seen any ghosts, disturbed my fantasies. I gave her a rundown of my day and the people I'd met so far. I even mentioned the strange occurrences in the bedrooms. She wished she could join me, but working flat out as a nurse at the Shadow Creek Veterinary Clinic allowed her no time for extra days off at present. Such a shame. My excitable daughter would have been an excellent ally.

I inquired about Shane, and she reassured me her dad was doing well, seeing it had only been a few days since my departure. They'd invited him over for dinner the following evening. Lucky him. No-one would pass up a free meal concocted by Gemma's housemate/boyfriend, Benji, a gourmet chef. I promised to send her more pics and keep her informed on the goings-on of the weekend.

After ending the call, I heard Whitby barking aggressively and scratching the door leading from the kitchen into the hallway. 'What is it, boy?'

When he persisted, I set him loose to investigate the rest of the cottage, but he instantly raced into the study and sniffed the carpet.

'There's nothing here,' I said, eyeing the room and checking under the desk to be sure.

He lifted his muzzle and whined at a breeze fluttering the lace curtains. In response, I glanced out the open window yet saw no activity outside, just a vacant, silent yard.

Returning my attention to the interior, my breath caught in my throat. The toe of a grimy boot peeked out from behind the pushed-back door. I snatched a metal letter opener from the pencil caddy on the desk and wrenched the door away from the wall, only to discover my attacker was a pair of Blundstone boots with thick woollen socks stuffed inside.

I sighed with relief and looked to Whitby for advice. 'Should we search the other rooms?'

He stared, eyebrows twitching, before refocusing on the window.

This time, when I edged out, I noticed flattened plants in the garden below and a smudge of a dirty handprint on the sill. My hand hovering over the print verified that someone had made it from outside. Had this someone been perving into the room, or had they already hauled themselves in? Where were they now?

I slammed the window shut and turned, hoping the person wasn't waiting in another room, when my eyes fixed on a yellow sticky note adhered to the computer screen. *CALL ME BITCH!* was written on the note in large letters.

A message left for Paisley? Or a request from her, as in, *Call me Ishmael.* Alternatively, maybe it was an affirmation, trying to talk herself up. In that case, I could confirm she had attained her goal.

With Whitby uninterested in any other room in the cottage, I hurried him outside and around to the window.

'What can you deduce, Watson?'

My tail-wagging assistant explored the garden soil. From there, he followed a winding scent trail across the lawn to the fence and barked in the direction of the bushland opposite. My eyes roamed. The peeping Tom could be far away now, or well hidden, watching me panic.

I returned to the mansion by car—no menacing trees this time, thank God.

24

ELODIE

January 1921

The Greenwoods leave early on Monday the tenth, Elodie's father using his art of persuasion to charm Zachariah into relinquishing driving the Studebaker to him. Safely delivered to Rosewood railway station, they board the train bound for Brisbane.

Elodie nabs a window seat just as the whistle blows. Clouds of steam and coal smoke engulf the platform with a mighty hiss, and the engine pulls the train out of the station. She half-heartedly watches the passing landscape of farming properties and undulating hills. Still reeling from her nocturnal encounter days before, she reasons heightened emotions had manifested evil and anticipates the city visit will provide a much-needed distraction. However, the vividness of the horrid event convinces her otherwise. Perhaps the lecture will help her refocus.

They reach their destination and travel from Central Station by tram to the premier Bellevue Hotel, where her father books two rooms on the top level of the three-storey brick building enhanced by grand verandahs and twin roof towers. Favoured by visiting politicians because of its position opposite Parliament House, the hotel is also the popular choice of accommodation for country travellers such as themselves.

Once freshened up from the journey, the Greenwoods enjoy a light meal before taking a stroll through the vibrant city.

Elodie is awestruck by the shop fronts lining Queen and Adelaide Streets. 'So many new styles to choose from,' she says with excitement, clutching her mother's arm.

They both purchase an outfit from McDonnell & East department store, and fabric from the drapery section for future dressmaking. Meanwhile, her father buys a ready-made suit from Finney Isles and an ebony wood smoking pipe from a celebrated tobacconist.

That evening, they dine with the Hawthornes at the Gresham Hotel. Samuel, the son, isn't as boorish as Elodie expected. Tall, charming, and attentive, he encourages her to taste culinary delights that would flabbergast Maggie, including a prawn cocktail, a standing rib roast, and an upside-down pineapple cake. Her slight intoxication from more than one glass of wine puts Elodie in an affable, yet giggly, mood.

On the morning of the eleventh, Sam and Mrs Hawthorne arrive at The Bellevue soon after breakfast and take Elodie and her mother for a walk through the Botanic Gardens. Eating ice cream from a vendor, they wander through exotic displays, inhaling sweet floral scents and listening to Schubert wafting from the bandstand.

Following a short ferry cruise down the Brisbane River, lunching on sandwiches while taking in the views, they return to the hotel in a vintage hansom cab.

'Just like in the old days,' Olivia says wistfully, recalling her youth.

After an afternoon nap, the two families meet outside His Majesty's Theatre at dusk and make sure they are seated in the stalls well before the lecture's commencement. Along with multitudes of other women, Elodie flicks open her oriental folding fan and joins them in flapping to the extreme in the stifled air caused by the summer climate and body heat of over a thousand people.

She leans forward in her wooden chair as Arthur Conan Doyle appears on stage to the warm applause of a packed house. Tall—six-feet or more—and thickset, with squinty eyes and an impressive walrus moustache, he addresses the audience in a powerful voice, his rolling accent hinting at his Scottish heritage.

'I want to talk a little to you tonight to help you understand the physiology of this subject. Though worked out scientifically during the last few years, a good deal of it has not yet reached the public's comprehension because of the Great War.'

He explains he is one of thousands of mourners who turned to Spiritualism for consolation after losing loved ones during the conflict. He shares how, deeply depressed by the deaths of his son, brother, two brothers-in-law and two nephews, he found solace in the claims of spirit existence and communication between the living and the dead. Outlining the strength of evidence from his scientific research, he refers to visits from his dead son, who told him he was 'so happy'. This, including the study of forty scripts of spiritualist messages published in *The New Revelation,* left him without doubt what awaits him on the other side of the bar. Death has now lost its terror.

Sweeping her gaze around the auditorium, Elodie's every nerve buzzes with amazement. It takes all her energy to remain seated and not leap up and exclaim with frenzy the added dimension her dreaded psychic ability has exposed. Though filled to the doors with patrons, spirits also cram the theatre, the dead clinging to pillars supporting the dress circle or hovering just below the ornate ceiling like bats. Several slip through the maroon velvet stage curtain and follow Sir Arthur around as he speaks, their grey-tinged flesh and sunken eyes giving proof that life for them has ceased. Surely, she isn't the only person witnessing this, especially if genuine mediums are in attendance.

Her attention returns to Conan Doyle informing his audience that, contrary to what some clerics and church leaders espouse, his views do not suggest one needs to suspend their Christian faith to believe in spiritualism. Rather, together, they validate the truth of the afterlife, with those who have passed, having the power to return at will to speak words of assurance to the bereaved.

Elodie flinches when her mother, tears in her eyes, squeezes her hand. Her father fingers his beard, his brow wrinkled in concentration. It's easy to guess where their thoughts lie.

Henry's hunched shoulders straighten when Sir Arthur details the purpose of mediums as intermediaries between the deceased and those left to grieve. He tells how he has met many a charlatan out to fleece money from the hopeful, but also those who are genuine, quoting cases where he's been a witness and proven no trickery was involved. He professes he isn't endeavouring to convert anyone, but to show evidence and let people make up their own minds.

As he speaks to the accompaniment of around forty pictures of psychic phenomena—'spirit photographs', he calls them—the crowd shows great astonishment, with a woman across the aisle fainting and falling off her chair.

Enthusiastic cheering follows the conclusion of the ninety-minute lecture, and it is a push for the Hawthorne party to safely exit the theatre amongst the jostling mass of attendees spilling out the doors into the foyer and onto the street.

Caught up in the throng, Elodie is shoved through a doorway into a side lobby, bringing her to a maze of corridors. Disoriented, she stumbles across a group of men gathered in a circle. They turn to face her, their mouths agape as she apologises for her interruption and asks for directions to the exit.

An elderly fellow in an outdated top hat speaks up. 'You can see us?'

'Of course,' she says, agitated. 'I'm not blind.'

'I'm not talking about physical sight.' He flings open his tailed coat, revealing a starched shirt stained with a blossom of red in the centre of his chest. 'I suspect you are clairvoyant.'

Elodie smacks a hand to her mouth on realising the man has suffered a mortal injury—a stab to his heart or a gunshot wound.

She studies the others in horror. A man in a black and white Pierrot costume has vomit splattered on his white greasepainted face and amongst the layered ruff at his neck. Another donning a paper mâché donkey mask displays sliced wrists leaking blood. A third, in a silk smoking jacket, has a hole for an eye and a shattered skull. All fatalities. But why are they so corporeal and able to speak with her? The dead she has seen up till now have uttered not one word.

Confounded, her voice trembles as she states, 'Yet none of you bear the pallor of death or ghostly appearance like those presently haunting the auditorium.'

'Our deaths were of our own choosing,' the masked man pronounces in an exaggerated tone utilised by stage performers. 'A release from our troubles. Though we do not harbour revenge or wish to contact the living anymore, we share regret for the pain caused to others.'

'My poor wife had to bring up five children on her own,' the man in the smoking jacket says, his lone eye downcast.

'My old mom and dad were distraught and blamed themselves,' sighs Pierrot.

The top-hatted fellow shrugs. 'I had no family to grieve my loss. However, my business partners were forced to shoulder the burden of bankruptcy while I took the easy way out.'

The donkey man spreads his arms to indicate the group. 'It is correct that we all died here, yet we do not haunt the premises. The veil between life and death thins out at certain times, and the commotion tonight in the theatre seems to have drawn us back.' A chuckle comes from beneath the paper mâché. 'It seems we've slipped through from the afterlife for an encore of sorts.'

'And the other spirits I have seen?' Elodie asks.

'Be careful,' the top-hatted fellow warns. 'You are an anomaly. Many dead will seek you out. Unlike us, they'll come clamouring, harassing you to pass on messages to loved ones.'

'Some may even try to possess you and use you for their own wicked purpose,' says the man in the smoking jacket. 'You don't want to entertain one of those.'

'Quick, get out now,' orders Pierrot. 'The damned are desperate spirits.' He points to a corridor opposite. 'Go that way.'

Elodie offers her thanks and escapes, soon finding herself in the foyer. She rushes out the entrance and locates her mother and Mrs Hawthorne waiting on the footpath.

Her mother taps her wristwatch. 'You took your time.'

'I got lost in the crowd,' Elodie says, shaken from her encounter.

'Well, as the menfolk are off to a gentlemen's club for drinks and a meal,' Mrs Hawthorne informs, 'I shall accompany you ladies back to the Bellevue for a light supper and a quiet glass of sherry before returning to my hotel and retiring to bed.'

Maybe multiple glasses, Elodie muses, frantic to get away.

25

Paisley wasn't overly concerned when I alerted her to the possibility of an intruder at the cottage, especially after assuring her that nothing was disturbed, with no evidence of ransacking. She said the handprint was probably left by Fletcher when gardening, and I tried to convince myself that if she wasn't worried, then neither was I.

The servants' quarters resembled a prison cell—cramped, sparse, monochromatic, and claustrophobic. It even had bars on the lone window—to keep people in or out? Although the room contained only a single iron bed, it could, with some effort, hold two beds or a double bunk. A tall silky oak wardrobe, a lowboy chest of drawers, and a corner chair were the only other furniture pieces. I sat on the bed after unpacking my backpack and noticed the springs lacked bounce. At least I wouldn't be tempted to oversleep and neglect my duties.

My phone bleeped. A message from my other sister, Skye. I was stunned that she had time to think of me during the working hours of her 'all-consuming' podiatry practice.

How are you faring in the wilds, Abbs?

I'm okay. Free for a call?

Sure. Got 5 mins between appts

Quickly phoning, I filled Skye in, giving details of my stay so far and some anecdotes about the guests. I also informed her of Fletcher's mental state, which surprised her because, like me, she'd assumed he'd sustained another injury due to being a bit of a klutz.

'I trust he's getting the help he needs,' she said.

'He's working on it,' I replied, not letting on he'd recently been 'cared for' by Joe.

Before saying goodbye, I mentioned my experience on the swing on the hill, and the flashback. Quizzed about the incident, Skye said she remembered it well. Playing with our dog in the yard, she saw me fly from the equipment and crash onto the ground. She was sickened by the odd shape my arm took after breaking.

'Did I slip off by accident?'

'You don't remember? You were crying out for Paisley to stop pushing the swing so high. Then she gave a mighty shove, and you lost your grip and fell.'

She could have knocked me down with a toenail clipper. 'No way. Paisley said it was all my stupid fault.'

'Then she's a liar. I can still see the sadistic grin on her face as she pushed the swing high, as if she enjoyed scaring you.'

'How could someone do such a thing to their little sister? And why would Paisley lie about it?'

'She's jealous of you. Always has been. You replaced her as the baby in the family and received all the attention. She still craves attention, I reckon. Look, I have to go. My next patient is here. A pain in the butt with a bunion the size of a golf ball.'

Hanging up, I mulled over Skye's words. What she'd said about Paisley explained a lot. I would have loved to have asked her about the Ouija board incident. Maybe it was Paisley and not Skye who'd tricked us into believing Grandad Bill spoke to us from the grave.

Needing to change tack, I opened my laptop to hunt for information regarding deaths at Grassington Estate. Bringing up an online research portal connected to the National Library of Australia, I searched archived Australian newspapers dating back to the mid-1800s. Henry's obituary appeared, so did an article reporting on the manner of his death, the details surprising and extensive.

SHOCKING DEATH AT GRASSINGTON ESTATE

(Saturday 22nd January 1921) The police on Thursday received information from Grassington Estate, near the village of Grimm, to the effect that the body of Henry Greenwood, aged 61, owner of the estate, who had left the house early that morning, had been found that afternoon at the bottom of a disused well close to the home. Upon rising and not finding Mr Greenwood at the house, Mrs Greenwood shared her concerns with the groundskeeper, Zachariah Bright, who organised a search party from the vineyard workers employed by Mr Greenwood to scour the property. Mr Bright, on seeing a hat and shirt hanging on a pole at the old stone well, climbed down and discovered the body of Mr Greenwood in the water at the bottom. The well was 20 feet deep and contained 8 feet of water. When retrieved, a gash on Mr Greenwood's forehead was the only visible injury possibly caused when jumping into the well. A length of rope found attached to one ankle was most likely used to tie his feet together. The deceased, a prominent businessman, left behind a widow and a daughter.

An old stone well? Cole had neglected to mention that. And Henry jumping into it was devastating. What drew him to end his life? I spent some minutes dwelling on this before continuing my search.

Funeral notices surfaced for young Thomas, baby Reginald Greenwood, and Olivia, including her obituary. Yet there was no account in any newspapers of a maid's death at Grassington, nor a hanging suicide, which would surely have been newsworthy. Interestingly, I came upon an article from the Gympie Times, dated 4 April 1872, regarding Gerald's discovery of gold.

SIZABLE GOLD NUGGET UNEARTHED

A splendid lump of gold was discovered at One-mile, Gympie, on the 2nd day of June by Mr Gerald Greenwood, who arrived from New South Wales to the area barely four months prior. The nugget weight after melting was 30.43 ounces. Valued by the Bank of England at £100, it was reputed to have been sold within days of its discovery.

100 pounds for a nugget weighing—I looked it up—around 865 grams would have been a decent sum back then. Had it aided Gerald in purchasing land close to Grimm and building Grassington?

I chanced on another article, dated August 1920, which mentioned Henry's closure of the timber mill and the sale of mill fittings and machinery. Financial strife? Could that be why he suicided?

I hunted for anything related to Elodie Greenwood, obtaining the dates of her birth and death, and her marriage to Samuel Hawthorne in 1925.

Bogged down in my investigation, I decided to offer help in the kitchen. To keep me occupied while Paisley and Cole prepared the three-course meal, they instructed me to set the table for dinner.

I spread a damask tablecloth, and added monogrammed silverware, crystal glasses, and antique cruet sets before completing the table setting with two elegant silver candelabras, and a fresh flower arrangement as a centrepiece. I sent a photo of my effort to Gemma and Benji, knowing they'd be impressed.

As an afterthought, I discreetly positioned a Bluetooth speaker of Paisley's behind a potted peace lily to play a compilation of vintage songs prepared on my phone for background dinner music.

Showering in the downstairs bathroom adjoining the servants' quarters, I did my makeup and hair and changed into a thrift shop-acquired outfit of a little black velvet dress with matching slingback shoes. I took a sexy pouting selfie of me hugging the newel post of the timber staircase and sent it to Gemma and Shane for a laugh. Was he missing me yet?

26

ELODIE

11 January 1921

Still overwrought from the lecture and subsequent incident, Elodie takes in the city lights from the hotel verandah while her mother turns in for the night. A disturbance at the far end draws her focus: a woman consoling a resisting child. Their strong accents identify them as British citizens.

'Billy, dear, I'll allow you fifteen minutes, then you simply must try again. We have another big day ahead of us. We may even venture out to visit an aviary. You like birds, don't you?'

'Hello,' Elodie says, moving over to the mother and child. 'Have you seen a cockatoo yet? They are splendid.' She grins down at the girl, around eight years of age, her eyes large behind thick-rimmed spectacles.

The girl's teeth protrude as she smiles and nods. 'I've seen a white one with a fluffy crest, and a pink and grey one.'

'A galah,' Elodie informs. 'The pink and grey ones are called galahs.'

'They're very noisy. And big.'

'They certainly are. We also have magnificent black cockatoos with yellow tails. If you spot a flock of them, it may be a signal of approaching rain.'

The girl glances up at the woman. 'May I try to draw one before I go to sleep?'

'Yes, darling.' Her mother enfolds her in a hug and watches as she rushes into their room through a French door. She turns to Elodie. 'Thank you. Billy ... that's our nickname for little Jean ... has had trouble sleeping. Not so her two brothers, typical boys, dropping off as soon as their heads hit their pillows. It's the heat, you see. It either exhausts or keeps one awake perspiring. We are not used to the tropics.'

Elodie chuckles. 'I've lived in Queensland my whole life and still have difficulty with our summers. Are you staying in Brisbane long?'

'A day or two more. We return to Sydney briefly before sailing to Adelaide and Western Australia. Then on to Ceylon and beyond.'

'Oh my, quite the pleasure voyage.'

'Mostly business, I'm afraid. Not that I'm complaining, it has been rather wondrous. We've already visited Melbourne, Sydney, and New Zealand. Have you heard of Sir Arthur Conan Doyle's lectures on Spiritualism?'

'Of course. My parents and I attended the lecture this evening. Eye-opening, for sure.'

'Well, Sir Arthur is my husband.'

Elodie clutches her face, embarrassed she hasn't recognised the short, round woman who has appeared alongside her husband in newspaper photographs. Blames her failure of recognition on the darkness, and the woman's casual attire. 'Oh, I'm so sorry, Lady Conan Doyle, I should have known.'

'I don't stand out in a crowd like your vivacious Nellie Melba.' Her warm smile is non-patronising. 'Please call me Jean.'

'I'm Elodie ... Greenwood.' She holds out her hand.

Jean's tender handshake becomes a firm grip. 'I sense an affinity. Are you also a medium?'

'No. But I see the dead, on occasions.'

'Magnificent,' Jean says, applauding. 'I am an automatic writer. I receive messages from the spirit world.'

'Truly? And what does that entail?'

'Well, I don't enter a trance as others do. I sit at a table with paper before me, pencil in hand. At the top of the paper, I make the mark of the cross. Arthur offers a prayer, and we wait until I feel the desire to write. I'm unconscious of what I'm writing, yet I know it is a direct communication from beyond the grave.'

Elodie's heart flutters. 'How fascinating.'

'Despite it being a gift, at times it is more of an affliction. Both a blessing and a curse.'

'I know what you mean. Most times, the spirits do not communicate with me. They are just visible, yet harmless. But I have been visited by pure evil on occasion.'

Jean studies her with a penetrating gaze. 'Was the wicked entity anyone you were familiar with? A relative? An acquaintance?'

Elodie shakes her head. 'I couldn't see it properly, yet its presence was ... powerful.'

'You must protect yourself,' Jean murmurs. 'Prayer. Obedience. Virtue. Don't give Satan a foothold.'

A call through the French doors. 'Mam. Can you tuck me in?'

'Please, go to your daughter,' Elodie urges. 'And thank you for your advice.'

Jean stretches up and gives Elodie's cheek a quick peck. 'Be strong, young lady. You are blessed. Therefore, use your gift for good. But prepare yourself mentally and physically lest you be dashed against the rocks.'

Wishing Lady Conan Doyle safe travels, Elodie tiptoes to her room, emboldened with a fresh purpose.

On the return train trip the following day, Henry notifies his wife and daughter of his plan to arrange a seance at Grassington in the near future. 'Sir Arthur gave me the name of a reputable medium for me to contact.'

'You spoke with Arthur Conan Doyle?' Elodie says with surprise. 'When did this happen?'

'Last night. I bumped into him after the lecture at the club. We had a brief chat, and he recommended Madam Maud Montague, one of the top mediums around town. I'm hoping she will accept an invitation to visit Grassington.'

Her mother gives a look of repugnance. 'For what reason?'

'Maybe she can contact my father and ascertain where he hid the gold nugget.'

'For heaven's sake, Henry, why do you not believe Gerald sold it all to purchase the property and build the mansion?'

'Because it's easier to believe he hid it out of spite to exasperate me. As you know, he was quite a malicious old rascal.'

'Who went senile in the end.' Olivia releases an extended sigh. 'That wretched nugget will be the death of you.'

Elodie groans, finding the conversation tedious. 'Maybe he stashed it away to ensure you built your personal wealth solely through your own efforts.'

'And so I have. Though circumstances aren't in my favour at present and I ... *we* ... could do with extra funds to set us right.'

Her mother rolls her eyes in frustration. 'I'd rather the medium contact Tommy. I'd do anything to hear from our dear boy and find out if he's happy, like Sir Arthur's son.'

27

***

One by one, people arrived for dinner. The O'Maras and Rowan were seated on one side of the dining table with the Michaelsons and Joe opposite, while Paisley assumed the role of host at the head. Fletcher's absence was notable in the vacant chair at the far end. Still, my sister abstained from commenting on his non-attendance and launched into a formal welcome, saying how she expected the guests' weekend stay at Grassington would be a memorable one. A stern nod to Cole and me standing dutifully at a distance sent us scurrying off to return with the entrees.

Pleasant chatter accompanied the meal. What I gleaned from conversations was that Vince was a solicitor of distinction, Daphne taught English and music at a private girls' school, Rowan helped run a podcast entitled *The Tell-Tale Heart*, and the Michaelson's were avid metal detectorists in their spare time.

Fascinated by their divulgences, I was also struck by anomalies. Luke—as reed-thin as he was—gulped down food like it was in short supply, while Daphne, more on the pudgy side, picked at her specially made vegan meal. Rowan, wearing a figure-hugging satin outfit with a revealing neckline worthy of a red-carpet appearance, blushed whenever attention turned her way. And Joe, failing to mention he was no longer on the force, entertained with jaw-dropping details of gruesome crimes he'd investigated. Even Paisley, appearing carefree, strangled the life out of the linen napkin in her lap.

I could not be excluded. Patiently waiting for her next command, I dreaded Paisley's gruff request. The combined escalation of her demands, odd experiences, and the trauma of the previous week in Shadow Creek—which I hadn't yet resolved—had me teetering on mental distress. Time would tell.

Besides noting falsehoods, I kept a sharp eye on Joe and Paisley, lest they dropped their guard and disclosed their true attitude towards one another. Inconceivable as it was, I had to consider the possibility of them having an affair. Why else would Joe unexpectedly appear—to the joy of my sister—neglecting Fletcher? Where did his loyalties really lie?

I 'accidentally' knocked naan bread off the tray I held. When it landed on the floor, I nudged it under the table with a nimble kick and used the excuse of retrieving it to see if Joe and Paisley were playing footsie. Both pairs of feet looked to be behaving themselves. Not so Luke's right elastic-sided boot, which seemed dangerously close to one of Rowan's black sequinned shoes. I put it down to his long legs just fighting for space.

The guests being engrossed in the main course, enabled me to sneak to the kitchen and plate up my own meal. Cole did the same.

'Awesome!' he said, dipping bread into his serving of Beef Rendang. 'Thought I was going to keel over from hunger watching that lot get stuck into their food.'

'Me too. I reckon we should have eaten beforehand. Would

have made our job easier. Here, try this.' I added a good dollop of lentil and vegetable korma to his bowl. 'It's sublime. Hey, do you know how I can contact that Darius fellow, the *ex-gardener*?'

He spoke through a mouthful. 'Why would you want to do that?'

'I need to speak with him. I doubt Fletcher can manage the grounds alone, especially now. However, that's not why I wanted to talk to the gardener again.'

'Again?' Cole squinted and wiped his mouth with his sleeve. 'You've met him?'

'I talked with him in the rose garden. He said he pops in from time to time to monitor things. So, where can I find him?'

'Well, if you're that keen, he's at the pub in Grimm most days. His chosen hangout since he's jobless.'

'Talking about Grimm, what's with the Yowie statue? A relative of yours?' I teased.

'Looks more like you.' A snigger. 'A pioneer explorer back in the old days was reported to have seen one hanging around. There have actually been a few recent sightings.'

'You're kidding.'

'Nope. There's some footage on YouTube. Not real clear. Could be a guy dressed in a gorilla suit.'

I said I'd check it out sometime.

Paisley disrupted us by poking her head into the kitchen. 'Any Rendang left? People are asking for seconds.'

Cole and I peeked into the large pot we'd just scraped the bottom of and shook our heads.

'In that case, bring in more bread. That'll have to do before dessert.'

• • •

We delivered extra naan to the dining room. Refilling Vince's wine glass with a top-shelf Shiraz, I pricked my ears to the crunch of gravel from the drive outside. A deep throb of a car engine caused everyone at the table to cease talking.

Paisley shot out of her chair and stood at the bay window, peering through the aged glass. 'Someone's arrived in a snazzy red sports car.'

Luke wasted no time in rushing over to view with her. 'That's a Ford Mustang,' he exclaimed, 'Who do you know has the letters *S-P-K-G-R-L* as a personalised rego plate?'

'Oh ...' Paisley cooed with delight. 'It seems our last guest has arrived a day early.' She turned to face our puzzled looks. 'Spook Girl.' Then she scooted from the room.

Chairs scraped on floorboards, and the rest of us moved as a mob into the foyer. Like a flood of ectoplasm, we oozed onto the porch just as the driver's door of the slick red beast flew open and a slender leg encased in black Lycra and a dark military boot appeared. Hilary Bloodworth slid out and stretched to her full height, the silver buckles on her leather corset gleaming alongside her multi-studded earrings as she shook her midnight-black hair.

A collective sigh echoed around me. This wasn't a dowdy elderly woman in costume jewellery and a kaftan; she was a statuesque seductress. I scanned our group. All seemed similarly transfixed. Were they also thinking this steampunk vision could have easily stepped from a superhero movie?

A husky voice broke the spell. 'Good evening, all.' Her scarlet lips parted to expose a flash of blinding white teeth. 'You, gym-junky, be a dear and collect my bags from the car boot.'

Heads swivelled as one, following her gaze to the end of our line-up.

Joe Teo, now perched on the bottom step, gave her a death stare. 'You talking to me?'

She arched a sculptured eyebrow. 'Yes, muscle man, unless that's just padding stretching your shirt sleeves.'

His hands balled into fists yet remained at his sides. 'So, you're Hilary Bloodworth, the ghost hunter.'

'I prefer *paranormal expert extraordinaire*,' she announced, thrusting out an impressive décolletage.

Joe laughed dryly. '*Faker*, more like it.'

She cupped a hand to her ear. 'I beg your pardon?'

'I know your sort, fooling gullible folk into believing what they want so you can make the big bucks. You're just a show pony.'

She sashayed forward, boot heels pulverising gravel. 'And you are?'

He waited until she was at arm's length before answering. 'Joseph Teo. *Detective* Joseph Teo.'

I drew in a breath. His introduction failed to add 'former' to his job title. He was sparring, that's for sure.

'Hmm ...' She tapped her chin with a blood-red fingernail. 'I met a Teo once. George Teo. He spoke to me from the afterlife during a lively seance back in 2015. An obnoxious trade unionist who met his fate at the bottom of the Brisbane River in the '60s after stepping on too many toes.' Her augmented height allowed her to come eye level with Joe. 'A relative of yours, by any chance?'

He scowled and pointed V-sign fingers to his own eyes and then at her. 'I'll be watching you.'

'I don't doubt that for a second,' she said with a wink. Nodding at Luke, his mouth gaping, she ordered, 'You, honey, fetch my bags.'

Luke scampered over to the car while Joe grunted in obvious disgust.

I hid a smile behind my hand. The weekend had soared to a whole new level of interesting.

28

———————

Hilary Bloodworth made a beeline for the vacant seat at the end of the dining table, her leather outfit creaking with every jaunty step. Treating her with the protocol of a visiting dignitary, all waited for Hilary to sit before seating themselves.

'Sorry I've landed on you like this. My plans fell through for the evening, so I thought I'd arrive early. You don't mind, do you?'

'Of course not,' Paisley gushed, starstruck. 'Your room is ready and waiting. Have you eaten? We can prepare a plate.'

'No, I'm good,' Hilary said. 'I stopped at a roadhouse along the way for a quick bite.'

'Oh ... you did?' Paisley didn't even try to hide her abhorrence that someone would choose to eat at such an establishment. 'We're about to serve dessert. An exquisite chocolate lava cake, or a frangipane tart if you're averse to dairy.'

'Either would be lovely.' She snatched up Daphne's unused wine glass. 'A splash of bubbly wouldn't go astray.'

A nod of command from Paisley and I obliged, pouring Hilary

a generous measure of Prosecco before following Cole to the kitchen to plate up the dessert.

'Don't you just love her outfit,' he raved. 'It's to die for.'

I laughed. 'At least if you did die, you could make contact through her.'

We returned with trays loaded to find Hilary in conversation about her profession.

'I absolutely love it. Investigating paranormal activity is the best.'

'And dangerous?' Rowan asked.

'Sometimes. Especially if you contact a vindictive spirit. Gotta know what you're doing with one of those. It's like wrangling a tiger.' She gave a purring growl.

'Are there many types of spirits?' Daphne enquired, taking the frangipane tart that I offered her and giving it a sniff. Did she not trust Paisley to respect her requirements?

'There certainly are.' Hilary leant forward on her elbows, eyes sparkling with the enthusiasm of unleashing knowledge. 'First—'

'Excuse me.' Rowan produced her phone and placed it on the table. 'Do you mind if I record your explanations for my podcast?'

A wide smile. 'Not at all. I'll make sure I speak clearly. Now, first, there's what we call an *interactive personality*. This is the most common of all spirits. Usually, a deceased person known to you—a family member, or even a famous figure. Friendly or not, they reveal themselves in a variety of ways, visibly or audibly. They can touch you or emit an odour, such as perfume or cigar smoke, to make their presence known. This category of ghost retains its former personality and often visits to comfort or inform you of something important. Chances are, if you encounter a deceased loved one, it's because you need to see them.'

Hilary took a break from talking so she could gulp down her wine. She licked her lips. 'Have you ever seen a swirling mist or fog?' A few heads nodded. 'Then you may have witnessed an ectoplasm or ecto-mist.'

Luke spoke through a mouthful of lava cake. 'Like in *Ghostbusters*? *He slimed me!*'

'Not quite. This vapour cloud often appears several metres off the ground and can move swiftly or stay perfectly still, as if it's orbiting. They can appear white, grey, or black in videos and photographs. Sometimes ectoplasms appear before becoming a full-bodied apparition. Outdoor sightings include places such as graveyards, battlefields, and historical sites.

'Then there's the poltergeist, which means *noisy ghost,* because it can move or knock things over, make sounds, and manipulate the physical environment. It's actually one of the rarest forms of hauntings, and to many, the most terrifying. Starting softly with scratching noises and gentle tapping, the sound, over time, builds to loud knocking, lights turning on and off, and doors slamming. Fires breaking out mysteriously are attributed to this type of spiritual disturbance. While much poltergeist behaviour is harmless and ends quickly, it can become dangerous. Experts say it is a mass form of energy that a living person controls unknowingly.'

Vince coughed, possibly to draw attention, or show his scepticism. 'How could someone do that?'

'*Why* would someone do that?' Sandy added.

Hilary flashed a smile, obviously unruffled by these questions. 'A poltergeist focuses on and around specific person. Documented cases have occurred when someone was under attack or in a high-stress scenario, like during a divorce.'

I shot a look at Paisley, catching her eye before she staged flicking crumbs from the tablecloth in front of her. I considered the poltergeist that visited us in the holiday house. Though Paisley hadn't believed a ghost had come-a-calling, she'd mentioned

Mum had difficulty controlling her temper back then. What if Mum's angst had conjured up a violent spirit, a poltergeist?

'I'm sure you've all heard of orbs,' Hilary continued. 'These transparent balls of light hovering over the ground or in the air are the most photographed peculiarities. Many believe an orb is the spirit of a deceased human or animal moving between places. They can move at speed, so if you get to photograph one, you are very fortunate.'

'Ahem,' interrupted Joe. 'Photographed orbs are just reflected dust particles or lens flares. Simple explanation.'

Hilary ignored him and pressed on. 'Now we come to the funnel ghost, which is typically sighted in homes or old buildings. Also known as a vortex, it is frequently associated with a cold spot. The general consensus is that they are either a loved one returning for a visit, or a former resident of the home. They appear as a wisp or spiral of light in photographs or on video.'

My skin prickled. I wondered if I should be more mindful about taking photos inside the mansion.

'And that about covers them all,' Hilary said, her leather clothing squeaking as she altered her position on the chair and held up her glass.

Getting the hint, I rushed over to refill it with more wine.

With the exclusion of Joe—arms crossed, scowling—the guests seemed enthralled with their newly gained knowledge of spirits. Though Paisley's grin, I suspected, was brought on by the excitement of capitalising on people's exaggerated interest.

'I guess we'll all be keeping a lookout for ghosts, won't we?' she said, getting to her feet. 'Coffee anyone, or a fortified wine? A tawny? Let's adjourn to the drawing room.'

29

Cole and I stacked the commercial dishwasher in the scullery, and tidied bench tops in readiness for breakfast preparation the following morning. Almost finished, Paisley entered, highly pleased.

'The group seems talkative, and Daphne's commandeered the piano. I don't think we need any parlour games.'

I dropped my lower lip, showing false disappointment. 'What, no Truth or Dare? I suspect several people are hiding secrets close to their chest tonight.'

My assertion must have hit a mark, for Paisley exited in a rush just as 'Getting to Know You' from *The King and I* filtered in from the sitting room.

'They could have at least given Strip Poker a go,' Cole said, a glimmer in his eyes.

A game I wouldn't want to witness with that lot. 'Quick, let's clock off for the night before Paisley finds more jobs for us. Are we allowed to join the guests in the drawing room, do you think?'

'You can. I have stuff to do.'

'Like what?'

He gave a sly smile as he untied his apron and hung it on a wall hook. Was a hot date on the cards? I hoped for his sake there was.

After hanging my apron next to Cole's, I went to cash in on the fun with the others when I was grasped and pinned against the panelling of the main staircase.

Dressed in wide-leg purple silk pyjamas and a crossover top with padded shoulders, Bridget looked to have raided a chest of vintage clothing from the 1930s. A distinct odour of naphthalene evoked a childhood memory of hiding in a blanket box belonging to my grandmother. Bridget glowered at me, her wrinkles seeming deeper in the dim hall light.

Had no-one delivered her a meal again? I could rustle up a sandwich or make two-minute noodles if she was hungry.

'Have you talked with the gardener?' she implored. 'I need to see him. I *have* to see him.'

'Not yet. I've been rather occupied. I'll try to find him tomorrow, okay? Arrange a time for you two to meet up.'

Her hold of my shoulders eased before she locked me in a bone-crushing hug. 'Thank you, Abby.' The embrace and strength of it were a surprise, yet I was more shocked that she'd remembered my name. 'Are they all in there?' She nodded towards the noise-filled room, the chatter interspersed with a tune I couldn't quite put my finger on being thumped out on the piano.

'The guests? I reckon so.'

She gave an enormous sigh. Before I could ask if she'd eaten, Bridget swung around, her fluffy mule slippers click-clacking as she climbed the stairs to the floor above.

The music built to the chorus. Ahh ... the theme song from *The Phantom of the Opera*.

. . .

Unnoticed, I sidled into the drawing room and settled into a club chair positioned against the wall, alongside a large Tree of Life tapestry. Piano music made it difficult to follow the drone of talk until Vince's resonant tone rose above the mishmash of noise.

'What's the story behind the three ghosts?' he said from his position near the fireplace. His elbow rested on the black marble mantle, a cut-glass whiskey tumbler in his hand.

Daphne stopped playing and rotated on the piano stool. 'Firstly, who *were* the three ghosts?'

Everyone looked at my sister, manning the drinks trolley. She went to answer but was cut off by Hilary sitting on a chesterfield sofa and thrusting her hand up like a traffic cop.

'No! Don't tell them, Paisley. Let the house do that.'

Sandy, seated on her right, edged closer. While Rowan, on her left, clutched the small vintage-style compass pendant hanging from a silver chain around her neck and asked, 'What do you mean, Hilary?'

Joe nodded in support from his position next to Luke on the opposite sofa. 'Yeah, unpack that for us, will you?'

'Certainly.' Hilary leant forward to retrieve a small glass of fortified wine from the coffee table between the sofas, her leather corset straining noisily. 'Rule one in paranormal investigation: Never assume myths and legends are true accounts. Leave it to the location or the spirits to reveal what actually happened.'

My voice croaked as I spoke up. 'How the hell can they do that?'

Surprised faces turned in my direction, astonished by my presence in the room. Joe, on the other hand, looked amused by my frankness.

Hilary pointed a finger, as if acknowledging my bid on a precious work of art. 'Abby, is it? To start with, you get a cold reading by using your body. Walk around to sense the environment, paying attention to unexpected noises, temperature variations, shifting shadows, feelings of fear, and chilly sensations. These are potential indications of unseen spirits. Let your physical self guide your investigation. Later, you can question the spirits.'

'And ask them what?' Joe jeered. 'Why do they open doors when they can walk through walls?'

Hilary's glare would have snap-frozen a steaming meat pie. She turned her gaze back to the rest of the group. 'Simple yes-and-no questions at first. The answers can come in the form of lights flickering or dimming, strange sounds such as tapping, banging, and scraping. At times, you may hear actual voices, though they are best picked up by electronic voice recorders, or tuning a radio to a static station.

'Another simple method is to use an old-fashioned compass to find changes in magnetic fields.' She pointed at Rowan's necklace. 'Sudden movement and quivering of the needle, or a more dramatic spinning motion, can indicate the presence of the paranormal.'

All eyes focused on the compass pendant nestled between Rowan's breasts. Her skin flushed, and she quickly covered her cleavage.

'I've brought along several high-tech devices we can use later to contact spirits.' Hilary indicated a black leather suitcase just inside the room near the doorway to the foyer. 'Let's postpone that until tomorrow night so I can arrange everything.'

A tingle of excitement. What wondrous tools did the case contain for contacting the dead? Joe, shaking his head and grumbling under his breath, looked to be thinking otherwise— *Hogwash! It's all trickery.*

'Can we do something now?' Paisley asked Hilary. 'A little basic reading?'

What was my sister up to? Did she suspect this would lead people to create their own spooky experience?

'Of course. If people are willing.'

Guests eyed each other before agreeing. I even gave my consent. With any luck, I'd be relieved of my duty of bringing the group's notice to eerie sights and sounds.

'Okay.' Hilary clapped her hands. 'Let's begin.'

We followed her into the foyer, jostling as we vied for a position closest to our guide.

'Please gather around. Before we commence, I like to address the spirits as a show of respect.' Not waiting for a response, she launched into a benediction. 'To the earth and those who lie beneath. To the paths we are about to walk and to those who tread them before us. To the home we will enter and to whom it once housed. To the rooms and their echoes. Know we come in blessing and wish you only peace.'

Daphne said 'Amen' and got elbowed in the ribs by her husband. 'Sorry, I couldn't help it.'

Hilary cleared her throat. 'As you stroll through the rooms, be alert to your senses. Take note of any feelings, noises, smells, and disturbances. Thirty minutes should do. Then we'll report back to the drawing room to debrief.'

'I have a dinner gong I can beat to denote when the time is up,' Paisley offered.

'Brilliant. At the sound of the gong, we return. Now spread out, no need to move around in a large, rowdy clump.'

30

ELODIE

20 January 1921

Madam Montague arrives a week after the Greenwood's return from Brisbane. Collected from the train station by Zachariah, she is brought to Grassington for an overnight stay.

Elodie's apprehension delays her joining her parents waiting at the front portico, choosing to stay upstairs until summoned. Yet, her anxiety vanishes the moment she meets the short, stout woman in her sixties, resembling a sweet grandmother rather than an eccentric spirit medium.

Madam Montague's small eyes disappear as she smiles. 'You must be the daughter. What a lovely young woman you are.' A pat of Elodie's cheek. 'An exquisite rosebud.'

The woman drops her carpetbag with a gleeful yelp and circuits the foyer, her arms outstretched, fingers wriggling in the air.

'Wonderful. A treasure trove of stimuli. I sense a powerful presence here—defiant. Also ...' The tapping of her heels on the terrazzo tiles ceases as she shifts her attention to Henry and Olivia. 'Loss. And great misery.'

Elodie's mother gasps, while her father frowns. He escorts Madam Montague into the drawing room where refreshments are laid out on the sideboard.

Elodie pours a glass of iced tea and perches on the armrest of the sofa, her gaze falling in turn on the spirit medium, the sunlit room, pulsing shadows. No trace of malevolence brings relief, her rebuke that horrid night in her bedroom successfully ridding the house of sheer evil.

'So, you'd like to get in touch with someone dear to you?' Madam Montague asks Henry between sips of her lime and grape juice.

He sucks in a lip. 'Not sure I'd use that terminology, but yes, I hope to contact my father and clarify certain matters he failed to answer when alive.'

'I see. And you, Olivia? Is there a person you'd like to hear from?'

'My little boy, Tommy. I am desperate, Madam Montague, to know if—'

She shoots up a hand. 'Shush. I don't wish to have any prior knowledge. Cold readings are my preference. Let the spirits do all the work. And please, everyone, call me Maud.'

Elodie's respect for the woman grows. Even the shadows have shrunk back into the corners. She answers Maud's questioning look. 'Sorry, I have no desire to communicate with the dead.' If she were brave, she'd plead with her to seek out the No Face Man and demand he confess his identity, explain his hounding of her. 'Though my ... friend ... Will, yearns to hear from his deceased mother.'

'You've invited Will Flanagan to the seance?' her mother retorts.

'Dad gave permission for him to join us.'

'But he's just a—'

'Valued worker and friend of Elodie's.' Henry winks at his daughter. 'Though I guess he is becoming more than a friend who, like us, has lost a family member. Why wouldn't we allow the young chap the opportunity to make contact? Class does not exclude involvement, Olivia. You've invited Maggie to take part, haven't you?'

'She's been with us for such a long time, she's like one of the family.'

Henry's moustache flutters as he releases a puff of air through his lips in exasperation.

Maud breaks the tension by coughing into her handkerchief. 'For anyone wanting to get in touch with a deceased person, an object linked to them can facilitate communication with the correct spirit.'

Elodie wonders if Will has anything to offer, being motherless since birth.

After Maud takes a catnap in the green room and shares an early dinner of cold cuts and seasonal vegetables, she chooses the private dining room beside the office in which to hold the seance. Curtains are drawn and the soft glow of candles replaces the electric lighting.

Six chairs encircle the round table, with Henry and Olivia sitting either side of Maud. Two seats, one on Elodie's right and another on her left, remain empty until Will appears dressed in clean shirt and trousers, his hair slicked back from a freshly shaven face.

Elodie's pulse quickens. Since the visit to Brisbane, she has kept their contact to a minimum, meeting only in public as a safeguard against igniting desire and stirring up evil. Still, it hasn't stopped her from conjuring the thrill of her experience in the grotto. *Prayer, obedience, virtue*, that's what Jean Conan Doyle had instructed.

Will sits between her and her father, who offers him a welcoming smile before introducing the young man to Madam Montague.

'Glad to have you on board,' the woman says.

The shake of Olivia's head doesn't go unnoticed by Elodie. *Snob* she mumbles under her breath. If only her mother approved of their match.

Moments go by in silence, though Will's jiggling leg hints at a restlessness that Elodie finds contagious, crossing and uncrossing her ankles in response.

'And when might Maggie be joining us?' Henry says, indicating the vacant chair.

The answer comes in the sound of hurried footsteps. The group's focus transfers to the doorway in time to catch Violet entering at a rush, her face flushed from the effort.

'My mother passes on her apologies. She's feeling pretty crook at present and asked me to take her place ... that is, if me being a stand in is acceptable, Mr Greenwood.'

'Of course, dear,' he says tenderly.

Olivia beckons her over. 'Sorry to hear your mother is unwell. She seemed to be fine at dinnertime. Hopefully, she'll be much better by morning.'

Violet sits between her and Elodie. Her eyes find the guest medium. 'You haven't started, have you? I'd hate to have missed anything.'

Maud assures Violet she has arrived just in time.

Elodie is relieved her friend is back to her more pleasant self, the bitterness of jealousy seeming to be no longer an issue. She puts it down to Violet capturing the new cooper's attention, a jovial young Irishman with a ribald sense of humour, not averse to flirting. The pink bruise on Violet's neck she's neglected to conceal fully with face powder is proof she's recovered from her obsession with Will.

'Let's begin,' Madam Maud says. 'First, to maintain the circle's shared energy, please place your hands on the table with your little fingers touching your neighbour's.'

A spark of electricity courses through Elodie's left finger as it connects with Will's right one. She banishes an impure thought and stretches her other hand towards Violet's, finding her friend's fingers are trembling. Their eyes meet in a sideways glance. Is she anxious about the evening's event? Fearful of what may happen?

'Secondly,' Maud instructs, 'I want you to clear your mind. Think nothing other than being present. Close your eyes and focus only on your breathing. Inhale ... exhale. And again.'

A whiff of Will's pomade tickles Elodie's nostrils, igniting an intimate scene—her face buried in his hair while his mouth explores the contents of her satin bandeau brassiere.

'Ease the beating of your heart,' Maud interrupts, as if reading her mind. 'Let it slow to a gentle pulse.'

Elodie sighs and attempts to refocus her concentration.

'Imagine those you wish to speak with standing beyond a thin veil, imploring you to sweep it aside and break the separation between worlds.'

A creak of a chair as someone nervously shifts weight in their seat.

'Come, spirits,' Maud says. 'Do not fear, you are welcome here. Make yourself known.'

Elodie gives a one-eyed peek, her breath catching when she spies unfamiliar mist-like entities easing out of the shadows, one circling the table as in a game of drop the handkerchief. Where will it stop?

'You may open your eyes. Now that the doorway to the afterlife is open, let's try to make contact. Who wishes to go first?'

Olivia answers eagerly. 'Me. I don't think I can wait any longer.'

'Have you brought along an item?'

She rummages within a skirt pocket and produces a toy train engine made of lead. 'It was a favourite of my son's.'

Maud rolls it to the centre of the table. 'To start with, we will pose simple yes/no questions.' Lifting her arms, she addresses the spirits in a loud voice. 'Knock once for yes, two for no.' She nods towards Olivia.

Olivia scans the room. 'Tommy, dear boy, are you here?' At first, nothing. Then a scraping noise. Her eyes double in size. 'Was that a knock?'

'Repeat your question,' Maud instructs.

Olivia does as told, yet Elodie fails to recognise her brother amongst the clutch of translucent figures.

A single knock comes from beneath the table. Various things could have caused that: a shoe tapping on the floor, knuckles rapping on the underside. Sceptical of the incident, Elodie notes Maud's hands are not in plain sight.

'Tommy! It's me, Mumma. Are you happy in heaven? Please tell me you are?'

Another rap, louder.

'Thank God,' Olivia sobs. 'I love you, my sweet boy. I miss you so very much.'

'We both miss you,' Henry says in a booming voice.

Olivia wipes glistening tears from her cheeks. 'I should have looked after you better. I regret letting you get so sick. Do you blame me for your ... passing?'

Two raps.

More sobbing from Olivia.

Doubting that the sounds were genuine, Elodie leans sideways and peers under the table. To her astonishment, Tommy is sitting cross-legged on the floor. Sad eyes lock onto hers and she shudders. Had he lied to ease their parents' pain?

She straightens and finds Violet observing her intensely. When younger, Elodie had confided in her about the sightings of Tommy, which Violet had regarded as harrowing. Now, as Elodie nods strongly in response to her silent question, Violet quickly tucks her legs under her chair, away from the ghost boy.

'My turn,' Henry announces, removing a smoker's pipe from his waistcoat and laying it on the table. 'This was my father's.'

'Well,' Maud says, 'ask away.'

Henry clears his throat and adjusts his tie, as if a ghost would care how smart he looked. 'Gerald Greenwood, are you here? This is your son asking.'

Leaves beating against the window glass in a stiff breeze outside, followed by the screech of a barn owl break an air of expectation.

'Are you here, Father, in the house you built?'

Everyone jerks when the clock in the hall starts to strike eight o'clock.

'Let's try something else,' Maud says at the chime's conclusion. She produces a sheet of paper and a lead pencil taken from the carpet bag near her feet. 'Has anyone heard of automatic writing?'

'I have,' Elodie says. 'Lady Conan Doyle has such a gift.'

'If your father wishes to contact you, Henry, he can do so by using me as a medium to write down his messages.' Gripping the pencil and hovering it over the paper, Maud sits ramrod straight and closes her eyes. 'Are you with us, Gerald?'

The group eases forward in their seats for a better view.

Sudden movement. Maud jots down a word and stops.

Henry leans over and reads it aloud. '*Yes.*' He clasps his hands together. 'Excellent! Will you address my concerns, Father?'

Another *Yes.*

Elodie scowls. How could a person prove Maud was fraudulent? Asking a question that she couldn't possibly know the answer to would be a good start.

Her father's impatience comes to the rescue. 'Let's cut to the chase. What did you do with the gold nugget?'

Hesitation. Then a scrawled *Grassington.*

'I'm aware you bought the land and built the house with funds gained from your discovery. But you didn't receive payment for all the gold. I know you kept a portion of the nugget. Where did you hide it?'

The pencil drops and rolls off the table.

Henry retrieves it and returns it to Maud. He smacks his hand on the tabletop. 'Where's the gold, you old fool? You didn't see fit to tell me when you were alive, so you'd better tell me now or I'll burn the ruddy place down!'

'Oh, Henry,' Olivia sighs, 'you wouldn't.'

'Wouldn't I? It will be no use to us when the bank comes calling.'

'You're overreacting again. Surely, things aren't that bad.'

'You don't know the half of it, Olivia, because I've protected you from reality. Return to your fantasy world if facing the truth is too challenging.'

Her responding glare is cold enough to freeze hell twice over.

Words are scribbled across the page before the pencil flies from Maud's grip and hits the wall opposite.

Henry snatches up the paper and studies the markings before waving it above his head. '*Ding dong bell?* What in buggeration does this mean?'

Maud's eyes open and she folds her arms across her chest. 'That's for you to work out. I am only a channel, remember?'

Henry grumbles and balls up the paper, stuffing it into his vest pocket. 'It's all blasted nonsense. I need a stiff drink.' He begins to rise.

'Wait,' Elodie says and turns to Will. 'Do you still want to contact your mother? Unless Violet has someone she'd like to speak with.'

'Me?' Violet looks horrified. 'No, I'm just here to make up the numbers.'

'What about Roy?' Olivia asks. 'Wouldn't you like to speak with your brother?'

Violet shakes her head. 'No. I'm sure he's fine where he is.'

Will removes an item from his trouser pocket and cups it in his unscarred hand. 'I was told this belonged to my mother. She died when I was born, so I never knew her.' He holds it up for all to see. Dangling from a short silver chain is a moth-eaten rabbit's foot.

A gasp from Olivia.

'May I hold it?' Maud asks.

Elodie rests back. *What can the great medium devise for this?*

Will stretches across the table and drops the hideous item into Maud's outstretched hand.

She strokes the worn charm. 'Let's see if anyone comes through.'

'I don't know her name,' Will says. 'My adoptive parents were never told.'

'That's all right. She'll know you, I'm sure. A mother's bond is strong.'

Will speaks with determination. 'If my mother is present, please give a sign.'

Within seconds, Maud's hand quivers, and the rabbit's foot leaps from her grasp, landing on the table. Her body shakes, the tremors as violent as a convulsion. Elodie deems the overacting has gone too far when the woman's eyes roll back. Yet her suspicion that Maud is a sham is dispelled when a moan bubbling up from her chest escalates into a shrill wail. 'Where's my baby?'

'I'm here, mother,' Will says, pushing up from his chair.

Maud's head pivots in his direction, her eyes showing only the whites. 'You're not my babe,' she says in the voice of a stranger.

'I have grown. It has been many years.'

'Where'd they hide you? I've been searching long and hard.' Standing and reaching out her arms, Maud's form takes on a strangeness, as if overlayed with another, like a superimposed image in a photograph. 'Come, my child. Let us never separate again.'

Her visage flickers, alternating between her own, those of a much younger woman, and a horrid featureless face. Green vapour pours from her mouth, creating a cloud that stretches towards Will.

Violet's hand squeezes Elodie's thigh. Despite witnessing this unnatural phenomenon, Violet can't possibly see all that Elodie can. The misty entities that were standing by have vanished into the darkness, while the soldier ghosts have reappeared to form a protective shield around Will. Are they sensing danger?

When Will moves forward, Elodie clutches his arm. 'Don't! Harm may befall you.'

He tugs free of her grasp. 'Don't be silly. She's my mother.' He takes another step, only to falter as the soldier spirits circle around him, faster and faster, creating a spectral force field.

'She's not your mother,' Elodie cries. 'Keep well away from this evil, my love.'

The whites of Maud's eyes twitch. 'What is this? An unholy coupling?'

A moan from Olivia attracts her attention.

Maud points a trembling finger at her and screeches, 'Murderer!'

In succession, a painting falls from the wall with a thud, a crystal vase on a shelf shatters, and a bird smacks into the arched window from outside, cracking glass. Terrified, Elodie observes the ghost soldiers being sucked upward and swallowed by a black hole in the plaster ceiling that instantly closes.

A disembodied scream starts up, the keening causing hands to cover ears.

'What's going on?' Henry yells, jumping to his feet. 'How do we stop this?'

He scans the group, all paralysed with shock. Everyone stays put except Olivia, who leaps up and rushes from the room.

Elodie finds her nerve. Springing from her chair, she reaches across the table and seizes the rabbit's foot. Holding it over a candle flame, it catches fire, scorched fur crackling, dried skin shrivelling. As acrid fumes fill the air, Maud shrieks and collapses onto the floor in a faint.

A deafening silence replaces the tumult.

31

Making sure I hadn't left any unmentionables out for people to ogle, I raced to the servants' quarters and quickly tidied the room. I lurched when a head appeared in the doorway.

'So, this is where your room is,' Joe said, leaning against the door frame. 'Hmm ... there's a depressing vibe in here, and not because of your presence. A splash of colour wouldn't go astray. A throw rug, or some scatter cushions. Definitely a fresh coat of paint.'

'It'll do me fine for a night or two. I've experienced worse.'

'You have? Fascinating. You're welcome to share my delightful room. There's only one bed, so we'll have to sleep top-and-tail ... unless ...'

His suggestion ground my gears further, and I pushed him into the hallway, shutting the door behind us.

'Where to now, Abby?' Joe asked.

'No need for us to stick together. We should work independently, per Hilary's suggestion.'

'I disagree. A shared experience is always more fun. I wouldn't have enjoyed Fletch and Paisley's wedding half as much if we hadn't—'

I slapped my hand over his mouth. 'Nuh-uh. Don't go there.'

Luke stepped out of the adjoining bathroom. 'I wouldn't recommend going in there, either.' He nodded at the door he'd closed. 'It won't be safe to enter for a good ten minutes. Have you been to the office yet? I'm told it has a jail.'

'It's not a jail,' I said. 'It's a strongroom with a grille door. Used for storing important papers and the like.'

'Wow, I remember that.' Joe's face lit up with childlike wonderment. 'Fletch and I once pretended to be outlaws, members of the Kelly gang. His dad joined in, taking on the role of a constable and locking us up in there for horse stealing.'

'He locked you kids in the strongroom?'

'Not really. We broke out easy enough and escaped to make more mischief. I've got to see it again.'

Both men took off in a hurry. Having already encountered oddities in the office, I took my time walking down the hall, only to stop at a noise coming from the servants' dining room—which I jokingly named the *puttanesca* room. Inside, I found Rowan doubled-up, groaning.

Appendicitis? Indigestion? Menstrual cramp? I clutched her shoulder. 'Where's the pain? Want me to get help?'

Her cries immediately ceased, and her body relaxed, although her hand trembled, jiggling her gold bangle when she wiped sweat from her forehead. 'I'm okay, but someone experienced a lot of pain in this room. I think I was a conduit for their agony.'

'Really? How did it feel?'

'Like something trying to burst out of me.'

That shocking scene from the movie *Alien* flashed into my

mind. 'That doesn't sound good.' My eyes darted to her necklace. 'Uh-oh.'

Rowan followed my gaze and gasped.

We both stared wide-eyed at the pendant's compass needle spinning crazily. When I dragged her from the room, the needle stopped its manic gyrations. I pushed her back in and it resumed. This time, Rowan removed herself.

'A hot spot for sure,' she said, clutching the pendant. 'Hilary has to set up equipment in there tomorrow.'

Curious as to what had caused havoc with the magnetics, I agreed.

With Rowan's necklace serving as a spirit barometer, we moved from room to room at ground level. Yet the only other area to disturb the compass needle—only a minor reaction in this case—was, unsurprisingly, at the foot of the staircase.

Rowan started up the stairs to continue our research on the next floor when I tugged her down. 'Can't ignore the cellar.'

'There's a cellar?' she asked with surprise.

'Don't all the best haunted houses have cellars? And attics. Though I'm not sure there's one of those. Just a rooftop observatory. Incidentally, did you sense anything eerie when you were up on the roof?'

'Not much. The view was spectacular, however. I had an impulse to become a bird, launch myself into the air and glide away on air current. You should go up there.'

I offered a weak smile, then led her to the door behind the stairs. I opened it and swung it wide. 'Here, you go first.'

Rowan baulked. 'But it's pitch black down there.'

She wasn't wrong. I leant in and slid my hand over the wall near the entrance until I found a switch. I gave it a flick, and the worn timber steps came into view, lit by the glow of a caged bulb.

Rowan crept down the narrow staircase with me following

close behind. When we reached the bottom, I coaxed her towards the brick arch, where we stopped and faced the inky darkness beyond.

'If I knew we were venturing into an abyss, I would've brought spelunking equipment,' she said. 'I don't even have my phone. What an idiot.'

Phone! I yanked mine from my dress pocket and pressed the torch symbol. Light flooded into the section where I'd seen Bridget do her hocus pocus, shadows fleeing into the corners.

'Can you voice record our experience?' Rowan asked, wrapping her arms around herself. 'Thanks,' she said when I opened the Voice Memo app. 'It's freezing down here in the Grassington mansion cellar,' she announced for the benefit of future podcast listeners. 'And it smells rank. Sewerlike, with a rotting sweetness.'

I aimed the torch at the floor near the brick wall. The silver tray was still there, the pineapple now brown and shrivelled. A scattering of colourful sprigs showed what Bridget had distributed.

Rowan picked up one. 'Verbena?' she whispered.

I examined the tiny pink flowers. 'I think you may be right.'

'Verbena flowers are strewn around a shrivelled piece of fruit,' she exclaimed in a louder tone. Grabbing my phone, she waved the light over the floor and up the walls. Darkness flittered and stretched, morphing into eldritch shapes. 'What's been going on here?'

A shiver accompanied my shrug. 'I caught Bridget Greenwood down here the other day slicing up the pineapple and casting a spell before scattering the verbena sprigs. No idea why.'

'You don't think she's a witch, do you?'

'I hadn't thought of that. Have you had many encounters with witches?'

'For a previous podcast, I interviewed a group of strange women known to lurk around Toowong cemetery in Brisbane smashing off the hands of weeping stone angels as a part of a ritual. But they weren't witches per se, just occultists. Then there was a lady, a successful businesswoman, who quit her job at a consulting firm to live in seclusion in a caravan in bushland, cultivating fungi to make potions for curing different illnesses. She resembled a witch—wild hair, crazy clothing. She even owned an assortment of wildlife she joked were her *familiars*.'

'So, more a gypsy.'

'Oh no, you can't say gypsy anymore. It's a derogatory term. *Romani people* is now more acceptable.'

'Duly noted. Do you enjoy being an investigative journalist of sorts? I toyed with the idea of studying journalism in my youth, but life took a different turn. Motherhood derailed things a little, and I ended up working in bookstores.'

'I love it. Meet loads of fascinating people, most who just want their story told. Not every story is an uplifting one, though. There's plenty of heartache out there.'

'For sure. So, what brought you here this weekend? Are you planning a Greenwood episode?' The folder I'd seen on her bed had indicated as much.

The light shook slightly as she spoke. 'I came to discover more about—' She tilted her head. 'Did you hear that?'

I listened hard. Nothing, until Rowan screamed and dropped the phone, plunging the cellar into blackness.

I groped around the paving until I located the phone. The screen came to life when tapped, showing no sign of damage. I illuminated Rowan on her knees, stroking her head and groaning.

'What the hell happened?'

'I heard a scuffling noise. Then something heavy hit me on the head.' She examined her fingers. 'How can there not be blood?'

Terror-struck, I scanned the torch, hoping to spotlight a trickster from upstairs. 'Who's there?' No answer. 'What's your compass doing, Rowan?'

She snatched back the phone and focussed the light on her pendant. 'Nothing.'

'Nothing? How can that be?' I lifted the pendant to eye level. 'Ah ... it's damaged. The glass casing is cracked. And one hand of the needle has broken off.'

Rowan studied it. 'It wasn't like that before we came down here.'

We shared a look of horror, which intensified when a wine bottle suddenly rolled across the floor and halted at our feet.

A gong sounded above, and Rowan and I were upstairs before Paisley struck it a second time.

32

We joined the others, streaming past Paisley and her oriental brass gong to enter the drawing room. Hilary stood rigid alongside the marble fireplace, waiting for everyone to get settled.

Rowan and I sat close on one of the leather sofas, shoulders touching, finding solace in each other's nearness like strangers brought together by a shared tragedy. I cast my gaze around the group, searching for signs of other spooky encounters.

Across from us, Daphne's white-knuckled grip of her husband's knee was substantiated by the pained expression on his face. Sandy pacing the floor near the windows, brow furrowed in apparent distress, contrasted with his son slumped in an armchair scrolling through his phone.

Joe ambled in, sipping from a glass of water—though it could easily have been vodka. 'Is everyone accounted for?' he asked, scanning the room. 'No-one taken hostage by demonic forces?'

No comments. Not even a rebuke from Hilary. The air was dense with expectation. We could have been family members in a hospital waiting room eager for news on the outcome of life-saving surgery or the safe arrival of a newborn.

'How did you all go?' Hilary asked. 'Any experiences?'

A babble of voices as everyone spoke at once.

Hilary whacked an iron poker against the brass fireplace screen. 'Speak in turn, please.'

For Rowan's benefit, I pressed the Voice Memo app on my phone.

Sandy went first. 'I heard scratching sounds in the hallway walls upstairs. It could be mice, which I can help with. Otherwise ...' His eyes bulged, leaving everyone's imagination to complete his thought.

Then came Daphne. 'I smelt perfume in our bedroom. A strong lavender scent that wasn't there before. And I found an antique pearl earring on my pillow, exactly like the ones Olivia Greenwood is wearing in her portrait on the wall. Isn't that right, Vince?' He nodded in agreement.

Luke spoke next. 'I'm not sure, but I think I photographed a ghost.' He held up his phone, the screen facing out. 'There's a hazy white shadow in this pic of the spiral staircase. I also captured three orbs in the sitting area upstairs.'

Excitement as people vied to view the evidence for themselves. Yet a hush fell when Rowan's voice rose above the din.

'I was attacked in the cellar.'

Hilary knelt in front of her and took her hand. 'Would you care to elaborate? How did it make you feel?'

'What do you think? Creeped out. One moment I was chatting with Abby, the next I was struck on the head. God, it hurt.'

Gasps and murmurs all round.

Hilary again demanded quiet. 'Did you see anyone, Rowan? See what you were hit with?'

'No. I dropped the phone, and the torchlight switched off. I don't even have a lump.'

My turn to be questioned. 'Did you witness anything, Abby?'

'Not then. But I saw a wine bottle roll across the floor by itself soon after. And Rowan's compass pendant broke while we were down there. The needle went wacko earlier when we were in the puttanesca room when Rowan felt her guts ready to explode.'

A barrage of remarks.

'Where's the puttanesca room?'

'Rolling wine bottles?'

'Guts exploding?' This came from Luke, who looked more amped up than concerned.

I only commented on the first one. 'The puttanesca room is what I call the smaller dining room.'

More frantic chatter between the group. However, Joe, being a wet blanket, reiterated there had to be logical explanations for everything.

'We recorded the event in the cellar,' I said, holding up my phone. 'Listen.'

I played the recording. Except for our initial pineapple and gypsies chat, the rest was just static.

'What a shame,' Hilary said, getting to her feet. 'Dropping the phone wouldn't have helped. Still, it was a successful venture for everyone. Several spirits certainly occupy the house, so it seems we're in for a lively time tomorrow evening. I trust we aren't too stirred up to sleep tonight.'

'Sleep?' Daphne reached for Vince's hand. 'How on earth am I going to do that with Olivia Greenwood hanging around?'

'Sleeping pills, dear. They'll do the trick.'

Sandy slapped Luke's knee and stood. 'C'mon, young fella. Best we turn in and get some shuteye. Another day awaits.'

'Remember, everyone,' Paisley announced. 'Breakfast is from

seven o'clock.' After ushering us all out, and turning off the room lights, she pulled me aside in the hallway. 'Thanks, Abby. You were brilliant in scaring Rowan like that. It's precisely what I wanted.'

'But I didn't do anything. It wasn't me.'

She winked and laughed. 'Good one, sis. Keep it up. I knew I could rely on you.'

Clenching my jaw, I proceeded to my prison cell.

Paisley must have used up all the good linen on the paying guests, for the sheet covering me was flimsy from age. With my mind abuzz with the events of the evening, I kept movements to a minimum in case I shoved a foot straight through the fabric.

The more I thought about it, the more I sided with Joe. There had to be logical explanations for what we'd just experienced. Although I was as keen as anyone to believe in the supernatural, I wasn't easily fooled. Facts needed weighing up first. Some of the encounters could have been manipulated. Paisley had pressured me into toying with people's fear factor, so what stopped her from convincing others to do the same?

What if Rowan was a mole, acting her part to perfection? After all, we only had her word for the eerie occurrences. There was also the folder of notes I'd seen in her room. Had she been swatting up on the Greenwoods?

An odd sound broke through my thoughts—odd for that late hour.

I sprang out of bed and opened the door to better hear the piano music drifting down the hallway. Flippin' heck! Who was out there playing the recurring melody of Camille Saint-Saëns' *Danse Macabre*? Was Daphne also battling sleep?

Throwing a bathrobe over my pyjamas, I tiptoed down the hall, the music growing in intensity as I neared the drawing room.

From what I recalled from my long-ago high school music studies, this piece was based on the legend of Death playing a fiddle on Halloween as skeletons danced on their graves. A chilling tune to perform in the dark in an old mansion in the middle of the night.

I edged into the drawing room, making out only silhouettes of furniture in the inadequate lighting filtering through the arched windows. Not wanting to switch on lights and draw attention, I tentatively crossed the floor towards the piano in the far corner and swore when I bumped into a sofa, jarring my knee.

The music stopped.

'Hello,' I said, rubbing my injury. 'It's just me, Abby.'

When no response came, I blindly felt my way over and recoiled when I discovered the piano stool unoccupied, and the leather upholstery cool to the touch. *What the?*

My voice trembled as I wheeled around and implored, 'Where are you?'

The Tree of Life tapestry billowed before settling around the contours of what appeared to be a person. Acting fast, I rushed over and lifted it, revealing nothing but a bare wall.

Moments later, footsteps in the hallway launched me out of the room. I almost peed my pants when the resounding chime of the grandfather clock in the foyer struck one o'clock.

I hurried through the etched glass doors and caught movement on the carpeted staircase. A diaphanous figure stood on the middle landing, both arms reaching out. Before I could get a clearer glimpse or holler out, the image took on a strange form, pulsating, then transmuting into a swirling, shimmering mist before evaporating.

Time stood still as my befuddled brain struggled to comprehend what I'd witnessed. It had to be a dream. I went to pinch myself, but the bile searing my throat proved I was in a conscious state. Panicked, I staggered down the hall to my room, when a cool breeze wafting towards me indicated the side door to outside was open.

I sped out onto the verandah, coming to a standstill on the cold mosaic tiles. The eerie cries of a curlew cut through constant chirping of crickets. My ragged breathing joined the nocturnal chorus until, in the distance, a light flashed above the vineyard on Fig Tree Hill. It took only seconds to discern it was torchlight giving a series of long and short bursts.

A crunch of gravel nearby alerted me to something emerging from the ebb and flow of shadows. A person. Desperate to discover their identity, I hurtled down the steps, rounded the mock orange hedge, and collided with the night walker.

33

ELODIE

20 January 1921

Elodie and Will talk on the upper verandah. Will's contact with his mother has shaken him, and he wavers between anguish and wonder, while Elodie questions why their relationship was deemed *unholy*.

Unsuitable, or *ill-matched*, might be a more fitting term. However, class differences don't exclude the possibility of a love match. One would expect his mother—if that's what she really was—would be more concerned about his happiness. And he is happy with her, isn't he?

'Marry me,' she says, wrapping her arms around Will. 'Make me your wife.'

'Where did this come from?' he says, looking far from pleased. 'Why bring this up now?'

'I love you and I think you love me, so why don't we make it official? Ask my father for my hand.'

Will steps out of her clutch. 'Elodie … it seems you might be jumping the gun.'

'But you said you wanted me. I'm giving you permission to have all of me … forever. In matrimony.'

'Cripes, Elodie. I want you, no doubt about that. But I can't marry you.'

A jolt of disappointment brings a sour taste to her mouth. 'Are you saying you don't *want* to marry me?'

'I'm saying you can do so much better. We're incompatible in the long term, surely you know that. Financially, socially, and—'

'Dad likes you. He respects you. I'll talk him into giving you a higher position … and with better pay. He'll give consent.'

'Are you sure about that? Your mother will definitely oppose it. There's never been a future in it.'

A crushing blow. 'I don't believe you. Our time spent together. What you said to me. What we *did*.'

'Trust me. We'll both find someone more suited.'

She struggles to breathe, her heart aching as if tearing apart. 'Who could be a better match for you than me? We'll make it work.' She presses hard against him, her body fitting perfectly into his.

Will clutches her shoulders, his fingers biting into her flesh. Is it passion he feels or abhorrence? She's pushed away when Violet rushes onto the verandah.

'There you both are. The sleeping draught I gave Maud should set the old luv right.' She grips Will's arm. 'So, how are you faring? That was all a bit nutty, wasn't it, your mother appearing like that?'

His face brightens, and he squeezes her hand. 'A shock to be true. Though amongst the terror, I was comforted.' His voice breaks as he says, 'She remembered me.'

'Of course, she remembered you. You're unforgettable.'

A look passes between them—fleeting, intimate.

Scales fall from Elodie's eyes. How could she be so naïve to believe she was the only recipient of Will's attention? The marks on Violet's neck. Whose mouth had caused them? A groan escapes her. She's been doubly deceived—betrayed by both her sweetheart and her friend.

'That thing wasn't your mother, you fool,' she lashes out. 'It was a monster saying what you wanted to hear. She's dead. Her rotting corpse food for worms, just like those poor soldiers you failed to save.'

Will's glare stabs Elodie like a knife.

'That's a horrible thing to say, Elle!' Violet admonishes. 'Insensitive.'

'That's the pot calling the kettle black,' Elodie snaps. 'Stealing another's woman's man is despicable. What happened? Had you tired of all the other men around here? Or had they tired of you, sharing yourself around like an alley cat?'

'Maybe Will wanted someone more focused on him than themselves and their standing in society, Miss High and Mighty.'

Elodie lunges, ready for a skirmish. Yet when Violet steps back, protecting her stomach with her hands, she halts her attack. Surely not! Glancing at Will, Elodie sees his discomfort and embarrassment.

She flees inside and locks herself in her room. Falling on the bed, tears soak her pillow.

Aware of someone stroking her hair, Elodie lifts her head to find Tommy crouched beside her, his lips quivering in empathy. 'Why?' she implores in her suffering. 'Why did they do this to me?' She reaches for his ghostly hand, only to pull back when her brother's mouth forms a menacing grin.

What has provoked his delight in her misery?

Beetles scuttle in her belly when Tommy's face transforms into the repulsive smudge of the No Face Man.

34

___

Flat on my back on the gravel drive, I stared open-mouthed as Joe got to his feet with torch in hand and dusted himself off.

'Fuck, Abby, what are you doing?'

'I could say the same of you. Why were you out so late? Piano playing? Signalling?' A glance up at the hill showed there was now no light flickering.

'Huh?' He helped me rise. 'I didn't know you'd be waiting up for me. Anyhow, I'm an adult. Free to stay out as late as I want.'

Whitby appeared alongside him. Unsurprised, Joe stroked the dog's head.

I spat grit from my mouth. 'Have you just come from the cottage?'

'So what if I have? It's got nothing to do with you.'

'You reckon? What were you doing with Paisley at this hour?'

He shone the torchlight in my eyes. 'Why? Are you jealous?'

'In your dreams.' I slapped the torch, redirecting the light away. 'Why are you here instead of keeping an eye on Fletcher? No way you only dropped in to lend a hand.'

'I needed to hear Paisley's side of the story. What Fletch has been experiencing seems more bizarre than the result of stress. I don't believe in ghosts, but I do believe in evil. I've seen enough of it in my profession to know it is the living we should fear.'

'Your *past* profession,' I corrected. 'Before you were turfed out of the police force for increasingly aggressive behaviour and nearly killing someone in custody.'

Joe clenched his jaw, showing I'd hit a nerve. 'I wasn't turfed out. It was my choice to resign, and I got help. Anyway, that mongrel deserved the beating he got.' He kicked the ground with the heel of his shoe and fell silent, as if enjoying the memory of the assault. 'Want to know a secret?'

I cocked an eyebrow. *Did Dracula have a taste for blood?*

'I came here for answers, Abby ... for Fletcher's sake. I'll show this place isn't haunted; a simpler, more sinister explanation exists for his delusions. Although I'm not a copper anymore, my detective skills are razor sharp, and I am determined to solve whatever is happening.'

'But why now? Why this weekend?'

'The sooner, the better. No use in leads going cold.'

'What leads?' Surely, he didn't suspect Paisley was intentionally sending Fletcher over the edge. Over his shoulder, I glimpsed the return of the light above the vineyard. 'There it is again.' I pointed. 'Somebody's up on the hill.'

Joe swung around and spotted it, too. 'Maybe it's a signal to someone inside.'

'That's what I thought.'

We both peered back at the house, but there was no responding blink, other than Cole's party lights wrapped around the roof tower shifting from gold to blue.

'I'll sneak up to the hill and see if I can nab the signaller,' Joe said. 'You go into the house, check if anyone else is awake.'

. . .

Armed with a freshly lit candelabra swiped from the dining room, I searched both floors, including the upper verandah.

Without forcing entry into bedrooms, I detected sounds of slumber filtering through gaps under doors—Rowan moaning in her sleep, steady snoring from one of the O'Maras, a trumpeting fart from a Michaelson. Even an ear pressed flat against Bridget's door failed to pick up notes of someone on the move.

The house, however, was awake. I heard it in the rattle of windows, the popping of contracting timber, and water hammering in aged plumbing as I wandered the vacant hallways like a pitiful ghost. Even the flicker of the occasional wall fanlight —as dull as they were—when passing by, and the start-up hum of the commercial display fridge in the kitchen as I entered, implied the house followed my every move.

In Henry's old office, a thud prompted me to aim the candlelight at the bookcase. My heart pulsed in my ears at the sight of Arthur Conan Doyle's work on spiritualism splayed on the floor in front of it. I picked it up, only to glance fearfully at the doorway when floorboards squeaked in the hall.

Joe appeared with Whitby in tow.

Breathing sharply from exertion, he informed me he'd found no person on the hill or in the vineyard, and I reported no-one roaming around the house. We decided to return to our rooms, hoping the new day would bring answers to the mysteries of the night.

Too churned up to sleep, I sat propped up in bed flicking through the book the house seemed eager for me to read. What was I meant to discover from *The New Revelation* beyond Conan Doyle's journey from scepticism to belief in communication with spirits?

A folded flyer slid from the pages and landed on my chest. It was an old programme for a pair of lectures to be held at His Majesty's Theatre in Brisbane on the 10th and 11th January 1921. The lectures entitled *Death and the Hereafter* and *Pictures of Psychic Phenomena* were to be given by Sir Arthur Conan Doyle as part of his southern tour. A statement at the bottom claimed that Melbourne, Sydney, Adelaide, and New Zealand had already received his presentations with much enthusiasm and commotion.

Had Henry or Olivia attended either of these Brisbane talks? Maybe that's where they bought the book.

In the hope of finding more clues, I discovered a faded signature on the book's title page, an autograph penned by Sir Arthur himself. Interesting, too, was a crinkled sheet of yellowed note paper inserted between pages in the back, bearing a printed letterhead for one *Madam M Montague, Clairvoyant.* The address beneath her name showed she had resided in Brisbane, at Vulture Street, West End. Scrawled large across the page in thick lead pencil were the words *DING DONG BELL* and below it, in a finer hand, the date *19th Jan, 1921.* Wasn't that the day preceding Henry's death?

A sound disrupted my thoughts. Dry-mouthed, I stared at the wardrobe to better discern the tapping coming from within. It became a banging noise. When it increased to a frantic pounding, I grabbed my phone and tore out of the room.

Upstairs, I had no sooner rapped on Joe's bedroom door when it swung open.

'Whaddaya want?' he slurred, blinking against the glare of my phone torch.

I slipped inside the room and lowered the light, unintentionally aiming it at his spandex Spiderman boxers. 'Sorry. I'm too scared to sleep on my own in that room. I'm imagining all sorts of screwy things.'

He groaned with irritation and kicked the door shut. 'Dammit, I'd just nodded off. You have the bed; I'll sleep on the floor.' Whipping a pillow from the mattress, and a blanket from the armchair, he made a nest on a mat beside a curled-up Whitby.

'It's not fair that you should miss out on comfort because of me,' I said, sliding between body-warmed sheets.

My comment was met with a grumble, and Joe—despite his bravado and suggestive banter hours earlier—chivalrously remained on the floor as I tossed and turned.

Though I was protected from the *unexplained*, sleep proved difficult. Not due to Joe's laboured breathing, but his lingering scent on the bedding, evoking long-ago moments infused with passion and deceit. When I eventually drifted off, a violent jerk caused me to wake with a cry.

'You okay?' Joe whispered.

'Yeah, just a nightmare where I fell out of a hot-air balloon.' I flipped the pillow over and wriggled to get comfortable, only to have Joe interrupt my settling.

'Why are you really here, Abby?'

'I told you. The room downstairs spooked me.'

'No, at Grassington.'

'You know, to help Paisley and Fletch with the opening. Muck in where needed.'

'Did it have anything to do with escaping from your troubles? Another of your ventures ending before it got going must have been a real kick in the guts.'

The gall of him! Who did he think we were, a couple of schoolgirls sharing secrets in a camp dormitory? God, I really didn't want to talk about it with Joe. I didn't need his judgement, now or ever.

'Maybe it was all for the better, Abby. I suspect there's a deeper yearning inside you than being a retailer. A need to break free and follow your own ambitions. To continue where you left off years ago.'

A sharp twinge in my chest. What else would explain the relief that accompanied the grief and guilt I'd been experiencing since the shop's destruction? Yet how was Joe able to identify the cause of my distress when I hadn't realised it myself until now? His clever psychoanalysis unnerved me, so I hit back with sarcasm.

'What are you up to now? Did I hear you were going to buy an outback pub? I reckon that's where you should be, far from civilisation.'

A long sigh. 'That was one option. I'm tossing up an additional idea, setting up my own business.'

'What, a Jim's Mowing franchise or a fast-food service? Pizzas never go out of fashion.'

'Something I'm more familiar with.'

'Like running a fight club? You could train people to beat the crap out of each other.'

'Fuck off!' he growled. 'I was trying to be civil. Obviously, I'm wasting my breath.' The sound of him punching his pillow.

Why did I have to be so snide? Was my sister's behaviour rubbing off on me? Joe may have indeed turned over a new leaf. I weighed up saying something conciliatory, but the silence from the floor becoming a gentle snore led me to face the wall and eventually drift off.

At some point I awoke, aware of being spooned from behind. I took comfort in the face nuzzled into my neck, the hand gripping my hip, until it registered that it wasn't Shane snuggled against me, but Joe. Rolling over to shove him out, I was shocked to find no-one there; Joe was still on the floor, mumbling in sleep.

I cocooned myself in the sheet and dozed fitfully until first light. Creeping out, I snuck back to my room.

35

Shaken awake by a cruel hand, I opened grainy eyes and cringed at Paisley's reptilian stare.

'Hey, Sleeping Ugly, you're needed in the kitchen.'

'What time is it?' The words grated against my throat.

'Eight o'clock. Most of the guests have begun breakfast. You'll need to do better than lazing around when you're on duty.'

'Not lazing. Four hours. That's all I reckon I got for sleep.'

'Well, that's your fault.' She pinched my arm, making me squeal. 'We need you in the kitchen, *pronto*.'

I growled and rolled over. 'I'll be there soon.'

A stinging slap on my thigh. 'Up now, sis.'

Paisley purposely left the door open as she exited, allowing the drift of voices and cutlery clinking on chinaware to further piss me off.

I slithered out of bed to kick the door shut and sat on the mattress with my head in my hands, wishing I could sleep for a week. A tincture of what caused Rip Van Winkle to nod off for twenty years wouldn't have gone astray. The craving for caffeine alone got me moving.

I warily opened the wardrobe to retrieve a purple denim overall dress and was more baffled than relieved to find no monster leaping out. What had made those godawful pounding noises that sent me fleeing upstairs to Joe's room? And what had crawled into bed to cuddle up with me?

Dressing, I dragged myself down the hall to the kitchen.

Slumped over the stovetop, Cole crumbled tofu into a pan of milky-looking mixture. 'Morning,' he grumbled, his bloodshot eyes viewing me from beneath heavy lids. He looked as bad as I felt.

'Rough night, huh?' I asked. 'Or too good of a one?'

He groaned and stirred his creation.

I wasn't much into small talk either and poured myself a huge mug of strong coffee.

'I swear I saw a couple of ghosts during the night,' Luke commented as I entered the dining room with a fresh pot of tea.

Paisley and Sandy were the only ones not seated at the table. Even Joe was in attendance, sitting in Fletcher's place. Irritated, I placed the teapot beyond his grasp.

'Your photo of the vaporous cloud in the hall was pretty convincing,' Vince said through a mouthful of bacon.

'Not that one. When I woke for a whizz at some point, I spied a woman carrying a light floating down the timber stairs.'

I twitched. Had I been spotted searching the floors?

'And returning from the loo,' Luke continued, 'I went in search of a kitchen snack and saw someone on the carpeted stairs. A translucent figure, kind of sparkly. And *poof*, it disappeared.'

He'd witnessed it too! Somehow, I found that unnerving. I

deliberated on sharing the image of elderly Olivia standing behind me on the stairs, and the experience of being spooned in bed. However, I kept them to myself. What if the early morning snuggle was a form of wish fulfilment? Repressed desires for ... who?

'There's something else.' Luke shot Rowan an inquisitive stare. 'What was that racket coming from your room last night? All that moaning and gagging sounded like you were dying.'

Her eyes wide with panic. 'You heard me?'

'And you didn't think to enquire if she needed help?' Daphne implored.

Luke shrugged. 'She stopped soon enough, and a light shone under her door. Thought she must be okay.'

Rowan eyed Hilary seated across from her. 'I dreamt I was gravely ill. My throat was so sore I could hardly swallow, as if I'd eaten broken glass. And feverish too, burning up. But I woke feeling perfectly fine.'

'Anyone else have a disturbed sleep?' I asked. 'The piano being played got me out of bed.'

Heads turned towards Daphne being served her plate of breakfast by Cole.

'Wasn't me,' she said. 'I was tucked up in bed. Isn't that right, Vince?'

'Yes. Snoring right alongside me. A little too close for comfort, but understandable.'

'How so?' I asked.

Daphne answered. 'The earring on the bed unsettled me and I had trouble nodding off. I heard a noise and saw a silhouette of a figure outside our window. Yet when I roused Vince, and he peered out, there was nobody there. Anyway, we drew the curtains after that.'

Had that someone also been me, peeking into a window or two

from the verandah to check if anyone was up? 'What size would it have been?'

'The silhouette?' Daphne chewed her lip as she contemplated. 'It reached halfway up the window arch. A rather tall person, in my opinion.'

That ruled me out. I glanced at Joe, thinking he might ask more direct questions, but he was busy trying to clean a splodge of tomato sauce off his shirt. What had happened to his sharp detecting skills?

'Ah-hah ...' Hilary leant her elbows on the table and steepled her fingers in front of the keyhole opening below the neckline of her slinky black top. 'Our presence has obviously stirred plenty of activity. I imagine it will be a hot time in the old house tonight.'

I squinted in puzzlement. She—who supposedly channelled the dead—hadn't shared any personal experiences from the basic ghost reading, or any nighttime incidents. Hilary was tall too. Joe may have been accurate in calling her a fake, here to dupe poor schmucks like me.

He abruptly rose and hurried out, his shirt bunched in his hand. Off to soak it in stain remover?

Paisley walked in from the kitchen. 'Everyone enjoying their breakfast?'

'Actually,' Daphne pointed to her food, 'this tofu scramble tastes rather like soap. I expected someone with your ability to have mastered such a simple recipe.'

Cole, snapping his head around to cast a fierce look in her direction, seemed ready to whack the woman over the skull with the oversized pepper grinder he held.

Paisley kept her calm. 'Sorry, Daphne. Can I offer you a replacement meal?'

'Don't bother. I have muesli bars in my bag to nibble on.'

As Paisley passed me, she growled her annoyance. 'What a

hag. Hey, can you pop into Grimm for me when you have a moment this morning? A few extra groceries need collecting from the store.'

I readily accepted, happy to escape Grassington even for a short time.

36

OLIVIA

20 January 1921

Unable to endure the séance any longer, Olivia bolts outside. Wandering the gardens gulping in moist night air, shadows lurch and take joy in accusing her. *Murderer!* The nightmare of twenty years earlier revisits her, the harrowing details standing out in stark clarity.

Hours pass.

Back inside the house, Olivia hears, 'Where were you?' and stops on the dreaded middle landing of the main staircase. She stares up at Henry standing at the top of the stairs, his eyes sparkling with excitement rather than concern. This nauseates her. How she despises him and his lack of control. If it wasn't for his lust, she wouldn't be facing the problems it has caused. Problems she alone must remedy before everything goes to wrack and ruin.

'I went for a restorative walk,' she says, stepping up to his level. Had he caught the waver in her voice? No matter if he had. The events of the seance alone were enough to unsettle anyone's nerves. 'Where is Maud? The others?'

'Maud's in her room,' he says. 'Violet has concocted an elixir to calm her down. Will and Elodie have gone to bed.'

Her heart pounds. 'Together?'

'What? No, certainly not. Will went back to the workers' shed.' He clasps her hand. 'I've worked it out.'

She pulls her hand away. 'Worked what out?'

'Maud's writings from father.'

'But you called it nonsense.'

'I initially dismissed it as ludicrous. But I've given it some thought, and I reckon it's a cryptic message.'

'*Ding dong bell* is cryptic?' Olivia lets out a sigh. 'Sounds like a nursery rhyme to me.'

'Exactly! And therein lies the clue. *Ding dong bell, Pussy's in the well.* Don't you see, Olivia? The sly rogue hid the gold in the old well. I must find the nugget.' He begins to descend the stairs.

She grips his shirt sleeve and jerks him back. Tells him he isn't going out there now. That it would be ridiculous. It was late. If he had to go on a ridiculous expedition, he should wait till morning.

'Of course. I'll search for it at first light.'

Olivia follows him into the bedroom. Tells him her head is still awhirl from the evening's events and that she will stay up a little longer.

Henry agrees it was quite a to-do, and that he'd seen nothing like it. He sits on the side of the bed and unbuttons his vest. His hand halts in easing the last button from its hole. 'Why did Maud … Will's mother … accuse you of being a murderer?'

A breath lodges in her throat. She forces a laugh. 'It was all silly talk. Maud was delirious.'

'And that rabbit's foot Will produced. I'm sure I've seen one like that before. Didn't—'

Olivia yelps as her shoulder is clutched from behind. Spinning around, she finds Maud standing in the doorway, her face expressionless, eyelids drooping. Is the woman sleepwalking?

'I don't blame you, Mumma,' Maud says in a familiar childlike voice.

Olivia clutches her chest, feels her heart pounding beneath her bodice. 'Tommy, is that you?'

Maud nods and gives Tommy's lopsided grin. She must be deep in one of her trances.

'Darling one,' Olivia responds with elation, 'we called the doctor as soon as we could, but it was too late. Scarlet fever had already taken its hold of you. We should have protected you. Vetted the health of the mill workers' children before letting you play together.'

'How could we have known they were ill?' Henry mentions, now beside her. 'They all succumbed so quickly, even their parents were surprised. We weren't the only ones grieving, remember?'

Maud clears her throat. 'Not the illness, Mumma. I saw you on the stairs with Claudette. Heard her tell you about the baby. I know why you were angry. Why you pushed her.'

A shiver runs through Olivia. Had Tommy's spirit been there on the landing, witnessing her transgression? She groans and sneaks a look at Henry, his eyes gaping along with his mouth.

Maud touches Olivia's arm. 'She wasn't the only one.'

Olivia gasps. 'But I've hurt no-one else.'

'No. Claudette wasn't the only one Daddy did bad things with. And not just in the house. In the shed. At the mill.'

Suddenly woozy, Olivia steadies herself against the door frame. 'Thank you, Tommy. You did well, telling me this.'

Maud sucks in a deep breath, then blinks and cocks her head. 'Sorry, what did you call me, Olivia?' Her voice is her own again, yet she appears confused, her head darting from side to side. 'What am I doing here?'

'Delivering a message.' Olivia eases the woman back into the hallway. 'You can return to your room now. Everything is fine.' She watches her stagger away.

Henry does not respond. Casually undressing, he slides into bed and rolls to face the window. Has guilt robbed him of speech?

Olivia closes the door behind her as she walks from the room.

Curled up on the child-size bed in Tommy's room with shadows pulsing around her, Olivia fails to fall asleep, her mind too cramped with thoughts.

A noise in the hallway causes her to look up from the pillow and discover a note has been slipped under the door. Fury ignites when she retrieves it and reads the message from Henry, stating that in the morning he intends to telephone the police.

If learning what she had done shocked him, then he has to accept full culpability for what occurred.

She goes downstairs to Henry's office. Retrieving her latest journal from its secret spot, she opens to a fresh page and takes up a pen. To stymie the madness that threatens, she reveals the full extent of Claudette's death.

August 1900

A scuffle. Claudette stumbling backwards. Falling.

'What was she doing here?' Maggie says, crouching with Olivia at the bottom of the stairs beside the woman's prone form. 'She doesn't work for you anymore.'

The young maid, Jane, inches forward and opens her mouth as if to answer, but Olivia beats her to it. 'I was coming down as Claudette was coming up. She said she wished to speak with me, then she slipped. Too much floor wax, I suspect.' She shoots Jane a warning look, and the girl blushes and cowers.

Olivia eases the blood-soaked head from her lap to the floor. 'What shall we do?'

'Let me double check.' Maggie presses her ear to the woman's chest. A few anxious moments pass. 'Praise God! There's a faint heartbeat. She's alive.'

Maggie gives the slack shoulders a brisk shake, and in disbelief, all three of them watch as Claudette's eyelids flutter. She moans in pain.

'We need to make her comfortable.' Maggie indicates the private dining room nearby. 'Let's move her in there.'

Olivia agrees, eager to get her out of sight before someone else enters the house. God forbid if Henry happens to walk in on the commotion.

They lift Claudette and transport her into the small room, laying her with care on the floor rug. After placing a cushion under her head, Olivia uses her silk scarf to bandage the damaged scalp.

'Has she broken anything?' Jane asks.

Maggie examines each arm before hoisting up Claudette's skirts to check the stockinged legs. 'All as straight as ...' Her eyes widen. 'Leave us, Jane. Close the door behind you.'

'Maybe I could help.'

'Leave us be, girl!' Maggie commands. 'And shut the door.'

Jane obeys, yet there is no noise of her moving away.

'Her bloomers are soaked with blood,' Maggie whispers.

Olivia gasps. 'Is she losing the baby?' Maggie's puzzled look causes her to add, 'Claudette is in the family way. She just told me.'

Maggie scowls. 'How far along is she?'

'I'm not sure, but she made me feel the baby kick.'

Maggie tugs the brocade shawl away from its owner and explores within the folds of the blue dress. 'She hid that well. Her belly is the size of a mature pumpkin and just as hard.'

A sharp cry causes them to flinch.

Claudette's eyes open slowly. 'Help,' she whimpers, clutching her stomach and attempting to rise. 'It hurts.'

Maggie eases her back down. 'We'll get help.'

'No,' Olivia cries. 'Can't you simply do what needs to be done?'

'This is serious, Mrs Greenwood. Beyond my capabilities.' Maggie pushes up and goes to the door, opening it a crack. 'Jane, find Zachariah. Tell him to fetch Dr Morphett. He may still be down at the mill giving aid to an injured worker. Say Claudette has had a nasty accident falling down the stairs and needs medical attention.'

The sound of running away. Maggie closes the door and returns.

'How was no-one aware of her condition?' Olivia asks.

'She's been gone for over two months,' Maggie reminds her.

Another moan. Claudette bares her teeth, claws the air, and groans loudly.

Maggie kneels and whips off the saturated bloomers. Parts the legs. 'Holy Mother of God. The baby's coming.'

'It can't be ... not yet,' Olivia shrieks and grasps a thrashing arm. 'Hold on, Claudette. Wait till the doctor arrives.'

'I reckon it's too late for that.' Maggie pushes her shirt sleeves up to her elbows. 'Lift her into a sitting position, Mrs Greenwood, and support her from behind.'

Olivia freezes, overwhelmed by what is happening. Not fifteen minutes earlier, she had been preparing for a pleasant stroll through the gardens, hopeful and unaware her day would be upended.

'Olivia, now!'

Ignoring the fact Maggie has called her by her Christian name, she sits behind Claudette and props her up against her, as if sharing a toboggan. However, the blood-smeared head writhing against her chest shows it will be no fun ride.

Maggie forces Claudette's knees up. 'Reach around and hook your hands under her thighs while I work down here.'

Olivia gives it her all, muscles straining to keep Claudette in position.

Maggie unfastens her kitchen apron, bundles it, and lays it between the legs. She then squats and delves under the skirts. 'The head is crowning. If you can hear me, Claudette, push hard now.' A groan. 'Good, another one. You're almost there.'

Claudette tenses against Olivia before releasing a high-pitched wail. Her skull smacks against Olivia's chin, causing her to bite her tongue and taste blood. She lets out a cry of her own.

'And again, dear,' Maggie encourages.

A grunt became a mewl, and Claudette droops in Olivia's arms, her head lolling to the side. Olivia pinches her arm, slaps her cheek. 'She's passed out.'

'I guess it's up to me to manoeuvre the baby's shoulders out.' Maggie frowns with concentration and eventually something small and glistening slides onto the apron pillow. It is grey, streaked with white scum and blood. Olivia has seen this before.

'Is it alive?' She croaks.

Maggie cradles the infant, still attached to its mother by the umbilical cord, and gives it a shake. No response, no sound. It could be a doll made of India rubber. She turns it on its side and pokes a finger into the tiny mouth, scooping out mucus. Then she massages the limbs and chest until a squeak is heard. With more kneading, the squawking comes good and loud.

She holds the child aloft. 'There you go, luv, you have a little baby boy.'

When Claudette ceases to stir, Olivia strokes the woman's pale cheek. 'Did you hear that, Claudette? It's a sweet boy.' She studies the blank stare and slack mouth of the head resting in the crook of her arm, then locks eyes with Maggie, sees her frown.

Maggie applies her fingers against Claudette's neck. She again listens to her chest.

Olivia breaks out in a cold sweat. 'What's happening?'

Maggie pulls away, her shoulders sagging. 'Nothing. She's gone.'

'Gone? You mean ... but how?'

Olivia shuffles out from under Claudette and crawls next to Maggie, who deposits the babe on the motionless chest before running off. She returns moments later with a pair of kitchen scissors and a length of twine. Tying the umbilical cord close to the baby's stomach, she snips it free, and together they observe the baby squirm atop his dead mother. While he pinks up nicely, she takes on an ashen tinge.

Olivia snatches the child and hoists up the skirt of her dress to wrap him in new chintz. 'What happens now?'

A voice calls out. A knock at the door before the knob turns.

Dr Morphett enters, clutching his black medical bag. He observes the scene with startled eyes. 'What in God's name?'

'Shut the door!' Olivia shouts. 'We can't let anyone else see this.'

Dr Morphett complies and approaches, darting a look at Olivia and her slew of petticoats shockingly exposed before scrutinising Claudette from a short distance. Removing a stethoscope from his bag, he fits the earpiece into his ears. Pressing the bell against her chest, he listens and shakes his head, confirming that she is deceased. Peeling Claudette's skirts up to her waist, he proceeds to give her a proper physical examination.

With horror, Olivia notices her body has partially expelled the afterbirth, as dark and meaty as lamb's liver.

'She obviously died during childbirth,' he says. 'That gash on her scalp. The fall that brought me here?'

'She hit her head when she tripped and tumbled down the stairs,' Olivia replies, surprised her voice sounds steady when her heart gallops like a racehorse.

'In that case, a brain haemorrhage may have caused her demise. We'll need to do a postmortem examination to prove the cause of—'

'No!' Olivia drops the baby into Maggie's arms and grasps Dr Morphett's sleeve. 'Just write a death certificate and state she died from a fall down the stairs. That's what happened.'

'But the birth, I'll have to mention—'

'Please, not a word of the birth,' she implores. 'No-one can know she had a baby.'

'But the father, surely he must—'

Olivia stamps her foot on the floor. 'He will never find out. Not while I live and breathe.'

The doctor averts his gaze as realisation dawns. 'Ah ... I see. We'll need to clean her up. I can do some of that, but you ladies will have to do the rest. A change of attire would be in order. You'll need to get rid of her bloodstained clothing and ... other evidence. Everything will need to be burned.'

He comes alongside Maggie and watches the infant sucking its fist, tut-tutting as he views the sharp features of a babe who hasn't had time to store fat. 'Clearly premature. It will be a miracle if he survives. Have you figured out what you will do with him?'

'Can't you take it?' Olivia says, frantic for the removal of the newborn from Grassington and prying eyes. 'Care for him until he ...' Tears threaten to spill. The thought of another baby dying in this house fills her with dread.

'You must know of someone who can give him the best chance,' Maggie pleads, collecting Claudette's shawl from the floor. 'A wet nurse, at least.'

'Not from Grimm, though,' Olivia entreats. 'Somewhere else.'

Dr Morphett sighs. 'Very well, I'll take the poor mite with me and see what I can do. But like I said, I have doubts concerning his survival. I will also arrange a mortician to collect the mother's body.'

While Dr Morphett finishes up, Olivia follows Maggie to the laundry to collect a bucket of water and a washcloth.

'The baby is Mr Greenwood's, isn't it?' Maggie murmurs, swishing a wire shaker containing a bar of soap through the water.

Olivia nods a heavy head and swaddles the baby in his mother's shawl, pinning the rabbit's foot talisman to it for extra good luck. 'She told me before she fell. I never suspected.'

'We were all in the dark, then. Never mind, it will be put right soon. And I will never mention it.'

'Not even to Zachariah?'

'Not even him.'

'What shall we do about Jane?'

'She'll be no worry. I'll warn her if she breathes a word about what happened, she'll be out of a job with no reference from me. She won't like that.'

Leaving Maggie to undress and bathe Claudette, and with the baby in Dr Morphett's care, Olivia rushes upstairs to find suitable clothing to dress the unfortunate woman in. When she reaches the landing, a recollection strikes like a lightning bolt.

A split second before Claudette fell, while rage engulfed her in a red mist, she saw—as if outside of herself—her arm thrust forward, the heel of her hand striking Claudette in the centre of her chest, propelling her backwards.

Olivia sets the pen down and drops her head into her hands. Relief in having written down the truth does not come. Instead, facts assault her like bullets.

Claudette's baby survived. Adopted by a couple nearby—curse you, Dr Morphett.

The boy grew to adulthood—his mother's rabbit's foot kept as a memento—and now works for Henry ... his father?

And worst of all, he and Elodie have shared intimacies. What if she really is his sister?

Olivia is even more determined to set things right. Put an end to Elodie and Will's shameful romance before things go too far. As Claudette said through Maud, it is unholy. But how can she accomplish this without revealing Henry fathered a child with one of his employees? A child who could well be the true heir to Grassington.

I breakfasted alone on the side verandah, slinking out of view when Sandy and Luke walked by carrying an item that looked the right shape for a whipper snipper—their metal detector, no doubt. Watching them once again head in the direction of the sawmill ruins, I almost dropped my fruit salad when Bridget materialised beside me, dressed like a normal person in linen pants, shirt, and a wide-brimmed straw hat.

She gripped my arm with a grimy hand. 'Abby! Have you talked with the gardener? Have you arranged the rendezvous?'

'No, sorry. I haven't yet had a chance.'

'If you could do so post-haste, it would be much appreciated. I am in urgent need of his assistance.'

'Can I help in the meantime?'

Her eyes swept over me, weighing up whether I'd be able to tackle whatever she had in mind. She held out a brown paper bag. 'Deliver this to the tower on the roof. It's becoming too difficult for me to use the spiral staircase. Arthritis,' she added like a badge of honour.

I wanted to play my trump card: Acrophobia. But that would seem petty, so I took the bag from her. A peek inside showed it was filled with cherry tomatoes. 'Why would you have me do that?'

'It pleases him.'

'Pleases who?'

'Him.' She stepped down to the lawn and pointed to the rooftop.

I joined her, and looked above, squinting against the sun's glare. For a fleeting moment, I thought I glimpsed a dark figure on the observation deck. A blink and the image vanished. A trick of the light? Heat haze?

I humoured her. 'Are tomatoes his favourite?'

'Sometimes he prefers apricots. So ...' Bridget paused, and I realised she was waiting for a response to her request.

'Er ... alright, I'll see what I can do.' I was sure I could rope someone in to deliver the tomatoes for me. 'Where should the bag be left? Or do you need to wait for collection?'

'Oh, no! You don't want to do that. Just leave the bag in the tower. He'll come for it when he's ready.'

'Who is *he*, Bridget?' Perhaps he was a bird, or a possum.

She pressed a crooked finger against her lips. 'I dare not say his name out loud.'

As she hobbled away, I could have sworn her infirmity was more pronounced. Was that for my benefit, to invoke sympathy?

The mansion interior was as quiet as a tomb. Where was everyone?

In the drawing room, I caught Daphne slumped on a sofa and snoring, presumably catching up on sleep from a disrupted night. A dog-eared paperback novel rested across her chest, its distinctive noir-style jacket evocative of an Agatha Christie mystery. As I leant close to read the title, the chugging of a computer printer reached my ears. Retreating slowly so as not to disturb Daphne, I reached the office, discovering it vacant and silent, yet the residual odour of tobacco seemed sharper.

A slightly open filing cabinet drawer hinted at a recent visitor. I rolled it fully out and noticed a manila folder protruding from a congested suspension file tabbed with the letter 'W'. Tugged free, I saw that the folder was labelled 'Wills'.

Was Bridget seriously contemplating changing her will?

I pressed the folder back into the file and closed the drawer. Leaving the house through the front door, I was about to head to my car to drive to Grimm when a voice interrupted me.

'A hot day already.'

Joe, seated on the front verandah in a fabulous wicker peacock chair, held a frosty glass in one hand, and a glossy brochure in the other, fanning his face. Having exchanged his white shirt and grey trousers for a cobalt polo and tartan shorts, he looked ready for a game of golf rather than giving vibes of a hardened ex-cop. 'Supposed to reach thirty-seven degrees with an 88% chance of an evening thunderstorm.'

'Thanks for that weather report,' I commented, unenthused. 'The early morning fog and deafening cicada chorus told me as much.' At least he hadn't led with mentioning our tense nighttime conversation and throwing out more accusations. However, the day was still young. 'What happened at breakfast? Some detective you were, more interested in removing food from your teeth and clothes than questioning the guests.'

He sat forward. 'I'll have you know, detecting is more than grilling suspects. There's also listening and observing. You'd be surprised what you can discover by keeping your mouth shut.'

I gave him a dirty look, this time refraining from retaliating.

Joe handed me the brochure. 'Look what I found in Hilary Bloodworth's room. I knew she was a fake. She was parroting information from this when she told us all about ghosts.'

I read the banner above a fuzzy image of a figure behind an opaque glass door:

Paranormal Investigating 101.
Tips on ghost hunting.

'You broke into her room?'

'I wouldn't call it a *break* in. No damage to any door fixtures. While you and the others were finishing breakfast, I gained access on a hunch I'd discover something, and I did.'

'So, the whole sauce spilt on your shirt was a ruse to sneak away?'

'Yep. I couldn't stomach listening to more shit-talk about ghosts, anyway.'

Unfolding the brochure, I browsed the text and recognised content from Hilary's conversations. Had she learnt this by rote? I studied the fine print at the bottom of the last page.

'Well, Sherlock, it's obvious you didn't read it all.' I pointed to the line that stated the copyright for the brochure belonged to *Bloodworth Inc.* and included a link to a website under the same name. 'Looks like Hilary produced this booklet. She was reciting her own work, you idiot.'

Joe snatched the brochure and examined it at close range. 'Oh, right you are. Don't know how I missed that.'

'You were too eager to denigrate Hilary, that's how. A case of jumping to conclusions. I reckon you're threatened by her.'

'Threatened?' He gave a dry laugh. 'Not in a long shot. Mark my words, there's something shifty about her.' He tapped the brochure against his chin. 'Still, my snooping wasn't in vain. I found out she suffers from insomnia, wears only black, and has a kid who lives with his dad.' He ignored my 'So, what?' comment and added, 'I also overheard Paisley speaking with Sandy. She's asked the Michaelsons to do a job for her.'

'Exterminating pests?'

'No, finding something with their metal detector.'

'What did she ask them to look for?'

'Gold.'

My eyes bugged out. 'A seam of gold? A motherlode?'

'No, just a nugget.'

'Oh ... like the one Gerald discovered on the Gympie goldfields?'

'You've heard about that?'

'I read an article about his discovery in an old newspaper report. But I'd assumed he'd used the funds from the sale of the nugget to buy this land and build Grassington.'

'There's always been a rumour that he'd kept part of the nugget and hid it on the property for safekeeping. I remember Fletcher repeating the myth when we were kids and making up a game we called *Eureka,* where we'd pretend to find the nugget in odd places around the mansion. We got into trouble for digging in the rose garden.'

'The complete nugget was worth a fortune back then,' I said. 'Imagine what it would go for now. Even a portion of it would be a major jackpot. Why has no-one seriously searched for it before?'

'Who says they haven't? Though it could still be just a tale. People fantasise about buried treasure, you know.'

'What if Paisley stumbled upon evidence that validates the rumour? Where is she, anyway?'

'Haven't seen her for ages.' He gestured at the paper bag in my hand. 'What have you got there?'

'Oh.' I held it out. 'Would you mind taking this up to the roof for me? Leave it in the tower.'

'What's in it? Hush money?'

'Cherry tomatoes.'

'Tomatoes?'

'From Bridget.'

He hesitated and glanced inside. I could see his mind working behind his eyes, scrolling through explanations, and coming up short. 'Who are they for?'

'No idea. Bridget's gone loopy again. Said they have to be left in the roof tower for some bloke to collect. Seemed afraid of him.'

'Hmm ... I wonder if she is referring to Gerald Greenwood. He took a nosedive off that very roof.' Joe placed the paper bag between his canvas loafers and sculled his drink, ice chinking against the glass. 'So, Bridget thinks old Gerald has a hankering for cherry tomatoes.'

'She leaves pieces of fruit all over the estate. I spied her slicing up a pineapple in the cellar the other day and setting it on the floor on a silver platter. I even found items in the cemetery, and a kiwi fruit on the staircase that the maid fell down.'

Joe hurtled out of the chair, ice cubes shooting from his glass and gliding across the verandah flooring. 'Aha! It all makes sense. Have you heard of Hungry Ghosts?'

'Nope. What's that?'

'Chinese ancestral worship includes a belief that, at a particular time of year, ghosts can be granted permission to return to the world of the living. Arriving hungry, these spirits unleash evil if their surviving relatives don't give them sufficient food offerings.'

'How do you know all this?'

He raised an eyebrow.

I grimaced. 'Sorry, I tend to forget your rich cultural background.'

'My mother used to tell me stories. Also, a Hungry Ghost Festival is held each year to honour hungry dead ancestors.

During this period, the gates of hell are supposed to open up, freeing starving ghosts to roam the earth in search of food and entertainment. Indulging them with offerings of food and drink is a way of warding off bad luck.'

'You reckon Bridget is doing this as a way of dealing with Grassington's ghosts?'

'A tainted version of the tradition. Bridget must have read about it somewhere and thought it would help with the hauntings ... what she *imagines* are hauntings, that is.'

The old gardener had mentioned her determination to keep spirits at bay. 'You still don't believe, do you? Why so sceptical?'

'Because it isn't logical. My reasoning indicates there is no such thing. To fully believe something is true, you need a high quality of evidence.'

'So, you want tangible proof that ghosts exist?'

'Yep.'

'Let's see what tonight's event offers up.' I retrieved the bag of tomatoes and shoved it into his hand. 'I gotta go into town. Do this for Bridget, will you? If only to ease her troubled mind.'

38

—————

ELODIE

21 January 1921

Henry fails to join the family for lunch and farewell Maud Montague when she departs for the train station. He is also not present for afternoon tea.

Zachariah's arrival in the kitchen for a handout of freshly baked goods interrupts Olivia and Elodie's concerned conversation with Maggie, and he quickly learns of Henry's absence.

'Missing, you say?' His expression turns solemn. 'When did you see him last, Mrs Greenwood?'

Olivia's brow furrows, though her eye contact with him remains steady. 'Last night when we retired. I woke early and he wasn't in bed. He wasn't downstairs, either.'

'There were no signs that Mr Greenwood had eaten before going out,' Maggie adds. 'And he hadn't taken leftover food from the refrigerator, which is a departure from his usual hurried habit when skipping a meal.'

'And you, Miss Elodie?' Zachariah enquires, biting a rock cake in half. 'When did you last clap your eyes on your father?'

She casts her mind back, clearly seeing him with a drink in hand, settled in the drawing room, deep in thought. She had been on the verge of launching into her tale of woe, informing him of Will and Violet's betrayal, but reconsidered. What concern would her heartbreak be to him? *It's part of life*, he'd probably have said.

'After the seance,' she answers. 'I bid Dad goodnight and saw no more of him.'

Zachariah returns his attention to her mother. 'Had he dressed this morning? Any clothing missing that might hint at where he was heading?'

Olivia bites her lip as she ponders. 'His work boots were gone, as well as a set of labouring clothes I'd seen slung over the dressing room chair.'

'Then he must still be on the estate.' Zachariah shoves the rest of the cake into his mouth. 'We'd better organise a search party from the few labourers that remain on the property.'

Olivia and Elodie watch from the first-floor verandah as the small group of men spread out and move in different directions.

Elodie's stomach knots at the sight of Will amongst them. She faces her mother. 'And you really didn't see Dad this morning?'

'You know he's an early riser, eager to get on with the day. I was busy entertaining Maud before Zachariah took her to Rosewood. It was only when he hadn't turned up for any meals that I began to worry.' She wipes a bead of sweat trickling down her cheek. 'I'm glad Maggie is well again. However, Violet is now poorly. A vomiting sickness, I'm told. She's been banished from the kitchen.'

Elodie evades her mother's intense gaze. Is she aware of what has been going on between Violet and Will? Their treachery? A probable pregnancy? She dares to broach a subject bothering her. 'You left the seance in a hurry last night.'

Olivia's eyes meet Elodie's before darting away. 'I was overcome with emotion after hearing from Tommy during the seance ... quite a shock. Though I have doubts it was real.'

Was she speaking the truth? Elodie knows her mother had slept in Tommy's room again, because she heard crying coming from there. Maybe her parents had quarrelled. Tension was obvious between them. In fact, there was tension between everyone last night. Despair falls like heavy rain, weighing her down.

Olivia grips the railing so tight her knuckles turn white. 'Let's pray they find your father safe and sound,'

Elodie cocks her head as an idea surfaces. What if her father hadn't gone out? Had anyone thought to fully search for him inside the mansion?

Following an unsuccessful hunt through every room, Elodie appreciates the lower temperature in the cellar as she searches in the dark space with a battery-powered torch.

She opens an unfamiliar door in a brick wall, revealing a storeroom packed with odd pieces of furniture, wooden crates, and tea chests—an Aladdin's cave of curiosities. Delving within a chest filled with packing straw, she extricates delicate cups and saucers belonging to a bone china tea set, along with a tarnished silver coffee pot. Elodie returns them with care and steps around the piles, stumbling in the dim light against a metal trunk. Despite it being dust covered and battered, she sees two letter Gs etched into the surface of the hinged lid. Her grandfather's initials.

She unfastens the latch and lifts the lid, exposing rusty digging tools, a hessian sack containing threadbare clothing, and a mouldy leather pouch. Unknotting the pouch's leather tie, Elodie pulls out a handful of yellowed papers and a cardboard mounted photograph. Faded in parts, the sepia image shows two men standing in front of a lean-to made of wood and corrugated iron. Protected by the roughly built structure are a wooden gold miner's cradle and a timber windlass positioned above a wide hole. She studies the men: a younger version of her grandfather bearing the familiar handlebar moustache, and a bright-eyed fellow with wispy face whiskers and a floppy felt hat. Someone had written '*Gerry and Clem*' on the reverse side of the photo.

A hasty perusal of the aged papers shows one is a document, a Queensland Miner's Right issued to *Gerald Greenwood* and *Clement Wallace* in January 1872, in the district of Gympie. Had the fabled gold nugget belonged to both men, sharing the fortune gained from its sale? If so, what had happened to Gerald's mining partner, and how had he used his windfall?

Elodie feeds the items back into the pouch and takes it with her into the main section of the cellar.

She chooses at random a bottle from one of the many well-stocked wine racks and frees the cork with a screwdriver found on a shelf. While gulping the rich, dark liquid, she wonders what her future will entail since it won't include Will. Is she doomed to die a frustrated old maid, destitute now that her father's debts have come to light? What will become of Grassington? Her mother? How will they survive? Desperation twists a dagger into her heart.

A hubbub of noise outside extinguishes her despondent brooding—excited voices, hurried footsteps.

Elodie moves over to the bulkhead doors and listens. Makes out words filtering through the timber slats.

'Found him.'

'The old well.'

'*Dead.*'

39

––––––––––

Grimm was less depressive on a Saturday morning. Although, daylight revealed deteriorated buildings that could benefit from a good sanding and paint job, with several needing a total restoration.

Townsfolk milled around, sitting on benches outside shops, or chatting in the shade of trees. Kids played handball against the toilet block in the Yowie park, and skateboarded down footpaths, enjoying the day before the sun reached its peak and sent them scurrying indoors. Even so, conversations paused, and cautious eyes trailed me as I walked from my car to the store. I was a stranger, an interloper, an oddity.

The store's air-con offered respite from the heat, even if only doing a half-arsed job. I waited at the counter for the attendant to finish slicing and dicing an iceberg lettuce and notice me. Only my deliberate knocking over a container of mints drew her attention.

'What can I do ya for?' the woman asked, wiping her hands on her denim shorts.

'Hi, I'm here to pick up an order of groceries for Paisley Croft from Grassington.'

'Oh ...' she sniffed, 'you're one of *them*.'

I scowled. 'One of what?'

'That lot.' She nodded her pink-frosted head towards the door before vanishing through a colourful PVC strip curtain.

Was her revulsion due to me being a tourist, or because of my connection with Paisley and Fletcher—the Greenwoods?

She returned with a cardboard box filled with the foodstuffs. 'That'll be eighty-nine fifty-five,' she said, keying the price into the cash register, her purple painted nails clicking as she typed.

'Okay, great, I'll let her know.' I went to lift the box from the counter when she slapped her hand down on top.

'Not so fast, darl. Payment first.'

'What?'

A deep sigh and an eyeroll. 'You need to pay before you take.'

'Oh ...' *Bloody Paisley*. She had better reimburse me. I paid by credit card.

A hint of a smile appeared on the woman's freckled face, exposing an unfortunate snaggletooth. 'Have a nice day,' she said, sliding her hand from the box.

It was then I read her name badge: *Brenda Sedgwick*. 'Are you related to Cole Sedgwick?'

A frown. 'What if I am? What's my brat-of-a-son done now?'

'Nothing. Well, nothing bad. All good.'

Brenda chuckled. 'Give him time.'

Not wishing to stir up more angst, I offered my thanks and carried the groceries out to my Vee-Dub.

Dumping the box on the front passenger seat, I spotted the hotel across the road and the signage secured to the fascia: *The Hairy Man*. A nod to the Yowie legend, or a rugged town pioneer? I shut the door and went in search of Darius the gardener.

The cramped and gloomy pub interior smelt strongly of malt and citronella mosquito repellent. A scrawny fellow slouching behind the long timber bar glanced up from his crumpled newspaper, no doubt alerted to my arrival by the Velcro-ripping sound made by the soles of my sneakers as I crossed the viscous beer-stained flooring.

He folded the newspaper and leant forward on bony forearms, his bulbous red nose protruding from the depths of his sallow complexion. 'Hello, luv, what can I get you? A cider? A cheeky chardonnay?'

'Umm ... I don't need a drink. I wondered if you could help me find someone.'

'What for?' His eyes brushed over my short overall dress, and he flashed a lopsided grin. 'I may be able to oblige.'

Filthy bugger! 'I'm looking for a local man named Darius. I was told this is his hangout.'

'And what does a blow-in like you want with him?'

'A chat. That's all.'

'About what?'

'Who are you, his minder?'

'Nah, he doesn't need my help. You're in luck. He's over there enjoyin' a cold pint.' He nodded to a spot over my right shoulder. 'You can take him another brew. Save me a trip.'

Turning, I noticed a tanned elbow jutting out from one of the timber booths along the side wall.

'Thanks,' I said, grabbing the beer and making my way over.

I slid into the bench seat opposite and placed the fresh beer on the table alongside two empty pint glasses. 'Great, I found you.'

My glee slipped away as I stared up at a middle-aged male with a shaved head and tattoos snaking up both arms. No workwear, just jeans and a black T-shirt emblazoned with the words *Save water, drink beer.*

'Oh, I seem to have made a mistake.'

I leant out of the booth and peered into the one behind, finding it vacant. I gave the bartender a questioning look, shrugging my shoulders. He cocked his head and pointed at the booth I was in. Was he enjoying a joke at my expense?

I angled in. 'Sorry. I'm seeking a man called Darius who worked as a groundsman at Grassington Estate.'

The bald guy smacked his lips together. 'Yep, that's me.'

I laughed. 'No, it isn't.'

'Ugh ... yeah, it is.' He thumbed his chest. 'Dylan Darius. I worked on the estate for fifteen years ... until recently.'

'But I'm looking for a much older man. Short, with a bushy white beard.'

His eyebrows bunched. Snatching his mobile phone from the tabletop, he flicked his fingers over the screen and held up a photo. 'Is this the fella? We both worked at Grassington for a time.'

I dropped my bag on the bench seat and inched forward. The image showed this bald guy across from me, standing with his arm around the shoulders of an older man—a little more tidily groomed, but recognisable as the individual I'd talked with in the rose garden. 'That's him. It's urgent I speak with him.'

Dylan considered me through narrowed eyes. 'If you're deadset he's the one you're lookin' for, there could be a problem. That bloke, Neville Darius, is me father. He's been dead for six years.'

I jarred my shoulder as I lurched back. 'He can't have. I spoke with him at length yesterday at Grassington ... *and* the previous day.'

'Impossible. Unless me dad pulled off a flamin' miracle and rose from the grave, he's buried in Grimm cemetery, right next to me mum.'

'But how could I have conversed with a dead guy?'

A moment of silence. 'Strange things happen up at Grassington. I've seen stuff that would make your flesh crawl.'

No shit! I grabbed the new glass and guzzled half the brew. My flesh wasn't just crawling, it was combusting in multiple tiny explosions.

Dylan eased forward, his scrutiny making me squirm in my seat. 'Who are ya, anyway? And why are you searchin' for me dad?'

'Paisley Croft is my sister. I'm staying at Grassington for a while to help with the guesthouse.'

'Paisley's sister, hey?' His eyes leered. 'You're nuthin' like her.'

Was that a compliment or a criticism? 'When I told Bridget Greenwood I'd spoken with the old gardener, she got excited, said she'd do anything to speak with him. I planned to arrange their meeting, however, it's impossible now because he's ... you know. Her dementia must have caused her to forget what had happened to him.'

'How bloody convenient for her.' He gave me another piercing stare. 'Tell that sister of yours I'm still waitin' to be paid. Jobs are close to none around here, and the sharks are nippin' at my heels.'

'Wolves,' I corrected.

'Hey?'

'Sharks circle, wolves nip.'

'Well, tell her they're both bloody after me and she'd better pay up!'

Blimey, somebody's jocks were in a twist.

We both flinched as a burly man burst into the pub yelling, 'Who the fuck owns that yellow bug parked on the other side of the street?' Dressed in a torn navy singlet and grease-smeared khaki shorts, he looked as solid and hairy as the town's decrepit Yowie statue, but way more beastly.

I edged out of the booth and raised my hand. 'Ahh ... that'd be me.'

He stabbed a soiled sausage finger in my direction. 'You're bloody well blocking my driveway, woman. Move it or I'll drive my truck right over it.'

I got to my feet. 'Sorry, thought I'd parked beside the kerb. I'll move it immediately.' I turned to retrieve my bag and tell Dylan I'd return to continue our chat, when I found he'd already scooted off and was nowhere in sight.

Rushing from The Hairy Man into a wall of heat, I sprinted across the road to my car, now surrounded by a mob of locals eager for a bit of action to liven up their day.

The car tyres skidded on loose bitumen as I made my quick getaway, no doubt disappointing many hoping to witness a monster truck pulverise a poor defenceless VW Beetle.

40

ELODIE

The coroner determines her father's shocking death to be a suicide by drowning.

Throngs of local folk and city contacts attend his funeral, eager to pay their respects. However, Will subsequently tenders his resignation, saying he is moving to Brisbane to work on the docks. Days later, Violet also removes herself from Grassington. Although no explanation was offered, the Greenwoods and Brights know precisely where she went and who she followed.

Olivia's idea of coping with grief is to summon the minister of the church in Grimm to exorcise the mansion of the evil that has brought the family so much misfortune. The use of bells, incense, and invocations creates a sense of peace that descends like a cleansing balm.

For added protection, Elodie performs a daily ritual of burning medicinal plants and purifying herself in the sacred smoke. She also employs her psychic ability to determine if any malevolent spirits haunt Grassington. With no fearful sightings—even Tommy has not reappeared—a new normality prevails.

Tempted by a morbid curiosity, Elodie visits the stone well a month after Henry's passing yet keeps her distance from the edge. The vision she'd seen here as a child—the corpse rising from the water—she now believes was a premonition. If only she'd been able to warn her father. The ball of grief kept imprisoned within her ribcage bursts free and tears flow freely. As wracking sobs force her to her knees, she beseeches her father's spirit, demanding to know what drew him to suicide. Was deciding to end his life the only answer to his financial problems?

It doesn't make sense. He was an innovator, a dream maker, a risk taker. Suicide would have been, in her father's view, a weakling's way out. And why did he choose to drown himself in the well? Wouldn't the dam have been a better location to do that, weighted down to submerge? Or he might have used a firearm from the property, a common method for rural suicides. Elodie harbours a strong suspicion there is more to her father's death than everyone is being led to believe.

She turns at a whispered *'My little gumnut'*, expecting to find her father standing behind. But she is alone. Her heart pains. It must have only been leaves rustling in a breeze.

Though a tough year ensues with Elodie and her mother struggling to manage the property, their early implementations succeed in ridding the mansion of sinister forces.

Zachariah and Maggie loyally stay on, caring for the household and the grounds as best they can. Nevertheless, genuine rescue comes in Samuel Hawthorne's offer to take on the role of property manager until Elodie comes of age and inherits Grassington. Yet, once she reaches the age of twenty-one, Sam proposes marriage to seal the deal. Elodie, seeing no other solution to their predicament, accepts his proposal with the proviso that he keeps the estate running rather than selling it off.

A swift society wedding that appears in all the Brisbane newspapers takes place, and the couple enjoy a short honeymoon in Sydney before sharing the position as owners of Grassington. Elodie's mother readily admits her satisfaction with the match, confident that the property will pass to her daughter and her daughter's future children.

Five trouble-free years go by. Though Elodie is saddened by her inability to bear children, Sam's proven worth in the marriage—offering stability and contentment in place of impetuous passion—bolsters her belief in lasting love.

Zachariah's sudden death from heart failure in 1928, and Maggie's move to Brisbane to be near her children and grandchildren, ushers in a new era for Grassington. The Estate even survives the years of the Great Depression by diversifying into growing crops and raising livestock to provide vegetables and meat, as well as milk from dairy cows, for the household. Along with other rural properties, they are more resilient during the hardship than their urban counterparts. With a devoted, hard-working husband, and an amiable mother willing to pitch in wherever possible, Elodie deems Lady Luck has smiled on them.

Until a ghost from the past returns one day in 1931.

41

I dropped the grocery box into the mansion kitchen and left before encountering anyone. A need for clarity brought me to the glade. If answers couldn't be found within the serenity it offered, then they couldn't be found anywhere.

I wandered around, all in a flap. How had I conversed with a dead guy twice, a man I'd seen as clear as day, who'd interacted with me and given me roses? I must have suffered psychotic episodes, disconnections from reality. Was I even here in this colourful garden right now, surrounded by twittering birds? I plucked one of the pink star-shaped lilies growing in profusion around me and rubbed it against my cheek. It felt real.

My sight drifted to the grotto and statue, the site of a hanging. What compelled a man to suicide in such a beautiful location? Despair? Or had he also suffered delusions?

Morbid curiosity coaxed me over and I climbed the stone stack below the dais. Stretching up and gripping the statue's jagged hem for balance, I stared up at the stony face, trying to fathom the horror her frozen gaze had witnessed that fateful day.

I visualised the man arriving in the glade, distraught, tormented, wishing to escape his struggles. Scrambling up the rocks to reach the statue, he looped his belt around his neck and paused, reconsidering his path to ultimate peace. *Was this the only way?* Maybe a calm took hold, giving him the courage to do what he must. Then, sucking in a deep breath, he attached the belt to the railing, offered an apology to those he was leaving behind, and jumped.

My eyes snapped shut. All the birds in the glade fell silent. In the space of several heartbeats, the only sound reaching my ears was the eerie creaking of a leather strap weighed down by a body buffeting the stones.

Opening my eyes, I found myself lying flat on the altar. A glance upwards stunned me as I caught sight of a stain trailing down the statue's face like a tear track. Was it there before? I tilted my head one way, and then the other. If I wasn't mistaken, her wide cheeks and tapered chin resembled features belonging to Elodie Greenwood. Had Olivia commissioned this statue in honour of her daughter?

Voices. Coming closer.

I scrambled down the rocks and bolted up the steps to hide inside the cave. The newly torn spiderweb, its drooping strands swaying in the breeze like cotton threads, gave an unobstructed view through the wall vent.

Rowan and Hilary appeared, stopping in my field of sight.

'How about here?' Hilary asked. 'What can you feel?'

Rowan paced in a circle. Then lifting her face to the sky, she raised her arms, palms flat, as if entreating the Almighty for guidance. Was Hilary also using her as a spirit indicator?

The ratchet-clicking call of a nearby crow caused Rowan to pivot towards the grotto and aim for the rock altar, where moments ago I lay spread out like a sacrificial offering. Rowan touched the rock surface, only to pull her hand away moments later.

'Something happened here,' she said with concern.

Hilary came alongside. 'Did you get an impression?'

Rowan's eyes fixed above as if locking onto the statue, then dropped to study the crevice. I stepped back against the wall, out of view.

Her voice carried. 'Let's go inside the grotto.'

Bugger! I didn't want them to catch me spying. Rushing out the opposite exit to the one Rowan and Hilary approached, I took the bushy path and stone steps leading up to the mansion.

Crossing the driveway, I stopped at a bleep from my phone. A message from Gemma, wanting to know who stood behind me in the pic taken the previous evening on the timber stairs. I'd thought I was alone when taking it, but when I scrolled through my photo album, I discovered she was right. Someone was on the step above me, near the wall. A scrawny, hollow-eyed woman resembling Olivia Greenwood in old age.

A voice drifted from the lower verandah: 'Hello? Hello?'

Addled, I ventured closer, only to glimpse Paisley pacing with her phone to her ear. 'Right, our connection's back,' she said, facing away. 'Yes, everything's going swimmingly.'

Curious as to who she was talking with, I concealed myself by the mock orange hedge in earshot of Paisley's conversation.

'The guests are lovely and are enjoying their stay. One night down and another to go ... Been a real help ... Getting the knack of any new role can be tricky.' A chuckle. 'No, I'm not pushing too hard.'

Was she conversing with Cole's mother? Brenda Sedgwick checking up on her son was a sensible act, but did she know how close the pair were?

'What's that? ... Well, there have been a few prickly moments

... yes ... Oh-my-God I agree, that attitude has to go, it's so childish.'

Poor Cole. He was still a kid. Teen angst came with the territory of youth. I stifled an urge to leap up there and grab the phone to enlighten Cole's mother on Paisley's immature outburst during the puttanesca dinner. I would have enjoyed sharing how my sister had ridiculed him and their family for no good reason. As leaves parted in a breeze, I saw Paisley now sitting on the top step and twirling a length of hair around her finger.

'To be totally honest, I think she's reaching her limit.'

She?

'Odd behaviour ... You know, scatterbrained, nutty thinking ... Yeah, probably stress, but I've seen it before. When it peaks, it's not pretty, right?' Another laugh. 'Shane, how did you cope all these years?'

Shane?!

The conversation wasn't about Cole. It was about me! And between my sister and my husband. My stomach gripped. How often had they shared similar criticisms, bad-mouthing me without my knowledge?

I swung around at a tapping on my shoulder.

'Abby, glad I found you,' Hilary said, drawing me out of the foliage. 'Want to go for a walk?'

Reeling from what I'd just overheard, I stammered, 'N-now? W-with you?'

Hilary frowned. 'Is that such a bizarre request?'

I looked back at the house verandah, catching Paisley walking inside. Were she and Shane still making fun of me? 'Sure. Okay.'

We strolled together, my diminutive form pronounced alongside Hilary's imposing height and confident gait. 'Is there a purpose for this walk?' I asked.

'We haven't had a one-on-one chat. I thought we could get acquainted.' She halted beneath a flourishing ivory curl tree, shadows from the windswept foliage dancing across her features. 'How do you interpret the cellar incident? Any idea who Rowan might have encountered down there?'

'Not at all. I only saw the wine bottle rolling across the floor.'

'What about Rowan's agony in the ... what did you call it? The Puccini room?'

'Puttanesca room. Yes, the pain doubled her over, making her scream. But I have no idea what caused it.'

Hilary nodded slowly. 'I've just taken Rowan to the grotto. Are you aware of the hanging death there?'

I mirrored her nodding.

'Oblivious to the incident, Rowan experienced being choked in the grotto cave. I had to drag her out for it to stop.'

'Geez, that would have been traumatic for both of you.'

'You bet. I now understand Rowan isn't being targeted by violent spirits. She is *clairsentient*. She manifests the pain of the spirits at their time of death. That is how they communicate with her.'

'You mean people actually died at the places where she sensed pain?' My mind checked off locations. 'That would include the stairs, the puttanesca room, the cellar, and now the grotto.'

'Don't forget her bedroom,' Hilary urged. 'I, incidentally, am *clairaudient*. I hear spirits speaking with me.'

'You hear dead people?' Why hadn't she mentioned that earlier? 'Have you heard any here at Grassington?'

'Of course. It's a real rabble at times. How about you, Abby? What have you experienced?'

I drew back. 'Why do you assume I've had any experiences?'

'You have a certain vibe,' she said with a smile.

A certain vibe? I wrapped myself in a hug. This was getting way too weird. Somehow, a confession tumbled out. 'I've … seen things. Things that defy explanation.'

'Visions? Ghosts?'

'Possibly. They seem so real. It's only since I've been staying at Grassington.'

'In that case, you may be clairvoyant, with spirits communicating visually. Inquisitive people like you search out answers, so there could be secrets needing to be revealed.'

'Secrets about the Greenwood family?'

'That's almost a given, though don't close your mind to other possibilities.'

'I think I photographed a ghost.' I scrolled through my phone to find the photo of Olivia with me on the stairs, however locating it proved difficult. Even the messages between Gemma and me regarding the pic were missing. 'That's odd. I'm sure I had an image.'

Hilary squeezed my arm, her touch sending a zap through me. 'Don't be afraid, Abby. *Trust your instincts and plough ahead*, that's my motto.'

I had promised Shane I'd be changing my behaviour, keeping my nose out of things. But after hearing him and Paisley enjoying a joke at my expense, I didn't give a hoot about conforming to rules.

'By the way, this is for you.' Hilary fished something from a pocket in her dress and dangled it in my face. A gold hoop earring similar to the pair I was …

I touched my ears and discovered an earring missing.

'Rowan found it in the grotto,' she said. 'I knew at once it was yours. I'd noticed them earlier at breakfast. They're lovely.' She fitted it into my ear, her nearness producing a deafening buzz, as if a thousand bees were making a hive of my brain. 'You didn't have to scurry away,' she whispered.

Had she seen me hiding in the cave, or had a blabbermouth spook snitched?

As we walked on, I noticed a small, lush, shrub growing alongside the path. Stooping, with the intention of plucking one of the many white trumpet-like flowers from its stem, my hand was whacked away.

'Be careful of this plant, Abby,' Hilary warned. 'It looks to be an Angel's Trumpet. Highly toxic. Touching or inhaling the flowers can be seriously hazardous to your health.'

I shoved my hands into my pockets. *That was close.*

We ended up at the cemetery, where Hilary recited her mantra, paying respect to the dead before entering. I introduced her to the inhabitants, pointing out those who'd died in tragic circumstances, and Hilary touched their headstones, nodding and murmuring, as if in conversation.

At Henry's grave, she gasped and dropped her hand. 'He didn't kill himself!'

'How do you know that?'

'He told me.'

I skewed round, fearing I'd catch his spirit floating nearby. 'Had he just fallen into the well and drowned?'

She gave a shrug. 'He said he'd been searching.'

'For what?'

'Let's find out.' She replaced her hand on the headstone and projected her voice. 'Henry, what were you searching for?' Her brow puckered and she caught my eye. 'I think he said *cold*.'

'He was searching for cold?'

'Yeah, that doesn't sound right. Maybe he's feeling cold.'

Hilary set both hands on the stone and repeated her question.

Moments later she turned to me. 'He said *gold*. Does that make more sense?'

I held my breath. Did Henry fall into the well while searching for the gold nugget? I hesitated, reluctant to disclose my limited knowledge to someone I barely knew. 'Ask him again if he fell by accident.'

She did and his response was a quick *No*.

An alarmed look passed between us.

'If he didn't jump on purpose or fall by accident,' I declared, 'then he must have been—'

'Pushed,' Hilary said, the same time I uttered, 'Murdered.'

'Who pushed you, Henry?' was Hilary's next question.

A lengthy wait, and Hilary shook her head and sighed. 'He's gone quiet. Seems like that's all we're getting today.'

I would have been happy to stay and keep trying, but she was keen to keep moving.

Hilary took another turn around the cemetery, with me trailing behind, until she suddenly paused. 'What's this here, another grave? I wonder why it's unmarked.' She crouched and hovered her hand over the spot.

A crow landed on the brick wall above her. It cocked its head left, right, and gave a rattle before issuing a protracted caw. Hilary startled me when, engrossed in using her gift, she craned her neck and met the bird's gaze. The bird immediately stiffened and toppled off the wall. Hitting the earth with a thud, it lay deathly still next to the sunken earth.

I stumbled back and tripped, falling hard on my bum. Fear nailed me to the ground when Hilary studied me with an icy stare, her pupils shrunken to pinpricks.

'He had to die,' she rasped in a voice unlike her own.

I cast a glance at the lifeless bird, wings spread, feathers stirred by the wind. 'The crow?' I groaned, my tailbone throbbing.

She pointed to the unmarked grave and growled, 'Him.'

The next instant, Hilary stood over me offering a hand up, her expression and tone showing genuine concern. 'Are you alright? That was a nasty tumble.'

What the hell!

Despite the agony, I excused myself and hobbled out of the cemetery, desperate to distance myself from Hilary and all the dead.

42

ELODIE

1931

Elodie consults a physician in Brisbane over fertility issues. After two days away, she returns to discover Sam has taken on another transient labourer desperate for work.

'The swaggie turned up yesterday. He's an alright bloke, just down on his luck like the others,' he explains. 'Has had experience with garden work, so I've put him in the groundsman's cottage. It's a little rundown, but I'm sure it's better than where he's been sleeping of late.'

Grateful her husband is a compassionate man, Elodie offers to put together fresh food and take it to the cottage. She baskets bread, cold cuts, and a flagon of milk, and follows the tree-lined track through stippled afternoon light. Rainbow lorikeets feeding raucously on flowering gums shower her with blossoms and leaves. She pokes a crimson bottlebrush flower through her hair clip and pats her newly cropped hair, styled in a modern bob with a fringe that her mother encouraged her to try.

'It's all the rage,' Olivia had said, showing her pictures from a women's magazine. 'Your appearance could do with an overhaul. You don't want Sam's attention roaming elsewhere.'

Elodie had bitten her tongue. What would lashing out at her mother achieve? In the end, she'd agreed. A change in style might lighten her mood.

A knock on the cottage door causes it to open a crack. All Elodie can see is a weathered and stubbled cheek, and a blood-streaked eye. She holds up the basket. 'Welcome to Grassington. I am Mrs Hawthorne. I thought these might help.'

'Leave it on the doormat,' the man mumbles.

'Oh, if that's what you prefer. If you need anything else, let me know.' Descending the steps, she looks over her shoulder, catching the man leaning out. Her eyes widen at the sight of a scarred arm reaching for the basket. 'Will?' she cries, turning around in shock. 'Is that you?'

He looks up, stupefied. The past nine years have not been kind to him. He's lost weight. His hair has thinned and receded, leaving a widow's peak in the hairline. Lines crease his sun-hardened face. Before he can shut the door, Elodie rushes back up the steps and slips past him into the cottage.

They stand in the entry, their eyes locked on one another.

'What are you doing at Grassington?' she asks, her vision swimming with pricks of light. She presses a hand on the wall to steady herself.

'I needed work.'

'But why Grassington? Surely you could find labouring jobs elsewhere.'

'Figured it would be easier here.' His face scrunches and he stares at the floor, his laceless boots shuffling on the worn linoleum. 'And ... I ... I needed to see you.'

Her chest constricts. 'But you didn't seem too eager to greet me just now.'

'I wanted to ... ah ... clean myself up a bit first.'

A study of his clothes shows they are tattered, with unmatched shirt buttons. There's dirt in the folds of skin around his neck and beneath his fingernails. He's been living rough for a while.

'What's happened to you, Will? Where is ...' Her mouth can't seem to form her ex-friend's name. 'Where's your family? I hear you've had a child.' Her stomach churns. 'Or maybe there are more now.'

'A daughter. She lives with her mother.' His eyes meet hers. 'We haven't been together for four years.'

Elodie squirms under his gaze, struggling to take in this news. Feels bad that she's pleased his life hasn't worked out well. 'Why did you want to see me?'

'Can we speak about this later? I've just run a bath.' He peers down at his grubby clothing. 'I need to change.'

'Of course. How long are planning on staying?'

'I do need the work, you know. I'm no slouch. Any money would greatly help in these tough times. Your husband seems like a good egg.'

'Sam is a Godsend. He's wonderful,' she adds, lifting her chin and smiling, boasting of her good fortune.

'Children?' he asks.

'Not yet.' Her heart aches with a stab of disappointment. 'Well, I'll leave you to it.'

Will holds the door open for her as she exits. 'Tonight?' he whispers. 'The usual place?'

Elodie frowns, brushing away flashes of stolen moments of ecstasy. 'The grotto?'

His lips pucker. 'I meant Fig Tree Hill. After dinner?'

She offers a quick nod and hurries away, wishing Will had never returned to upset her life's balance.

She arrives soon after sunset, feigning an evening stroll in the rose garden, while Sam retires to the office. Sitting on the swing, her heart pounds as she waits for Will. Hates that she took extra care with her appearance. *Stupid girl*, she chides herself. *Calm down. He hurt you, remember?*

Time passes. Almost giving up, she sees a light weaving through the old vineyard. Fusses with her hair, her dress, until footsteps reach her ears.

Will crests the rise, his breathing laboured. 'Crikey, it's still a mighty climb.' He hangs a kerosene lantern from a tree branch and leans against the trunk.

In the dim light, Elodie notices he has changed into better quality clothing. His hair is slicked back, and he is now clean shaven, the hollows in his cheeks more visible.

He gives the same smile that once charmed her. 'You're looking good, Elodie.'

She folds her arms across her chest lest he see the thumping of her heart. 'So, Will, what is the true purpose of your visit?'

'First, to apologise. I was beastly to you.' He rubs a hand across his mouth. 'It was all a big mistake. I wouldn't have gone if it wasn't for the baby. I never meant for that to happen.'

'The baby? Or cheating with my best friend?'

'Both, I reckon. It was madness, I know.'

'How long had it been going on, this madness with Violet?'

'Vi turned up at my quarters one night. We had a few laughs and got tipsy together. Things happened and she visited a few more times. It was easy with her. No expectations, just ... fun.'

Elodie slides from the swing to confront him face-to-face. 'And it wasn't with us? I'm sorry I was such a bore. So inexperienced.'

'She wasn't the marrying kind … not for me. You were. Then the baby changed everything. I couldn't let the kid grow up without a father.'

'Yet, that's what is happening now. You left her and her mother.'

'Vi left me. She ran off with another bloke. A travelling salesman. Took young Claudia with her.'

Claudia. A derivation of his mother's name.

Will's eyes glisten with tears. 'I've got nothing now. No family. No steady job. I'm dirt poor. It's humiliating.'

'What is it you're wanting from me? Cash? We're not as flush as we look. The depression has taken its toll on all of us.'

'You never found that gold nugget your father was so fixated on?'

'The gold? It's a myth. We all know that.'

'What if I tell you I don't go along with that notion? That I have reason to believe it is hidden somewhere on the property. Would you see fit to pay me a spotter's fee if I found it? Or a portion of the proceeds?'

'Are you suggesting a reward?'

'Yeah, something like that.'

Elodie takes a step backwards, paces around the swing. 'That's ridiculous. Why would you suppose such a thing?'

'That is why your father was at the well. I've thought long and hard about it. Don't you remember the message the clairvoyant had for him? *Ding dong bell.* It's a children's nursery rhyme. The second line being, *Pussy's in the well.* A hint of where to find the nugget.'

Elodie freezes in contemplation. 'You think it could still be there after all this time?'

'Has anyone else searched for it?'

She shrugs.

'If it's not there. It must be on the estate somewhere.' He grips her shoulders, her pulse racing at his touch. 'Give me time and I'll find it for you.'

'You're as loony as my dad. So, you're saying he didn't go there to kill himself?'

'I reckon he fell in before he had the chance to find the nugget. That's why it's got to still be there.'

'Unless ...' Elodie pulls away, her thoughts wandering, visiting a scene from the past. 'What if someone followed him and helped him fall?'

'Helped? You mean pushed him in? Who would do that, and why?'

'It's just a thought,' she says, searching her memories.

She yelps. 'Quick, turn the lantern off. I think someone is looking for me.' She points down the hill at the house, where a light bobs along the lower verandah.

Will twists the wick dial, extinguishing the flame. 'Is it your mother?'

'No. She's in Brisbane, visiting a cousin. Won't be back for a fortnight.'

They remain side-by-side on the hill, watching in the dark as the light weaves its way across the lawn and heads in the direction of the rose garden.

Will's fingers brush against hers. 'I'm sorry I was such a fool. I didn't mean to hurt you like I did.'

'It's all for the best.' A lengthy sigh. 'I'm happy with Sam. Really, I am.'

Another moment of silence.

'I should go back,' Elodie says, yet lingers, unwilling to break the intimacy of their nearness.

43

By the time I'd reached the mansion, I was convinced the incident in the cemetery was an illusion due to emotional strain, or maybe another mind flip. I'd certainly had enough of those recently.

Joe, standing at the main entrance, blocked my escape inside. 'Can I have a word?' he asked.

I attempted to pass, each sidestep countered by a move from him. 'Stop it, Joe. I need to get inside and rest or maybe drown myself in hard liquor.'

'Please, Abby, it's important.'

'So is my sanity.'

'That bruise on your head. How did you say you got it?'

My hand went to my forehead. At least the lump had shrunk away. 'I hit my head on a pantry shelf.'

'How'd that happen?'

'I don't know. I think I tripped. It made me dizzy and see double. Then I felt a migraine coming on.' I gave him a shove. 'Get out of my way, will you?'

He stood firm and gripped my arm. 'Any other symptoms?'

'Before or after I brained myself?'

'Either.'

Strangely, the strength of his grasp and regard for my health eased my distress. 'Well, I've been seeing wacky things—nature attacking, swirling visuals.' *Dead people. Hilary possessed by something evil.* 'Stuff like that.'

'Hallucinations, eh? Have you ingested any strange substances that might have caused this?'

'You mean drugs?'

'Anything. Food or beverage.'

My anxiety soared. 'What's with the twenty questions? I've been eating normally. I even ate a healthy muesli with fresh fruit for breakfast yesterday. Left an interesting aftertaste. Though Paisley tossed hers in the bin.'

'Where'd you get the muesli?'

'From Paisley's pantry. It was stored in a glass Mason jar.'

'Show me.' Joe tugged me down the steps and onto the lawn.

I dug my heels into the grass. 'You want to go to the cottage now?'

'I'm concerned you were mirroring a little of what Fletcher said he'd experienced.'

He guided me to his car ... well, Fletcher's car.

'We could walk there, Joe. It's not that far.'

He eased me into the front seat, placing his hand on top of my head like a cop with a perp so I wouldn't whack my skull on the door frame. 'I want to make sure you don't do a runner. Put your seat belt on, or I'll do it for you.'

'Not going to handcuff me to the steering wheel?'

'Now that's an idea.' The car rocked as he slammed the passenger door.

. . .

In the cottage kitchen, I searched the pantry for the jar.

'It's here but it's empty.' I held it out for him to view. 'That's odd.'

'Check the bin.'

I pressed my foot on the pedal bin and the lid flipped open. Someone had recently emptied it.

Joe groaned. 'Are there wheelie bins outside?'

'Probably.'

He opened drawers, found disposable gloves and a fresh bin liner, and together we went outside. Two large bins sat against the back of the cottage, one with a yellow lid designated for recycling. Did rubbish collection come out this far, or did they dispose of it themselves?

Feeding his hands into the gloves, Joe searched the general waste and found a recent white bin liner. Carefully ripping it open, he sorted through the kitchen scraps.

'Someone's tipped a heap of what could be muesli in here.' He scooped out a handful of dry oat mixture. 'Look at those dark grainy bits. That ain't just nuts or dried fruit. Something else has been ground down and added.'

'Like what?'

'Shrooms is my guess.'

'What? Magic mushrooms?'

He dropped the handful of muesli into the fresh bin liner and was inside and rummaging in the pantry before I'd made a move. I joined him just as he extracted a Ziplock bag from a high shelf. Held it up to the light, it looked to be half-filled with dried long-stemmed mushrooms.

'Boom!' he cried. 'There's our answer. Ingest these bad boys in any form and you'll be off your head in no time. Fletch wasn't seeing or hearing ghosts. He was just tripping on psilocybin.'

'So, that's what happened to me? Can I be tested to make sure?'

'A hair follicle drug test would determine it.'

Before I could object, Joe reached down and plucked several strands of hair from my scalp.

'Hey,' I cried, grabbing my head. 'A little warning next time, okay?'

Joe found a fresh Ziplock bag in a drawer and fed my hair inside.

'Why would Fletch want to trip on shrooms?' I asked. 'For fun?'

'I wouldn't think so. He's never been one to experiment with drugs.' He dropped the Ziplock bags into the bin liner with the muesli remnants. 'I reckon Paisley has been slipping hallucinogens into Fletch's meals. That's why she didn't touch her breakfast. And later, fearing she may be found out, she dumped the contents of the jar.'

'But where would Paisley get the shrooms? Was she trying to poison him?'

'More to make Fletch think he was going loco, I'd imagine. It wouldn't be too difficult to obtain them. Who knows what is grown out here in the country?'

'For what reason were they given to him?'

'That's what we'll have to determine. Were you aware Paisley had talked Fletch into going off his anxiety meds? Urged him to try more natural, noninvasive methods, such as meditation and naturopathy.'

'I guess magic mushrooms are pretty natural.'

'They can also be harmful in excessive doses. Imagine driving while hallucinating.'

I didn't have to imagine. Being a passenger in a car while tripping was bad enough.

'Fletch, with his mental health issues, wouldn't have purposely taken anything to distort his reality,' Joe said, his face filled with worry. 'Someone has been playing games with him. Deadly games.'

'I don't get it. How would Fletcher being deemed *non compos mentis* help Paisley?'

'It all depends on her reasons for doing such a thing. She could be holding a grudge and acting in retaliation.'

A bitter taste in my mouth. 'Has Fletcher done something wrong? You can tell me. If the scumbag has been up to no good—'

'Hey! I'm just postulating, offering theories. If Paisley were anyone else ... if I were back on a case like in the past, I might suspect she has her eyes on his inheritance.'

'Wouldn't he have to die for that to happen? Can magic mushrooms kill you?'

'Other mushrooms are more poisonous. There's a higher likelihood of Death Cap or Autumn Skullcap causing death if eaten. Not nice. Vomiting, diarrhoea, hypothermia, liver damage, and coma before dying. However, Fletch showed no such symptoms. Yet, like I said, if he'd been disoriented enough, a serious accident may have occurred.'

'That's intense.'

Joe agreed. 'In the eventuality of Fletch's death preceding Paisley's, there's a likelihood his inheritance would pass on to her, being his spouse. But you'd have to examine his will for that.'

His will. The open drawer in the office filing cabinet. The folder jutting out. Had Paisley been checking on the legalities of Fletcher's will?

'But what about Bridget? Wouldn't both she and Fletcher need to die before Paisley inherited anything?' My heart pounded when I saw Joe confirm this with a nod. 'Neville said he needed to keep a watchful eye on Bridget. I assumed health concerns. Perhaps he suspected something far more alarming, like a safety issue.'

'Neville who?'

I hesitated. He'd surely consider me bonkers. 'Neville Darius. He … er … spoke with me.'

A puzzled look from Joe. 'But he's dead. I'd say there was more chance you'd talked with Keith, but even that's far-fetched.'

My turn to be baffled. 'Who's Keith?'

'Neville's brother.'

'Neville had a brother?'

'Yeah, dead ringers for each other. Fletch and I used to call them Tweedle Dee and Tweedle Dum. They both worked here as groundsmen.' Another jaw-clenching. 'What makes you think you spoke with Neville?'

I babbled. 'I chanced upon him in the rose garden the other day. Then I drove into Grimm this morning in search of him, and ended up speaking with his son … who told me his father was dead … which threw me because it implied I'd spoken with a ghost in the garden …. and I thought I was going bonkers … and now you're telling me there were lookalike brothers?'

I stopped to catch my breath, thoughts tumbling like fruit symbols on a poker machine. 'What if I hadn't seen a ghost at all? Maybe I'd been talking to this Keith fellow.'

Joe clicked his tongue. 'But you couldn't have because they locked him up in 2013. He's been serving time in prison for killing Neville in a fit of rage. Terrible business.'

'You're kidding me! He killed his brother? Are you sure he's still behind bars?'

Joe held my gaze for a moment. 'We should get back.'

I agreed. 'First, let me grab some extra clothes.'

I found a reusable shopping bag in the kitchen and stood confused in the doorway to the spare room. 'Who's been sleeping in my bed?'

Joe stood with me, his attention on the mess of sheets and

skewed pillow. 'Who are you, one of the three bears? You didn't leave it unmade like that?'

A huff. 'Of course not.'

He walked over and examined the bedding. Pinching the surface of the pillow, he raised his hand to his eyes. 'A strand of hair. Green.'

'Cole,' we said in unison.

In the wastepaper basket, I discovered a dry facial wipe smudged with mascara and glitter eyeshadow. 'I'm certain he said he was going out for the night. Looked pretty rough this morning, too.'

'Maybe he crashed here afterwards. He might sleep here for convenience.'

My eyes zeroed in on the graphic novel in the bookcase. Not Paisley's. 'Does he usually live with his mum? I think I met her in Grimm, working in the store. Not the warmest personality.'

'Brenda never was the cheery sort.'

'You know her?' I held up both hands. 'Don't tell me. You met her when you were kids when you stayed here with Fletcher.'

'Spot on. Her parents owned the grocery store, known back then as Sedgwick's Corner Store and Teashop.'

'But it's not on a corner.'

'I know, and it served little in the way of tea. Weird, huh? Nice assortment of lollies and smokes, though. We sampled both on the sly. Fletch's dad would have truly locked us up if he'd caught us puffing away.'

Joe scanned the room and, leaning forward, frowned. Sticking a foot under the bed, he dragged out the missing purple vibrator. He raised his eyebrows as he regarded the gnawed and lint-covered dinosaur. 'Lost something? The teeth marks are interesting.'

I kicked it back under the bed. 'It isn't mine. Whitby ran off with it the other night.'

'Curiouser and curiouser,' Joe said with a lopsided smile. He lifted the worn tobacco tin from the bookshelf and turned it over in his hands, giving it a rattle. 'What's in this old thing?'

'No idea. I found it in the cemetery, but it's rusted shut.'

'Might contain something of worth.' He twisted the lid without success. 'So, you've met Dylan Darius. What's your take on him?'

'Did you know he was employed here until recently?'

'Not sure if you'd call it work. According to Fletch, he's a bludger. As lazy as a toad. That's one reason for firing him when they took over this joint.'

'What other reasons were there?'

'Well ... ugh ...' He grimaced while attempting to lever open the tobacco tin lid with a fingernail. 'Fletch suspected him of helping himself to some bits and bobs from the estate.'

'You mean stealing? Bridget told me valuables have been going missing from the mansion, but she crazily blames Paisley for doing the pilfering. She's been keeping a list.'

'An inventory, hey? That could prove helpful.' I could almost hear the gears turning in his head. 'A shame we can't catch Dylan in the act now that he's not working here.'

A metallic clink as the rusty lid fell on the floor.

Joe fingered what was in the tin and held up an item for me to see—a bronze medal hanging from a rainbow striped ribbon.

'It's a victory medal awarded to those who served in the First World War,' he said, pointing out the winged figure of Victory on one side and the words *THE GREAT WAR FOR CIVILISATION 1914-1919* inscribed on the other. He lifted out two more medals— one with a red, white, and blue ribbon attached to a four-pointed bronze star. The other, a blue, white, and gold ribbon with a silver medallion showing the head of King George V. 'Whoever owned these, saw military action in The Australian Imperial Force.'

'Any name on them to show who they belonged to?'

'No. But there's a postcard photograph here of a guy in a military uniform.' He handed it over.

I studied the creased black-and-white image of a soldier in a World War I military uniform, crouched beside an archaic machine gun mounted on a tripod stand. Written on the back was *Will Flanagan, Amiens 1918,* and a service number. He appeared to be in his late teens, and ruggedly good looking. I recalled Hilary's ominous words in the cemetery: *He had to die.* Was this the person buried in the unmarked grave?

'How is he connected to the Greenwoods?'

Joe shrugged. 'Beats me. The service number should make him easy to research.' He removed a wad of tissue paper, which unfurled in the palm of his hand. 'Look, there's also a pressed flower and a lock of hair.'

I recognised the dried bloom as the star-shape flower growing in abundance in the glade. The hair fastened by a thin blue ribbon was blonde, almost pure white.

44

—————

Someone had already arranged picnic hampers on a cloth-covered trestle table on the eastern verandah. I counted them to make sure no more needed to be brought out from the kitchen and noticed one tied with a tag marked with the name *O'Mara*. Making sure Daphne's dietary requirements were met, no doubt.

Joe came alongside, whistling the tune of *Teddy Bears Picnic*. I sang along in my head. The words, *If you go down to the woods today, you're sure of a big surprise*, striking fresh fear into my heart.

Paisley appeared, quick to chastise us. 'Where have you both been? I could have done with some extra help.'

'We've been at the cottage,' Joe said.

Her glare bounced between him and me. 'And what were you doing there ... all alone ... out of sight?'

I stiffened. *What was she implying?* On the verge of bitch-slapping my sister, I felt Joe's hand press into the small of my back to still my anger.

'We're here now, Pais,' he said in a calm tone. 'What can we do?'

Ignoring the question, she turned and addressed the guests congregating around the table. 'Picnic wherever you like,' she announced. 'The baskets are ready for collection. Vince and Daphne, yours is tagged. Oh ... and while everyone's here, has anyone come across Rowan's gold bangle? She seems to have misplaced it somewhere in the house.'

'My Rolex watch is missing, too,' Vince said. 'I'm sure I'd left it in our room.'

'Have you checked in the ensuite?' Daphne asked. 'Didn't you take it off in there before showering last night?'

'Of course I've checked. That's the first place I looked.'

'Hopefully, the items will turn up soon,' Paisley said with a cursory look of concern.

Most chose shaded areas close to the mansion. Luke and Rowan aimed for a blanket under a jacaranda, while Sandy and Joe—accompanied by Whitby—sat at a picnic table beneath a Moreton Bay fig. Hilary took her basket to an old bullock dray used as a garden feature, setting her food items in a row on the weathered timber like condemned criminals facing a firing squad. The O'Maras, meanwhile, decided to 'luncheon' in the rose garden.

With no string quartet on the premises, I went to collect the Bluetooth speaker to play soothing music suitable for a garden party. Unable to locate it behind the peace lily in the dining room, I asked Cole if he'd moved it when cleaning up last night. He looked anxious, and I agreed Paisley would be furious if she found out it had gone missing. I talked Cole out of doing his own search and left him drizzling lemon syrup on a sponge cake while I hunted elsewhere.

I eventually found the speaker where it wouldn't have gone

unless it had grown legs, propped up on the window ledge in the drawing room near the piano. Who had moved it and when? Then it struck me. Was that how I'd heard *Danse Macabre* being played at midnight? Had someone deliberately set it up, playing music from their own device as a wicked joke?

I returned to the verandah to question my sister when the O'Maras rounded the corner of the building, Vince with his arm wrapped around his blubbering wife.

Paisley raced down the steps. 'What's happened? Daphne, are you hurt?'

A commotion ensued as the guests hurried over and crowded around.

'Did you see something spooky?' Hilary asked, her eyes alive with excitement.

When Daphne raised her head, we all gasped at her bright red face, resembling a severe case of sunburn. 'Anna-pilac-thith,' she blurted through lips as swollen as a celebrity's trout pout.

'Anaphylaxis?' Paisley drew back. 'Do you have an EpiPen with you?'

'Yes, thank God.' Vince stroked his wife's cheek. 'You should have seen her moments ago. I thought we were going to lose her.'

Daphne shot Paisley an icy stare. 'It happened after I'd eaten.'

Paisley scowled. 'I can assure you, Daphne, every item in your picnic hamper was safe for you to eat.'

Luke came to my sister's defence. 'Maybe it was one of your muesli bars, Daphne. Did you check the ingredients?'

'Definitely.' Vince said. 'She's had them before, with no reaction.'

'Are you allergic to bee stings?' Sandy jumped in. 'There are plenty of bees around the rose bushes. Or pollen? I've noticed several casuarina trees here in flower.'

'What about toxic plants?' Rowan's input. 'You may have

brushed against a bush. Certain plants secrete oil or sap that can cause allergic reactions.'

'No, she only has food allergies,' Vince said sternly.

Daphne gave a moan. 'It wath thumthing I ate, I tell you. Take me to our room, Vinth. I think we thould return home.'

'No, dear, we can't leave yet. A lie down will put you right. You always recover quickly after treatment.'

Paisley trailed them up the verandah steps to the side entrance. 'I'll bring you a cup of tea or a cold drink. An ice pack, even. Whatever you need.' Grovelling was an awkward fit on my sister.

If she had been ultra-careful when preparing Daphne's meal, like she said, had someone else taken the opportunity to do harm? Who would have a motive? I glanced at Cole standing near the trestle table. Was that a smile tweaking the corners of his mouth?

'Come with me,' Joe demanded, tugging me away from the melee.

He took me to the rose garden. At the wrought iron table in the gazebo, he stood over the spread of food items left by Vince and Daphne.

'Do you notice anything unusual? An item? An ingredient?'

'Why didn't you drag Paisley down here? She'd know better than me.' His harrumph and disapproving glare caused me to add, 'Oh ... you reckon she's a suspect. What about the possibility of it being Cole? You weren't there at breakfast when Daphne complained about the scrambled tofu he'd cooked.'

'And that would give him reason enough to poison the old girl? I don't think so. Poisoners derive pleasure from seeing their victims suffer, and I can't imagine young Cole being so vindictive over a little criticism. He'd be more likely to spit in Daphne's drink.'

'Yet you can imagine Paisley doing it?'

'If she can drug her husband to make him think he's going insane, who knows what else the crazy bitch is capable of.'

'But what motive would she have had for exacting revenge that may have proven fatal?'

Joe examined a container of strawberries, lifting a nibbled one up by the stem. 'Could be as simple as payback for griping about her recipe. People often commit violent crimes on impulse, arising suddenly under intense emotional pressure.'

Which described my sister's current state of mind to a tee. I pondered for a moment.

Joe gave me his full attention when I said, 'Maybe it was something else. Before I ran into you on the verandah this morning, I discovered the office filing cabinet open and a folder poking out labelled "Wills". Paisley mentioned Bridget had thoughts of changing hers and bequeathing Grassington to the Heritage National Trust. Vince is a solicitor. What if he's covertly working for Bridget? Paisley might have found out and didn't like it. Took her anger out on his wife as a warning to back off or leave. One way to get rid of him.'

Joe seemed unconvinced. 'Why would Bridget do an idiotic thing like handing over the estate at no cost? I thought she cared about her nephew.'

I threw up my hands. Everything was becoming too complicated for my tiny brain.

'Let's first find evidence of something that induced anaphylaxis, hey, Abby?'

While Joe resumed his inspection of the picnic food, I removed a partially eaten bread roll from a plate and separated the two halves. Picking off the salad mix, I sniffed the savoury spread, smelling hints of garlic, lemon, curry powder, and ... Was that pureed cauliflower or ...

I handed the bread roll over to Joe. 'You might want to get this spread tested for chickpeas. Where's the nearest forensic testing centre?'

'You mean a crime lab? In Brisbane, but I don't plan on travelling there right now.'

'Then bag it. Perhaps bag everything and get the lot tested for fingerprints or DNA or whatever, along with my hair follicles.'

'I'm no longer with the police, remember? I don't have the same privileges as when I worked on the force.'

'You were willing to submit the shrooms as evidence ... or do you intend to keep them for personal use?'

'Go to hell!' He dropped everything into the hamper, including the dirty plates and cutlery. 'I'll try to call in some favours. But I'm not leaving here now that things are heating up.' He thrust the basket into my arms. 'Take this to your room and hide it well.'

I hid the hamper in the wardrobe in the servants' room. Realising Paisley would discover it missing, I took a cardboard box from the kitchen and emptied the hamper's contents into it before slipping the box under the bed.

In the office, I faced the filing cabinet and wondered whether Vince, or another, had removed something from the Wills files. How could I determine what had been extracted when I didn't know what the folder had contained?

'Abby, there you are. Copy this, will you?' Paisley stood in the doorway holding up a sheet of paper, a form. 'It's an incident report for my own records. You can never be too careful.'

'For what happened to Daphne?'

'For what I *know* about what happened.'

'Which is?'

'That I have no knowledge of what transpired and wasn't involved in anything suspicious.'

How long had she been rehearsing that line? 'Is that an accurate statement?'

She gave me snake eyes, and I expected a forked tongue to dart from her mouth when she hissed, 'Are you calling me a liar? What kind of sister are you to doubt my word?'

I could have boomeranged that statement straight back at her. Scared I might be her next victim, I cowardly shifted ground. 'I meant, Cole may have mistakenly added an ingredient causing Daphne's reaction.'

'Cole? I was the one who prepared the lunches and packed the hampers.'

Would her confession be admissible as proof against her in court? 'What if he snuck something in on the sly, or transferred the O'Mara's name tag to another hamper?'

'Why would he do that? You obviously watch too many crime shows.'

Because I did, I knew that anyone with a strong motive could be driven to dark deeds. Even my sister.

Paisley sniffed the air. 'I think something's burning in the kitchen. Print two copies and file them in the folder in the filing cabinet marked OH & S.'

I should have followed and confronted her, but without Joe as reinforcement, I piked. 'Hey, you owe me money for the groceries,' I yelled.

'Take it from the petty cash tin in the bottom drawer of the desk,' she shouted from down the hallway.

I removed a sheet of paper left under the scanner cover and replaced it with Paisley's report. Pressing the print button, I swept my eyes over what I'd dropped on the desk, finding it to be an original document from a bygone era. A thrill ran through me when I read the words: *The Last Will and Testament of Henry Arthur Thomas Greenwood.*

I scoured the text, noting that Henry's remaining fortune and properties were to be left to his wife, and on her death, his eldest living child, or in the absence of children, his closest surviving relative. No preference given for the legitimacy of the said child, nor the sex. Meaning illegitimate daughters possessed equal inheritance rights to legitimate sons.

Was this what I'd heard being printed earlier? Someone making a copy? But why, and for whom?

I printed my own copy of the will and filed the original in the cabinet, along with Paisley's Incident Report forms. Before leaving, I tugged out the desk's bottom drawer, prised the lid on the unlocked cash tin inside, and relieved it of a handful of notes. The drawer stuck halfway when sliding it back in. Jiggling it, and giving it a few good thumps, something dropped onto the floor beneath.

I fed my hand under this section of the desk and dragged out a vintage cast iron key. A strip of adhesive tape attached to it showed someone had secured it to the underside of the drawer. I stared across the room at the velvet curtain obscuring the strongroom.

Tugging the drape aside, I inserted the key into the grille's rim lock and gave it a turn. A rotation of the brass knob and the grille door opened a fraction, the hinges creaking when swung wider to allow me to slip inside. Other than empty wall shelves, it really was a bare space. What if it contained a hidden panel like the upstairs hallway?

I patted the brick walls, stamped my feet on the floor, and studied the ceiling. No secret panel, no trapdoor, and no manhole. It was just what it was, a strongroom for storing valuables. I was about to leave when the grille door clanged shut. Twisting the knob did nothing. I nervously squeezed my hand through to manoeuvre the key in the lock when my fumbling made me lose my grip, the key dropping to the floor. Groping for it, the key shot across the floor out of reach, as though tugged by an invisible force. *Shit!* I rattled the bars in frustration.

The house held me captive, but for what purpose?

I examined the interior with fresh eyes and, to my amazement, discovered *BEWARE CW* gouged deep in the brickwork beside the door. Who had done this, and when? It had to be a clue of sorts.

A sudden click, and the grille opened a crack all by itself. Having found the scratched message, was I now free to leave?

I rushed out. After locking the door, I stashed the key in the desk drawer, took Henry's will, and hurried to the servants' room.

45

I pushed aside the shopping bag of clothes retrieved from the cottage and cleared a space on the bed for Henry's will and Arthur Conan Doyle's book on Spiritualism. Lifting out the tobacco tin I'd also dropped into the bag, I added it to the array. My heart fluttered. Right then, I didn't believe in coincidence. With these items and the *BEWARE CW* message, what puzzle did the house require me to solve? Or maybe there were multiple puzzles.

I flicked through the pages of the book and extracted the notepaper with the letterhead. Who was *Madame M. Montague*, and why was the note dated *19th Jan, 1921*?

An internet search on my phone for this woman led me to the newspaper archive site. According to several articles, Madame Maud Montague was an eminent Brisbane clairvoyant during the 1920s, in demand for holding seances and crystal readings. Henry's ownership of Conan Doyle's spiritualism book showed he'd had an interest in communicating with the dead. Had Madame Montague held a seance for him, by chance, the day before his death? Was *DING DONG BELL* a message received from the afterlife?

And the items in the tobacco tin. Who was William Flanagan?

I visited The Australian war Memorial website, typed in the service number written on the back of the photograph found in the tin, and up came his full name, *William Brody Flanagan*. A click on a tab took me to a scanned copy of his enlistment papers, which stated he'd joined up in Ipswich in April 1918 at age eighteen. The contact person was his father, *Colin Flanagan*, living at Rosewood. It also mentioned when and where he served overseas, and the injuries he sustained in the Battle of Amiens in August of that same year.

An additional search on the family history website gave electoral roll information on a William Brody Flanagan who had resided at Grassington Estate, Grimm, in 1921, and worked as a vintner. Then in 1924 he lived in Hamilton, Brisbane, and worked as a labourer. A *Violet Flanagan* lived at the same address, listed as employed in home duties. His wife? No listings for William on any rolls after that, though Violet's name appeared at various addresses until the late 1960s.

Unsure who *CW* was or why this person inspired fear, I had to find Joe. I needed a clever mind and his, however convoluted, would suffice. In the meantime, I hid all the articles in the shopping bag and shoved it into the wardrobe.

He wasn't in Bridget's room. I knocked and waited with my ear pressed to the door, yet it remained shut.

'If you're looking for the old girl,' Sandy said from the top of the stairs, 'she's foraging for food in the kitchen and piling a tray with fruit.'

'Oh, right. You haven't come across Joe, have you? He's the one I want to see.'

'Nope. Sorry.'

'How'd you go at the sawmill today? Find anything interesting?'

He held up what looked to be a plastic fishing tackle box and gave it a rattle. 'Quite a bit. Plenty of nuts, bolts, and horseshoes, as you'd expect. Though old coins, a cigarette lighter, and a gold ring made the find more worthwhile. A little cleaning and they'll come up a treat. Paisley said we could keep anything not of worth to her.'

'Great.' An idea formed. 'Did you locate a well while exploring the grounds?'

'A well?'

'Henry Greenwood drowned in one somewhere on the property.'

'What bad luck. No, we haven't come across one yet. Though there is a cairn I'm keen on checking out. At least that's what it appears to be on the map you gave us.'

The stone circle. What if it was the site of the well? 'Would you be prepared to have a look now? I'd love to come with you.'

Sandy's face lit up. 'Sure. Let me get my metal detector from the car. I'll find Luke and meet you outside in about fifteen minutes, okay?'

I fetched a hat from my room and opened the wardrobe door to retrieve my joggers. For a second time, I searched for evidence of someone having hidden within, ready to pounce. Scuff marks from shoes or handprints would do. Even a blob of used chewing gum stuck to a panel would ease my mind in knowing a living person had concealed themselves in the wardrobe.

I examined the woodwork, patting the sides and rear for a false panel. Excitement surged when I discovered a small notch at the back, perfect for a finger grip. After some manipulation, a section slid sideways, exposing an opening in the wall behind, just the right size for someone to crouch and sneak through.

Dauntlessly, I did just that and entered a narrow space between the bedroom and bathroom walls. Perhaps the nighttime tapping and pounding had come from within this cramped area, not from someone hiding inside the wardrobe.

Dust and the smell of mice made me sneeze as I shuffled crablike through the cobwebbed passageway until I hit a dead end. Intrigued by a set of metal rungs screwed to the end wall, I didn't hesitate to climb up and go through a hole in the ceiling to reach another level. Here, I moved from the rungs to a platform upon which a wooden ladder rested against a side wall.

As I tackled the ladder, my foot slipped, jarring my knee. I swore. I cursed again when I reached an air vent and peered through tiny curlicue holes into what I realised was Rowan's bedroom. So, a ghost had not emitted the voice that had called my name through this same vent, but someone with a penchant for spying. Another theory debunked.

I jumped as the door flew open and Rowan burst into the room. Lifting the mattress on the spare bed, she extricated the blue manila folder I had seen yesterday. After shuffling through typed pages, she removed a sheet and underlined occasional words with a pen, making notes in the margin. I itched to know what she'd added to her info on *The Greenwood Curse*.

Too slow to stifle a sneeze brought on by the dust, I ducked back when Rowan looked up and cocked her head questioningly at the noise she'd heard. I climbed down the ladder with care, only for my shoulder to bump against the timber wall frame. Something tiny fell off and shot down the front of my overall dress. Dreading it was a mouse, I shoved my hand inside and yanked it out, shuddering when I saw it was neither alive nor a mouse. Shrivelled, leathery, and fastened to a metal clasp, it looked to have been a paw of a small animal before it became a ... what ... a talisman? A charm? For good luck or bad? By finding it had I hexed myself?

I staggered back against the end wall, which swung open and pitched me into the mansion's upper hallway. Splayed on the carpet runner, I realised my clumsy entrance was gained through a secret door in the wall panelling. Hearing noises from Rowan's room, and fearing she was about to open her door, I dropped the paw into my bib pocket and pressed the wall panel shut, choosing to take the staircase down to the lower floor like a normal person.

What was the hidden passageway's original purpose? Ease of access between floors for the servants? Or something more debauched, such as assignations between upstairs residents and downstairs help?

Who here would know of its existence? Bridget, Paisley, Fletcher, and Cole were the most probable people. Even Joe might have been aware of it. Yet, I couldn't imagine Bridget having the mindset of a trickster to frighten me in the wardrobe last night, let alone the agility to climb the iron rungs. And Joe would have had to move at warp speed and pull off a good performance to fool me into believing I'd just woken him. Paisley too would have had to hightail it from the cottage and creep into the passageway without me twigging to her presence. That left ... *Cole.*

Just because he'd hinted he was heading out on a date after dinner—or I'd assumed that's where he was going—didn't mean it had occurred. Cole's enthusiasm may have resulted from his involvement in spooky games. At my sister's request, he could have orchestrated all the strange goings-on last night. In that way, Paisley could claim her innocence by being absent from the mansion when the incidents took place. But that didn't stop her from pulling the strings on her puppet, her loyal devotee, drawn over to the dark side with the promise of a monetary reward or a brighter, more fulfilling future. Paisley may have even coerced Cole into 'poisoning' Daphne.

My tolerance reached its limit. It was imperative that I confront my sister and call her bluff. However, it would have to wait until after tonight's dinner. I had a well to find.

46

ELODIE

1931

Elodie walks through the glade in the late afternoon, impressed with the gardening work Will has achieved over three weeks of clearing undergrowth from the tree-lined slope below the manor house. He has successfully rid noxious lantana and giant devil's fig, created rockeries and pathways, and planted many flowering shrubs. Sam, pleased with taking a chance on a stranger, is unaware of Will's history with Grassington and past relationship with Elodie. And she is determined to keep it that way.

Ascending the stone steps, Elodie enters the grotto as planned and adjusts her vision to the gloom. Will is already there, sitting on the stone bench, puffing on a half-smoked cigarette. His eyes light up at her appearance, and once again, her heart skips a beat. Regular meals and labouring work have given him a more healthy, muscular frame, and the hollows in his face have filled in.

Dropping the cigarette and grinding it into the ground with his boot heel, he pats a spot beside him.

Elodie flops onto the bench. 'How's it going, Will? No success yet in finding the nugget?'

He sighs deeply. 'I thoroughly searched the likely locations. It's not down the well, as you're aware, after giving me a hand in climbing out again. Or in the logging sheds. Neither has Gerald's old hut in the bush revealed anything. I suppose he could have buried it underground. But where? The possibilities are endless.'

'Yes, it's like the proverbial needle in a haystack. I've been working my way through the mansion. Thus far, my search has been a failure.'

'I'm thinking I might have to stay here a few more months.'

Elodie's whispered response is emotion-charged. 'Would that be so bad?'

Will gives her knee a squeeze through her gaberdine skirt. 'Of course not.'

The potency of his gaze heats her cheeks. She glances away and wrings her hands. 'If I were still a single woman ...' The guilt of contemplating such desires twists her heart into a tighter knot. 'We need to be cautious in meeting like this. Wouldn't want Sam to think we're up to no good.'

Will lifts her chin, turns her face towards his. 'What if we were? No-one needs to know.'

'You're not suggesting—'

His mouth on hers ignites an internal blaze so strong she fears it will turn her to ash. Since his arrival, Elodie has imagined this moment. Wrestled with the right and wrong of it. Now, as her fantasy comes true, she surrenders, her soul falling, spinning like a gum leaf in a breeze. Down, down, down.

Menacing laughter breaks the spell.

It isn't emitted by Will, nuzzling her neck, his hand inside her blouse. It emanates from a dark corner of the grotto. Has Sam followed her, snuck in, and caught them?

Elodie shoves Will away and springs from the bench. The laughter echoes, bouncing from one rock wall to another. She covers her ears. Nearing the shadowy nook, she inhales an offensive odour. Two burning coals stand out in the inky blackness.

She screams.

Will crushes her within an embrace. 'What's the matter?' he demands. 'What's upset you?'

Had he not heard the cackling? Seen the hideous thing watching them? She wrenches free at another disturbing sight.

They're back.

The dead soldiers huddle around Will as if guarding him against ... what? The evil in the corner ... or her?

She escapes outside and takes the path up the slope leading to the mansion.

47

___

The Michaelsons had waited for me on the front steps, and together we walked the grounds. Skirting the perimeter of the rose garden, we crossed an elevated area towards a line of trees and found the remains of an old stone well, crumbling and shrouded in milk thistle. Removing the timber covering, the well proved to be deep, although it contained barely enough water to drown a rat, much less a man. However, Sandy and Luke seemed enthusiastic about the possibility of finding something about which they wouldn't elaborate. Of course, I knew it was the gold nugget. I would have quizzed them about it if I hadn't glimpsed movement nearby in scrub—a figure, human-sized. Was Henry's ghost watching us? No, it appeared to be large and hairy.

I left the detectorists to do what they did best and went to investigate. If in luck, I'd sight the legendary Yowie.

I followed the snap of dry twigs and rustle of foliage and pushed deeper into what became a dense forest of wild bushes, lantana, and gnarled trees. At some point, the noises ceased. Momentarily disoriented, I glanced around for signs of the creature's whereabouts. A shuffle through leaf litter urged me to edge round a large wattle tree, only to spy a huge goanna stretching its neck upwards and tasting the air with its forked tongue before clawing its way up the trunk to safety.

Using my limited knowledge of bushcraft, I tracked vegetation disturbances of scuff marks in dirt, flattened grass, bent and snapped plant stems. Something had also trampled on a clump of bright leathery fungi growing at the base of a tree trunk. There was an air of mystery in branches swaying and creaking, some catching in my hair like stick fingers as I passed. Yet the subject of my search remained beyond my reach.

Just when I'd given up hope of finding my quarry, a flash of blue through breaks in foliage directed me to a small clearing where a pop-up tent stood amongst the ruins of an old bush hut, the timber stumps and rusted strips of corrugated iron being the only visible traces of a simple dwelling. The coals and ring of rocks surrounding an extinguished fire pit were cold to the touch, the billycan amongst the ashes empty of water. As no-one appeared to be present, I thought it safe to inspect more closely.

I unzipped the tent a fraction and poked my head in, discovering a single inflatable mattress topped with a sleeping bag and, resting alongside, an LED lantern. The planned encampment, evidenced by food tins, packets of ready-to-eat meals, and stainless-steel cooking utensils, suggested more than an overnight stay. After so long in prison, was Keith Darius's house near Grimm no longer available, forcing him to construct a bivouac?

A crunch of dried leaves caused me to pull out and scan the bush. My legs buckled as a shaggy figure slunk from behind a flaking paperbark tree.

'What the hell,' I gasped, realising it wasn't a Yowie or a wild animal, but someone dressed in a leafy ghillie suit. When the person removed the hood, revealing a face streaked with khaki face paint, I let out a cry. 'Holy smoke! What are you doing here?'

'I could ask the same of you,' Fletcher said, his deep voice grating as if he'd spent the night spurring on a footy team to victory. He was a right mess. Unruly hair, bushy beard, bloodshot eyes, he looked to have not slept for days.

'You're supposed to be at Joe's convalescing,' I said with concern.

'And you're supposed to be helping Paisley.'

A thought bungee-jumped into my brain. 'Did Joe bring you yesterday?' Fletcher's silence spoke volumes. *The bastard had lied to me.* 'Were you signalling him last night, flashing a light from Fig Tree Hill?'

Fletcher gave a nod. 'He dropped me on the grounds before he arrived at the house the other day. We arranged to meet up, check up on what each had discovered. Joe's adamant that Paisley doesn't know I'm here. He suspects she's up to something, though I'm unconvinced. I still reckon it's the others who are after me.'

I gathered he wasn't referring to the guests—not the living, breathing kind, anyway. Had Fletcher been the one creeping around the property, spying on people? Maybe he was the cottage intruder, sneaking into the study and leaving a note, demanding Paisley—alias Bitch—call him.

'I've heard about your unusual experiences. Your breakdown,' I dared to mention. 'What makes you think the ghosts are targeting you?'

'Breakdown? Bullshit! Isn't it obvious? I'm a Greenwood descendent. They're energised by their need to torment me.'

'And Bridget? Are they treating her the same way?'

'Have you met her? She's going batty trying to deal with that lot.'

'But why are they so angry with your family?'

A harsh screech cut through the forest. A cockatoo? Fletcher had other ideas.

'Quick, they're watching.' He pushed me behind the tree and forced me to crouch with him, shielded by the wide trunk. I scrunched my nose. He ponged like a hundred-year-old swamp. Where else had he been? Was he in the habit of scaring folks near Grimm? I wondered if I'd recognise him in those Yowie videos on YouTube.

'*The sins of the fathers are visited on the children,*' he muttered ominously. 'Have you heard that Gerald found a gold nugget on the goldfields? It's rumoured that a remnant of it is hidden on the property.'

'Yeah,' I said, 'Joe spoke of that.'

'It sent us on a few treasure hunts as kids. My mother told me a few years back, before she took ill, that Gerald kept a portion of the nugget and used the funds from the sale of the rest to set himself up here, build Grassington. But that he wasn't the only one who discovered the gold.'

'He wasn't?' Fletcher needed to read the old newspaper report. Surely it wasn't fake news.

His mud-smeared Adam's apple bobbed as he swallowed hard. 'Gerald had a partner on the diggings. A partner he killed after they found the nugget together before anyone else knew of its discovery. Just so he could get his hands on the whole fortune.'

'No way! How long had your mum known this?'

'Her mother confided in her and Aunt Bridget before she passed away. It seems Elodie found evidence that proved it. She also believed her father, Henry, also knew about it. Maybe Gerald let on something as his health declined. Maybe it was guilt that made the old bloke go loco in the end. My mother reckoned the house was cursed because Gerald killed the man. That's why she hardly visited Grassington after she married. She couldn't stand the place. I now understand why.'

'Could that be why Bridget is considering palming Grassington off to the National Trust?'

His eyes bulged. 'You know about that, too?'

My mind reeled with all who had died horribly at Grassington. Who was next? 'There's a plan to get in touch with the deceased tonight, which, if what you say is true, mightn't bode well for any of us.'

Fletcher gripped my shoulders. 'Don't let them do it, Abby. All hell could break loose. Did Paisley organise this?'

'Hilary Bloodworth, the paranormal expert, offered her services. Paisley's pushing for it as entertainment for the guests.'

'No, no!' Fletcher tugged his hair so hard I thought he'd rip out handfuls. 'Why can't the silly bitch see she's playing with fire? I've warned her time after time, but she thinks I'm cracking up from stress. I'm not.' He punched the tree trunk, sending paper bark flying.

He was certainly showing signs of distress now.

Fletcher winced and rubbed his hand. 'Anxiety doesn't make you see the dead, hear them crying for their baby.'

'What? Olivia cries for her babies?' That was news to me.

'Not Olivia. The maid. She wanders the mansion, searching for her child.'

'Why is she looking for her kid there?'

He shrugged. Yet I held my breath. What if Cole's story about an illegitimate Greenwood child was more than gossip? If so, what had happened to it?

The *coo-ee* call of a storm bird stirred me to view the sky, see grey clouds swirling with menace. 'I need to return,' I said, straightening to stand. 'I'd feel so much better if you were at Joe's place. There's a storm brewing, and a tent doesn't seem safe enough. Maybe you can stay at the cottage tonight while we are at the mansion ... clean yourself up a bit.'

'I'll be fine,' Fletcher said, though his trembling hand on my shoulder suggested otherwise. 'Safer for me to stay out here and wait for Joe. He'll find out soon enough the ghosts are real.'

I deliberated on whether to mention the shrooms and their part in his mental breakdown.

'Well, call me or Joe if you change your mind and need help.'

He shook his head. 'I don't have a phone anymore. Spirits can make contact through electronic devices.'

Then how had Paisley spoken with him? Of course, she'd lied about calling Fletcher. 'Well, take extra care, okay? The supernatural aren't the only ones to fear out here.'

'Don't worry, Abby. Everything will be sweet once Grassington is exorcised of ghosts, once and for all.'

And how the hell was that going to happen?

'Where'd you get to?' Luke asked from the mansion portico.

Sandy gave me a stern dressing down. 'You had us waiting for quite a while. When you failed to return, we came back here. The weather is definitely on the turn.'

I stepped up the front stairs to their level. 'I ... er ... went for a walk. Did you find anything worthwhile at the well?'

Sandy rattled a glass jar filled with odds and ends. 'A bunch of old coins and some nails. The metal detector locates objects up to twenty centimetres below water, which is ample for the murky puddle remaining at the bottom of the well.'

'We also found something else.' From a canvas backpack Luke produced a rusty metal implement with a pointed end on one side and a broad flat blade opposite.

'What is that?'

'A head off a pickaxe.' Sandy said, grinning. 'The handle has rotted away.'

'Why so happy about this find?'

'It has initials scratched into the metal.' He wiped the flat end with his shirtsleeve and held it close to my face.

I cringed at the sight of the same initials I'd seen scratched into brickwork of the office vault. 'Who was this CW?'

'No idea. But I'm betting he was a miner.'

A gold miner, like Gerald's partner. 'How'd you get into the well? It looked pretty deep.'

'And dark and slimy.' Luke said, pulling a face. 'I abseiled down. Always carry rope, just in case.'

I imagined him crawling down the wall of the well on his long spidery legs, connected to the surface by a freshly spun thread, or in this case, a length of rope.

My jaw dropped.

Wasn't rope discovered tied around one of Henry's ankles? Had he been climbing down to search for the gold? What if his death wasn't an accident? An axe or gardening shears would have sufficiently severed the rope from what it was tied to on the surface. Executed by someone out to snaffle the gold Henry was looking for ... or as payback for the suffering Henry had caused them. Either way, it would have been ... *murder.*

'Are you okay, luv?' Sandy asked. 'You're looking a little seedy.'

'It's just the heat,' I lied.

'Yeah, it's a killer,' Luke said with a groan. 'I've been sweating like a pig all day.'

Sandy pinched his nose. 'And you stink like one too, son. We'd better get cleaned up for dinner.'

So should I. But first, I had to haul someone over the coals.

48

────────

'You,' I barked at Joe, catching him seated in the drawing room scrolling through his phone. 'Come with me.'

He gave me a dirty look. 'What … now?'

'Now.'

He eased up from the sofa, and I shoved him towards the doorway, then down the hall and into the servants' quarters.

'Sit,' I said, pointing to the chair. Seeing it loaded with discarded clothing, I pushed him onto the bed instead, the springs creaking under his weight.

'What's this all about, Abby?' He gave a slow smile and leant back on his elbows. 'Had a change of heart, have you? Up for a little afternoon delight?'

I stood tall in front of him, my voice catching as I yelled, 'You barefaced liar!'

He sat up straight. 'In what respect?' he said with a squint.

'In that you claimed Fletcher was recuperating at your place when, in fact, you'd brought him to Grassington with you so he could go camping in the bush. Also, last night's hilltop light was his signal to you, not a stranger's message to a guest. I bet you never went to talk with Paisley at the cottage. You were probably waiting for that cue to meet up.'

'Let me—'

'Nuh-uh! You're scum. You played me like a fool. The two of you must have had a good ol' laugh about me hunting through the mansion looking for evidence of trickery, when it was you doing the hoodwinking. Highly juvenile.'

He started to rise. 'I had to, Abby. The truth is—'

I forced him down. 'Nope. Don't want to hear it. You can't be trusted with telling the truth.'

'Well, if we're throwing out accusations, I could say you can't handle *facing* the truth.'

'What the hell are you talking about?'

'I reckon I've been reasonably open about things, other than meeting up with Fletcher. Whereas you deny reality as a way of avoidance.'

'Hah! You're so full of it. You're deflecting.'

'Am I? If I've learnt one thing from my mistakes, it's prizing being honest with yourself.'

'And I haven't?'

'You refuse to accept your life is going nowhere. I remember when you had such high hopes, dreams of becoming a valued journalist, being a champion of the underdog. But you threw it all away to marry boring-as-bat-shit Shane and turn domestic. Now you're floundering, flitting from one dissatisfying job to another. If you don't do something worthwhile, regret will gnaw at you until you're as hollow as an empty suit of armour.'

An odd analogy. Yet what Joe said did more than touch a nerve. It cut me to the bone. My throat constricted, and tears stung my eyes. Slumped on the bed beside him, I was too dispirited to protest when he pressed my face into his chest to muffle my sobbing.

'I knew it!' came a cry from the doorway.

I sprang away from Joe, my heart sinking to new depths at the sight of Paisley simpering, pleased with herself. 'It's not what it looks like,' I explained. 'Joe was ... um ...' I stared at him, my watery eyes pleading for help.

'Comforting her,' he said.

'Is that what you call it?' Paisley stepped into the room and lowered her voice. 'Were you also being comforted last night, Abby? I saw you leaving Joe's room early this morning. And this afternoon you both slipped away to the cottage for a quick rendezvous before lunch. I'm not stupid. I'm tempted to call Shane and tell him what's been going on.'

Lord, give me strength! 'Pais, believe me, nothing happened. Do you really think I'd cheat on Shane with Joe? You know how I feel about him.'

'And how do you feel about me?' Joe implored, his posture stiffening.

I pretended to stick my finger down my throat to vomit.

He snorted. 'There you go, lying to yourself again. And here I was thinking my empathy was breaking down walls between us.'

We exchanged a glare filled with loathing.

'Well,' Paisley clapped her hands to regain attention. 'Whatever is going on ceases now. No way will my weekend be ruined by infidelity.'

'For cryin' out loud,' I groaned, 'how many times do I have to—'

One bounding stride brought Joe face-to-face with my sister. 'At least we weren't intentionally harming someone.' He grinned like he'd delivered the winning jab in a boxing match.

Paisley recoiled. 'I've already said, I put nothing in Daphne's lunch that would set her off.'

'Maybe I'm not referring to that.'

'Then to what might you be referring?'

He brought his phone to life and showed her the photo of the handful of discarded muesli. 'What do you see here, Paisley?'

She leant in. 'Oats?'

Joe swiped the screen and zoomed in on the pic. 'And what else?'

'Raisins? Sunflower seeds? Looks like muesli.'

'And those brown chunks? Care to guess what they might be?'

'No.' She glanced at me and made a face, as if to suggest Joe had gone bonkers.

'Shrooms,' he said.

'You mean magic mushrooms?' She threw her head back and laughed. 'You think I put them in the muesli? What use would that be? Shrooms are just hallucinogens, right? If I wanted to do real harm, I'd have used the lethal kind. Hidden Death Cap mushrooms, say, in a veal stroganoff, or a creamy mushroom fettuccine.' She poked Joe in the shoulder. 'What do you think you're doing, mate?'

'Accusing you of assaulting your husband, among other things.'

'Fletcher? Oh-my-God! You're delusional if you think you're still a detective. You're pathetic. A has-been. A discredited cop booted off the force for lack of self-control. Lack of brain cells too, it appears.'

Joe gritted his teeth, his face turning a deep shade of red. 'Okay, where's your phone?'

'My phone?' Paisley patted the back pockets of her wide-leg pants. 'Must have left it in the kitchen. Why?'

Joe shoved a hand into the pocket of his shorts and held up a sparkly silver phone case. 'Contains some interesting text messages.'

She lurched forward. 'Give it back, you arsehole. That's an invasion of privacy.'

Joe twisted away, blocking her move with his shoulder. 'Who's Didi?' he asked, holding the phone above his head, out of reach. 'They're keen to get a hold of you. Ten unanswered calls and a few choice text messages. Rather offensive. Obviously not the right hire company, hey?'

A flush crept up her neck. 'How did you get into it?'

'Easy. Your password is the date of your wedding.'

She scowled. 'You remember that?'

'Of course. How could I forget such a memorable event?' His wink in my direction elicited a groan from me. 'My guess is you've been pilfering valuable household items, Paisley dear, and getting this *contact* to sell them on the sly. Seems they're not happy you've paused the venture. Get a little jittery, did you? I don't blame you. Theft is also a serious crime, especially when stealing from an older relative. It's called elder abuse.'

My gut compressed like the bellows of an accordion, squeezing a similar pipe organ noise from my throat. So, Bridget's assumption that Paisley was stealing from her was correct. Perhaps she'd also stolen from the guests. My mind became a tangle of all the things my sister was involved in, which now included swindling. Her greed and duplicity were beyond measure.

'It's not theft if it's your own property,' she said flippantly.

Joe's eyes bore into hers. 'Grassington's contents are not yours to sell.'

'By marriage, they are. What is Fletcher's is mine.'

'But they don't belong to Fletcher ... not yet, anyway. Bridget's still alive if you haven't noticed.'

She flung her hands in the air. 'Good God! The stuff's just

sitting around, collecting dust. What's the harm in selling unused items and using the money to enable improvements? The guesthouse wouldn't have gotten off the ground without my initiative.'

'You're selling without Bridget's consent.'

'She won't give consent. She's gone batty. I'm just running a side business on her behalf. Doing everyone a favour.'

'Especially yourself. I reckon Grassington will only get the dregs after you've lined your pockets. On your behalf, I told Didi to bugger off. Told them the cops were sniffing around, and Detective Teo was sussing things out. That should put the wind up. Who are they, anyway? Someone you met online in a dodgy chat room for lowlifes?'

Paisley gave a sardonic laugh. 'You're so way off, Sherlock. I have no idea how you lasted so long on the force.'

I'd had enough of her smarmy bullshit. Seizing the pillow from the bed, I chucked it, pelting my sister in the face. 'What's happened to you, Pais? You were never like this, resorting to crime to get what you want. A perfect opportunity landed in your lap, and you destroyed it by becoming a thief.'

She punted the pillow back, missing me completely. 'Life's been easy for you. Everything handed to you on a platter. You were spoilt even from birth. Mum and Dad overlooked me, leaving me stuck between the revered firstborn and the perpetual baby of the family.'

'What a load of crap.' I unlatched my emotional cage and set my fury free. 'You've always been the extrovert, the centre of attention. So clever, so entertaining. If anyone was the favourite, it was you, Miss Perfect. And look at what you've achieved in your work life, amassing experience in brilliant establishments, winning awards and public acclaim in hospitality. While I've always struggled to find my footing. I am once again unemployed, with no grand plans in the foreseeable future. Add to that a mocking husband and tell me again how life is rosy for me.'

Joe nudged my arm. 'I have some ideas that might lift your spirits.'

I shot him a frosty glare. 'Quit it, will you? News flash: you're not God's gift to women. Far from it.'

His face fell, his bruised ego offering Paisley an opportunity to snatch her phone back. Clutching it, she fled the room and down the hall.

'I wasn't talking about sex,' Joe said with a huff before storming out and bolting in the opposite direction to Paisley, no doubt to escape outside.

Screaming with rage, I snatched my hairbrush from the chest of drawers and hurled it at the wall. Buoyed by the release of tension, I was about to throw an empty glass tumbler in the same direction when thumping sounds come from inside the wardrobe. I wrenched open the door and couldn't have been more surprised when Bridget tumbled out.

'What are you doing in there? Listening?' I took in her scruffy appearance, including a cobweb covering her head like a hairnet. 'Have you climbed down the ladder from upstairs?'

She pressed a finger to her lips. 'Shh ... our secret. I have something for you. Something to keep safe.' She leant into the wardrobe and extracted an antique round leather hat box.

I went to take it, but she held her grip and we ended up in a game of tug-o-war, the items within scraping back and forth.

'Bridget, do you want me to have it or not?'

She released her hold, and the box hit me in the chest. 'Ouch! For God's sake, what does it contain?'

'The truth,' she said in a hushed tone. 'The truth about the Greenwoods.'

'Why give it to me? Why not Fletcher?'

'Because he's not here and I trust you.' She clasped my free hand. 'Thank you for arranging things with the gardener. He wants to meet in the rose garden this evening.'

'Oh ... which one?'

She cocked her head birdlike. 'The last time I looked, we only had one rose garden.'

'I mean, which gardener. Old or young?'

A smile tweaked her lips. 'Keith will always be in his prime to me.'

I sucked in a breath. 'You've been in contact with Keith Darius?'

'He wrote me a note. Slipped it under my door this afternoon while I was taking a nap.'

'Is that right?' With what I'd learnt about Keith, I doubted the wisdom of Bridget rendezvousing with a convicted killer in the night. 'His sneaking into the mansion is a bit of a concern, don't you think?'

Bridget's flippant shrug in response irked me. Along with hauntings by the dead, we now had numerous flesh and blood entities gadding about, free-ranging not just on the property but through the house. No wonder valuables disappeared easily.

I shook the box, curious as to what was inside. 'Am I allowed to open it?'

'No!' she squealed. 'I just want you to hang onto it. Don't want the cook getting her thieving mitts on it.'

The cook. My sister. Suspicious of Paisley, I couldn't agree more. 'Okay, I'll take care of it for now.'

Bridget nodded and stepped back into the wardrobe, reappearing seconds later to exit more sensibly via the room door.

I studied the hat box, noting it bore an old P & O Cruise passenger sticker marked with the name *Elodie Hawthorne*, and itched to prise open the lid. Either I would discover something fascinating, or something mundane, important only to Bridget. By sheer willpower, I resisted the urge to snoop. Having placed the box back inside the wardrobe, I covered it with my hoody. Now I had more strange objects hidden in my room: the O'Mara's picnic food, the shopping bag of clues, and the box of secrets. Oh, yes. I removed the wizened animal claw from my bib pocket and dropped it into the shopping bag.

Were any of them safe in my care?

I locked the wardrobe door and hid the key inside one of the socks I kept along with my underwear in a lowboy drawer.

49

OLIVIA

1931

She can't believe her eyes. Collected by Sam from Rosewood train station, Olivia almost passes out when they arrive at Grassington and she notices a man planting agapanthus along the driveway. He looks familiar. Her initial thought being someone from Grimm, until the sudden realisation of his identity chills her to the bone.

She corners Elodie in the kitchen kneading dough for bread.

'What is the meaning of this?' Olivia demands, slamming her handbag down on the table and sending up a cloud of flour. 'Why is Will Flanagan here?'

Elodie's hand trembles as it brushes loose strands of hair from her face. 'Sam has taken him on to work in the gardens. Help clean up the glade area.'

'But what brought him to Grassington?'

Elodie blushes and says he's had the devil of a time attaining employment, and he thought he'd have a better chance here.

Olivia asks if Sam knows of their past liaison, and groans when Elodie shakes her head. 'Where is Violet? Their children? Are they here too?'

'They only have one child. Violet left Will and ran off with a travelling salesman, taking the girl with her. Will hasn't seen them for years.'

Olivia tells her it is a disaster, and that it won't end well. 'He must go as soon as possible.'

'We can't send him away yet,' Elodie urges. 'He hasn't finished his project. It would disappoint Sam. Will has done such wonderful work.'

'On you too, I see,' Olivia responds. 'You've certainly changed your tune. You hated him the last time you saw him. We were both pleased when he left.'

Elodie plonks the ball of dough into the large porcelain mixing bowl and covers it with a cloth. 'He has changed. We've all changed, Mum. Much has occurred since then.'

'Yes, you've married. Need I remind you of that?'

A throat being cleared turns their heads. Sam stands in the doorway, bewilderment written on his face.

'Why would you need reminding that we're married?' he says to his wife.

Elodie and Olivia share a look of horror.

Olivia reveals that Will had worked here before Henry's passing. That he and Elodie were once in a relationship.

'But I broke it off,' Elodie jumps in.

'A relationship? Is that causing ... er ...' Sam casts his eyes, as if hoping to find the correct word written on the cupboard doors. '... problems?'

Elodie quickly denies it and assures Sam it is well in the past. She hurries around the table to clutch his hands and confess she loves only him.

He caresses her cheek. But as his gaze drops, he peels back the collar of her blouse, exposing an intimate scarlet bruise at the base of her throat. He demands an explanation.

Olivia knows she should depart and let the couple resolve their issues alone but is determined to hear the extent to which her daughter has defiled herself with her brother. She edges back into the dim recess of the pantry.

In the heat of the moment, with anger consuming them, Sam and Elodie seem oblivious to her presence.

'It's nothing,' Elodie sighs, the wind knocked out of her sails.

Sam tugs the apron from around her waist. 'Where else did his mouth roam? Show me,' he pleads.

Elodie crosses her arms over her chest. 'Nowhere else.'

'How can I trust you when you've just lied to me?' Sam forces her arms apart, and rips her blouse open, buttons clattering on the floor. He drags her skirt down to her ankles. 'Now you remove the rest.'

Elodie's eyes meet her mother's. Olivia expects terror, or pain, but sees humiliation.

She slips from the kitchen. Too weak-kneed to attempt the staircase, Olivia leans against the wall in the hallway. She hears Elodie sobbing, and porcelain smashing. Followed by the unmistakable sounds of a husband taking back physical ownership of what is legally his.

50

I was stoically determined to continue as normal. Showered and changed into a flowing dress with a bright macaw print— a leftover from a Pacific Islands holiday several years earlier—I had a memory of the last time I'd worn it. We'd enjoyed a romantic sunset dinner cruise, followed by a moonlight stroll on the beach, and hot sex in our bamboo bungalow. If only every day could be like that—fun, uncomplicated.

Having received no text messages from Shane, I checked his most recent post on social media. Pics of him with his mates, barhopping in the city. Having a blast without me.

Closing the door, I went to assist in the kitchen.

With no mention of the incident in my room earlier on, Paisley was back to barking orders and nitpicking. Finding fault with the way I handled the food prep, she sent me to set the table.

Nerves on edge, I fumbled with the glassware and cutlery, bringing sharp glances from Cole, wearing an electric-blue satin shirt I recognised as a gift I'd given my sister on her last birthday.

Paisley's attempt to rankle me by offering the shirt to Cole failed, for I was pleased that it looked way better on him. He was also in Paisley's firing line, being chastised for not mastering the simplest of tasks by putting out the wrong crockery set.

It was a relief when a hum engulfed the dining room as guests arrived eager for dinner, including Daphne, who seemed to have regained her usual vigour, entering in a cloud of mauve chiffon. Hilary—no surprise—wore a slinky black split-thigh dress, which competed nicely with Paisley's in-your-face gold halterneck. Even Joe had spruced up in a maroon shirt and tie, and grey dress pants, though he could barely look me or Paisley in the eye, cold-shouldering us for our treatment of him. The Michaelsons had, at least, changed into fresh button-up shirts and chinos.

The appetisers eaten, Cole and I received an invitation to sit with the guests at the table for the main course. I'd only just taken a seat next to Rowan—all sparkly in a pink sequinned outfit and velvet choker with a locket—when, to everyone's surprise, Bridget shuffled into the room. Her cowl-neck sheath dress and vintage gold turban embellished with rhinestones, along with her Cleopatra eyes, gave off ageing movie star vibes. Yet to her credit, she'd made an effort, and I almost leapt to my feet and applauded.

Paisley rose from her place at the head of the table and ushered Bridget into it. 'So glad you've decided to join us, Aunty.'

Bridget eased onto the seat and scanned the array of guests staring wide-eyed with shock at her presence. 'Welcome,' she said in a steady, confident voice. 'Thank you for visiting Grassington Estate. I do trust you are enjoying your stay.'

Mumbles in the affirmative, except for Daphne, who held her tongue and pursed her lips. Bridget's normality led me to suspect she'd medicated sufficiently to counteract her anxiety when in the company of strangers.

We chatted in moderation, feasting on roast pork, grilled salmon, and tasty accompaniments, while Daphne picked her way through the butternut squash risotto allotted to her, checking for nasty surprises. Out of an abundance of caution, I chose not to partake of the stuffed mushrooms.

Vince pushed his empty plate aside and coughed into his fist. 'Ms Hawthorne, can you tell us anything about the maid who fell down the stairs?'

Bridget flinched, clearly rattled by this question. 'I ... I beg your pardon?'

'What was her name?' he asked. 'And when did this tragedy occur?'

She squinted and frowned. 'Have we met before?'

Vince cocked an eyebrow and fidgeted with his aqua-coloured pocket square. 'No. I don't believe so.'

Interesting. That eliminated him from colluding with Bridget about changing the will. Perhaps he was in cahoots with Paisley.

Bridget turned to Paisley, as if hoping for a prompt. 'I'm ... I'm sorry I can't help. The unfortunate incident happened well before my time.'

'Her name was Claudette Renouf,' Cole jumped in. 'And it was in the early 1900s. Like real early.'

'How'd you find that out?' Paisley asked with indignation.

'My grandma told me. A relative worked here as a maid during that time.'

'You've never mentioned that before.'

'I wasn't aware until this morning when I phoned her.'

'And somehow it just came up in conversation, did it?'

Cole glared back at her and turned his attention to his plate, stabbing a baked potato with his knife and hacking it into pieces.

Renouf? Where had I heard that name recently? No, I'd *seen* it ... on a folder label. *The Renouf Question.* I fixed my attention on

Rowan, who leant forward over the remains of her meal, her interest in the topic evident. Was she researching the maid for a podcast episode, or for personal gain?

'Why the need to know?' Paisley asked Vince.

'I'm intrigued by the Greenwood family. Anyway,' he glanced around the table, 'aren't we all interested in the truth behind the maid's accident? How simple is it to trip on the stairs and die?'

Chair legs screeched across floorboards as Hilary got to her feet. 'We can ask Claudette tonight. I'll skip dessert, if you don't mind, Paisley. I need to set things up for our paranormal experience. The drawing room will be required, along with the cellar, and ...' Her eyes found mine. '... the *puttanesca* room.'

A cry escaped Bridget. She pushed away from the table. 'You can't do that! No seance, please,' she demanded. 'No forcing spirits from their world into ours. I've worked so hard to keep them at peace.'

A distant rumble of thunder added to the ominous mood.

Hilary acquiesced. 'Fine. There are some other, simpler approaches we can use to communicate with spirits, and only if they desire to. No forcing, no angering. Will that be okay, Bridget?'

A brief pause preceded the older woman's nod.

'Need help with the equipment?' Sandy asked Hilary.

'That'd be great. Forty-five minutes preparation should do, and then we'll all meet in the drawing room like last time.'

Hilary and Sandy removed themselves, spurring Cole and me to collect the used dinnerware, and return with desserts and a cheese platter.

'We need to talk,' Joe whispered as I handed him his Banoffee tart.

'If it's got anything to do with lewd suggestions for my future, count me out.'

He gripped my wrist, his fingers squeezing tight. 'Get over yourself, Abby. It's not always about you.'

With dessert finished, and the table cleared, I was about to query Rowan on what she knew of the maid, when Joe drew me into the foyer.

He held up his phone. 'I made a call. Apparently, Keith Darius was released from prison a week ago. Therefore, I presume it was he you spoke with and not Neville's ghost.'

'Yeah, Bridget confirmed it earlier. She's meeting with Keith tonight.'

He looked aghast. 'Where? When?'

'In the rose garden. Didn't give a time. A lover's reunion, I'd say.'

'I'd better have a serious chat with her. By the way, we should remain vigilant. My gut still tells me there's something not right about Hilary.'

I was of the same opinion. I also had no trust in my sister. However, if Paisley hadn't contaminated the muesli, who had? I put this to Joe.

'I'm still working on that,' he said. 'Perhaps the same person who tried to hurt Daphne.'

Could Cole have done both? For what reason?

'I thought I saw a ghost today,' Joe said casually. 'It floated up the carpeted staircase to the first landing and hovered, glowing and flickering. Sort of see-through. Then it vanished.'

Shock momentarily robbed me of speech. 'I ... I saw the exact same image a few days ago. Thought I was going mad. Do you now have second thoughts about the validity of ghosts?'

He gave a laugh. 'Not on your Nellie. I examined the balcony on the floor above that landing and discovered a small device. By my guess, we both witnessed a projected image of a woman.'

'You're kidding! Who set that up? Paisley?' I said in response to him arching his eyebrows at me. 'Where would she get her hands on the necessary equipment to do that?'

'Good question. Maybe Hilary has contacts.'

It was getting to where nothing surprised me about my sister anymore. 'Incidentally, where exactly did Keith murder Neville? It wasn't here at Grassington, was it?'

'As a matter of fact—'

'Let me guess. Was it in the cellar?'

'Correct. He died as a result of a blunt force head trauma leading to a brain haemorrhage.'

'What brought that on?'

'Keith pleaded self-defence. A dispute arose concerning Neville stealing from the Greenwoods. A fight ensued and Keith struck Neville on the head with a bottle of vintage Muscat, proving fatal.'

'That explains Rowan's experience of being clobbered on the skull in the cellar. Why didn't you say anything last night?'

'Biding my time. Assumed Rowan was playacting.'

A thought niggled me. When speaking with Dylan Darius at the Hairy Man, he'd mentioned how convenient it was that Bridget's dementia helped her forget what had happened to his father. Was he implying she knew more about his death?

'Hey,' I said. 'Are you familiar with an old animal's foot charm? A brooch, maybe?'

'Like a lucky rabbit's foot?'

'I guess that's what it could've been. It's in an awful condition. I found it in a secret passageway here.'

A glint in his eye. 'The one leading from your room up to the first floor?'

'Of course, you'd know about that. Yes, it was hidden in there. Who might it have belonged to?'

Joe pulled me over to the wall photo of the group of ladies having tea outdoors and pointed to a woman seated behind the child at play. 'Is that what you're talking about?'

I examined the item attached to the bodice of the woman's lace blouse. 'Why, yes, that could be it.' Unfortunately, the shadow cast by her wide-brimmed straw hat obscured her face. 'Who is she?'

'The maid who took a tumble down the stairs.'

'Claudette Renouf?' Tingles crept from my fingertips up to my elbows. 'What was the charm doing in the secret passageway?'

Joe seemed as perplexed as I was.

I stared open-mouthed at my room in a total shambles. Linen had been ripped from the bed, leaving the mattress askew on the iron base and pillows scattered about. Clothes dangled from open lowboy drawers, and items from my toiletry bag and backpack were strewn on the floor. However, the wardrobe was still locked, and the key remained hidden in the sock. Opening the wardrobe door, I found the contents safely in place. Whoever had ransacked my room—in search of God-knows-what—mustn't have known about the secret passageway and entry through the wardrobe. Then again, perhaps a poltergeist had made the mess.

I quickly tidied up and fished Bridget's hat box out from its concealment. *Had someone been searching for this?* My conscience battled with my intrigue. To open it would be a breach of trust, yet it might illuminate family secrets, possibly explaining their tragedies. With a sudden compulsion, I unlatched the lid and spewed the contents onto the bed.

My eyes fell upon several bound journals—each bearing the name *Olivia Greenwood* in tarnished lettering—and a bunch of loose pages torn from such notebooks and filled with handwriting. There was also a weathered leather pouch, which, when untied and upended, spilled out more items.

I stared at a creased and brittle newspaper clipping from The Gympie Times, dated 30th May, 1872.

GOLD RUSH TRAGEDY AT GYMPIE.

Today a fatal accident occurred at the Chester claim at One-mile, whereby a man named Clement Wallace was killed by the fall of a bucket. From what was learnt, the deceased was working at the bottom of the shaft while his partner, Gerry Greenwood, acted as the braceman. It is said that the hook was defective, and that Greenwood missed securing the bucket to the hook, causing the bucket, heavy with tools, to fall on the poor man below, crushing his head and killing him on the spot.

Now that was a tragic piece of news.

Included with the clipping was a miner's licence, and a sepia photograph of two men standing outside a lean-to which sheltered mining machinery. According to the notation on the back of the photo, the men were *Gerry* and *Clem*. This matched the miner's licence being made out for *Gerald Greenwood* and *Clement Wallace* as partners in a mine.

I again viewed the newspaper report. It appeared Clem's death was a wretched accident. But what if Fletcher's ramblings about his great-great-grandfather were true? Not wanting to share their fortune, Gerald had brought about an 'accident' to kill his partner. By delaying the discovery announcement for several days, he could have made it look like he'd found the gold on his own. In that case, he had built Grassington with money obtained through murder—money that didn't wholly belong to him.

A sudden thought. The 'CW' marking on the pickaxe head

discarded in the well had to refer to this Clem Wallace. So had the letters scratched on the strongroom wall. Could dead Clem be haunting Grassington, exacting retribution on the Greenwoods? If so, who or what had warned me by directing me to the message? The house or another spirit?

I carried out some quick online research and began perusing Olivia's journals and paperwork in the hope they'd hold answers to these and many other questions. What would I learn about the Greenwood family from these writings?

51

Time flew. I tore myself away from the journals and changed into a sage-green jumpsuit and red Chucks before joining the others. What I'd just read distressed me. Fletcher's disclosures about his ancestors were only the tip of the iceberg. I faced a choice: help cleanse Grassington by revealing tragic truths about the Greenwood family, or tempt fate by being complicit in cover-ups that had lasted over a century. Nonetheless, my top priority was focussing on interaction with the dead. In doing so, I hoped to grasp clarification.

Candles provided subdued lighting within the drawing room, while the arched windows framed an exterior illuminated by electric verandah fixtures. I found a spot amongst the huddle of guests.

'Let me explain things,' Hilary said, moving in the semi-darkness to the coffee table. 'Here we have dowsing rods, used for tuning into cosmic energy.' She clasped two copper L-shaped bars by their shorter ends. 'Held side-by-side, the rods move in response to yes/no questions. The longer ends signify *"yes"* when crossed, "no" when apart.'

Were the Michaelsons, like me, wondering if the rods could also detect gold?

'Might find us some water,' Joe scoffed. 'Hope they don't lead us to underground plumbing.'

Hilary let out a heavy sigh, and moved to the piano stool, from which she collected a small black device with a display screen—a cross between a mobile phone and a walkie-talkie. 'This is a spirit box.'

Simultaneously, we moved closer.

'Is it a ghost trap?' Luke asked.

Hilary gave a weak smile. 'It scans radio frequencies—*white noise*—to allow spirit communication. When asked a question, spirits have been known to talk through this device due to their electromagnetic presence.'

'What type of questions?' Rowan asked, holding out her phone, recording the goings-on.

'Who they are? What do they want? Can we help? Stuff like that.'

All eyes followed as Hilary placed the box back on the stool, everyone, no doubt, eager to get their hands on the device.

She beckoned us to follow her through the foyer into the dining room, now lit by a multitude of candles. Stopping at one end of the dining table, she indicated a vintage mirror mounted on a stand, its elaborate gilded frame glinting in the flickering glow.

'The idea is to stare into the mirror and observe if your reflection alters. It may show you at different ages. Or it may take on another form, possibly a deceased person known to you. Be receptive to your senses. How do you feel? What do you hear? Is that person communicating with you? What are they saying?' She placed a simple wooden metronome atop the fireplace mantle and moved the pendulum all the way to the right. Released, it began a steady swing, the mechanism ticking at two beats per second. 'The pulse will help with concentration.'

'Or put us to sleep,' Joe said.

Hilary glared at him. 'Listen buddy, your snide comments are really annoying. No-one's forcing you to take part in the activities, so if you're bored, go find something better to do, like search for your decency.' She stopped the pendulum from swaying and patted Sandy on the shoulder. 'Lastly, my good friend here helped me set up a laser grid device in the cellar, which is able to map out the physical aspects of a spirit. All you have to do is sit and watch for one to pass by.'

A clever laser dance performance I'd seen on *Australia's Got Talent* came to mind. Would it be like that?

Hilary rubbed her hands together. 'Are you ready? Choose an item, have a go, and after twenty minutes, swap.'

'I'm off to talk with Bridget,' Joe hissed into my ear.

'Chicken,' I taunted. 'Too scared to join in the fun, hey?'

He harrumphed and slunk away.

No surprise that Sandy made a beeline back to the drawing room to fetch the dowsing rods. The O'Maras hurried out into the hall, heading for the cellar door, while Luke and Hilary commandeered the spirit box. That left Rowan and me to tackle the mirror.

Rowan opted to go first, pulling out a chair and placing her phone on the table. 'I'm sitting in front of a mirror,' she said, projecting her voice for the recording. 'Let's see if anything appears in the reflection.' Then she sat motionless, while I stood nearby, waiting.

I yearned to witness something thrilling. I was open to having a truly supernatural experience; something that would definitely prove the existence of ghosts. Yes, I'd seen and heard uncanny stuff here at Grassington, much of it explained away. I wanted tangible proof, hard evidence, not some vague mumbo jumbo up for interpretation. Even Hilary's little show in the cemetery could have been a prank. I wanted to witness it with my own eyes, touch it with my own hands. A personal experience was what I desired. I now knew how Doubting Thomas had felt when all the disciples, bar him ... and Judas, had seen the risen Lord. C'mon—bring it on!

The stillness in the room heightened sounds—the rumble of an approaching storm, the clicking call of a gecko. I remembered the metronome and rushed over to flick the pendulum, returning in time to catch Rowan's reflection in the mirror blur and—as a challenge to my disbelief—transform into a raven-haired beauty with cupid's-bow lips.

I blinked several times, but the vision remained.

'Can you see her?' I whispered to Rowan, my pulse pounding in my ears.

'Who?'

'The woman in the mirror. She has substituted your face with hers.'

'She has? OMG! What does she look like?'

'You can't see her?'

'No. Only my reflection.'

My mouth fell open in awe. 'She's beautiful. Dark hair, dusky complexion. Kind of exotic.'

Rowan touched her own cheek, and the image smiled. 'Is it Claudette Renouf?'

'Claudette, the maid? Why would—'

'She's my relative. My great-great-aunt,' Rowan gushed. 'I'm researching her for my podcast.' Without taking her eyes from the mirror, she removed her velvet choker and unthreaded the locket, handing it to me. 'This was passed down through generations of my family. Open it.'

Stunned by her revelation, I complied, holding the small ornamental case up to the light of a candle. Inside was a tiny portrait photo of a woman similar to the one in the mirror.

'This is Claudette? My God! Is she telling you anything? What do you feel?'

'Sad. I feel so very sad.' Rowan frowned in concentration and huffed through her teeth. 'Now I'm fuming with anger.'

The reflection turned forlorn and opened its mouth wide in what appeared to be a yawn until I perceived it as a muted scream.

The metronome ceased ticking, plunging the room into silence.

Moments later, Rowan's ear-splitting wail shattered the quiet. I lurched and went to comfort her. However, she shrugged my hands from her shoulders and leapt from the chair, blood trickling from her nostrils. She snatched her phone and ran from the room.

Too astounded to move, I stared at the empty doorway. Had no-one else heard Rowan's cry and bothered to check what had happened? I viewed the mirror. Now it was my turn.

Restarting the metronome, I sat in the chair and cringed. In the quivering light, my reflection looked like shit: hollow-eyed, sallow-skinned, and droopy-lipped. I expected candlelight to improve my appearance, not make me look deathly ill. The mind-numbing pulse of the metronome became the stupefying beat of Visage's 'Fade to Grey' as the song played in my head.

In time, my face took on the form of both my parents, the inherited features taking turns to stand out—my father's nose and forehead, my mother's lips. Even Grandad Bill emerged in the jutting chin he'd passed on. Emotions stirred and tears welled. I fixed on the hypnotic *tick, tick* lest the lump in my throat became a sob.

Drowsiness took hold, my eyelids heavy, threatening to close. On the verge of my drifting off, a blaze of light cleaved the surrounding darkness. Immediately followed by a crack of thunder that rattled windows.

I squealed and vaulted from the chair. As I peered across the room, external lighting was now non-existent. A blackout? Leaves pelted against the large bay window like hail.

A second blinding flash almost turned me to stone, not due to its abruptness but because it revealed a dark-clothed figure standing on the verandah. The floor shook as God's giant bowling ball rumbled down heaven's alley to knock over celestial pins. I bounded over and pressed my nose against the glass to see into the night, hoping it wasn't Fletcher exposed to the elements.

Another explosion of light.

In the split second before the inkiness returned, I glimpsed a face on the other side of the window, centimetres from mine— black eyes within a sea of pulpy flesh and bone. I backed away, covering my ears against the resultant *boom*.

A gust of wind burst from the fireplace, blowing out all but a lone candle flame. Movement in the twitching light sent icy tingles down my arms—a shadow crouching, slinking behind furniture, edging near. *No, no!*

This time, my fear response was to arm myself in readiness to attack. I snatched up a fireplace poker. Idiot! How effective would such a weapon be against a demon, a creature of the night? A silver crucifix and holy water would be more helpful. I scarcely had a chance to react when the shadow sprang from behind the table and knocked me off my feet.

The hefty weight of a hairy whining beast crushed me as I lay sprawled on the floor, its large, slimy tongue swiping my face.

'Whitby?' I wheezed, just as he burrowed his head into my

armpit. 'You don't like storms, either,' I said, squeezing him tight, his trembling contagious.

Voices. Swift footsteps. Guests returning.

I shoved Whitby off and joined them in the foyer, where torches beamed in every direction like strafing searchlights. Wind whistled through gaps around the double front doors, and something tumbled across the portico. The wicker chair?

'You guys won't believe what just happened,' I croaked.

'There's no electricity,' Daphne shrieked, panic in her eyes.

'Yep,' Luke said, confirming it by reaching over and twice flicking the wall switch connected to the overhead chandelier without success. 'Wonder if the house received a direct hit.'

'Could be just a power surge from the lightning,' Sandy offered, waving his yellow Eveready dolphin torch around. 'Anyone know where the circuit board is located? Might just need to reset the safety switch. Otherwise, there may be a generator that needs firing up.'

'Check in the kitchen.' I suggested. 'Or in the cellar if you're brave enough. But first I want to tell you—'

'Okay, I'll give the cellar a squiz first.' Sandy receded into the shadows.

'How'd the spirit box go?' Daphne asked Luke. 'Contact anyone otherworldly?'

The penlight torch held below his chin gave a creepy half-shaded effect to his face. 'One voice came through rather strong, hey, Hilary.' He glanced around with a start. 'Oh, she was here just a second ago.'

'Was she?' I exclaimed. 'I never saw her. What I did see was—'

'But I could have sworn she was hot on my heels.' Luke's bewilderment overrode my third attempt to share what I'd witnessed. 'We were trying the spirit box out in the small dining room.'

Daphne gripped his arm. 'Did Olivia speak with you?'

'Not sure. A female enquired about a baby. I guess it could have been her. Then came a male voice. Gruff. Telling us to get out of his house. How'd you go with the light grid in the cellar?'

'Very pretty, all those little green lights. Rather mesmerising. But nothing scary occurred. I must admit, I nodded off while waiting for an apparition to show up. A thunderclap woke me.'

'Was Vince with you?'

'At first. He headed upstairs to the toilet soon after we got down there. Said he felt queasy.'

We all jolted at a blast—glass smashing in the drawing room.

Rushing in, we discovered a tree branch had speared through one of the arched windows, littering the floor with sparkling splinters. Curtains flapped in the flurry of wind and rain.

'Look,' said Luke, his torch lighting up the mirror above the fireplace mantle. Scrawled across the glass in dripping red were the words: *Blood for blood*.

A sudden scream and muffled thuds prompted us to sprint through the other doorway into the hall. A crumpled heap lay at the foot of the carpeted stairs, the rhinestones on the gold turban dazzling with reflected light.

52

ELODIE

1931

Elodie sits on the stone bench near the pond, the lantern at her feet illuminating the rose garden in a faint arc of light. She splashes her puffy, burning eyes with water and breathes in dewy air. A stone of emotion wedges in her throat as she waits.

Sam said Will hadn't resisted when told his services were no longer needed and he was to depart first thing in the morning. He must have guessed the reason for the abrupt dismissal.

Has Will seen the note she'd slipped under the cottage front door, asking him to meet up? What if he decides not to appear? He might be packing his belongings at this very moment and planning to leave Grassington tonight.

Elodie stares at her hand, at the lock of hair she's snipped from her head and tied with a satin ribbon, a simple gift to remind Will of her. What would he choose to give her in return?

She touches her lips, her neck, recalling the urgency of his longing. Wishes they'd experienced more than just a few hasty kisses. Maybe she should meet him at the cottage. Seclusion would allow passionate intimacy, creating a cherished memory for them both.

Rising to leave, she sees Will round a rose trellis, his spectral protectors following close behind. Their eyes meet. Elodie recognises the torment in his gaze, for she'd seen the same in her bedroom mirror only moments earlier.

He drops his rucksack, and she runs into his outstretched arms.

'Don't go,' she pleads. 'Not yet. We have time.'

'Time for what?'

'Let's go back to the cottage. Make love at last.' She doesn't care they might have ghostly witnesses.

He holds her at arm's length. 'We can't do that. It'd be wrong.'

'But you were prepared to do that last night, hang the consequences.'

'Sam didn't know about us then. He does now. It would be a blatant act of betrayal after he paid me more than my work was worth. Double the amount, in fact, because I didn't kick up a fuss about being let go prematurely.'

'You chose money over love?' Has she gotten it all wrong? 'So, lust was your motivation, Will. Lust for me and a damned gold nugget.'

'Not at all. I just wasn't sure. Do you love me, Elodie?'

She pulls his face down and plants her mouth on his, her tongue parting his lips, surely, he can taste her hunger.

He breaks contact. 'Then what are we to do?'

'I'll run away with you. We could hit the road and create a new future together. Go wherever the urge takes us. Two travellers living on love and our wits alone.'

'You'd leave all this? Your well-heeled life? And what about your inheritance? I don't think I'm worth all that.'

A wave of nausea pummels her. She would be giving up a lot, as well as bringing disgrace upon the family. Still, how could she live without Will? 'Maybe I'm being hasty. There will be things to sort out. It might be better to wait and contact you when everything is formulated.'

His face falls. 'I'll need to know sooner than later so I can plan my next move. I'll give you until midnight to tell me of your intentions.'

'Midnight? Today? That's only a few hours away.'

'I'll be waiting in the grotto. If you don't turn up, I'll know you've changed your mind, and I'll leave.'

Darkness envelops him as he strides away.

Elodie remains, annoyed that Will has set such a brief timeframe, forcing her to be brave enough to follow through with an immediate course of action.

A sound draws her attention to the mansion's upper verandah. Moonlight briefly reveals a figure standing at the railing before the person disappears.

Elodie sneaks inside. Her mother is at the piano in the drawing room, her rigid fingers butchering a Chopin nocturne, a bead of sweat trickling down her neck to slip beneath the collar of her dress.

'Where's Sam?' Elodie asks, scanning the room.

Her mother's hands hover over the keys. 'He's been drinking all evening. He has gone to bed early.'

The accusing look directed her way brings a tightness to Elodie's chest. Why does her mother judge her so? Has she no compassion? In desperation, Elodie heads to the office.

Closing the door behind her, she rifles through the desk drawers in search of the strongroom key. Upon finding it, she flings back the velvet curtain, feeds it into the grille door lock, and twists the heavy brass knob.

Inside the vault, she tugs the cord to switch on the lone bulb hanging from the ceiling and finds the large metal box belonging to her on a middle shelf. A peek inside confirms it still contains a wad of banknotes she'd been secretly stockpiling. That, together with the rarely worn jewellery kept here, which she could pawn, would set them up for the time being if she left with Will tonight. She fingers the paperwork regarding her inheritance. Yes, she would take that too.

Her gaze lands on the worn leather pouch owned by her grandfather, which she'd discovered in a trunk along with other items on the day her father died. Being of historical importance, she'd deemed it worth keeping. A strange urge now compels her to search within the pouch.

There is the Miner's Right document, and the photo taken at the Gympie gold diggings. Also tattered papers, including receipts and old newspaper clippings. Elodie reads one clipping for the first time, gasping in horror at the detailed report of the tragic death of Clem Wallace. Gerald's mining partner had not lived a fortuitous life as he had after discovering gold but had died with his head crushed from an incident at the mine.

She reads another news clipping reporting Gerald's discovery of the nugget just two days after his partner's fatal injury. Thoughts bombard her until a heightened sense of dread convinces her Clem's death was no accident. Greed had led to murder.

Had her father known this? Was it possible Gerald had confided in his son in a moment of weakness? Or maybe Henry had, at least, suspected his father of foul play, being there as a child on the goldfields with him. That could be why he was so hellbent on discovering the nugget. He knew its existence wasn't a myth.

Elodie returns the pouch to the box and replaces the lid. The light above flickers, and the room's temperature plummets. A putrid odour causes her eyes to water. Turning, she finds she is not alone. The man without a face is with her in the vault. As ghastly as ever, he is no longer nameless.

'Blood for blood,' he rasps, his voice grating like fingernails scraping on a chalkboard.

She clutches the box to her chest and confronts him with newfound courage. 'I am not afraid of you, Clem Wallace. Be gone from this place. Your revenge from the grave must cease.'

A nightmare laugh reverberates in the small space. He glides forward, and she cringes, preparing to fight off the inevitable clawing. But it never comes. Clem vanishes the instant the lightbulb above explodes with a resounding pop, sending glass shards to rain down and litter the floor. Immediately, the grille door slams shut. Elodie feeds her hand through the bars, but the key in the lock is missing, and the door won't budge no matter how hard she rattles the knob. She is a prisoner.

Her screams for help go unanswered.

Collapsing on the floor, she convulses amongst broken glass, limbs contorting with fear and loss. Her teeth clamp on the only word she can muster: *Will.*

53

'Bridget!' I dropped to my knees and rolled her over, only to gasp and pull away.

My sister lay motionless on the carpet runner.

Paisley might be a gorgon, but I hadn't wanted her to meet a terrible fate. I went to scoop her up, but Daphne held me back.

'Best not to move an injured person,' she advised.

My chest constricted. 'What if she's—'

A moan became a sharp cry of pain, and Paisley's eyes flickered open.

'Thank God you haven't had the same outcome as the maid,' Daphne said in a soothing tone.

'Where does it hurt?' I asked frantically. 'Can you move your arms and legs? Any tingling in your spine?'

Paisley gave me a helpless look. 'My ankle hurts. And my ribs.' She eased her head from side to side. Blood dripped from a cut chin. Whitby, sensing her discomfort, hunkered down beside her, resting his muzzle on her shoulder.

'What happened?' I asked. 'Did you trip in the dark?'

'No, I think I was pushed. I was on my way down the stairs, being very careful in the dark. I'd just reached the landing when I swear someone shoved me from behind.' She touched her left side and winced. 'Who would do such a thing?'

'Well, it wasn't any of us,' Luke said. 'Who isn't here?'

Daphne was quick to reply. 'Vincent must still be in the toilet.'

'Joe went to talk with Bridget,' I said, 'and Sandy went to find the circuit board.'

Luke repeated that Hilary had been with him in the bedroom. 'What about Rowan? Wasn't she with you, Abby, looking into the mirror?'

'She ran off earlier. Got scared.'

'And don't forget young Cole,' Daphne added. 'Did anyone see him before the blackout?'

'He wasn't here when Hilary was giving us the lowdown on the paranormal equipment,' Luke offered.

Paisley jerked my arm to get my attention. 'He was in the kitchen, stacking the dishwasher. But that was ages ago.'

Luke moaned. 'It could be any of them ... barring Dad, of course. But why would anyone target you?'

My sister stiffened, lost for words. So was I. Could Cole's anger towards Paisley extend to doing her serious harm? I thought of Fletcher and the hallucinogenic muesli. And Daphne's anaphylaxis. Paisley also clashed with Joe and Bridget. With the proper trigger and reason, any of us could commit an act of violence, *even murder*. However ...

I eased the jewelled turban from her head. 'Why do you have this? What were you doing upstairs?'

'Putting away washed linen while you lot were chasing ghosts. I found Bridget's turban in the hallway. Wondered what she was up to stripping out of her clothes.'

'Did you find her?'

'No. She didn't answer my knock on her door.'

'So, you wore the turban for safekeeping?'

'Ahh ... yeah ... something like that. Help me up, will you?'

Carefully manoeuvring my sister into a sitting position, I took charge of the situation. 'Daphne, help Paisley onto a couch. Luke, check the loo, and see if Vince is okay. I'll search for a first aid kit.'

I headed into the kitchen, highly suspecting someone had mistaken Paisley wearing the turban for Bridget. Rain now lashing the windows added to the eeriness of the blacked-out mansion, and every gloomy nook had the potential for harbouring an assailant ready to leap out and attack. Waving my light, I spied the first aid kit on a wall shelf. I also noticed the door to outside was wide open. Had someone recently entered or exited? I boldly crept out.

Though shielded from the downpour by the overhead verandah, sheets of water cascading from the overfilled guttering obstructed my view of the grounds. I cocked my head as shouts from the direction of the rose garden cut through the tumult. Tugging an old raincoat hanging from a hook near the doorway, I threw it on and slipped the hood over my head before running through the waterfall.

I sloshed over the soggy lawn littered with leaves and twigs to reach the garden wall, when two figures ran out through the ivy-covered archway. A flash of lightning glinted off a wet bald head. Was that Dylan Darius? I pressed flat against the brickwork and switched off the torch. Being only several metres away, I saw him trip and fall onto his knees, sending up a great splash. Keith appeared in front of him and slogged him hard in the face.

Dylan rebounded like a punching-bag clown. 'She's a murderer,' he spluttered, rising and planting his feet in mud. 'She killed me dad.' He ploughed into Keith's stomach with his head, propelling him into a hydrangea shrub.

I aimed my phone and videoed the brawling men as best I could in the flares of lightning strikes. The rain at least seemed to be easing.

A drenched Keith struggled to extricate himself from the dripping vegetation. 'Bridget caught your father stealing from her,' he wheezed. 'Neville went for her, and she walloped him in self-defence. Do you think I'd let her go to prison for that?'

My mouth hung open. *Keith had taken the punishment to protect Bridget?*

Dylan dragged his uncle out of the bush and shoved him to the ground. 'You should've made her stand trial and face conviction. The mad bitch deserved it.'

Keith lay in a puddle, panting with exhaustion while being pelted with erratic raindrops. 'Is that why you enticed her ... into the rose garden ... pretending to be me? So you could kill her?'

Kill? God, no!

Dylan wiped water from his eyes. 'Drawin' her out was easy once I knew you were free and hangin' around. Yet I wasn't gonna kill her, you old fool. I was tryin' to make her 'fess up about what she did to me dad. I planned to blackmail her into payin' me a pretty sum to keep me mouth shut. You turnin' up just now spoiled everything.'

'Lucky for Bridget I did. You'd better not have seriously hurt her.' Keith staggered to his feet, his soaked clothing adhering to his body. 'You've already got money from her, though. You've been thieving from Grassington just like your old man.'

'I didn't get all the dosh. The other bitch got the bigger chunk.'

'What other bitch?'

No. I didn't want it confirmed.

'Fletcher's missus. Paisley's the one who approached me. She swipes objects, and I sell 'em for her. She still owes me heaps of cash, but she's ignorin' my messages, so I had to come up with another way to get me hands on some coin.'

I gasped, sucking in a spritz of precipitation. Didi ... DD ... *Dylan Darius*. He and Paisley had been in partnership. I couldn't wait to tell Joe if I ever found him.

The next minute, Dylan was on the ground with Keith straddling him, the tines of a garden fork pressed to his throat. How many times had Keith needed to do that in prison? He must have found the fork while amongst the hydrangeas.

'Listen here, dumb-arse. You're gonna stop stealing and pay Bridget back every cent you made from the sales. I don't care how you bloody do it, but it's gonna happen, or I'll hand you into the cops myself.'

Dylan laughed. 'No-one's going to believe you, Keith ol' boy, an ex-con. It'd be your word against mine.'

I took this as my cue and stepped into view, my sneakers squelching in the sludge. 'Actually, there's a witness.'

They twisted around, eyes wide with shock.

'I heard everything you said. Even recorded your confession.' I waved my phone, hoping I'd captured something useful. 'Now, where's Bridget?'

A search revealed she was no longer in the rose garden. Yet the punch-up between uncle and nephew had left someone dead in the pond. Broken from its pedestal and half-submerged in the water was the now decapitated statue of Gerald. It must have been hollow because something odd protruded from the neck of the severed head.

I helped Keith frogmarch Dylan into the mansion, his hands fastened behind his back with a trouser belt. My heart skipped a beat when his muddy boot prints on the kitchen floor perfectly matched the ones I'd seen on the path below the front steps on my first morning here. I wouldn't have been surprised if he had also left his handprint on the cottage study windowsill.

We used the grille door key I had found earlier to lock him in the strongroom, the best course of action given the circumstances. Naturally, he wasn't happy about being incarcerated and screamed abuse as we left him on his own in the pitch black.

'I'll go check for Bridget outside,' Keith said. 'The poor dear must be in hiding, scared witless.'

I peeled out of the raincoat and handed it to him. 'You may need this.'

He took off in a rush.

Excited voices and candlelight directed me to the puttanesca room, where my sister lay stretched out on the sofa. Daphne dabbed her injured chin with a gauze square taken from the kitchen first aid kit—no ill feelings between them now, it seemed.

Luke bounded over. 'What's been going on?'

Without disclosing Paisley's part in Dylan's thieving, I explained to my shocked audience what had just occurred. Thankfully, my sister's discomfort stopped her from reacting to my mention of her accomplice. I wasn't sure how I'd have responded if she'd shown concern for his wellbeing.

'Has anyone else turned up?' Shaking heads answered my question. 'That's worrying. I'm going upstairs in case Bridget escaped back to her rooms.'

54

———

Her door was half open.

'Hello,' I called. 'Are you okay, Bridget?'

The only response was the wild wind rattling the sash windows and whispering through cracks like murmuring voices. I fed my way between stacked furniture and display cabinets, recoiling with a yelp when my phone torch hit on the glimmering eyes of the tiny stuffed dog in the glass container, its needle teeth bared savagely. Reaching the sitting area, I searched her bedroom, kitchenette, and ensuite. Bridget had not returned.

Back in the hallway, a squeak from behind halted my return downstairs. Swivelling, my light caught the elephant pull-along toy rolling forward on the carpet runner. I watched in dread fascination as it sped up and stopped only centimetres from my feet.

A shadow moved at the far end of the hall.

I aimed my torch towards the timber staircase and spotlit a child wearing outdated knee breeches and a white tunic top, his dark sunken eyes filled with despair. My skin bristled. Another projected image to scare me?

'What do you want?' I rasped, playing along.

The boy silently turned and faced Rowan's room.

I inched forward. But as I neared, the apparition grew less distinct, to the point when I reached the door, the boy had vanished. However, a residual vapour in the vicinity where he'd been standing, cold and moist to the touch, challenged the idea of a set-up. Every nerve in my body buzzed with excitement. I wiped my pooling eyes, thrilled—and somewhat terrified—at having seen an actual ghost. In fact, hadn't I glimpsed several ghosts this night? There was also Claudette's image in the mirror and that ghoulish thing looking through the drawing room window. The boy spirit was, by far, more to my liking.

My breathing remained shallow and rapid as I opened the bedroom door and swept my light around. I shuddered. A body lay face down on the floor.

'Rowan!' I fell to my knees and grasped her shoulder. 'Are you alright?'

She moaned and turned her head, her gaze meeting mine. 'Has he gone?'

'The boy?'

'No, the man. At least I think it was a man.' She sat up with difficulty. 'A dark figure, at least. I ran up here after seeing Claudette in the mirror and tried to compose myself ... and then he ... it ... was here, in the room. It had some strange evil power over me, and I couldn't move, even when he lashed out and clawed me. I must have blacked out with shock. Look at what he did.' She held out her arms.

In the torchlight I saw no visible lacerations or bruising. No proof whatsoever of an assault.

Rowan rubbed her skin. 'I'm not lying. It stung.'

'I believe you. I reckon I saw this ... whatever it was ... after you left me. It peered at me through the window from outside. So gross.'

'What was it, a demon? Have we opened a portal by trying to contact the dead?'

Fletcher's warning rang in my ears: *Don't let them do it, Abby. All hell could break loose.* 'Maybe the door to the portal was already ajar, and we just helped kick it wide open.'

I assisted Rowan to the staircase. Scratching and fumbling noises in the hallway walls as we passed sounded like the house had a definite rodent problem. Were they trying to scrabble free out of a sense of danger? Thumping from behind timber panelling had me wondering what other critters lived within the walls.

I sent Rowan downstairs without me, saying I needed to check on something. She didn't object.

Pressing my ear against the red cedar veneer, I heard a muffled voice. Startled, I responded with a feeble 'hello'. Sharp cries for help interspersed the pounding. By my calculation, this section of the wall hid the entrance to the secret passageway.

'I'll get you out,' I called, and pushed with the heel of my hands to make the panel swing open, yet it failed to release.

I took three steps backwards, and ran at the wall, putting my total weight behind my shoulder on impact. The panel clicked and sprang open, shunting me in reverse. I stumbled but regained my balance. Shining my torch into the narrow passageway, I discovered Cole on his hands and knees, his face blotchy and dripping with sweat.

'Finally! I thought I'd die in here, only to be found years later as a skeleton.'

'What the hell have you been doing?'

'I couldn't open the hidden panel, and the wardrobe downstairs in your room must be locked. It's freakin' scary in the dark with spiders lurking all around.'

I'd locked the wardrobe to keep secrets away from prying eyes. 'You didn't answer my question.'

He gripped both sides of the doorway and pulled himself up.

'What's in that?' I pointed to a bulky pillowcase on the floor between his feet.

'Ahh ... I ... umm ...' Cole struggled to fabricate a convincing lie. 'Found it in here ... someone's ancient stash.'

'Did you now? Empty it.'

Stalling, he lifted the pillowcase and tipped it upside down. Clinking and jingling as an assortment of jewellery, keys, a wallet, and other costly trinkets tumbled onto the floorboards.

I leant in and studied the contraband in the torchlight. 'Not so very old, I see. So, we have a pickpocket ghost, do we?'

Cole gulped. 'Maybe.'

'Cut the crap, kid. You're a thief. One of a few in this house, it seems. Is that what you've been doing while we've been tackling spooks? Sneaking into rooms and helping yourself to valuables?'

'So what? They've got plenty of money to buy replacements.'

'Did Paisley coerce you to do this on her behalf, to earn some Brownie points? Just like she convinced you to play ghostly pranks on me and the guests?'

'No. I did it myself, to help my dad.'

'Why would a father need that kind of support?'

'Because Paisley owes him money, and it was a way to get him some.'

'And who is your dad?'

'Dylan Darius. He—'

I shot my hand up to stop him. 'I know who he is and what he's done. Holy shit, Cole, that loser's your father?'

'Yeah. He and Mum never seriously got together ... except for that one time when they made me. He and I have only really connected since I've come to work here. But now he's been given the boot. Paisley and Fletcher need to pay for what they've done.'

'Was it your idea to put shrooms in the muesli, or his?'

He gave a smug grin. 'It was just a bit of fun.'

'Fun? It was cruel and dangerous.'

'I was just helping Fletcher to chill, that's all. Free his mind.'

'Upping his anxiety more like it. You're barbaric. Have you been doing the same to Bridget, making her appear demented?'

A chuckle. 'Nup, not me. I reckon she's just getting old. My grandma was the same. In the end she didn't know who anyone was.'

'What about Daphne's lunch. Did you purposely change the O'Mara tag to another basket?'

'Well, she was such a cow. Nasty for no good reason.' His scowl added ten years to his age. 'What are you gonna do about it, hey? Dob me in to Paisley?'

It would be difficult to turn him in to my sister, who was far from perfect herself. 'Joe might have a few things to say. He can't arrest you, of course, but he'd give you a proper dressing down for being a stupid idiot, and I'll support him. You'd better return every single item now, or you can go downstairs and confess your misconduct to all the guests.'

He slouched and sighed. 'You won't tell Paisley if I return everything?'

'Only if you promise to behave in the future. No more stealing or poisoning. I'll not be so sympathetic next time.'

'Hey, I did you a favour. I messed up your room, so it looked like someone tried to rob you. That way no-one would blame you for stealing.'

'Why would they blame me? I'm no thief.'

'Well, there's been talk. You were found in Rowan's room, snooping around. And you have access to room keys.'

'I wasn't snooping. I was looking for the source of the coldness.'

'And you're nosey. Sneaking around, spying on people.'

'What? That's ridiculous. Return those things to the rooms you stole them from, you numpty, before I change my mind.'

Supervising Cole in returning the items he'd nabbed, we arrived at the puttanesca room.

Rowan sat hunched at the table, sipping from a bottle of spring water that shook in her hands—obviously still traumatised.

'Great, you're safe too, kid,' Luke said, raising his hand for a high five and receiving a resounding slap. 'Though now Dad is missing. He's not in the kitchen and hasn't answered his phone.'

Daphne, wrapped in a self-hug, paced back and forward. 'Vincent wasn't in the bathroom. He's unaccounted for. Along with the others.'

I stated that Sandy was probably still in the cellar dealing with a fried circuit board. 'Perhaps Vince returned there. They could be working together to get the power back on.'

'Hope it's just a power surge,' Paisley offered from the sofa. 'If it's an outage, the generator is as good as useless. Fletcher was supposed to fix it, but I'd put money on him not getting around to it.'

'Someone should go check to see if they're there.' I locked eyes with Luke.

He coughed under his breath. 'I should stay here. Someone needs to protect the womenfolk.'

Wimp! 'Okay, I'll go find them. If anyone else turns up, keep them here.'

Luke handed me his tiny penlight torch. 'Take this.'

'Guess it'll do. My phone's power is getting low.' I slipped my phone into my pocket and moved into the hallway.

I ducked as window glass shattered somewhere, and wind howled through vents. Thudding of rapid footsteps seemed to come from upstairs, along with doors banging. Timber creaked like an ancient sailing ship tackling rough seas, and I fell against a wall when the floor appeared to pitch and roll. The building's horrendous noises as it withstood the squall, could easily be construed as ghosts trying to contact the living. Yet, what if neither the storm nor the dead generated these noises? Supposing it was the mansion, struggling to rid itself of existing evil. At least there was a reprieve from the lightning and bomblike blasts of thunder.

I shook out my fear and rounded the staircase. Opening the door leading to the cellar, I flicked the light switch to confirm the power was still off down there—it was. I wasn't so stupid as to forget to use my torch when descending into the blackness. This was no corny B-grade slasher film. Though, what I found seconds later almost proved that assertion wrong.

I crossed the stone flooring to pass through the brick archway and slid on something sludgy, losing my footing, and landing flat on my back. The torch, knocked from my hand, spun in an arc on the paving, spotlighting the cause of my fall: a puddle of red, and next to it, a smashed wine bottle.

Struggling to my feet, I retrieved the torch and wiped it dry on the leg of my jumpsuit. A metallic scent: the sticky red liquid wasn't wine, but blood.

'Sandy!' I called. 'Vince! Are you here? Are you hurt?'

An echoing moan drew me to a corner, where I discovered Sandy hunched behind an oak wine barrel, gripping his head to stem bleeding from a nasty gash on his scalp. Crimson trickles streaked his face.

I tried ripping a strip of fabric from my jumpsuit like they do in the movies and found it near impossible. 'Keep the pressure on your head. We'll bind it when we get upstairs.' I helped him to stand. 'Who did this to you?'

Sandy inhaled deep breaths. 'I don't know. A man? He tackled me before I got a good look at him. Clobbered me with a bottle then bolted. I was shittin' myself he might return to finish me off.'

In any case, this attacker appeared to be a live human and not Rowan's demon assailant.

'Where'd he go?'

A nod of his head indicated the bulkhead door, now open to the elements with light rain spraying in. 'I was in too much godawful pain to see who it was.' A groan. 'Why'd he do it?' Sandy sounded close to tears. 'I was no threat. Just fiddling with the generator which, for the record, is totally stuffed.'

'Maybe you got in his way.' Of what, I didn't have a clue. I aided him to the stairs. 'Where's your Dolphin torch?'

'Dunno. The mongrel must have taken it.'

I delivered Sandy to the rest of the group. Daphne, as a way of curbing her worry about Vince, readily accepted her role as ER nurse. Seizing the first aid kit, she shoved Paisley to the end of the sofa to make room for her next patient. Luke informed me he had called triple o. However, because ambulances were dispatched from Rosewood instead of Grimm, there would be a lengthy delay.

55

OLIVIA'S JOURNAL

1931

I had to stop this nonsense once and for all. After seeing Elodie and Will continue their filthy carry-on in the rose garden last night, I spoke briefly with my daughter before making for the cottage to once again right a wrong. Certain that revealing the facts would be the only means to conclude the sordid romance, I had to tell Will who his real father was. But relief came when I spied him collecting his belongings, intent on leaving of his own accord. That was until I watched him head down the path leading to the grotto. Were he and Elodie to share a more intimate goodbye, or were they planning on running away together? I had to act quickly.

My entrance into the cave surprised Will. But he was more shocked to learn that Elodie was his sister, which I gladly shared after keeping it to myself for so long. Empowered with determination and a boldness not my own, I enlightened him about the slut that was his mother. The poor fellow lost the ability to speak for several minutes. Then he had the audacity to call me a liar. I may have become aggressive in my approach, inflating the truth and telling him how his mother had bewitched hapless Henry. Yet I convinced him of the reality of the situation. No person has shown more despondency than he when I suggested he do something permanent to end the depravity.

He had many options. He could have left with the money Sam gave him and started a new life. How was I to know when leaving him in his misery that Will would use his leather belt to hang himself from the grotto railing? A worker found him this morning lying on the stone altar below the sculpture Zachariah had commissioned for Elodie's twenty-first birthday, the belt broken in death from Will's weight. As fitting as any Shakespearean tragedy.

Not unexpectedly, Elodie is inconsolable, which is of great concern to Sam, even though he now has no rival for her affections. Seems she locked herself in the strongroom last night. Aware of her fragility, she'd taken desperate measures to curtail any impulse to abscond with her lover and tossed the key out of reach. I am consoled because her loyalty to Grassington and her family saved her from making a colossal mistake.

I feel no regret for my actions—if indeed they were my own—because any decent parent would have done the same. However, I am not lacking compassion. I have agreed to Will being buried in our little cemetery at a respectful distance from the other graves.

56

I really needed to pee.

On my way back from the toilet, a cry from the first floor prompted investigation. Though when I climbed the timber staircase and walked the hallway, I was met with silence. As I passed the spiral stairs, a clanging high up indicated the tower door was unlatched and swinging. *Who was up there?*

My phone buzzed. I tugged it from my pocket and cringed at a message sent by Shane. *Abby* was all he'd typed. This was followed by three dancing dots that disappeared soon after. I had no time for his crap.

I negotiated the winding steps up to the landing and pushed the door fully open. Summoning courage, I stepped out.

The tower comprised a rectangular cubicle with archways at both ends, each leading to a separate observation deck. I edged out through the right one. Though the rain had lessened to a drizzle, my hair writhed in a gale. Cole's party lights must have been solar powered, for they still flashed gold and blue, offering intermittent snatches of the surrounding stone parapet. Unless I dared to gaze over it, the formidable distance between the rooftop and the ground was out of view.

A sound puzzled me, like someone being repeatedly struck by an open hand, until I saw it was the flag high on its pole slapping against itself. My relief was short-lived when a malformed figure stepped out of the tower, having crossed over from the left side observation deck. I shrank back against the parapet.

'Is that you, Abby?' came a recognisable voice.

'Joe! What are you doing hiding up here?'

I moved towards this odd-looking silhouette when a stern order brought me to a halt.

'Keep your distance!'

'What for?' A blinding light forced me to shield my eyes. 'Hey, cut that out!'

The light bobbed away, and I glimpsed Joe's distorted form breaking apart as someone with a torch moved out from behind him—the reason for his peculiar appearance. That someone also seemed to be gripping Joe's arm and poking a handgun into his ribs.

'Vince? What are you doing?'

'I caught Joe red-handed, rummaging through my luggage,' he said rather proudly. 'Thought he could help himself to my belongings. He's a thief. He's already stolen items from other guests.'

'I sure as hell have not!' Joe snarled. 'I'm a cop.'

Vince laughed. 'Cops aren't immune to stealing. And to be correct, you *were* a cop. And not a very reputable one.'

'He wasn't the one stealing from the guests,' I said, inching closer. 'It was somebody else. They've confessed.'

'Who?' Vince again shone the LED light in my face, making me squint.

'I won't tell you until you get that bloody light out of my eyes.'

He lowered the torch to my chest, where deep inside, my heart hammered with panic.

Seizing the chance, Joe whirled around, reaching for the gun. He changed his mind when the weapon was raised to his eye level.

'You don't have the guts to shoot that thing,' Joe said.

'Ya reckon?' Vince aimed the gun higher and shot into the air.

I recoiled at the blast and the acrid bite in the breeze that wafted my way.

Vince pressed the muzzle against Joe's forehead. 'Willing to take another chance?'

'What's going on?' I demanded. 'All this because you thought Joe nicked something of yours?'

'There's more to it,' Joe said. 'I discovered a copy of Henry Greenwood's will in Vince's briefcase before we scuffled. As well as a copy of a birth certificate for a living male child born to Claudette Renouf in August 1900. She's the maid, remember? The certificate showed Grassington Estate as the place of birth but omitted the father's name. Vince is either working for Bridget or Paisley. I've grilled him, but he won't come clean.'

'Are you?' I asked Vince. 'Has one of them offered you big bucks to discover if Henry fathered an illegitimate child?'

'Hmm ... I'd prefer to keep that secret for the time being. I had a larger audience in mind for the big reveal.'

'Why? For effect?'

'Yes, definitely for effect.'

'Then remove the gun from my skull,' Joe said, 'and we'll gather everyone together for the announcement.'

A clatter drew our attention to the hipped roof beside us.

In the flitting gold and blue brilliance, I saw a furry monster slide down the corrugated iron. There came a *thud* as it collided with the masonry of the observation deck.

Something large and hairy heaved itself over the balustrade

and landed on the deck in front of us. Still in his ghillie suit, minus the hood, Fletcher beat his chest like a scruffy King Kong. Had he gone stark raving mad? Ingested another dose of shrooms?

While Fletcher dazzled Vince with zany martial arts moves, Joe grabbed a section of the electrical cord belonging to Cole's party lights and lassoed it around Vince's neck. Tugging him against the tower, he pressed a knee into the older man's groin to hold him there.

Vince thrashed, dropping both the torch and the handgun.

The torch rolled and stopped, while the gun skidded across the timber deck in my direction. I picked the gun up, finding it much heavier than expected, and pointed it at a writhing Vince.

'Keep still, everyone,' I shrieked. 'I don't want to shoot the wrong person.'

'Aim it away!' Joe cried. 'Do you even know how to fire it?'

I sure didn't. But I kept it focused on Vince as best I could. In the blinking lights so close to his face his features took on a Jekyll-and-Hyde malevolence—alternating gold for good and blue for evil. A swollen eye showed Joe must have got in a swipe before being seized by Vince earlier.

Fletcher retrieved the Maglite torch and shone it in Vince's eyes. 'I don't think we've been introduced. I'm Fletcher Croft, heir of Grassington. Who might you be and what do you think you're doing?'

As Vince had trouble speaking while being throttled, I spoke for him. 'He's Vincent O'Mara, one of the guests. He's here with his wife, Daphne.'

'Oh, the lawyer fella. Why do you have a gun?'

'The revolver's mine,' Joe offered. 'Legally owned. Vince somehow grabbed it from me.' Joe tugged on the cord to stifle a garbled comment from his captive. 'I was in the main bedroom, glancing inside Vince's briefcase, when the lightning strike plunged everything into darkness. Heard a scream from the hallway and Vince rushed in. We had a bit of a conversation, which led to a dust-up and him taking off with my revolver. I chased him outside, but he bolted back into the mansion and up here. Unfortunately, he got the upper hand.'

'I thought you'd gone upstairs to speak with Bridget,' I said.

'I had beforehand, but she wasn't in her rooms. Found the note Keith left her, telling her to meet up tonight. But it wasn't from him.'

'How do you know?'

'It had a dirty thumbprint on the back. One made by a person with a particular injury.'

'A partially severed thumb on his right hand?' Fletcher queried, scowling. 'Bloody Dylan Darius. What's he up to?'

I frowned back. 'Hang on, how did that injury occur?'

Fletch and Joe shared a sheepish look. 'We may have had a part in the accident that saw Dylan lose the end of his thumb as a kid.'

'It was just a game that went wrong,' Joe explained. 'We hadn't expected him to hesitate in withdrawing his hand as the axe came down.'

Geez! Boys and their idiot games. I was surprised I hadn't noticed Dylan's injury at the pub. But then again, my thoughts were focussed elsewhere.

'Why did he want to meet with Bridget?' Fletcher asked Joe.

'He's been helping Paisley steal from her,' I said.

Fletch gasped. 'Paisley's been stealing from Bridget?'

'Yes,' Joe and I answered together.

Joe continued. 'Paisley doesn't trust Bridget to keep ownership of Grassington in the family and wanted to sell the treasures for herself before they were given away.'

'Dylan also blames Bridget for his uncle's death,' I added. 'He was going to confront her tonight, give her a scare, and demand the truth about his dad's death. Pilfer more money from her. But Keith stopped him. Dylan is now locked up in the strongroom.'

'So where is Bridget?' Joe asked, concerned.

'She's missing. What brought you up here, Fletcher?'

'I was in the neighbourhood,' Fletcher said with a wink. 'I heard a commotion up here from the ground, followed by a gunshot. Thought I'd climb up the drainpipes to have a little look-see. Didn't know I'd find a crazy old guy threatening my best mate.'

I wasn't aware my brother-in-law was so nimble.

Vince, struggling against his bindings, struck out, his shoe connecting with Fletcher's shin.

Fletcher wailed and raised the Maglite as a weapon.

'You wouldn't hit a relative, would you?' Vince rasped.

'Relative?' Fletcher looked stupefied. 'What in blazes are you talking about?'

Joe eased the cord's tension slightly, while pressing his knee harder into Vince's crotch. 'Yeah, what do you mean?'

'We're related. After researching my family, I discovered some interesting info. I visited to discuss this matter with your aunt a while back. However, she showed no interest in past events. Got a little antsy and slammed the door in my face.'

'And so she should have,' Fletcher growled.

'I intended to inform her that my great-grandfather was the rumoured illegitimate child. He was the first surviving child of Henry Greenwood. Elodie came later. The inheritance, as stated in Henry's will, should have passed to him, and down his line. Therefore, I am, in actual fact, the true heir of Grassington. This is all mine, and you are trespassing.'

'The hell we are.' Fletcher rammed the torch into Vince's stomach.

Vince buckled and wheezed, fighting for air.

'Then why did you push Bridget down the stairs?' I asked.

Fletcher's head swung around. 'Bridget fell down the stairs?'

'No, it was actually Paisley, mistaken for Bridget. She's okay, though.' I shifted my attention back to Vince. 'Why hurt Bridget, given the will supported your claim?'

He gave a repulsive smile. 'Call it a whim. A guarantee she wouldn't get in the way.'

His head jerked sideways when a fist ploughed into his jaw.

'You have me to deal with, shithead,' Fletcher snarled, shaking out his hand.

God almighty! Enough of all this testosterone. 'Just tie the bastard up with the electrical cord and bring him to the office. He can join Dylan in the lock-up.'

As I approached the tower to head downstairs, a yowl made me spin around.

Vince, his bindings loosened, had Fletcher bent backwards over the parapet and was strangling him with the electrical cord. Fletcher fought back, smashing glass light bulbs strung around Vince's chest.

Meanwhile, Joe had collapsed on the deck, a large knife embedded in his thigh. *Was that Bridget's pineapple-hacking implement?* Vince must have snaffled it while in the cellar with Daphne.

'Holy fucking hell.' Joe winced as ink-dark blood oozed from the wound. His eyes met mine. 'Give me the revolver!'

I slid it across the flooring into his open hand.

'Stop!' Joe yelled, taking aim at Vince. 'Let Fletch go or I'll shoot.'

Vince turned his head and gave a sinister grin. Grasping Fletcher by the ankles, he was about to heave him over the stone barrier, when there came a sickening blast of pistol fire and Vince slumped like a deflated air dancer.

Fletcher, teetering on the parapet ledge, lost balance and disappeared.

I rushed forward and peered over the stone wall, fearing the worst, and caught Fletcher dangling, his hands gripping the electrical cord still attached to Vince. If it snapped, my brother-in-law would slide over the curved verandah roofing and plunge to the ground far below.

With adrenaline pumping through me, I grabbed hold of the cord and ordered Joe to assist. His belt now used as a tourniquet, he dragged himself over and struggled to his feet. With a combined effort, we hauled Fletcher back up to safety.

Leaning against the parapet, catching my breath, a light flickering through trees on the ridge above the glade caught my eye. A dog howled and then yelped, followed by a woman's cry for help.

'An ambulance is already on its way,' I told Joe and Fletcher, both attempting to give aid to Vince, splayed out on the deck with blood soaking the front of his vest. 'I gotta go.'

57

The abated downpour enabled the moon to shine between dispersing clouds and dripping branches, giving light to the steep muddy trail leading to the glade.

A rustle in the bushes alongside caused me to skid to a stop. Whitby sideswiped me as he pushed through the tangle of foliage and limped past, favouring a back leg. I went to offer help, but he whined and scurried towards the mansion. Hopefully, he wasn't seriously hurt.

As I raced through the bougainvillea arbour, a concert of frog calls greeted me, the gleeful clicking and tinkling contrasting with what I saw at the far end of the clearing. Shimmering in the moonlight like a celestial being, the statue mounted on the grotto platform above the boulder stack wobbled, as if preparing to break free of its fixture. Transfixed by this oddity, I drifted near, just as an eerie lament rose above nature's chorus.

I froze and clamped my hands over my ears to muffle the anguish, when clarity showed it was Bridget in her cream sheath dress, swaying on the platform and wailing. I also saw she stood outside the railing, precariously close to the edge. One wrong move and she'd fall, her body hitting the rock altar below, shattering frail bones.

'Stay where you are,' I shouted. 'I'm coming up.'

I ran up the central steps and subsequently took the ones on the left. Instead of entering the grotto from this side, I veered onto the path leading higher to reach the ledge above.

'Bridget. I'm here to help.'

Her cries ceased, and she cocked her head. In the half-light, she looked skeletal, her cheeks more sunken, her eyes bulging from their sockets. 'Abby,' she croaked.

'Yes, it's me.' I leant over the guardrail and offered my hand. 'Come to me, carefully now, and I'll help you around the railing.'

She frowned, studying me with suspicion, then shuffled sideways. At one point she teetered, sending small rocks at her feet plunging and smashing apart on the altar. Still, she moved closer until I gripped her arm and assisted her to safety.

Bridget shivered in my grasp. 'Keith's hurt. He might be dead.'

I was appalled. 'Where is he? What happened?'

'He was strangled in the grotto trying to rescue me.'

'Strangled? By who?'

'The demon who abducted me.'

I struggled to make sense of this. Maybe I didn't want to. 'Is the demon still in there?'

The whites of her eyes appeared luminous as she darted looks left and right. 'I hurried up here to escape.'

'Okay, let's go have a look together, shall we? See how Keith is?' The calm lilt of my voice was an attempt to ease the situation. Within, my stomach squirmed with terror.

Bridget clutched my arm as we followed the path down to the cave. Nearing the entrance, a scraping sound alerted me to someone inside. A strange hissing followed, much like static produced by radio interference.

'*Be gone, she's mine,*' came a sputtering command from the dark interior. A man. Not Keith.

I positioned myself in front of Bridget and squinted to make out details in the shadows. 'Why is she yours?'

The voice growled, '*Revenge.*'

Step-by-step I moved into the cave, the surrounding air chilled to freezing.

A repugnant stench like rotting meat filled the space, and I lurched back, the heel of my sneaker connecting with something that shifted. I crouched and fumbled, appraising a sturdy plastic object by touch. My fingers encircled the handle of what I suspected was a dolphin torch. *Sandy's?*

I pressed the rubber button, and a weak circle of light shone on the dirt floor. Within this lit patch was Hilary's spirit box. It suddenly crackled to life, and I snatched it up, holding it to my face. 'Revenge for what?' I asked.

The box emitted words that were indistinguishable through the noise distortion.

'Please repeat that.'

More hissing preceded an audible murmur: '*Murder.*'

My flesh itched. Was this happening? Was I speaking with the dead? I chanced on the spirit wanting to converse further. 'Whose murder? Yours?'

White noise punctuated by shrill whistling, followed by a distinct, '*Yes.*'

I turned at a dragging sound coming from the opposite side of the cave. I aimed the torch, my breath snagging at a disturbing sight. Entering through the opening was Hilary, hauling Keith's body behind her by his shirt collar. Blood dripped from his lips, leaving red splotches in the dirt.

A cry beside me, and Bridget crumpled to the ground.

Hilary stopped and stared, mascara smudged under vacant eyes, froth hideously gathered like sea foam in the corners of her mouth. She pointed at the unconscious Bridget. 'The old woman must die,' she stated in a gravelly voice, her words accompanied by puffs of mist. 'So too, the nephew.'

I stared at the spirit box lying lifeless in my grip. Had the entity possessed Hilary? Had this happened to her multiple times since arriving at Grassington, like that instance in the graveyard? Not a prank, then.

The torchlight twitched as I trembled. Had the spirit entered her again during the paranormal activities and forced her to escape outside through the cellar, bashing Sandy in the process? That would explain him thinking a man had attacked him, also who had taken his torch.

I took a punt. 'Clem Wallace, is that you?'

Hilary's face contorted, briefly transforming into the monstrosity I'd seen in the lightning flash outside the sitting room window. If evil possessed her, courage now possessed me.

I thrust my shoulders back, straightening my spine. 'It's time to quit your retribution, Clem. It has no place here.'

'The Greenwoods must pay. Blood for blood.'

'It was wrong for Gerald to kill you out of greed. But his descendants are innocent.'

'Blood for blood.'

'It's not right! You've made them victims of your hatred.'

'He stole from me.'

'And you stole from him. So much unnecessary tragedy. No more. It has to stop.'

'Blood of his lineage, for the blood of mine.'

Hilary gnashed her teeth, and a hideous groan slithered out of her mouth. 'I was still alive after the bucket he dropped crushed my head. He could have saved me. I clawed at him, pleaded for help. But he left me to die. So, I cursed him.'

A twinge of sympathy for Clem's misfortune was overridden by a possible solution. 'What if I had the cure? Gerald hadn't used your portion of the gold nugget to build Grassington. He hid it. It won't be any use to you, being dead and all. However, a relative may find it highly valuable.'

'I have no relative.'

'Oh, but you do.' My hurried online search after dinner regarding Clement Wallace gave me the ammunition I now needed. 'Your wife, Prudence, who was pregnant when you died, gave birth six months later to a son she named Albert. She later married a man called Hawthorne, and he gave his surname to this boy. In a strange twist of fate, Elodie Greenwood married Albert's son Sam. Therefore, Bridget Greenwood is your great-granddaughter, and Fletcher is your great-great-grandson. If you harm either, you harm your own descendent.'

'Liar!' Hilary lunged, seizing me by the neck.

I dropped the torch and clutched her arms. When I failed to wrench her hands from around my throat, she squeezed harder, her thumbs as strong as vice screws. Specks of light danced in my vision as I fought to breathe. I stomped on her foot, to no effect. On the verge of blacking out, I pitched forward to knock her off-balance and slammed her against the rock wall.

Winded, Hilary eased her grip for a second. But I missed the opportunity to pull away. She continued to choke me, this time crushing my larynx. Thinking quickly, I shoved my hand into the back pocket of my jumpsuit and extracted the item that had fallen out of Gerald's head in the pond.

Hilary gazed down at the chunk of gold balanced in my palm. 'Is that my portion?' She locked her dead eyes onto mine.

With her attention transferred, I pulled my arm back and slammed the nugget into her face.

Her hands dropped from my throat, and she slid to the floor.

A train-like whoosh coincided with a whirlwind of cave-borne dust. Grit flew into my eyes and coated the back of my throat. The earth rumbled beneath my feet and the stone walls split in a series of cracks. Was the grotto collapsing around me? I ducked, ready to scramble towards an entrance, when calm returned in a rush.

Hilary peered up at me with blood flowing from her nose. 'Abby! What's going on? What have you done to me?' Her voice sounded fragile, yet it was now her own.

Coughing, I wondered if she was truly unaware of what had occurred. Was she now free of Clem's hold over her?

'I could ask the same of you,' I wheezed. 'Let's just say you haven't been yourself.'

Bridget whimpered as she regained consciousness and crawled over to Keith, while I slumped to a squat, my head in my trembling hands.

Sharp sounds I never thought I'd be so relieved to hear cut through the night.

Sirens wailing.

58

ELODIE

1943

Elodie enters her mother's sickroom carrying a tray of food. 'Here you go, Mum, homemade pea and ham soup. Just what you need.'

Olivia's emaciated frame barely causes a ripple in the layers of bed linen, her angular features showing the effects of her week-long illness. Elodie repositions her, sitting her upright and leaning back against the extra pillows.

'No food,' Olivia whines. 'I'm not hungry.'

'C'mon Mum, regain your strength. The twins are missing you. They keep asking when you'll be up to teaching them how to play Patience.' She feeds a spoonful of thick liquid into her mother's mouth. 'That's good. And another.' Elodie wipes a dribble of soup from the creased chin and several more offerings are eaten without complaint.

Olivia points a shaking finger towards the bedside table. 'My journal.'

'Not now. You don't have the strength to write. You wouldn't be able to decipher your own writing, anyway. It's gotten worse over the years. The entries in your past journals are much more legible.'

Her mother takes a swipe at the bowl, knocking it from Elodie's grip. It overturns, soup soaking into the coverlet.

'Look at the mess you've made. I've just changed the sheets, you silly old woman.'

'You've read my journals?' Olivia rasps.

'What if I have? Got something to hide?' She studies her mother. Waits. No response.

She sits on the edge of the bed and releases a drawn-out sigh. 'I've had suspicions about the Grassington deaths for a while now, Mum. Yesterday, Bridget discovered your old journals tucked away in the wardrobe in the disused servants' room during a game of hide-and-seek. Lucky for her she wasn't interested in opening them; what six-year-old girl would be? But I did. Certain dates interested me more than others. And though not explicitly stated, it wasn't difficult to read between the lines to understand the truth.'

Elodie clenches a handful of linen, her fingers hurting from the strain. 'You killed the nursery maid, Claudette, didn't you, with one purposeful shove. She didn't die, right away, of course. She first had to give birth. And Dad. I had trouble sleeping the night of the seance, and caught you leaving the house, out for an early morning stroll. Didn't put it together till much later that you were heading to the well. I didn't want to believe you were that vile. It makes me wonder if you had anything to do with Tommy's fatal illness,' she says with spite.

'Never!' Her mother's head rises from the pillow. 'It was Gerald's fault. He brought the curse upon the Greenwoods. Your father told me early on in our marriage that, as a child, he'd witnessed Gerald kill his mining partner in Gympie. Told me that his father, before he died, ranted about this dead man haunting him, seeking revenge. I assumed it was the words of a guilt-ridden lunatic.' Her voice having thinned, she clears her throat, wiping spit from her lips with the sleeve of her nightgown. 'But when tragedy after tragedy occurred, I came to believe it was instigated by evil. The house and all who live in it are contaminated by wickedness. Gerald was right. A vengeful spirit walks the halls of Grassington, and there is no stopping it.'

Elodie is taken aback. Everything her mother has said resonates with her. Hasn't she experienced similar incidents? Her initial infertility and strained marriage, temptation, and great sorrow. No, it had to be her mother's fault. Otherwise ...

'Mum, you're delusional blaming the deaths on a ghost. You are a murderer who needs to pay for what you've done.'

'No. You're mistaken. The demon used me. He possessed me to do the unspeakable on his behalf. He's the wicked one.'

Elodie leaps to her feet. 'Stop! You're pathetic. You killed Claudette out of sheer jealousy. Dad wasn't perfect, but he didn't need to die for threatening to report your actions to the police, which I'm sure he wouldn't have followed through with. And Will ...' Elodie vividly recalls the day they found him lying dead on the grotto altar. Overwhelmed by shock and loss, remorse consumed her for not leaving with him when he'd asked. For years she blamed herself for his death. But that was before learning what really led him to suicide. Before yesterday. Her voice breaks as she says, 'You killed Will by revealing I was his sister and pressuring him to end his life.'

Olivia falls back on the pillows in a coughing fit. 'Any parent would have done the same. In the end it was his choice. He would have destroyed everything for you. Stolen your birthright.'

'If you'd only told me the truth at the time,' Elodie whimpers.

'Keeping it to yourself was the cruellest thing you've ever done. We could have learnt to live as siblings. Shared the inheritance.'

'He'd have dumped you like a bag of rubbish. Kicked you out of Grassington.' Another hacking cough. Olivia's eyes widen, the pupils contracting. She clutches her chest and winces in pain. 'What have you given me?'

'Today?' Elodie gestures towards a vase of tall-stemmed flowers with bell-shape blooms on a table by the window. 'You like foxgloves, Mum. Did you know ingesting any part of the plant is poisonous to humans? Especially the leaves. Just a couple can affect the heart and cause death. Some may have found their way into your soup by accident.'

A strangled cry. 'But why? I'm your mother.'

'Because of what you've done.'

Olivia claws the nightgown's bodice. Her lips lose their colour. 'It was all for you. I succumbed to evil because of you.' Her eyes dart away and then glower at Elodie. 'You see them now, don't you, dear?'

A small group surrounds the bed. Those who've passed. Amongst them, Elodie's father, a clutch of infants, and sweet Tommy. Zachariah Bright is there too and, inexplicably, Claudette, the maid. But not Will, for good reason. Yet it is the fiendish presence skulking in the room's corner that causes the hairs on Elodie's arms to stand on end.

'He's all yours now,' Olivia wheezes, her face taking on a greyish hue. She presses her hand to her heart and fights for breath, gasping fishlike for air. Then silence. Stillness.

Elodie stares into the vacant eyes, startled at the rapid cessation of life, before plucking a candy-pink lily from the flower arrangement on the bedside cabinet. Known botanically as *Lilium Elodie*, they had first flowered in the regenerated gardens in the glade during the spring after Will's death. Blossoming every year since, she believed he had sown them as a surprise gift—a regular reminder of his existence and affection. Instead of organising a headstone that would have displeased both Sam and her mother, Elodie had planted more of these lilies near his grave, filling vases within the mansion in the height of their bloom. Having always lamented that she and Will had not consummated their love, the recent knowledge that they are brother and sister reassures Elodie their blood connection runs deeper.

She sniffs the lily and places it on her mother's chest, not as an act of tenderness but as a token of retribution. An eye for an eye.

A mist-like form rises from the body and joins the ghostly figures standing bedside. As if startled, they all suddenly wheel around to face the shadowy shape in the corner. With a mighty whooshing noise, the figures merge as one and disappear in a swirl of glimmering motes.

Elodie twitches as Clem Wallace steps into the centre of the room. The room quakes so violently she has to grip the bedstead for balance. A mighty tugging is felt, as if her soul is being extracted through every pore. The pull of his control drains her of energy.

Realisation dawns. He has the power to possess the living as well as dominate the dead. Is this how he carries out his twisted malice, by using others? Shifting her gaze to the shell of her mother on the bed, regret encompasses Elodie like a murky fog.

'*Like mother, like daughter,*' is hissed into her ear.

She winces with profound horror. Was that true? Has she also become his instrument of devilry? Caught in a whirlwind of emotions, her world spins and she slumps on the floor, helpless.

A flutter of wings snatches Elodie from the depths of despair. Her vision clears, revealing a black crow perched on the window ledge, its glossy feathers ruffling in the breeze. Swivelling its head, the white eyes ringed with blue stare directly at the hideous spectre. The beak opens, expelling a startling *caw*. Instantly, Clem vanishes.

Elodie rises and rushes towards the window, only for the crow to launch into the air and fly away before she can offer words of gratitude. She makes a pledge to protect herself and her children at all costs. When the priest arrives to offer comfort, she'll implore him to cleanse the house with prayer. Then it will be up to her to remain vigilant lest the demon returns.

Steeling herself, she opens the door and prepares to inform the family of Olivia's demise.

59

R oads blocked by fallen branches and powerlines held the emergency services up as had flooded creeks and a mudslide. Though when gaining access to Grassington Estate, they were in luck. The manual override allowed them to open the electric gates affected by the power outage and drive unhindered up to the mansion.

The paramedics explained this to me as they transported an equipment-laden stretcher through the main door. A police officer bustled in soon after, called in for additional assistance.

I escorted them to the candlelit puttanesca room, where all the wounded had gathered to make it easier for assessing cases. I waited with the emergency crew as they took in the scene.

Hilary, her nose swollen and packed with gauze to stem the bleeding, sat on a chair guarded by Rowan in case she transitioned into Clem Wallace. Fletcher—divested of his ghillie suit and wearing only a blood smeared singlet and shorts—plumped up a cushion for his best mate reclining on the sofa with a shish-kebabbed thigh. Luke administered aid to his head-bandaged father, while Cole was being useful by offering buttered scones to the injured, including Whitby, who sat with his injured hind leg stretched out.

Paisley, her foot buried in a tub of ice, yelled, 'Shut up,' and banged her fist on the wall in response to Dylan on the other side, screaming for justice from his incarceration in the strongroom.

'Sweet Jesus!' the officer exclaimed. 'Wasn't expecting this. It looks like a war zone.'

'Wait till you see what else we have for you,' Joe said, then took a long swig from a 'medicinal' bottle of Scotch.

Unable to take any more of this shit show, I went outside.

Righting the overturned peacock chair on the verandah, I sank into the wicker, feeling twice my age. I considered my optimistic arrival days earlier. *Grassington will be the perfect refuge for recuperating from my troubles. A godsend.* Yeah, right! A better plan would have been to stay home and binge watch *Derry Girls*, with a bottle of Fireball as company. My head fell into my hands as I succumbed to my misery.

The cop located me. He leant against a cast iron column with his arms folded over his protective vest. 'So, Abby, is it? Are you able to describe what occurred here overnight?'

I glanced up at him and laughed dryly. 'How open-minded are you to paranormal phenomena?' Then I burst into convulsing sobs.

The officer likely found my zigzagging, back-and-forth story perplexing. However, his encouraging nods and reflective exclamations helped spur me on. Though he was most likely thinking I was totally off my rocker.

When he returned inside, I stayed on the verandah, the events of the last few days scooting around my brain like ball bearings in a pinball game. They defied comprehension. Last night I'd asked for proof of ghosts and my plea was granted. I was now a genuine believer. Yet I had a lingering thought. Had I uncovered the secrets the house had tasked me with? In finding the gold nugget and confronting Clem, had I delivered it of evil?

In answer, the exterior lights came on, flickered, and then remained.

Cheers erupted from inside as the few rooms that were lit during the paranormal activities were illuminated again. More bulbs came on, the blaze of the foyer chandelier hurting my eyes when I re-entered.

Bridget and Keith sat huddled on the steps of the carpeted staircase, two bottles of pale ale at their feet. The old girl had scratches on her forearms and a cut knee, whether due to fending off Dylan or a demon I wasn't sure. As for Keith, except for bruises around his neck and a split lip, he looked none the worse for his ordeal.

I stood in front of them. 'Can either of you tell me when the statue of Gerald was made for the garden pond?'

The couple shared a look, yet it was Bridget who answered first.

'From what I remember my mother telling me, Zachariah commissioned its manufacture soon after Henry's death.'

'That would have been for the thirty-fifth anniversary of Grassington's construction,' Keith added with a lisp, the result of biting through his tongue when throttled by Hilary.

I shared my theory. 'If Zachariah had indeed discovered Henry's body in the well, as the newspaper report claimed, could he have also chanced upon the nugget there? Though, not wanting anyone to get their hands on it, he hid it elsewhere.'

'But why?' Keith said. 'Why wouldn't he want the Greenwoods or himself to use the money from the sale of the nugget? They were all in dire need of funds at that time.'

Bridget's eyes widened. 'Because he saw it as a bad omen. No more tragedy was needed.'

'Gerald may have concealed the gold and Clem's pickaxe in the well for this very reason,' I conjectured. 'Then Zachariah, being the loyal servant and knowing what was best for his employers, found the nugget when discovering Henry's body and somehow fitted it inside the head of Gerald's statue to make sure no-one other than himself knew of its existence.'

'What happens to the gold now?' Keith asked. 'Has that hellish fiend really been banished to ... to wherever?'

'He's gone,' Bridget said with conviction. 'I can feel it. Clem Wallace is gone for good. See, I can say his name now.'

'Yep, Clem has left the building,' I announced.

I turned as a hissing sound emanated from the walls, like air pressure changing. I trusted it was just the house sighing with relief.

'The nugget is rightfully yours, Bridget. You can do whatever you want with it.'

'Keith, you'll help me put my thinking cap on, won't you?' she asked.

He planted a kiss on her forehead. 'Of course, sweetie.'

With Bridget in the mood for recalling the past, I asked her a question that had niggled me since reading Olivia's writings and learning of Will Flanagan's suicide. 'Out of curiosity, Bridget, how was the relationship between your mother and grandmother towards the end?'

'Oh ... mostly good, I think. From what I saw, they were civil towards each other. Though it became strained just days before Grandma Livvie died. They were barely talking. Mum got us girls to ask if she needed anything, took up her meals. Maybe Mum knew what was coming. But then the day after her death, my mother went crazy from grief, digging up flowers in the garden and burning them and other things belonging to Grandma. I remember the bonfire we had in the paddock. A huge blaze. I still have a scar on my arm where a stray ember scalded me.'

'That's interesting. Do you recall which flowers she burnt? What type they were?'

Bridget scrunched her face as she thought hard. Her eyes lit up. 'Foxgloves, and white flowers with large hanging blossoms, trumpet shaped. I think they still grow in a flower bed somewhere. So pretty.'

'Yet poisonous,' Keith butted in. '*Brugmansia,* or Angel's Trumpets, are very dangerous. Inhaling their scent or ingesting any part of the plant can cause vomiting, diarrhoea, and hallucinations. Sometimes seizures and coma occur, and even death. So too the foxgloves. No wonder your mother wanted to destroy them.'

My intrigue skyrocketed. 'But why get rid of them at that point in time? Why the day after Olivia's death?'

Daphne suddenly appeared on the landing above us, her vacant stare as lifeless as a zombie's. As she made her way down the steps with Vince's bloodstained pocket square pressed against her chest, Bridget and Keith moved aside to let her pass. Words of comfort failed me as she meandered around us and entered the sitting room. Poor lady. What would become of her now that her husband was dead? Would his spirit now join the other poor souls in haunting the mansion?

What would become of Joe, who had fired the fatal shot? Wouldn't a plea of self-defence come to his aid? Then there was Hilary. What charges would they bring against her? Assault while possessed by a deceased person?

I turned at the muffled sounds of a heated argument, and then a door opening.

'Nope, you can stay in your cell for the time being,' hollered a voice I recognised as the police officer's.

An angry response and metal rattling. A door slamming. Boots stomping down the hall.

Would Paisley also face charges of stealing? Although, unlike Dylan, she hadn't conspired to take Bridget hostage, which stood in her favour.

Harsh crunching of gravel suggested a vehicle had skidded to a halt in the driveway.

'Good, backup has arrived,' the officer said, rounding the staircase. He jogged through the foyer and out the front door.

Seconds later he edged back through the etched glass doors, scowling. 'Damn! It's a bunch of bloody locals out to get a scoop.' He studied the three of us at the stairs in turn. 'Which idiot posted something on their socials?'

We all shrugged, yet I suspected someone younger must have done such a thing. Rowan or Luke? No ... Cole, for sure, the rascal.

The cop must have read my mind, for his eyes darted to the doorway of the puttanesca room. 'I'd better corral the mongrels,' he said with a sigh, and disappeared outside.

A piercing screech made me wrench around in fright. *What now?*

Relief washed over me when I saw the female paramedic wheeling a noisy trolley into the hallway. As it rolled by, Joe, lying on the stretcher with eyes glazed from a mix of painkillers and Scotch, grabbed my hand.

He tugged the green whistle inhaler from his mouth. 'Hey, Abbs, you did a ripper of a job. Want to join my team?'

'What team?'

'I'm setting myself up as a PI.'

'A private investigator? Hells bells! You want me to be your

Della Street, answering phone calls and running errands, supplying cups of coffee. Is that it?'

'Della who? Nah, I'm offering you a proper job, with proper pay.' He sucked on his green whistle some more. 'We could tackle cold cases and shit. Run a podcast even. Whaddaya reckon?' His silly grin revealed all his teeth.

'I reckon you're away with the fairies.'

He pulled a face. 'No fairies here.' He jerked his head left and right. 'Hey, have you seen that kid ghost? He freaked me out back in the day. But when I saw him while chasing that bastard, Vince, I just pitied the little fella. He looked so sad.' *So, he had seen ghosts!* Joe's lips twitched and tears rolled down his cheeks as he whimpered.

The paramedic raised her eyebrows at me. 'Don't worry. It's the analgesic.'

I wasn't worried. I enjoyed seeing tough-guy Joe's weaker side, even if it was medicinally induced. 'Let's talk about this job prospect once you're on the road to recovery,' I said, squeezing his hand.

Joe nodded, his eyelids closing. 'I knew my charm would win you over.'

'What charm? I need the money, that's all.'

The second paramedic appeared and helped manoeuvre the trolley out the front door and down the front steps.

I stood on the verandah, watching Joe being conveyed into the rear of the ambulance. The darkness was thinning, the sky pinking at the edges. Cicadas began their shrill summer racket, and a large black crow perched on a lamppost greeted the onset of dawn with a reveille of caws, rattles, and clicks.

'Hello there, I am Rowan Twomey,' I heard, coming from the wicker peacock chair where Rowan now sat, her phone up to her mouth.

I gave her a questioning look, and she returned it with a wink.

'This is *The Tell-Tale Heart*, the podcast of true spooky stories guaranteed to make your hair stand on end. Welcome to Episode 13, *Grassington Manor and the Greenwood Curse*.'

I opened my mouth to speak, but she pressed a finger to her lips.

'Lovely listeners, are you ready to hear the spookiest of tales? Ready to feel chills, thrills, and pop a few pills to steady your nerves? Then sit back and prick your ears to what I am about to tell you. It has it all, an historic country mansion, a family haunted by a tragic past, ghostly encounters, possession, danger ... and, best of all, *death!*'

'Really?' I cut in, shaking my head in disbelief. 'A little too soon, don't you reckon?'

She tapped a red button on her phone screen. 'It's not live. Just a recording. If you're up to it, you can come on the show as a guest, the *hero of the hour*, so to speak.'

The shriek of approaching sirens stopped me from telling Rowan what I actually thought about her loathsome invitation. It also disrupted the commotion made by the social media hopefuls arguing with the officer beside their van. One keen gawker, filming the exterior of the mansion, swung his camcorder around to capture the arrival of more police vehicles.

'Any publicity is good publicity, right?' Paisley said, standing close.

I glared at my sister, disgusted by her heartlessness. After the evening's traumatic events, how could she continue to be so self-absorbed? I stabbed my finger in her chest. 'You do realise you'll be implicated when the full details are reported. And who's saying Bridget won't decide to gift Grassington to the Heritage National Trust?'

'She wouldn't do that. *She can't.*' A worrisome look. 'Bridget made a deal with us.'

'Which she has every right to renege on,' Fletcher said, joining us. I was happy to see Whitby bore only a hint of a limp as he pulled up beside him. 'Bridget is still the rightful owner. She alone has the power to decide Grassington's fate.'

Paisley clutched Fletch's arm for balance as she took the weight off her injured foot. 'But Bridget's in no fit mental state to decide anything. She has dementia.'

'Does she, though?' I asked, my tone adding substance to my scepticism. 'The gardens here contain interesting vegetation. It wouldn't be the first time someone used plant life to their advantage.'

'Wha-a-t?' She rolled her eyes as if I was the crazy one, yet I noticed a flush making its way up her neck. 'Hey, don't tell Mum and Dad about all this, okay? Leave that to me.'

'Only if you promise to have an honest conversation with me real soon. I reckon it's time for you to spill your guts.'

'Yeah, I'd like to be a part of that too,' Fletcher said.

'Alright.' Paisley's shoulders sagged in defeat, and she diverted her attention to the clutch of uniformed police officers heading towards us. 'But first, let me brew some coffee for this lot.'

Watching her hobble back into the foyer, I had a hunch she would appreciate emotional support in the very near future. Hence, I needed to be the better person. After all, she was my sister.

Fletcher nudged me with his elbow. 'Thanks for everything. One thing Paisley got right was asking you here to help. You saved my life. Consider yourself welcome anytime at Grassington.' He grinned, the wrinkles fanning from his eyes still embedded with khaki face paint. 'As long as it's still ours, that is.'

'I think I'll leave my next visit to a much later date. There's only so much excitement a girl can take.'

I still clung to the notion that the house had been waiting for a deliverer to help purge the damned. Yet, why had it chosen me to be its hero? I was a mere mortal with no supernatural ability other than a rousing curiosity. Perhaps it had tried with others over the years, attempting to gain their attention by creating disturbances. Was I the only one to respond correctly, believing they were more than indications of a haunting? In this case, my snooping had paid off. *Take that, you naysayers!*

Whitby bumped against me and stuck his nose inside my jumpsuit hip pocket.

'Sorry, buddy, nothing there for you today.' When I exposed the lining to prove it, a milky white marble dropped from the folds of fabric and bounced across the terrazzo tiles. 'How did that ...' The sound of giggling caused me to look up and catch a child peeking around the corner of the verandah.

Why was Tommy still here? Surely, heavenly rewards awaited the little boy. As I returned his smile, his image faded until he was just a twisting funnel of mist that was carried away by a flurry of wind.

What awaited me beyond the confines of Grassington?

The crow atop the lamppost gave a prolonged rattle and ruffled its feathers.

'You know how crows are given a bad rap as harbingers of death or misfortune,' Fletch said, following my line of sight. 'They are also symbolic of transformation and wisdom.'

Viewing the bird with fresh interest, I sensed my life was about to alter direction—one rich with the promise of brighter outcomes and deeper fulfilment. Still, given who I was, could it ever truly be free of chaos?

ACKNOWLEDGMENTS

Stirring Ghosts was inspired by my lifelong fascination with Gothic horror and twisty mysteries. I thoroughly enjoyed playing with familiar tropes and tucking in a few Easter eggs throughout the pages—a playful nod to the classic tales that have thrilled and chilled me over the years. A visit to Woodlands of Marburg, an historic and reputedly haunted mansion west of Brisbane, sparked the idea for the setting and several of the characters who inhabit this story.

I've dedicated this book to my two sisters, not because our relationship mirrors the thorny one between Abby and Paisley (not completely, anyway 😉) but because these wonderful women have shaped my life profoundly. Our shared history and devotion to family binds the three of us together forever.

Heartfelt thanks to Graham Toseland from Fading Street Publishing for polishing my prose and offering invaluable advice, and to Writers Rendezvous members for their constructive feedback and encouragement. I'm especially grateful to Jane Ireland walking this precarious creative path alongside me, her honesty and humour sustaining me.

And, of course, I could never have achieved any of my writing goals without the unwavering love and support of my family. You are the light in the darkness—the reason I can overcome my fears and battle the ever-lurking monsters of procrastination and self-doubt. You are my heroes.

ABOUT THE AUTHOR

Vicki Stevens is an Australian mystery/thriller author living in the lush countryside on the rural outskirts of Brisbane. Her keen interest in genealogy motivates her to write compelling and evocative stories inspired by lives and events from the past. *Stirring Ghosts* is the third book in her Abby Eaton Mystery series.

If you enjoyed this story please leave a few words or a rating with your retailer or on a book review website.

For more info: www.vickistevens.com.au